TAKING UP SERPENTS

Ian Sutherland

ISBN: 0-9930056-3-2
ISBN-13: 978-0-9930056-3-3

For Fiona, for playing Daniel O'Donnell when it counted and everything before.

CHAPTER 1

IGNORING THE TIGHTNESS IN HIS CHEST, MURDO MacLeod fell into a hypnotic rhythm, pedalling slowly but consistently, his practised eyes scanning the weave for any breaks in the coarse thread. The seductive clacking noise of the loom — its cogs and wheels moving in mechanical precision, the shuttle flying left and right across the warp, the beater beam flipping forwards and backwards — overpowered the tinny radio on the shelf behind him.

His gaze fell on the familiar vista through the loom shed's panoramic window. In the distance, black clouds formed across the ocean's horizon. Like an army's initial frontal attack, Atlantic waves threw their might against the ragged cliffs, sea foam dancing gently in the mounting breeze like dandelion fluff from the summer yet to come.

Lost to the rhythm, Murdo's thoughts roamed freely. He thought of his daughter Morag, preparing for her final law exams on the mainland. In two weeks, she would finally return home. He hadn't seen her for two months, not since his check-up at the specialist hospital in Inverness. He would drive carefully across the winding single-track roads of the Isle of Lewis, and collect her from the ferry port in Stornoway, the island's capital. One glance at the slant of her lopsided smile and the depth of the furrow in her brows would tell him all he needed to know about whether she had passed or not.

The Victorian grandfather clock standing in the corner of the shed began its quarter-hour ritual, its church-like chimes just audible above the clatter of the loom. As he absently reached an arm behind in an attempt to rub his now aching upper back, Murdo wondered what his own grandfather would have made of the noisy old piece of furniture now located in the loom shed, long since banished from pride of place in the croft's hallway. Murdo smiled wryly as he attempted to formulate the stream of Gaelic curses that his grandfather would have let fly had he been alive to see the sight.

The chimes gonged twice. As usual, time had escaped him. Perhaps he ought to stop for a bite of lunch with Caitriona, his wife of twenty-four years. By now she would surely have finished feeding the croft's livestock and would be preparing a late lunch. He wondered if she had come up with a new panini recipe or whether it would be brie-and-tomato for the fourth day in a row, a concoction she had filched from the brand new Starbucks in Stornoway. She'd already let slip that she wanted an espresso coffee machine for Christmas. God knows how he would be able to afford that. He would need —

A lightning bolt of pain shot through Murdo's chest. He clutched his fist to his heart as he felt his body rapidly weaken from the wrenching attack. He gasped for breath but found he couldn't breathe. His legs stopped pumping the cast iron loom as he listed to one side, the agony overpowering. Powerlessly, he watched the slate floor rush towards him.

Unable to reach his hands out, his face took the full force, mercifully knocking him out cold.

Murdo MacLeod never regained consciousness.

David Dougan looked straight at the camera with the green light and gave his trademark smile, the one he knew viewers melted over.

"Now that the onions are caramelised to perfection …" He gave the burnt onions one more stir. At least the cameras couldn't pick up the acrid smell emanating from the pan. "… stir in one tablespoon of plain flour."

Dougan followed his own instruction and sprinkled some over the onion roux. He stirred vigorously with his wooden spoon, hoping the speed would prevent the camera mounted directly above from picking out any black bits. "This will help thicken the soup, but just a touch. We're not making an onion stew, are we?" He turned to his guest. "How're you getting on with grating the Gruyere?" He already knew the answer. Out of the corner of his eye, he could see that Davinda Rural, internationally famous Bollywood singer, had already finished the block of cheese. She'd made a bit of a mess and he just about stopped himself from shouting at her, remembering he wasn't in his own kitchen and that the show was being broadcast live.

Gritting his teeth, he let her answer, allowing his peripheral vision to appreciate the substantial outline of her breasts bursting through the low-cut black top she had donned to impress the British viewing public. He wondered if his high-def audience could see her nipples jutting through the tight-fitting top as clearly as he could. What a woman. He'd presumed such a well-regarded Indian actress would have worn a sari, but no, here she was, in Western garb revealing as much skin as his son's hot new fiancée. He was definitely looking forward to this week's after show party.

"Almost done, Chef," she answered politely.

He appreciated the use of his title. It reminded him of the days in Dublin, when he ran his first Michelin-starred restaurant. The period when, God forbid, one of his sous-chefs would have botched French Onion Soup like Dougan had done this morning. A thunderous bollocking, laden with quality Irish expletives, would have been guaranteed. Fortunately, no one would ever taste the concoction he was stirring right now. There was another waiting, pre-prepared by the show's cooking stylist, glistening to perfection in the warm oven to his left. That would be the one his other celebrity guests would taste in a few minutes before they cut from live to a pre-recorded segment.

While Dougan stirred and Davinda grated, he took the opportunity to ask some of the planned questions about

Davinda's new BBC television series set in colonial India. It may be a live cookalong show, but Davinda was no cook. She was only here to promote her new show to the viewers. He half-listened to her answer while ladling in some beef stock from the huge pan on the other hob, pleased to see the burnt bits hadn't floated to the top. In a pause between her long anecdotes, he jumped in for the benefit of the small handful of viewers he suspected were actually cooking along live. "Add the stock a ladle at a time."

Davinda droned on. Behind the cameras, technicians worked flawlessly, catching everything. Dougan purposely avoided looking at her tits. He didn't want the camera to catch him at it. He'd end up on the front page again, and he'd had enough of that.

Once all the stock was in, he reached for the bottle of white wine. "Add a good glass of dry white wine. Make sure it's quality, but don't go mad now. A good Australian Sauvignon Blanc or maybe a decent Italian Pinot." He looked sternly at the camera, deliberately smirking to let the viewers know a punchline was coming. "It maybe French Onion soup, but only you and I will know that you didn't use your best French Chablis."

Davinda laughed at his joke. Dougan appreciated the additional irony that the white wine he was actually adding was some cheap plonk the food stylist had dug up, a strategically placed blank white label preventing product advertising on the Beeb.

Dougan finally reached for the brandy, the last ingredient, other than seasoning of course. Finally, he'd be able to swap the pigswill he'd made live on television for the pre-prepared stuff the stylist had worked on overnight. He unscrewed the cap and splashed some in the pot. As he held the bottle, the most excruciating pain struck him right across his chest. At first he held himself rigid, trying to mask his agony, the brandy pouring continuously, but the pain didn't abate and he felt his body quicken, his ears blocking out all sounds, and blackness began to form around the edges of his vision.

Absurdly, Dougan became annoyed that the encroaching

blackness prevented his peripheral vision from taking in the profile of Davinda's gorgeous tits. But then it constricted further, striking him blind. He felt his legs give way completely and heard a scream as he dropped to the plastic floor, his arms flailing madly. The huge pot of soup crashed down on top of him, its boiling contents scorching his face and chest. He felt the heat only momentarily before the blackness swallowed him whole.

The cameras kept rolling while Davinda Rural kept screaming.

The crofter and the celebrity chef were two amongst many deaths in an otherwise unremarkable day of death in the UK.

In a retirement home in Newcastle, Ellie-Rae Granger had fought off the barmy ones suffering from dementia to gain control of the television. She bemoaned being one of the few with all her mental faculties intact, incarcerated within the bloody home because her body rather than her mind had let her down. The last stroke may have rendered all feeling from her left side, but it didn't stop her using her right arm to slot the remote control down by her hip in her wheelchair, allowing her to continue feasting her eyes on her favourite celebrity chef, the good-looking Irish charmer, David Dougan. As Ellie-Rae watched him and the Indian actress make onion soup, she vacantly observed the chef drop behind the stovetop counter. It was the last thing Ellie-Rae ever saw as she too quietly slipped away, her numb left side masking any pain. An opportunistic fellow patient spotted Ellie-Rae loosen her grip on the remote control and grabbed it, turned the channel over and settled on a cartoon.

Off the Cornish coast of Padstow, Winston Jones was hauling in the nets after a long morning's trawl. As the nets deposited their contents into the hold, he smiled, pleased to see it was a good catch. He'd be back in time for lunch, just in time to see his wife before she left for work in the coffee shop in the centre of town. But it was the last thought he had, as his body went rigid, causing him to lose his balance and topple over the side. Winston Jones' half-eaten body was washed up at the foot of the cliffs four days later.

Darren Raymond pumped his hips back and forth with all his might. He looked down at the stunning young redhead naked beneath him and, noticing her lips were parted, her breathing heavy and her eyes shut, grinned lasciviously at his good fortune. He had no idea what her name was, but it wasn't the first time he'd awoken hungover to find a gorgeous woman next to him, and no memory of how she'd got there.

Well, they weren't always gorgeous, he admitted to himself; that was one of the downsides of right-swiping every profile in the immediate Edinburgh vicinity displayed on his Tinder dating app. When you were drunk and in need of a quick fuck, you couldn't be choosy and swipe to the left, throwing away potential hook-ups. Darren felt his cock harden even more and knew he wouldn't last much longer. He was sweating now and the headache from his hangover was starting to get in the way. Suddenly, the pain in his head shot right down across his body, forcing him to arch his back almost to breaking point, and inadvertently causing him to thrust deeply. He heard the redhead exclaim a breathless, "Yes!" before his body slumped on top her, now a literal dead weight.

In the Midlands, Surinder Patel traipsed up the stairs to the top floor of the block of flats, disheartened to see the local gang lying in wait. What would it take for the sorting office manager to accept that he could no longer deliver to this block on his own? A courier's uniform was no protection against the drug-fuelled gangs that roamed the Leicester housing estate. Hesitantly, he moved forward, knowing that he had to pass by them on the balcony if he was to successfully deliver the Amazon parcel to number 96. Predictably, they blocked his way, shouting racist taunts at him. Two of them began pushing him. But in the middle of their hustle, he screamed with pain, his body going rigid, and, as a result, he was unable to offer any resistance to the final push from the biggest kid, the one with the ring in his nose. Surinder's body flipped backwards over the balcony and dropped to the ground below with a sickening thud, just missing a small girl playing on her scooter. She screamed as blood splattered over her brand new white coat. Five floors above, the gang of kids looked at each other briefly and, without a word, scarpered.

The deaths continued to mount that day in May. A man eating his fried breakfast in a greasy spoon in Hatfield fell facedown into a plate of baked beans, never to finish his meal. A woman running round Lake Windermere stumbled and tripped into the dark water, offering no resistance as she sank to the bottom. An old woman on a Ryanair flight from Bristol, excitedly looking forward to seeing her grandchildren in Spain, was unable to be awoken upon landing in Alicante. And many, many more.

The bodies were all processed properly, each taken to a local hospital or morgue, analysed fully and cause of death ascertained. Surinder Patel was treated as a murder, while Winston Jones' half-eaten body offered little to determine cause of death, and was recorded as accidental. But the others were each diagnosed as heart failure.

As pathologists around the country separately wrote the cause of death on the certificates, there was no one to notice that the times of death were all within a few minutes of each other. Only the deceased chef made the national news, but then it wasn't every day a celebrity dropped down dead on live television.

MONDAY

CHAPTER 2

Brody looked at his watch. Damn, he was now officially fifteen minutes late for his job interview. The car pulled up and he exited the taxi, throwing cash at the driver, and ran up the steps to the GCHQ visitor reception. His train from London had been delayed en route, using up all of his hour-long contingency allowance. He'd had to queue for a taxi outside Cheltenham Spa station, forgetting that *Uber*, the app he used all the time in London to request cabs, wasn't available out in the sticks yet. Then the busybody guard at the security post set within the razor wire-topped perimeter fence hadn't helped either. He'd taken ages to check off Brody's name and raise the barrier to allow the taxi through.

He'd expected the UK government's intelligence headquarters to be located within acres of undulating Cotswolds countryside to avoid unwanted observation, but instead the striking doughnut-shaped concrete-and-steel campus was situated on the edge of Cheltenham, surrounded by residential suburbia.

Brody hurried over to the receptionist and, straightening his slim, plain black tie, and smoothing back his white blond hair, gave his name. She consulted her computer, confirmed he was expected and asked for his identification. He reached into the leather man bag hanging from his shoulder, pulled out his driving licence and handed it over. Brody mentally hopped from one foot to the other as she studiously examined both sides and then paused to compare his face against the miniature image embedded in the plastic.

He smiled cheesily. "I'm hardly going to use a fake ID in here of all places."

"I wouldn't put it past you of all people, Brody," boomed a male voice from behind him.

Brody whirled around, pleased to see the massive form of Victor Gibb, who was smiling from within his cavernous cheeks. Gibb's hand engulfed Brody's as they shook.

"Glad you came, Brody. I half expected you to bail out."

"Of course I came. I'm just sorry I'm so late. Will it be a problem, Doc?"

Gibb wasn't actually a doctor, not as far as Brody knew anyway. 'Doc' was a reference to Doc_Doom, Gibb's handle on the CrackerHack hacker forum where they had originally met and formed an online friendship over the last two years. Brody had only met the man in person six weeks ago and still found it difficult to adapt to his real world name.

"It's okay. I had planned some time for a grand tour and a pep talk before your panel interview, but I guess you'll just have to bluff it." He reached beyond Brody to take a red badge from the receptionist. "Here. Put this on and I'll escort you to the lions' den."

Brody clipped the visitor badge to his lapel and followed Gibb to a security turnstile, next to which stood a uniformed guard and an electronic scanning machine. Brody automatically placed his bag on the conveyer belt and started emptying his pockets as if he was at airport security.

Gibb held his hand out. "Mobile phone, please."

Reluctantly, Brody handed over his Samsung Galaxy. Gibb handed it to the guard.

"You'll get it back when you leave."

"I thought phone signals were blocked inside the Doughnut?"

Gibb carried on walking. "Been doing some research on us, have you, Brody?"

Brody shrugged and passed through the metal detector, absurdly pleased with himself when it didn't go off. Of course he had done some research. He rarely walked into an office building without having thoroughly cased the joint first. But then he was usually testing security procedures, attempting to penetrate a secure data centre, or gain unauthorised access to their private computer network from inside the firewall. And although today was a legitimate meeting and not a penetration test he'd been hired to carry out, by habit he had researched GCHQ as much as was feasible. He considered it good practice.

Brody caught up with Gibb, who was surprisingly sprightly for his size, and asked, "So this is the Street, is it?" He indicated the long corridor that curved off into the distance, walkways above it crossing between the outer and inner rings of the building. Natural light streamed through a glass roof high above. On either side of them, glass-walled partitions gave views of open plan offices, although some windows were obscured by blinds. Groups of staff traversed the corridor and walkways, some in business suits, most dressed casually. Whenever they clocked Brody's bright red visitor badge, their conversations hushed and they stared at him as if he was a leper. Brody had never experienced such paranoia in employees before.

"I'm impressed. Yes, this is the Street. It encircles the building. We have restaurants and coffee shops further along. Need to keep the six thousand staff based here fed and watered. There's also a gym, shops and even a prayer room."

They reached a circular stairway next to a bank of lifts. Gibb chose the stairs. Brody was mildly annoyed. He didn't want to be uncomfortably hot and sweaty in a suit during a job interview. Two floors above, they entered an open plan office and marched across it, passing lines of staff working on computers. Brody automatically glanced at their screens, naturally inquisitive, but they'd already become aware of the visitor, either turning off their monitors or minimising any open windows so that only their official background wallpaper was visible: an aerial shot of the building they were in.

"Well, here we are," announced Gibb, having halted outside the door to a large boardroom. Vertical blinds hid whatever lay behind its glass walls. "I'll be here when you finish later. Let's grab a coffee and debrief afterwards."

"Sounds good. Especially the coffee part."

"Let me give you a piece of advice, Brody."

"Yes?"

"Remember one thing. We know far more about you than you think we do."

"Fair enough, Doc. Wish me luck."

Brody took a deep breath and entered the room.

Two men and one woman sat along one side of an enormous oval boardroom table. One lonely chair remained, directly opposite them. None of them stood to greet him, making Brody realise that his vision of a pleasant chat was somewhat misplaced.

"Take a seat, Mr Taylor," commanded the older man in the middle, peering at him over reading glasses perched low on his long nose, thinning grey hair combed over his balding skull. He wore a dark tweed jacket over a dark shirt, open at the collar. His expression was surly, as if Brody was inconveniencing him by showing up.

Brody did as he was told, pushing the chair back from the table so that he could cross his legs, casually resting his left ankle above his right knee. He knew this would make him appear relaxed and in control. He clasped his hands lightly and dropped them in his lap.

He waited.

The woman, who sat on the right, coughed and then smiled. She was in her late thirties, attractive and buxom with a low-cut top that exposed lots of cleavage. Brody consciously held her eye and smiled back.

"Mr Taylor, my name is Jane. This is Edward." She indicated the spectacled man in the centre who had already spoken. "And on his right is Graham."

The man called Graham hadn't acknowledged Brody once since he'd entered. He was busy swiping on his smartphone, seemingly oblivious to Brody's presence. He wore a pinstriped three-piece suit with a silk handkerchief protruding from the top pocket. His chestnut hair was cut with precision and his nails were manicured. Brody decided that of the three, he looked like trouble.

Graham dropped his phone into his inner suit pocket, sat forward and turned to face his colleagues. "Is it Mr Taylor? I'm a little confused."

"Or is it Mr Brody?" suggested Edward, pushing his glasses up his nose, as if to get a better view of Brody.

Brody sighed and spoke for the first time since entering. "I've already been through this three times with Doc … sorry, I mean Victor. He promised me that my real name would be revealed to the interview panel only to complete the vetting process before I'm asked to sign the Official Secrets Act. If you choose to employ me, I get to continue under my assumed identity of Brody Taylor. And that's how everyone round here would know me. That was the deal."

"Yes, I'm aware of your conversations with Victor. But you have to appreciate our issue with that, Mr …" Jane stumbled over his name.

"Taylor", insisted Brody. "This is non-negotiable."

"But the whole purpose of GCHQ is to protect the country from anonymous cyberthreats. We have to be above board in how we conduct ourselves, especially with each other."

"Really? Seems that everyone here hides his or her real identities. Do you guys even know each other's surnames?" Brody looked at each of them. Edward was about to speak, but Brody continued, indignant. "And then there's Victor, our friend waiting outside. He spent two years grooming me on the internet under an anonymous identity, attempting to lure me into meeting him in the real world so that he could invite me to sign up. Seems that double standards are the done thing round here."

"But why the need for an assumed identity at all?" asked Edward.

"Online I go by the handle of Fingal. I'm sure Victor's already told you that. As Fingal, I've made a lot of enemies in cyberspace. Many of them are dangerous. But online, I can hold my own against anyone. *Anyone.* But, like everyone who enters the deep web, I operate anonymously, masking my real world IP address so that it's almost impossible to track me down in the real world. Even GCHQ's prying eyes have failed at this. That's why it took Doc two years to track me down, and even then it was someone else that stumbled across me. But they only managed to expose one of my fake identities, not my real one. It's my final defence and I use it to maintain complete separation from my family. I will not risk their lives because of what I choose to do for a living."

"Okay, I understand all that, Mr Taylor. But why also here in GCHQ?" asked Edward.

"I'm sure you three are all nice, honest people, but you do hire hackers to work here. Hackers can't be trusted. Ever. If any one of them linked me to my online persona of Fingal, they might decide to expose my identity online. They probably couldn't help themselves."

"You seem to have a high opinion of yourself, Mr Taylor," stated Jane. Brody noticed that she'd used the surname from the identity he wanted to use. He'd won that argument.

"Perhaps," he conceded. "Let me try and explain. Online, Fingal is regarded as one of the world's most prestigious elite hackers. Fact. Getting one over on Fingal would bump up the online reputation of any person who achieved it. To a hacker, status in the hacking community is everything. And exposing Fingal might be enough to tempt even the white hat hackers you have working here if they found out I was among them. I won't risk it." He paused and then added, "And that's disregarding any financial inducement. After all, the Russian mafia has recently upped the bounty on my head to five million dollars."

"So you're concerned that another GCHQ employee could expose you online and lead the bad guys to you in the real world," Jane summarised.

Brody nodded.

"Not very trusting, are you?" This was Graham. He'd only spoken twice now and it seemed each time was an attempt to provoke.

"Not when it comes to protecting my family and those close to me. They would be fair game to the Russian mafia. Leverage against me. One of my close friends was killed because I slipped up. I'm not going to repeat that mistake."

"And this is why you want to join GCHQ?"

The gruesome image of Danny's lifeless body, with the back of his head blown off, blood and brains all over Brody's front room, inserted itself into Brody's mind. Danny had indeed been Brody's friend but, more importantly, he had been the soul mate and long-term partner of Brody's closest friend, Leroy.

When Brody's identity had been uncovered, Vorovskoy Mir, a Russian mafia-funded cybergang, had deployed a hitman to take out Brody in retaliation for years of continually disrupting their online scams, which in turn cut off their illegal revenue streams. Under his anonymous online handle of Fingal, Brody had long been on their public Most Wanted list, where they offered financial rewards for information leading to the capture of any of the hackers listed. At the time of the hit, Fingal was third on the list with a $1 million bounty. The hitman had carried out the attack in Brody's apartment, where Leroy and Danny had been staying. All three would have been eliminated, his two friends simply casualties of war, but the police had arrived just in time. Well, in time to save Brody and Leroy, but not Danny. Brody now topped the Most Wanted list, priced at $5 million.

Shaking the image of Danny from his mind, Brody focused on his objective. "Yes. Together, I think we can bring down Vorovskoy Mir. GCHQ has failed to bring them down for years. I believe we can help each other."

"Let me get this straight," said Edward, incredulity in his tone. "You want a job here so that you can access GCHQ's resources to bring down a Russian cybergang?"

Brody made a show of thinking about it and then nodded. "Yes, Ed."

Edward's jaw dropped. Graham burst out laughing. Jane shook her head.

Brody continued. "Vorovskoy Mir has state sponsorship from Moscow. It's on record for attempting to hack the nuclear power stations at Sizewell and Torness as well as our national grid. And that's ignoring all the lucrative drugs and human trafficking rings it supports. Given GCHQ's main purpose is to protect the UK's critical infrastructure from cyberthreats like this, I'd hazard a guess that you have a whole team dedicated to bringing down Vorovskoy Mir. And I can increase their chances of success."

"We're not in the business of hiring externally for one-off projects, Mr Taylor," said Jane. "We recruit analysts who are looking for a rewarding career combatting cyberterrorism in all its forms."

"And I'm happy to be deployed wherever you want," offered Brody, "*after* we've brought Vorovskoy Mir to its knees."

Edward and Graham glanced at each other.

Brody knew he had their attention now.

Graham turned back to Brody, all business. He leaned forward. "What do you have that GCHQ doesn't already have?"

"Three things." Brody counted off on his fingers. "One, I think like them. Two, they're after me and so we can use that to lure them out." It was time to play his trump card, which he'd not even revealed to Victor Gibb. "And three, I've seen Contagion's face."

Brody was referring to the leader of the Russian cybergang. While Brody, Leroy and Danny were being held at gunpoint by the hitman, Contag10n had Skyped in to personally observe Brody's execution over the remote live video feed. Safe in the knowledge that Brody was about to be killed, Contag10n had revealed his face. The image of the tattooed, metal-studded young cybercriminal was indelibly imprinted on Brody's retinas.

"You've seen Contagion?" asked Graham, disbelievingly.

"Better than that, I've talked to him."

Graham folded his arms and sat back in his chair.

The interview carried on for another fifty minutes, but Brody knew the hard part was over. Jane steered the conversation back to the benefits of a career working for Her Majesty. She grilled him over his psychometric test results, probing into Brody's lack of respect for authority, which he found amusing and didn't deny. It became clear that she was representing the human resources department and, as such, Brody paid lip service but nothing more. It wasn't her he needed to impress.

Edward, on the other hand, appeared to be on the panel to

determine Brody's technical competencies. His questioning began with an examination of Brody's programming abilities. He commented favourably on the results of the online tests Brody had completed the week before. He then turned the conversation into a discussion on the pros and cons of a range of computer hacking and social engineering techniques, visibly impressed at Brody's balanced approach to exploiting weaknesses in computer systems, digital or human.

Meanwhile, Graham contented himself with observing Brody intently, and offered no comments nor asked any further questions for the rest of the meeting. Brody concluded that Graham must work on the Russian desk and had made his decision, one way or the other, back at the beginning of the meeting during Brody's revelations about Vorovskoy Mir and Contag10n.

Half an hour after the interview finished, Brody and Victor Gibb were back on the ground floor of the building, enjoying coffee in one of the cafés located on the Street. During their journey back, Gibb had diverted him into a small onsite museum. Brody had been surprised to see displayed the first Enigma decoding machine, which had cracked German signals during the Second World War. His interest was also piqued by the notes handwritten on JRR Tolkien's application to join the code breakers at Bletchley Park, the original location for the organisation that would eventually become known as GCHQ. He wondered what the notes would say on his own application following his earlier interview.

Brody savoured the bitter flavour of his espresso and nodded at his host to show his appreciation.

"Not too bad, is it?" agreed Gibb, sat opposite Brody on a double leather sofa, his massive frame spread over both cushions. With one hand, Gibb lifted his own coffee to his lips, an oversized mug of caffè latte; his other hand maintained in position a few centimetres below, palm side down, to capture any drips that might otherwise spill onto his considerable girth. Brody could see it was a practised manoeuvre.

"Considering we're in the back end of beyond, I'm quite

impressed," commented Brody.

Victor leaned forward carefully. "So, how do you think the interview went?"

"I'm not sure the panel appreciated my honesty. They're probably used to recruiting gullible, whiter-than-white graduates rather than the likes of me, with my scars and a damn sight more shades of grey."

"I'm sure they've seen worse."

"Maybe, but probably only when interrogating captured Russian or Chinese black hats."

Victor placed his fingers over his mouth, feigning shock. "You're not a Russian black hat double agent, are you?"

Brody smiled obligingly. "Maybe Graham wondered that when I demanded to be attached to his Russian desk."

"Did he agree?"

Gibb's innocent question was all the confirmation Brody needed that Graham led the Russian desk.

"I think they're reticent about letting me go after Vorovskoy Mir. They pretty much said revenge is not a good motive for joining GCHQ."

"What did you say?"

"I told them to like it or lump it. If they want me in the service of Her Majesty, that's the only way they're getting me."

"Jesus, Brody."

"It's not like the pay's attractive."

"Well, that's for sure," confirmed Victor.

"Did they agree to you maintaining your Brody Taylor identity?"

"They didn't like it. But I think so."

"Aren't you concerned Vorovskoy Mir will track you down again?"

"Come on, Doc. I'm sure you've been fully briefed on my vetting process. You already know full well I've assumed a different identity."

"Well, yes, of course. Brody Charles Taylor instead of Brody Kenneth Taylor. You sure that's enough to keep the bastards off your scent?"

Brody knew he should have chosen a completely different name to better ensure his own safety. Perhaps it was a tiny rebellion against having to give up so much following the attack. Losing his apartment was just about bearable but severing all use of the Brody Taylor name he'd used for the last ten years would have been tough. However, to prevent the Russian mafia tracking him down in the real world again, he'd immediately dropped the original Brody Taylor identity and all ties to it.

Fortunately, his secret cache of legitimate pre-prepared alternatives, which he'd applied his hacking skills to set up many years before, included one other 'Brody Taylor'. This version had a different middle name and date of birth as well as a distinct passport number, national insurance number and other identifying factors that gave credence in the real world. But at least he could continue operating under the same name, albeit four years younger than his real age of 32.

"It will work fine. Anyway, there's no way I'm signing up here under my real name. That was the deal we made, Doc. If I ever spot it on any database or correspondence, I walk. Okay?"

Victor nodded soberly. "So, what is your real name then?" He gulped some more coffee and then gave a cheeky smile. "You can tell me, we're amongst friends." He waved his free arm around, pointedly indicating the groups of other government employees enjoying their coffee breaks or having informal meetings.

"Either you've got clearance to know my real name, or you haven't." Brody sat back and folded his arms. "But you're not getting it out of me."

"Correct answer," said Gibb with a grin. "We'll make a good GCHQ network operations specialist out of you with responses like that."

Brody shrugged. He'd found the whole vetting process far too intimate and didn't appreciate Gibb needling him. He'd felt completely naked when he'd finally exposed the identity he was born with when asked to sign the Official Secrets Act, but it was the only way he could apply for the job. While his alternate identities were good, they weren't up to fooling GCHQ.

They chatted amiably for a while and, when their cups were empty, Gibb escorted Brody back to reception. Brody picked up his phone from the security guard and turned it back on.

"Do you think they'll take me on, Doc?"

Gibb thought for a moment. "I would think so. Having the infamous Fingal working for the government is too much to pass up, even for them. I guess we'll know in a few days. Assuming the outcome is positive, when could you start?"

"Pretty much straight away."

"Will you move to the Cotswolds?"

They passed through the final turnstile and stood in the reception area next to two imposing pieces of art sitting on black onyx plinths. The frosted glass rock structures were still rough, as if they had been hewn out of the ground by giants. Their centres had been polished into round convex transparent lenses. Aptly, they reminded Brody of the All-Seeing Eye in Tolkien's *Lord of the Rings*.

"Not sure. I'll probably rent a flat in Cheltenham during the week." Brody looked up suddenly. "You do get decent broadband speed out here in the sticks?"

Victor chuckled. "I think it's probably no secret that with GCHQ being headquartered here, we generally have the fastest speeds in the country."

Brody smiled. "Well, that's settled, then."

"Have you told that beautiful police detective of yours that you plan to stay down here midweek?"

The smile dropped from Brody's face. No, he hadn't told Jenny that his plans required him to leave London, just as their relationship was getting going. He wasn't sure they'd survive as a long-distance relationship. Few people could.

Just as he was pondering how to talk to her, his phone buzzed three times in his pocket. This close to the entrance, it had picked a signal. But three buzzes meant someone had just posted something on the CrackerHack forum that included one of four keywords Brody was monitoring. Any time one of the keywords was used, an alert was sent to him immediately.

Brody reached for his phone and read the message. Frowning,

he looked up at Gibb and asked, "Do you remember BionicM@n from CrackerHack?"

"Yes, why?"

"I don't suppose GCHQ has his real world name and address, does it?"

"Even if it does, I'm not sharing it with you until you're a proper employee."

"Come on, Doc."

"What's going on, Brody?"

"He's on the Vorovskoy Mir Most Wanted list."

"So what? So are you."

"Well, they've just killed him."

DI Jenny Price placed the phone back on its cradle and punched the air in triumph, but then quickly withdrew her hand before anyone in the incident room spotted her reaction. She composed herself, just about suppressing a smile. Noisily, she pushed her chair back and stood from behind her desk, where she'd been trapped for weeks under a mountain of paperwork.

DS Alan Coombs and DC Fiona Jones looked up.

"Alan. Fiona," said Jenny. "Drop whatever you're doing. You're coming with me." She headed towards the exit of the incident room.

"What's going on, Jen?" asked Fiona, grabbing her jacket from the back of her chair.

"Dead body. Suspected snake poison."

"You can't be serious," stated Alan, rushing to catch up. "That means …" His voice trailed off as he processed the implications.

Jenny finished for him. "… that we've got a possible linked murder."

"Bloody hell, Jenny," said Alan, "Da Silva will jump for joy when he hears this."

Jenny halted at the door and made an exaggerated show of looking back across the incident room, as if searching for something. Ahead of her, the Holborn murder investigation team's officers and civilians diligently worked the phones and computers, a general hubbub of activity.

"Thought so," said Jenny.

"Thought what?" asked Alan.

"DCI Da Silva's not here. Nor is DI Knight." She turned to her older colleague. "Which makes me what, Alan?"

Realisation dawned on his face and he smiled conspiratorially. "Which makes you the SIO."

"While the prat's away ..." chimed in Fiona.

Jenny turned and flew down the stairs two steps at a time, her colleagues right behind her. Yes, Alan was right. With DCI Da Silva out of the picture, she had defaulted to becoming the Senior Investigating Officer on a new murder case.

"Da Silva will go apeshit when he gets back."

"Well, if he wants to go gallivanting up to Bedford, chasing a spurious lead, then that's his call."

"You ought to phone him, Jen," cautioned Alan.

"Don't you worry, Al, I will," said Jenny, opening the back door leading out to the police station car park. "After we confirm it's linked to the first poisoning."

"But that'll take a day or two. Da Silva will be back later today."

"So when he gets back, I'll update him. But until then, I'm in charge."

"You're pushing your luck, Jen."

"Maybe. But by then, I'll be point on this new case and he'll no longer be able to palm me off with shitty background tasks."

Jenny had fallen foul of her DCI during a recent double murder case. Newly promoted to the rank of Detective Chief Inspector and never having led a murder investigation, Da Silva had relied heavily on Jenny's greater experience and natural leadership ability to make it through the investigation, despite her lower rank. But, when a major break occurred, he had deliberately sidelined Jenny so that he could apprehend the suspect himself, seizing all the glory in the full glare of television cameras. However, Da Silva had inadvertently arrested an innocent man, which had backfired on him publicly. In the meantime, Jenny and Fiona became the ones to collar the real killer, thus receiving all the plaudits, much to Da Silva's infuriation.

In retaliation, Da Silva had spent the last six weeks since the killer's arrest making Jenny's life miserable, assigning her the most menial of tasks and keeping her focused on building the evidence pack for the Crown Prosecution Service. He had also seconded another DI to his murder investigation team alongside Jenny; an overweight, sleazy barrow boy-style cockney called Kevin Knight. Da Silva and Knight were colleagues and friends from Da Silva's brief time with the Met's kidnap unit the year before, and it was obvious to everyone that the inexperienced Da Silva was now relying on Knight's advice a bit too much.

The phrase 'the blind leading the blind' had been muttered more than once over the last few weeks.

Jenny had bitten her tongue and got on with the work. She told herself that packaging all the evidence to ensure that CPS secured the conviction of a serial killer was important, no matter how mundane the activity. While labouring under the mountain of paperwork, she had observed Da Silva and Knight lead her very own team on a series of new cases. From what she had overheard, the most interesting of them had occurred just last week when a thirty-year-old man in Highgate had been bitten by a poisonous snake and died. There were other factors that indicated foul play, but Jenny had only overheard snippets and so wasn't close to the details. But she innately knew that another snake poisoning within a week in another part of London was far more than coincidence.

And with Da Silva out of the picture for the day, Jenny resolved to grab the opportunity with both hands.

Sod him!

"Ah, Mr Brody, Mr Brody. Good to have you back."

Brody slumped into his favourite chair at the front of Bruno's coffee house and looked up at Stefan, the owner and head barista. His black hair was waxed back as always, reminding Brody of an Italian gangster from one of the *Godfather* movies. He wore his usual uniform, a black apron over white shirt and black trousers.

"Thanks Stefan, it was a long journey back to London."

"Long journey, Mr Brody says." It was as if Stefan was talking to himself. "And is warm outside, no? Hmm, in that case, I know what he will drink." Stefan turned his attention back to Brody and, with a flourish, concluded, "A double espresso and a glass of iced water."

Brody enjoyed their regular game. Even if Stefan guessed wrong, Brody rarely corrected him. The coffee here was good in whatever form it was served, hot or ice cold, short or long, with or without frothed milk. And now that Brody rented the flat above and Stefan had become his landlord and neighbour, Brody took extra care to stay on his good side.

"Perfect! A double espresso would be great. Thanks, Stefan."

Stefan shuffled back to the counter to make the coffee, effortlessly lifting empty cups and saucers from other tables en route.

Brody thought about the strange message he'd received earlier. He'd spent the journey back from Cheltenham mulling over its implications. The 'honourable' hackers, known as white hats, who'd made it onto Vorovskoy Mir's Most Wanted list were all professionals, completely adept at masking their locations. Brody's recent run in with them had only occurred because he'd been discovered in the real world and linked back to his Fingal identity, not the other way around. The precautions Brody took meant that no one could ever track him from his activity on the internet. So he was surprised that BionicM@n had tripped up. His status in the hacking community was not far behind Fingal's and his contributions to hacking discussions in the CrackerHack forums were incredibly technical, with his programming skills probably even more advanced. But the message he'd received was unequivocal: BionicM@n was dead.

He reached into his bag for his PC. He wanted to read the message one more time. After all, it contained far more than he'd disclosed to Victor Gibb. He pulled out an ethernet cable and plugged one end into the network point on the wall by his feet and the other into a dongle hanging from his tablet's USB port.

When Brody had moved into the flat above a few weeks ago, he'd convinced Stefan to allow him to extend the hard-wired network he'd installed in the flat down into the coffee shop, right by his favourite seat. Not being accustomed to doing physical jobs himself, Brody had bodged the network cable through two floors after borrowing Stefan's power drill to make the necessary holes. But, if he wanted access to artisan coffee while working, it was absolutely necessary. After his old apartment's private Wi-Fi network had been hacked six weeks before, which had led to the exposure of his previous identity, Brody now took greater precautions. Hard-wired was more secure than Wi-Fi, especially as he'd also configured his firewall router to block connections from unrecognised MAC addresses. That way, if any other patron tried to plug their computer into the network point located by his favourite seat in the coffee house, they would be denied access and would no doubt revert to the coffee shop's public Wi-Fi network.

"I see your penchant for good coffee is as strong as ever, Brody."

Brody glanced up quickly. The speaker was hidden behind a large potted plant but Brody could see through the leaves that he was slowly pushing himself up from an armchair. The gravelly voice with its Welsh lilt sounded familiar. Brody's instinctive reaction was that it was Leroy, but then his conscious brain took over, reminding him that his best friend was no longer on speaking terms with him, blaming him for Danny's death. An elderly black man stepped out from behind the plant and Brody immediately recognised the grinning face and understood why he had thought of Leroy. The similarity between father and son was just as spooky as the last time he'd seen them together.

Brody stood up and, hesitating briefly, shook the proffered hand.

"What are you doing here, Mr Bishop?"

"Less of the Mr Bishop. I've told you before. Call me Vernon. Mind if I take the weight off these old legs?"

"Here, take this chair." Brody hopped away from the chestnut leather high back he'd been using. "It's the most comfortable one in this place."

"Bless you, son."

Vernon lowered himself slowly into the chair. Brody sat on a rustic green Chesterfield sofa opposite, a coffee table between them.

He'd last seen Leroy's father two years before, during a week-long stay at his alpaca farm in Wales along with Leroy and his sister, Hope. Leroy had begged Brody to come with them, saying he would go mad with boredom otherwise. But Brody had always enjoyed visiting Leroy's parents in the North Wales countryside and so hadn't put up much of a fight. In the capital, Brody rarely spent time outdoors and certainly never disconnected from the internet. But at the Bishop farm, which had no broadband and an intermittent mobile signal, Brody was forced to switch off completely. He even enjoyed mucking in with the farm workers, caring for the strange South American beasts.

"I was hoping to see you," announced Vernon gravely.

Brody noticed that Vernon's short curly hair had turned even whiter at the sides, contrasting against his dark brown skin. His eyes were also much more lined, but the sparkle in them was as bright as ever. Age had lent Vernon Bishop a distinguished look, accentuated by the dark suit he was currently wearing. Brody had only ever seen him wear a suit on Sundays when he attended church service.

"You were waiting for me here?"

"I knocked at your flat across the road, but the old lady who lives there now said you'd moved out a while ago. No forwarding address. I remembered how much you liked this place and wondered if you might show up. And if you hadn't, well at least I'd have had a good cup of coffee."

Brody was relieved. It had been a risk to only move across the road from his old abode, even under his new identity. But Brody had reasoned that Vorovskoy Mir would assume he'd run and hide far from the location of their recent encounter and so he'd decided on the exact opposite. Anyway, they'd cost him so much. Danny's life. Leroy's friendship. His luxury apartment.

Even his orange and black custom-designed Smart Fortwo coupe, which he'd quickly sold for cash. Brody was damned if he was going to give up everything. Vernon had used the one thing Vorovskoy Mir didn't have access to in order to track him down: inside knowledge of Brody's real world habits. He was still safe.

"I had to move out …" Brody hesitated, realising he couldn't explain why, " … but I decided to stay in the area." He wasn't going to disclose the fact he'd moved into the flat two floors above.

"Shame, that was a nice apartment you and Leroy used to share."

"What's going on, Vernon? Is Leroy with you?" Brody's eyes scanned the coffee shop, his gaze settling on the door to the men's toilet at the back of the room, expecting it to open at any moment.

"No, he accompanied me down to London for my doctor's appointment. But right now, he's auditioning for the part of Jaques in *As You Like It* at the Barbican. I helped him rehearse his lines all the way down on the train. You should have seen the other passengers staring."

Leroy made his living as an actor. He'd been in many West End shows over the years but had mostly only had parts in the chorus, singing and dancing. A couple of times he'd won auditions for supporting comedy roles, which suited his ebullient personality. It seemed he was continuing this trend, but Brody knew his lifelong dream was to play Hamlet in Shakespeare's Globe theatre on the South Bank.

"Doctors? Is everything okay?"

"Yes, of course." Vernon patted his chest gently. "I just used my pacemaker check-up as an excuse to trick Leroy out of the house. He's been wallowing around at home for weeks now. And thank the good Lord I did; he managed to land the audition at the same time."

Brody vaguely recalled Leroy once explaining that his father had had a pacemaker fitted following a series of fainting episodes when Leroy was a teenager. The cause turned out to be a slow heartbeat. Something to do with a blocked artery in the neck.

"You're not having it checked, then?"

"Well, yes, I just did. At the specialist in Harley Street. Battery's got at least another couple of years. Everything's good. Amazing how they can tell all that without opening me up. They just connect a meter to it over radio waves or something. Dead easy … Anyway, so while Leroy's otherwise engaged I thought I'd pop in to see you on the way back to Euston. Still got a couple of hours before my train leaves."

Stefan returned carrying a tray, his eyebrows raised inquisitively at Brody's companion, but he didn't say anything. He placed Brody's beverage down in front of him along with a glass of iced water and checked if Vernon wanted anything, but Vernon joked that if he drank any more coffee he'd never sleep again. Brody thanked Stefan and he left them to it.

Brody lifted the glass of water to his lips, wondering what the hell Vernon could possibly want with him.

Vernon looked around to check the coast was clear, lowered his voice, as if he was revealing a great conspiracy, and leaned forward. "I'd always thought you and Leroy were … you know …" He shuffled in his seat. " … lovers."

Brody coughed and spluttered out a mouthful of water. Spray filled the air in front of him. Recovering from the shock, he placed the glass back on the table, grabbed a serviette and wiped his mouth. "What the hell made you think that?" Brody didn't stem the flow of outrage he felt at the accusation.

"Well, just the way you two are. You've been close friends for years, living together on and off. Neither of you ever brought a girlfriend home. And Leroy's always been … what's the word? Camp."

Blimey, this was a revelation. For all the years Brody had known Leroy, his best friend had lived in abject fear of coming out to his parents, suppressing his homosexuality from them completely. It was why he'd chosen a London university, leaving home for a place where he at least had a chance of meeting another man, in complete contrast to the narrow-minded Welsh village where he'd grown up. Leroy had told Brody that he suspected his mum may have known, but never did anything to broach the subject. And he'd dreaded ever raising the subject with his dad, unsure how the devoutly religious man would react. And with his father's heart condition, Leroy didn't want to cause any shock.

Yet here was Vernon, casually admitting he'd always known. Or did he? Perhaps he was fishing for confirmation.

Brody decided to focus on himself, not Leroy. "But I have a girlfriend."

'Yes, I know that now. Leroy told me." Vernon winked. "A policewoman, so I hear. Good on you, son."

Brody ignored the wink and focused on the more important fact. "I'm surprised Leroy's been talking about me."

That was a good sign, wasn't it?

"Because of what happened to Danny?"

"He told you about Danny?" Now Brody really was surprised.

"Yes, so very sad." He clasped his hands together and shook his head. "But it's because of Danny's death that Leroy's finally admitted to us that he's gay. When he moved back home six weeks ago, he was a complete mess, moping around feeling sorry for himself, but without explaining why. First of all, Gloria and I thought it was about you. That you'd split up or something. But we couldn't say anything as neither of us had ever broached the subject."

"What happened?"

"Eventually, he broke down in the kitchen and told us everything. We couldn't believe it when he told us that he'd had a partner for the last five years. And that it was someone else."

"Not me, you mean."

"Yes. I just wish …" Vernon took a gulp of air. His emotions were cracking. " … That we'd found a way to talk about all this before now. That way, we'd have met his Danny. We'd have met the person who tamed our wild son." Vernon offered a wan smile.

"I must say you don't seem concerned about Leroy being gay."

"I think we've always known. I'm just glad that it's all out in the open now."

"Leroy always thought you'd blow your top. Sever all ties. Be embarrassed of him."

"And maybe he was right. But seeing him grieving so deeply these last few weeks has helped me understand that his love for Danny was as deep as mine is for his mother."

"Well …" Brody didn't know what to say. "Danny was a great guy."

"He's so grief-stricken right now he's in danger of losing himself completely. Gloria says he should go to the doctors, get some anti-depressants. But I think all he needs is his best mate. You two were always great together. I'm sure if you came up to the farm you could help him through this."

"I'd love to help him, Vernon, but that would be the last thing he'd want. He blames me for Danny's death."

"Is that why you're not on speaking terms?"

Brody shrugged in acknowledgement. "He's right to blame me. I was the root cause."

"But you didn't pull the trigger."

"I may as well have."

"So you won't help?" Vernon's voice took on a shade of steel.

"If I could, I would. But if I show up at the farm, he's likely to kill me."

"I think he's past that, Brody."

"I doubt it. You didn't see his face at Danny's funeral."

"Grieving is a process. The anger's gone now. He seems calmer, more withdrawn than anything."

"That's good to hear. But if he sees me, I'm pretty sure I'll set him back. I'm sure you don't want that."

A phone rang loudly. It was an ancient polyphonic ringtone. Vernon pulled a silver Nokia 6610 out of his jacket pocket and peered at its black and white LCD display. Brody couldn't believe anyone could operate without a smartphone these days.

"Talk of the devil," Vernon announced, and put the phone to his ear. "Hi son, how did the audition go?"

Brody picked up his tablet and began randomly scrolling through emails, trying to give the impression he wasn't paying attention.

"That's great, son … told you the Lord works in mysterious ways, didn't I? … no, I don't remember Julian … sure, that's no problem, I'm already at Euston." At this, Vernon glanced at Brody and raised his eyebrows. "I'll be fine, son, of course I will … yes, you stay over and go out with Julian … don't worry, I'll let your mum know when I get home … tomorrow, sure … yes, of course, we can still go fishing on Friday … yes, I'll be fine … you go enjoy yourself, son … what about seeing Brody if you're staying over? You know you should."

Brody shook his head at Vernon, but Vernon ignored him and continued listening. Eventually, he said, "Well, I think he'd want to see you … you two can't throw away that many years despite what happened to Danny … well I think he would, in fact I know he would … okay, you think about it. See you in a couple of days." Vernon said goodbye, clicked off the call and placed the handset back inside his jacket pocket, each movement over-exaggerated to emphasise how pleased he was with himself. He leaned back in his chair, folded his arms and allowed a huge grin to spread across his face. "Maybe I will have another coffee."

CHAPTER 3

JENNY DISPASSIONATELY STUDIED THE GRUESOME SIGHT IN front of her, trying to breathe through her mouth to dismiss the stench.

The corpse lay sideways on the carpeted floor, tightly bound to an oak dining chair. Acrid-smelling vomit was everywhere. It looked as though the man had puked violently in all directions and all over himself before toppling over, taking the chair with him. Jenny couldn't tell whether he had been pushed or had overbalanced during his frenzied struggles against the ropes. Having fallen, he had continued retching, forming a large pool of sick under his head. Blood had also oozed from his nose.

"That's disgusting," said Fiona, covering her nose and mouth with the sleeve of her jacket.

"If that's the best you can offer, DC Jones, then you can get the fuck out of my crime scene." Jason Edmonds, the crime scene manager, was on his knees behind the body, examining the rope knots. He was dressed head to toe in white Tyvek coveralls and spoke from behind a respiratory mask. Two other members of his team were present. One was actively photographing the body from all angles. Another was dusting the doorknob on the living room door.

Fiona muttered a muffled apology and then retched. She turned and hurried out of the room.

Edmonds shook his head at Jenny. "Bloody amateurs."

Having attended numerous murder scenes with Fiona in the past, Jenny was surprised at her reaction. Perhaps she'd had a late night and was feeling particularly delicate. Although Fiona was perfectly presented as usual, with her precision-cut dark haired bob and perfectly pressed, tight-fitting suit.

"Talking of amateurs," said Edmonds, looking up at her, "how come your guvnor's not here?"

"Da Silva's in Bedford following up a lead on the first snake attack." Jenny crossed her arms and smiled, faking innocence. "So you've got to put up with me, Jason."

"Thank fuck for that." He resumed studying the rope knots.

Jenny crouched and turned her attention to a second wooden chair, which had been placed opposite where the dead man must have sat before falling over. She gave voice to the thought that occurred to her. "It's as if someone just sat there impassively and watched him die."

She heard a rustle behind her and turned to see Dr Gorski, dressed in his distinctive green coveralls, enter the room. The local pathologist spoke with an accent that always reminded Jenny of vampires from old black-and-white Boris Karloff movies. "If that is true," he said, "then whoever it was was sitting for one, perhaps two hours."

"What makes you say that, Doc?" asked Jenny, standing up.

"Black mamba."

Jenny stared blankly.

"Black mamba. Is a snake."

"You found the snake?" Jenny's eyes darted in all directions.

"No, no. Perpetrator took snake away."

"But while it was here," continued Edmonds, still kneeling, "it bit our friend Mr Gowda here multiple times on the hand and wrist." He pointed at the victim's left hand, the only limb not tied to the chair with rope.

Jenny leaned in closer, but couldn't see any obvious external marks. "I thought there would be massive swelling around the bite area?"

"Most snakebites do cause swelling. But not the black mamba, which Dr Gorski and I are now experts on following the first attack in Highgate last week."

"So that's how you know it would have taken him a couple of hours to die?"

"Yes," confirmed Gorski, "but is a horrible way to go. Once bitten, the victim would have been in excruciating abdominal pain, hence all the vomiting you can see. After a while, he would have had severe convulsions and eventually his lungs would have slowly shut down, placing him in coma before finally dying."

Jenny shuddered. Apart from his free arm, the poor man had been tied up the whole time. "I heard your working theory is that the previous victim placed his hand into a container with the snake inside?" During the drive over from HQ, Alan and Fiona had brought Jenny up to speed with the facts from the crime scene and subsequent autopsy, where a thirty-year-old man called James Butler had died in the same way; tied to a chair and bitten by a snake.

"The operative word is *placed*," clarified Edmonds. "As in *not had his hand forced*."

Gorski nodded. "Yes, autopsy revealed absence of bruising around Butler's wrist. If someone had forced his arm into a box containing snake, Butler's resistance would have caused bruising against perpetrator's grip."

"And there wasn't any?" asked Jenny.

"No," said Edmonds. "Lots of bruising over his body where Butler struggled against the ropes, but that would have been from the violent convulsions caused by the venom. None around the wrist or forearm where the snake bit, which wasn't tied up."

"And is it the same with Mr Gowda, here?"

Gorski kneeled down next to the dead man, carefully avoiding any vomit, and peered closely at his bare brown-skinned arm. It was a strange sight, the two men covered head-to-toe in plastic, kneeling either side of the victim, who was still tied to the wooden chair. "I will confirm during autopsy, but there doesn't seem to be any bruising here either."

"How do you know there was a box at all? Couldn't the snake have been thrown or placed on the victim?"

"A mamba is incredibly dangerous. It's not a pet snake you

can carry around over your shoulders. It would need to have been brought inside in some kind of container."

"And, as you can see, the bite marks are contained around the area of the hand and lower arm. This was the same on Butler. Only that area was exposed to the snake, meaning it had to be in a container."

"If one hand was free, why didn't he just untie himself?"

"Presumably because the perpetrator remained sitting opposite him and would have stopped him," suggested Edmonds.

Jenny tried to visualise placing her hand into a container holding a poisonous snake. "Are you saying it's some strange form of suicide?" she asked, incredulity in her tone.

"Not quite." Edmonds pointed to the rope knots behind the victim's back. "It's impossible to tie yourself up like this guy has. So, it's one of two things. Either it's some kind of assisted suicide. Or …"

Gorski finished off. " … or the victims were tied up and verbally coerced to put their free hand in the box with the mamba."

"Blimey, what could you say to someone to make them place their hand inside a box with a deadly snake?" asked Jenny, rhetorically.

"That's your job, Jen." Edmonds looked up at her, a glint in his eyes. "Not ours."

Brody slammed shut the door to his apartment, but then recalled that he was directly above Bruno's busy coffee shop. The patrons downstairs would no doubt have heard the bang. He grimaced and offered up a silent apology to Stefan.

Leroy's father's unexpected visit had brought everything back into focus. With Leroy out of sight and out of mind during the six weeks since Danny's death, he'd allowed the GCHQ recruitment process to fool him into thinking he was actually doing something about Danny's murder. But Leroy was already back in town. How could Brody possibly face him without something tangible to say about gaining revenge? Brody was convinced that if he could prove to Leroy that he had a plan to make Contag10n pay, then they would have a chance of returning to normality.

Brody missed his best friend being the noisy thorn in his side, forever remonstrating about how much time Brody spent online with his anonymous contacts, always pointing out that digital friendships don't qualify as such. He missed his flatmate just being around his apartment, even the grumpy, hungover version usually found barely alive late mornings or early afternoons, lolling about Brody's apartment, waiting for his alcohol-induced symptoms to pass before he would go back to work, put his all into another stage performance and then have the energy to go out partying in Soho until the small hours. But during the last six weeks, every time Brody pictured Leroy, he was haunted by the raw, brutally hurt and utterly betrayed expression that had adorned his friend's face when he'd stared accusingly at Brody across Danny's grave.

Brody realised he needed to stop procrastinating. He should be doing something else while also working his way through GCHQ's long-winded recruitment process. He estimated it would now take them a few days to communicate their decision. Assuming they hired him, it would probably take another few weeks before he commenced work. Even then there would no doubt be a probation period, during which he would have limited access to key systems while they monitored his activities, making sure he was truly trustworthy. He knew it would take months before he would be allowed to properly get his hands on their infamous toys. But once he finally did, he was sure his skills, coupled with GCHQ's mass-surveillance capabilities, would enable him to track down Contag10n in no time at all.

But all that would be months away. He needed to get going now. He owed it to Danny. And Leroy. He should be chasing down Contag10n with or without GCHQ's help. And with that finally decided, he remembered that he now had a new angle he could exploit. After all, the unexpected death of BionicM@n, his compatriot from the Vorovskoy Mir Most Wanted list, offered up a promising new attack vector.

Brody pushed himself up from the sofa and sat at the desk facing the window onto Upper Street. He powered on his tablet and brought up the private message from BionicM@n he had received that morning while he'd been with Doc_Doom at GCHQ. He'd read it three or four times on the train back to London and still couldn't believe what it said.

Fingal,

If you are reading this, I am dead.

I have set up a failsafe so that if I don't personally check in within five days, this email is automatically sent to you. Ever since fucking over Vorovskoy Mir two years ago, I have successfully checked in every day since. Therefore, I can only assume I am now dead.

Occasionally, I update this death letter, changing who its recipient will be, based on who seems up for (and capable of) bringing down Vorovskoy Mir the most. These days, that's you. You recently took them on and somehow survived, although paying a heavy price according to the rumours on CrackerHack. But I know you want to destroy them and so I now choose you. I also know from your recent temporary outing that you live in the UK. So do I.

Or I did, I suppose. :-(

I'm hoping that your public condemnation of those Russian bastards means you have the motivation and the means to bring them down. And assuming you do live in the UK that means that you'll have the ability to track me down in the real world. Because if you do, I have some information you will find helpful in your quest.

Obviously, I'm not just going to give you my real world name and address. After all, it's theoretically possible that I'm not dead and this death letter has gone out prematurely. Maybe I'm just temporarily incapacitated, perhaps stuck in hospital after a car accident, in a coma. Or maybe I've finally reached old age, got a sudden attack of Alzheimer's disease and forgotten all about this little email. But somehow I doubt it.

I am dead.

Track me down IRL. Or should I say IRD? ;-)

If you do, I will help you place a hex on those bastards. I want them to pay for killing me.

Go get 'em cowboy,

BionicM@n

Brody had never considered writing a letter like this himself. Even if he did, what would be the point? He'd be dead. And to whom would he send it, anyway? There was no one on the hacker forums he held in high enough regard or who he thought would care. Yet here was BionicM@n singling him out. Although Brody knew he'd publicly pissed off Vorovskoy Mir, he hadn't realised he'd become the unofficial champion of other white hat hackers disgruntled with the cybergang's heavy-handed, bullying behaviour. But to write a death letter to him … well, that was freaky.

Brody hoped BionicM@n wasn't dead and that his automated trigger had fired for a more prosaic reason. Deep down, Brody knew it was a forlorn hope. BionicM@n was a decent white hat, regularly active on the CrackerHack forums, talking mostly sense. He was smart enough not to slip up and allow his death letter to be sent inadvertently. No, this hacker was dead.

Dead or alive though, the part of the letter that really caught Brody's attention was the promise of information to help him track down Vorovskoy Mir. Brody wanted to get his hands on that more than anything. It was strange that BionicM@n had mentioned cursing them with a hex. Was he into black magic or something along those lines?

Brody thought about how he might track BionicM@n down in real life; IRL, as written in the letter. Or 'in real death', as BionicM@n had darkly joked. The only fact BionicM@n had disclosed about his identity was that he was British. Would it be as simple as searching the news sites in the UK for recent murders and narrowing down from there? He only had to identify all murders over the last week. Brody reasoned that there wouldn't be that many. After all this was the United Kingdom, not the gun-toting United States.

Brody fired up his tablet and began Googling news sites, using the keyword 'murder' and narrowing down the timeframe to a week. Annoyingly, news stories from all over the world popped up instead. He tried various ways of narrowing the results to just the UK, but still found that the stories varied between fresh crimes and updated stories on older crimes.

It would be much quicker if he had access to the national police database called HOLMES. He considered asking Jenny for help — as a police detective she had access to it via the Metropolitan Police IT systems — but then immediately discarded the thought. He was still regaining her trust after an initial bout of lies and deceit during their first week together. The last thing their burgeoning relationship needed was anything to make her think he was doing something dodgy once again. He was pretty sure asking questions about recent murders fell into that category.

He needed to get smart about this.

Surely BionicM@n would have given him more to go on than his nationality? Brody reread the death letter carefully, looking for clues. After reading it a few times, he realised that one sentence jarred with the rest of the letter. It was the line where BionicM@n had signed off, saying, "Go get 'em cowboy". Why would he use that phrase? First of all it was American slang, not British. Now that he thought about it, there was nothing about Brody's online persona that would naturally make someone refer to Fingal as a cowboy.

Brody guessed it had to mean something.

There was perhaps one other clue he could work with. BionicM@n as an online handle. Most hackers chose something that had some reference to them in the real world, even though it was a pretty stupid thing to do when you needed to stay anonymous. Brody himself was guilty of this. He'd chosen Fingal because it referenced his real identity in multiple ways, but only to anyone who really knew him. First of all, the name he was born with was Finn Brody, a fact that up until recently had only been known to Leroy. However, following the events surrounding Danny's death, he had disclosed his real name to Jenny, to regain her trust, and also to the higher echelons of GCHQ, to pass their stringent background checks. The second reason he chose Fingal was because of the famous Scottish poem, *Fingal's Cave*, where the meaning of the name Fingal was 'white stranger'; a phrase Brody thought aptly referred to his chosen profession of white hat hacker. And lastly, Brody had Scottish ancestry. So, in numerous ways, Fingal had meaning. Perhaps BionicM@n would too.

Feeling better armed, Brody fired up a freeware utility that dumped the text from all web pages listed in Google's search results. He pointed it at the first two hundred results for murders in the last seven days. Having all the text in one place would make it easier to scan through.

Knowing it couldn't possibly be that simple, but hoping anyway, he ran a search through the file for 'Steve Austin', the character name of the Bionic Man from the old Seventies TV series, *The Six Million Dollar Man.* As expected, there were no results. He was pleased BionicM@n hadn't been that dumb.

Next Brody searched the internet for a program that could scan pages of text to single out people's names. He found one that achieved this through a combination of semantic analysis of text and lookups of global name databases. A lot of work must have gone into developing the application, which probably explained why the program's vendors charged a small fortune for it. Undeterred, and with no intention of paying, he quickly accessed the deep web, first of all routing through two proxy servers and then TOR, to mask his location in the real world, hiding his IP address from prying eyes.

Once within the online underworld hidden beneath the surface internet used by normal people, he searched through the nefarious online marketplaces for the name extraction application. He was careful not to browse the marketplace for long. From experience, he knew that everything from drugs to guns was available for purchase, as well as the most disgusting pornography. With no ability to police the deep web, it really was the Wild West where anything and everything was for sale.

After a few minutes, Brody found a cracked version of the program and downloaded it. He wondered if the original developers had any idea that their expensively priced pride and joy was being made freely available in the deep web. After scanning it for viruses — one of the dangers of downloading anything from the internet, deep web or not — he installed it successfully. Within a few minutes, Brody had automatically extracted a long list of people's names from the top two hundred web pages referencing murders from the last week.

Brody then wrote a quick script to cycle through every name on the list so that it performed an internet search of the name with the keyword 'cowboy' added to the search criteria. He scanned the results and, although there were some spurious ones, finally narrowed down on one name: James Butler. It turned out that the first names of the famous cowboy, 'Wild Bill' Hickok, were James Butler. James Butler Hickok.

Back within Google, Brody searched for all news stories in the last week featuring 'James Butler' and the word 'death'. A long list of articles popped up from various well-known newspapers, mostly British.

It appeared that James Butler, a single man who traded stocks and shares from his home, was found dead a week ago in his family home in Highgate, North London. He had been poisoned and the police were treating it as highly suspicious.

This puzzled Brody. Poisoning didn't fit the profile of how Vorovskoy Mir dealt with people on their Most Wanted list. He knew that first hand. Maybe he had the wrong person, despite the connection to cowboys.

Brody did some more research and discovered that James Butler was a handicapped ex-marine, having lost both his legs in Afghanistan in 2007 during Operation Achilles. In 2011, Butler had become the guinea pig for some advanced prosthetic legs. There had been extensive press coverage at the time, with TV footage showing Butler's proud parents' tear-ridden faces watching their son walk towards them after four years of being wheelchair bound. Brody was impressed with the technology — the first prosthetics with powered knee and ankle joints that operated in unison, with sensors and microprocessors monitoring and predicting the user's motion, giving Butler the ability to walk almost normally.

Butler truly was a bionic man.

Brody had definitely found his hacker.

Now all he needed to do was find Butler's home address in Highgate.

A message popped up on his computer screen. It was Doc_Doom inviting him to a private chatroom. Brody followed the link.

Doc_Doom: Okay, Fingal. I didn't give you this. But I've got BionicM@n's identity like you asked earlier.

Fingal: Thanks, Doc. Do you mean James Butler?

Brody couldn't help showing off to Victor Gibb. At the very least, it would remind the government agent how resourceful Brody was.

Doc_Doom: Bloody hell, Fingal. How'd you do that so quickly? I've got all the resources of GCHQ behind me and it took us until now.

Fingal: Trade secret ;-)

Doc_Doom: Sometimes I think it's GCHQ who'll be working for you rather than the other way around!

Fingal: Of course not. By the way, if you'd like to save me a few minutes, could you let me have Butler's address in Highgate?

Doc_Doom: This is what I'm reduced to, is it? A glorified directory service?

Fingal: What do you mean, glorified?

Brody noted the address, shoved his tablet into his man bag and left the apartment.

"Mrs Gowda?"

The tear-stricken, pregnant woman in the hospital bed stopped wringing her hands and looked up. Spotting Jenny and Fiona standing there, she resumed twisting her fingers around each other and gazed off into the middle distance and shook her head. She spoke with a soft Welsh lilt. "I would have been Mrs Gowda if it weren't for the government and all their immigration shenanigans. We were hoping Rajesh's spouse visa would finally come through in the next couple of months, so that we could get married before the baby was born. Then I'd have become Gwenda Gowda." She smiled sadly. "We both joked that my new name would sound like a character in a superhero comic. Like Lois Lane or Peter Parker." She gulped and then sobbed loudly, "But not anymore. Just plain old Gwenda Bevan."

Fiona glanced at Jenny and nodded her head towards the exit, suggesting they should leave the woman and return when she was in a better state of mind. For a few moments, Jenny considered the idea, doubly so given Gwenda's condition.

Blonde curls fell all over her face, some matted to her cheeks by tears. Despite being heavily pregnant, Gwenda Bevan was so tiny the hospital bed appeared to swallow her up. She seemed such an unlikely partner to the overweight Rajesh Gowda, his body still lying on the floor tied to a wooden dining room chair in their home a few miles away, surrounded by scenes of crime officers.

Just as Jenny decided to return later, Gwenda inhaled deeply, looked up and asked, "Who are you?"

Jenny pulled out her police warrant card, offered her condolences and introduced herself and DC Fiona Jones. "We've just got a few questions about what happened, Gwenda."

"What happened? You make it sound like an everyday occurrence. But it's not. My beautiful Rajesh is dead. Murdered, even. It doesn't make any sense. Why would anyone want to kill Rajesh?"

"That's what I was going to ask you, Gwenda," said Jenny.

Gwenda studied her hands. "I've been racking my brains and can't come up with a thing."

"Did Rajesh have anything to do with snakes in his normal life?" asked Fiona.

"Snakes?" She threw them a surprised glance. "No, of course not. Why are you asking about snakes?"

Ah, no one had told her. Jenny explained their belief that he had died from snake poison. Gwenda shook her head in bewilderment as she listened.

"What did he do for a living?"

"He's a database analyst, working for MedDev Labs. They're a medical device manufacturer based in London. It's where I met him. I temped there last year. I'm a receptionist."

"You've only been together a year?" Jenny held her eye, avoiding the urge to glance at her swollen belly and come across as judgemental.

"Yes, a wonderful year," she said, wistfully. "He swept me off my feet with his cute smile. He worshipped the ground I walked on. And then, before we knew it, he had moved in and I was pregnant. Everything was going great, until …"

Jenny saw that it was all about to come crashing back. Quickly she deflected her with another question. "What do you remember about last night? Was anything different to normal?"

"Not really." Gwenda pushed herself upright in the bed. "We went to bed early, just after nine. I suppose that was different, normally we go to bed after the ten o'clock news. But I was feeling tired. I dozed off while he was working on his laptop in bed. He said he was remotely reindexing the MedDev Labs supplier database."

"And when did you wake up?"

"In the morning. But I woke up on the sofa in the living room with a blinding headache. I've absolutely no idea how I got there. And the room stank to high heaven of vomit. First of all I thought the morning sickness had come back and I'd been sick in my sleep or something. But then I turned round and that was when I saw Rajesh …" Gwenda trailed off at the memory.

"So, you have no recollection of anything between going to sleep upstairs and waking up in the morning downstairs in the same room as your fiancé's body?" asked Fiona.

Jenny thought Fiona's question was a little blunt. But it was an important point to confirm.

"No." Gwenda's voice began to rise. "I can't believe I never woke up. I could have stopped it."

But there had been little hope of her waking up. Jenny was waiting for toxicology results on Gwenda's blood and hair, but fully expected to be told that the drug, GHB, was present in her bloodstream. The other crime scene had established that GHB had been administered to James Butler's sleeping wife and child.

It acted as a sedative, preventing them from waking to Butler's death throes. It also caused short-term amnesia. And Gwenda's reference to waking with a headache also pointed to the presence of the substance.

"We think that you were drugged, to prevent you disturbing the killer."

Jenny thought of the perpetrator as *the killer* even though technically there was some debate as to whether this was a bona fide murder. Forcing someone else to commit suicide was usually tried in the courts as a murder case, although Jenny knew the conviction was likely to be dropped to the slightly lesser charge of voluntary manslaughter. Either way, to her it counted as killing someone.

"But how? They would have had to come into my room. I'm normally a light sleeper. Surely I would have woken up?"

"And maybe you did wake. But the drug we think they used causes short-term memory loss."

She wrapped her hands protectively around her belly. "But they could have harmed my baby."

"We've already told the doctors about the drug. They're doing extra tests to make sure everything is okay. But so far they say all your vitals are good."

"And the baby's," added Fiona, even though they'd not actually been told that.

"But how did I get downstairs?"

"Depending on how much of the drug you were given, you either walked down yourself or—"

"Or someone carried me?" she blurted out.

"It's possible, yes," confirmed Jenny.

GHB in the right dose would have put Gwenda into a very suggestive state, enabling the perpetrator to talk her into doing anything, like going downstairs. Jenny knew this was why it was the date rape drug of choice for many rapists. With its amnesiac side effects, she wouldn't have recalled doing so. Or, if the dosage was too high, then it would have sedated her completely, and she would have needed to be carried down the stairs. But either way, she was moved downstairs.

"I don't get it. Why not just leave me upstairs? Why bring me downstairs to watch Rajesh die when they knew the drug would make me forget everything I saw?"

Jenny didn't want to upset Gwenda even more by sharing her working theory that the killer forced Rajesh Gowda to put his hand in a container housing a poisonous snake by threatening the life of his wife and unborn child. By bringing Gwenda into the same room, the killer could have put a knife to her throat or held a gun to her head, forcing the hapless Rajesh Gowda to sacrifice his life to save theirs.

She decided to pick up on an earlier point. "You said Rajesh needed a visa?"

Gwenda nodded, sniffing.

"How come? Didn't you say you met him here in London where he worked?"

A nurse entered pushing a trolley. Efficiently, she started wrapping a blood pressure pad around Gwenda's upper arm.

"Rajesh is originally from Colombo." Seeing Jenny's quizzical look, Gwenda clarified, "In Sri Lanka. He's been in the UK for two years on a work visa supplied by MedDev Labs. But that doesn't give him leave to get married. So we've been going through the process of applying for a spouse visa. You need one of those to be able to get married. And even then, it only lasts six months. Then he would have needed to apply for permission to remain. The whole thing's a bloody nightmare. We've been on holiday for the last two weeks. But because he didn't want to risk not getting back in the country, we drove to the Brecon Beacons instead of going to see his family in Sri Lanka. Why can't the government just let people who love each other get married without all this bureaucracy?"

Jenny chose not to answer, avoiding turning their conversation into a debate about UK immigration policies. Instead she asked, "What kind of work visa did he have?"

"I don't know. You'll have to ask MedDev."

Jenny added it to her mental to-do list. "Is there anyone you can think of who would want to harm Rajesh?"

Gwenda pursed her lips and shook her head. *No.* Tears began to form at the edges of her eyes.

The nurse turned around and, with a grim face, put both hands on her hips. It was obvious what she was about to say. Jenny dropped a business card on the edge of the bed and started backing out of the room, pulling Fiona with her.

"We'll leave you to it, Gwenda," said Fiona.

"If you recall anything, no matter how small, give me a ring," Jenny added, pointing at the card.

The nurse stood sentinel until they left.

Fiona at her side, Jenny walked back the route they came, lost in thought. The whole case was incredibly strange. From what she had understood so far, it was an exact replica of the James Butler killing from last week. Thanks to their involvement, Fiona and the rest of the team had already got their heads around the strangeness. Jenny was dealing with it afresh and was unable to postulate any theory for the murderer's behaviour and choice of victim.

With a thousand unanswered questions and no clear idea of where to get the answers, she desperately hoped forensics would offer up some leads. Because, right now, she had very little to go on.

Wearing a matt black open-faced crash helmet, the tall, good-looking man exited his penthouse apartment via the lift that had opened exclusively into his palatial hallway. As he descended, he watched the floor numbers count down one by one and —

The noxious smell of piss broke through the illusion and hurled him back into reality. He'd even stepped in a puddle of urine on the second floor of the block of council flats where he lived. If he saw those drugged-up kids once more he'd strangle them one by one and … he forced himself to stop that line of thought.

Silently, he recited a prayer of atonement to Jesus.

Exiting into Allerton Road, he turned left down the shitty, downtrodden street towards the centre of Borehamwood. He tried to block out reality by conjuring up the childhood memory of traipsing down the mile-long pier at Southend, but he was troubled by the thought of piss molecules resting on his nose hairs. He poked around inside his nostrils with his index finger and then wiped it on the inside of his trouser pocket.

As he knelt, the opaque white plastic box he carried under his arm nearly slipped free but he caught it just in time. Anyway, it had two stretchy clips wrapped around it to ensure the lid stayed on, so he knew he was safe. But he was sorry to have knocked it, knowing the sudden movement would upset the animal inside. It didn't deserve that, not after its exertions last night.

An old woman came slowly towards him on the pavement with the aid of a four-wheeled walker, a basket containing her meagre grocery shopping attached at the front. He slowed down and deliberately brushed her coat with the white box, taking pleasure in the fact she had no idea she'd been millimetres from the most deadly snake in the world.

He repeated the game five more times on the way to the bank of garages located behind the local shops. It was where he locked up his matt black Vespa scooter. Leaving it out on the street was asking for it to be stolen or, at the very least, pushed over by the local gangs of kids. He strapped the white plastic box onto the rack on the rear, making sure it was held firmly in place.

Games and illusions were how he made it through each day. He'd honed the craft of inventing impromptu mind games and summoning lucid illusions during his ten-year stretch inside. It was how he'd survived the monotony, especially during those violent first five years in Woodhill, a category A prison. Exeter had been easier and then Maidstone had been a walk in the park by comparison.

Ralph Mullins was a huge hulk of a man, whom the other inmates initially nicknamed 'Wrecker Ralph' after he laid out three idiots who jumped him one day in the laundry room, while one of the screws was distracted. When Disney came along later with a kids' movie called *Wreck-It Ralph*, his nickname was adapted to match, especially as he had the same shock of brown hair and huge fists as the title character. After the laundry room incident, the other inmates mostly left Mullins alone. His mum, God bless her soul, said her Ralphy was like a cross between a basketball player and a shot putter. But he'd never played in a team or thrown a shot put. He was just a big loner who preferred his own company to others.

Well, except for his best friend and his pets.

Mullins pulled up outside his destination. He dismounted, untied the white box and walked around the back to the rear entrance. Once inside the building, he unlocked the door in the hallway, switched on the light using the pull cord, carefully closed and locked the door behind him, and then descended the wooden stairs to the large basement room, which was warm and damp thanks to the automatically controlled temperature and humidity.

"We're back, did you all missssss us?"

He laughed at his little joke, but there was no response from the banks of caged snakes, each in their own enclosures, stacked floor to ceiling on either side of the room. The enclosure sizes varied, depending on the breed within. The largest was six by four feet and contained a fifteen-year-old red-tailed boa constrictor over twelve feet long. The black mambas varied between four and eight feet and were housed in cages half the size.

Mullins placed the white box on the floor and carefully removed both stretchy clips, rolling them up and pocketing them. He then took off his fleece hoody and hung it up, revealing his immense muscular arms, bare up to the white T-shirt stretched tightly across his torso.

Before he lifted the lid of the white box, he closed his eyes for a moment. Allowing his fertile imagination to take over, Mullins wondered where it would take him this time. He was pleased with the result as orchestral music began to fill his ears. Opening his eyes, he noticed that each reptile cage now housed a snake playing a miniature musical instrument. He wasn't sure how a snake could play a violin and so didn't peer too closely, not wanting to break the spell.

To the magnificent sounds of the snake orchestra, he removed the lid from the box. Disregarding the thick, puncture-resistant gloves lying on the small shelf, he grabbed the medium-sized snake tongs from the rack on the wall below. He inserted them slowly into the white box and leaned over to see where the inhabitant was positioned.

The snake was uncoiling, a graceful, leisurely movement he always enjoyed observing, and the head levitated upwards towards the light, inquisitive. In Mullins' mind, the orchestra reached a crescendo, drums booming and cymbals crashing, just as he clipped the tong behind the head in a quick, practised movement, applying just enough pressure on the handle to grab the serpent but not so that he hurt it. Once secure, he lifted the animal out, its tail trailing behind.

He swapped the tongs from one hand to the other, careful to maintain even pressure. Now that his dominant right arm was free, he reached behind the head of the snake and grasped it between thumb and middle finger, placing his index finger on top of the head. He released the tongs and took up the weight of the snake's seven-foot long body with his now free left hand.

Mullins brought the animal up near to his own face and gazed into its dark, beady eyes, which he could tell were angry at being ensnared. He couldn't help trying to outstare it, even though he knew he would never win *that* battle; snakes having no eyelids, after all.

The mamba's long body writhed around beneath and wrapped itself around the same arm Mullins was using to hold it. He loved the feel of snakes on his skin, constantly surprised at the lack of sliminess. He noticed that this one felt cool, which meant its body temperature had dropped overnight. Mullins would place it back in its cage in a minute, where it could bask under the heated lamp and return its cold-blooded body to a more comfortable temperature. He would even treat it to a live mouse after last night's performance. After all, it had sunk its teeth into the little Indian man called Rajesh Gowda when he'd placed his shaking hand inside the white box. Just one bite would have released enough deadly venom to fell a hippopotamus, but it had inflicted four in rapid succession across Gowda's hand, wrist and lower arm.

Mullins wondered if the mamba had any venom left in its

glands. He wasn't about to risk finding out, though. He'd been bitten by this exact mamba once before and, thanks to the will of the Lord above, he'd survived to tell the tale. It certainly wasn't something he wanted to repeat, especially after calmly observing Gowda writhe about on the carpeted floor of his living room, screaming and frothing at the mouth in abject agony as the venom shut down his nervous system.

Mullins brought to mind Gowda's missus, prostrate on the sofa behind her dying fiancé. He hadn't realised she had a bun in the oven and was still horrified that he'd fantasised about fucking a pregnant woman. If he'd known about her condition beforehand he could have tried something different to avoid drugging her. He hoped the unborn child was unaffected, although now that he thought about it, it was sinful that she was expecting a baby while unmarried, so maybe she deserved it. Anyway, it wasn't for him to judge. Still, it had been the best way to obtain Gowda's compliance. What else could Mullins have done, anyway? Threatening him was out of the question. Forcing his arm into the box surely defeated the point? To have any chance of survival, Gowda needed to take part of his own free will.

Just like James Butler the week before.

Each time the snake struck, Mullins always tried his very best to help the victim. But no intervention had been forthcoming. He'd now failed twice in a row. First Butler. And now Gowda. He felt guilty because he knew his own lack of concentration was partly to blame. He shouldn't have allowed his mind to drift off into one of its illusions.

With Butler, he'd been intrigued by the man's prosthetic legs and had wandered into a daydream where all his own limbs had been replaced by soft plastic ones, like the rubbery *Stretch Armstrong* toy he'd had as a kid. In his dream, six black mambas had attacked him, Mullins laughing gleefully at their frustration that he remained alive despite bite after useless bite into his fake arms and legs.

With Gowda it had been the wife straddling him, riding him up and down, her swollen belly bouncing in time, the half-formed baby inside … he stopped himself thinking about that.

Next time he would get it right. He would keep his mind focused on the job at hand and do his best to block any of his illusions from penetrating. No distractions.

CHAPTER 4

ON JENNY'S REQUEST, THEY HAD ALL ASSEMBLED back at Holborn Station. The incident room was full to the brim. Surrounded by other detectives, uniformed officers and civilian staff, Jenny's team huddled together in the centre. DC Fiona Jones, prim in her trouser suit, flipped through pages in her notebook intently. She sat next to the unruly DS Karim Malik, who was whispering something into DS Alan Coombs' ear. Jenny assumed whatever he said contained expletives because Karim rarely spoke a sentence without including one, a technique she knew the Muslim officer used to gain acceptance. Karim leaned back to laugh at his own joke, while Alan, the father figure of her team, stoically shook his head.

Even Edmonds, the crime scene manager, and Dr Gorski, the pathologist, had turned up, fresh from processing the scene at Gowda's home. The corpse was now en route to the morgue where Gorski would carry out the post mortem later.

Jenny stood at the front and called the room to order. Silence descended respectfully, unlike the last briefing the squad had attended a few days before, or so Jenny had been told afterwards (she'd still been locked away preparing the CPS submission for the squad's last major case). True to form, DCI Da Silva had ducked hosting the session himself, in contrast with every other competent chief inspector in the police service. It was common knowledge now that this was because he lacked street-level investigative experience, the black officer having been pushed too quickly through the ranks in the Met's quest for minority representation in senior roles. Instead, he had delegated to Kevin Knight, his newly appointed DI, who was loud and full of cockney bluster, but not enough to mask his own inexperience in murder cases. Rapidly jumping from one random line of enquiry to another, rather than structuring them into overarching strategies, Jenny had been told that the squad had become restless and began talking amongst themselves, offering opinions and ideas. It was only when DCS McLintock, Da Silva's immediate boss, had made a rare and unexpected appearance in the room that everyone had sat up and paid attention. Whether he was there to support Da Silva and Knight or to check up on them had been water cooler gossip ever since.

Jenny was grateful for their rapt attention now. And for the absence of Da Silva and Knight.

"As some of you know, I've not been involved in the Butler case to date," she began. There were a few sniggers at this: those in the know fully aware that the unit's most competent DI had been deliberately sidelined. Jenny smiled and continued, "So, I'm obviously no expert on the details of the first crime. You lot are." She scanned the room, catching an eye here, an eye there. "However, I want each of you to think about the case afresh. Your previous investigative approach treated it as a one-off. But now, with Rajesh Gowda, we have a second killing with an almost identical MO. Someone out there is playing some kind of sick but deadly game and we need to catch him — assuming it's a him — before he strikes again." She paused for effect. "Because he most certainly will. Fiona, could you come up and do the honours?" Jenny held out a whiteboard marker pen. "Your writing is far more legible than mine."

Again, a few more jovial sniggers, the crowd enjoying Jenny's subtle self-deprecating reference to a moment six weeks before when Da Silva had humiliated her in front of the squad by abruptly sending up Fiona to replace Jenny at the whiteboard for the same reason.

"Let's take each aspect in turn and compare notes between the two cases. I'll lead from my understanding of the Gowda case. You lot," she indicated the room, "need to determine how similar each is, or if there are any deviations. After that, we'll assign actions. Okay?"

Lots of nodding heads. She had their full attention.

An hour later, the whiteboard was full of notes in neat columns under six headings: *Method of Entry, Incapacitation of Victims, Snake, Motive, Victim Selection*, and *Other*. Fiona had captured lots of bullet points in blue, only circling a few in red where there were differences between the two crime scenes.

Compared to the other lists, the bullet points under *Motive* and *Victim Selection* were much sparser and mostly had question marks after them, indicating these were guesses with no evidential basis, but ideas worth exploring nonetheless.

The killer had gained access to both homes while the families slept. It implied some level of surveillance to ensure peaceful entry. The Gowda residence had a fake alarm box visibly mounted on the front wall, but it was unclear as to how the killer would have known there was no alarm system. Unless, proposed Alan Coombs, he had monitored the Gowda family's comings and goings, and determined from the absence of warning beeps usually heard during the setting of an alarm that there wasn't one. As for access, it seemed that the killer had improvised. At the Gowda home, he had simply shoved in the back door with his shoulder. Jason Edmonds explained that trace fibres from his clothing were being analysed. In contrast, he gained entry into the Butler residence after finding a spare key hidden in the flowerpots outside, again causing speculation of additional surveillance. However, Jenny had collared enough housebreakers over the years to know that checking flowerpots for spare keys was a common burglary tactic. She wondered if people would ever learn.

Neither property had a CCTV system outside or webcams inside. After her last case where a murderer had secretly exploited hidden webcams to target victims, Jenny had made a point of checking.

Having gained entry, he casually sauntered via the kitchen to fill a glass with water and then made his way to the main bedroom. Although Butler's wife and Gowda's fiancé had no recollection of being drugged, a glass of water that they had not placed there was next to the bed. In both glasses, trace elements of GHB had been discovered. How he had forced them to drink it was unclear, but speculation of being held at gunpoint was rife. How else could he have kept control of two adults in a room and make one drink the drugged water? Perhaps he threatened to shoot the male to force the female to drink. It also made sense that the two males were each led downstairs at gunpoint where they were then tied to a dining room chair.

The knots used in the ropes binding both victims caused some speculation among the squad. One of the older PCs was a qualified boat skipper and, while examining photos of the knots, pointed out that someone with sailing experience would be familiar with them. But one of the younger PCs handed round his phone with the results of a Google search for 'rope knots', pointing out that anyone can learn pretty much anything from the internet. Even so, an action to cross reference future suspects against sailing databases was noted.

The rope itself had been brought to the crime scene by the intruder, but Jason Edmonds pointed out that it was cheap yellow polypropylene available from most DIY stores. Impossible to trace.

The major difference in the two crimes was the family member chosen for inducement. In the Gowda case, pregnant Gwenda had either been coerced or carried downstairs. However, in Butler's case, Gemma, his six-year-old daughter had been used to compel Butler to place his hand in the snake container. She had also been drugged with GHB. Fiona Jones had recounted the bleak testimony of the surviving Butler family members, where the daughter had awoken in the living room to the spectacle of her dead, tied-up father lying in a puddle of vomit and blood. She had run upstairs screaming to her mother. Little Gemma was being treated for shock even now, a week later, not having spoken a word since.

The team felt *Snake* offered the most promising lines of

enquiry. Black mambas were rare as pets. Being dangerous wild animals, they needed to be licensed. And importing them into the UK required special customs clearance. All easily traceable. Unless, as Karim pointed out wryly, the snake had been smuggled into the country illegally. Actions were listed to canvas exotic pet shops and London Zoo, as well as to visit each of the forty-five registered black mamba owners in the Greater London area.

The other aspect was the design of the container for the snake, the main question being, what type of box would allow you to place your hand into it but prevent the snake from escaping? One of the detectives in Knight's team had already visited a snake specialist to find out and explained that a simple plastic box with a removable lid was most likely the answer. Apparently, the snake gets used to its habitat and doesn't typically seek rapid escape just because the lid has been removed. But placing your hand in from above would most likely provoke the snake, which would be fearful that a predator was attacking it. It would likely strike in defence and, being a black mamba, bite multiple times in quick succession. "Which," commented Gorski, "would explain the numerous marks on both victims' left hands and forearms."

Motive had elicited guesses, none of which seemed plausible. One of the uniformed PCs proposed that maybe it was some form of Russian roulette. But the burglary and the use of another family member to incite the victim to place his hand in the container seemed to discount this. If the perpetrator had a gun, why go to all the trouble of using the snake? Alan Coombs suggested that maybe it was the killer's way of disassociating themselves from the killing. Talking this through with a psychologist became another action. Fiona wrote it on the board.

"Okay, onto *Victim Selection* now," instructed Jenny. "Butler and Gowda were not random choices. They were targeted for a reason. Let's start with the obvious one. Did they know each other?"

"Not according to Helen Butler or Gwenda Bevan," stated Fiona from behind Jenny.

Harry O'Reilly, the murder squad's computer expert, spoke for the first time. "I've been through Butler's computer with a fine-tooth comb already. Haven't found anything that sheds light on why he was killed. I've just finished a scan looking for any link to Gowda's known email addresses. Nothing."

"What about social media?"

"I've cross-referenced their social media profiles, so I have. No direct linkage on Facebook. There's one person on LinkedIn who is connected to the both of them. An IT head-hunter based in Paddington. He says he's never met either of them, just reached out on LinkedIn to expand his influence network. Apparently, it's standard practice for recruitment firms."

"What about professionally?" Jenny asked. "Gowda worked in IT for a medical device manufacturer called MedDev Labs. They're on the Stockley Park industrial estate not far from Heathrow Airport. What's Butler's story?"

"He served in the army up until about ten years ago," Alan replied. "He was discharged from duty after losing both his legs in a mortar attack in Afghanistan. After that, he was wheelchair-bound and worked from home as a day trader. He made bloody good money, according to his tax returns."

"Is it possible Butler served in Sri Lanka during his time in the military?" asked Jenny.

"It's possible. But, to be fair, Da Silva's in Bedford, meeting with the Army Intelligence Corps to get some background on Butler's time in service."

"But he doesn't know about Gowda yet," pointed out Fiona. "So he won't be asking the right questions."

Jenny turned to face her. "Yes, that's true."

Suddenly, Fiona's eyes widened as she looked past Jenny.

"That's DCI Da Silva to you, DS Coombs," shouted a Brummie accented voice from the back of the room. "And if no one updates the Senior Investigating Officer of a major new case development, how do you expect him to ask the right fucking questions?"

Jenny froze and slowly turned around. Every head in the room swivelled round to face DCI Da Silva and DI Knight, who were now marching towards the front of the room. There was a collective muted gasp.

How long had they been there? She hadn't noticed the door at the back of the room open to admit them, but then it was half blocked from view by a pillar. She had thought he was out of the picture until much later today or even tomorrow.

She realised she'd never heard him swear before, either.

This was going to be bad.

Brody stood at the bottom of a small stone staircase that led up to the Butler residence, a four-story, end-of-terrace Georgian townhouse located on one of the private roads between Kenwood Park and Highgate Cemetery. Brody was intrigued. For a computer hacker, James Butler had access to serious money when he'd been alive.

The house was within a stone's throw of Highgate Village, which sat on a hilltop and rose above the hustle and bustle of surrounding London. During the walk from the Tube station, Brody had passed plenty of independent shops and cafés, a refreshing change from the usual chains that populated most British high streets. He made a mental note to return one Sunday afternoon with Jenny.

Brody ascended the short flight of steps and pressed the bell, hearing it chime inside. He drew in a deep breath and let it out slowly.

The door swung open halfway, revealing an unusually tall woman, at least Brody's height. From the step below, Brody looked up into baggy sleep-deprived, red-rimmed eyes. She wore black jeans, a loose black jumper and black pumps. The only colour was a light blue hanky she held defensively in her hand.

Brody spoke first, forcing his voice to be soft and sad. "You must be Helen." He offered a half smile and then let his expression drop back to sadness.

She looked him up and down, suspicious. "Do I know you?"

"Wild Jim and I were close friends back in the day. I came to pay my respects." Brody shrugged slowly. He hoped using Butler's old army nickname would do the trick. "I'm so terribly sorry for your loss."

Helen Butler stared blankly.

"I'm Richie." Brody held out a hand. "Richie Williams. Jim used to call me Rhino when we trained together in ATR Winchester."

She shook it gently. "I don't recall James mentioning you."

"Really? I suppose it was a long time ago. Once we passed out, our army careers went in different directions. He went to Intelligence Corps with the likes of Big Dave and Jonas. I went into the Parachutes Regiment up in Catterick. Only saw him a few times after that, but whenever we got together it was just like old times. But everyone lost track of him after he was forced to return to civvies. I guess cutting of ties was his way of dealing with what happened."

He'd used his best line, referencing two of Butler's real friends and subtly letting her know that he knew about Butler's injuries.

"I remember Dave and Jonas." She gave a thin smile. "I think they're coming to the funeral. Well, assuming the police ever release his body."

"I hope to be there as well. That's actually why I called round. If I give you my number, will you let me know when it is? I'll need to leave enough time to get down from Dundee, where I'm based now."

"You're based in Scotland?"

"Yeah, I'm heading back up tonight." He watched her make up her mind about him.

Helen opened the door the rest of the way and stepped back. "Well, as you've come so far out of your way, the least I can do is offer you a cup of tea."

Brody shrugged as if making his mind up there and then. "Well, I do have some time before the train leaves. Thank you. Tea would be lovely."

He was in.

A few minutes later they were sitting at a table in the kitchen. Helen poured tea from a pot, idly asking him whether he wanted milk or sugar. Their conversation so far had been small talk. Some chocolate-covered biscuits lay untouched on a side plate.

Brody had spent the last half-day preparing for his encounter with Helen Butler. He'd approached it like any other social engineering hack, doing his research and finding out as much about his target as possible in order to sneak past perimeter security. Usually, that involved hoodwinking his way past a receptionist or security guard to obtain unescorted access to the interior of a secure corporate building. This time, the perimeter security was the front door of a suburban home, with the resident the equivalent of the security guard. He wasn't particularly pleased with himself for having to deceive the recently widowed Mrs Butler, but he knew it was the quickest way for him to learn as much as possible about her late husband.

After all, the truth was guaranteed to have had the door slammed in his face: *Hi, I'm Brody Taylor, a hacker friend of your husband, who you may or may not know was also a hacker. Although I've never met him in the flesh, he sent me a letter this morning, a week after his death, asking me to exact revenge on the Russian mafia gang who had him killed. Do you mind if I take a look at his computer for a minute?*

No, he'd had no choice but to deceive Helen Butler, as shameful as it now made him feel.

After he had uncovered BionicM@n's real identity, Brody had gathered as much background information as possible from publicly available sources. It gave him some basic facts, but nothing that would have put him on the inside track with the dead man's widow. For that, he'd contacted two of Butler's army friends, both of whom he'd discovered from a twelve-year-old newspaper story reporting that they'd got themselves arrested in a pub fight in Aldershot. Pretending to be a *Telegraph* journalist researching James Butler's obituary, Brody had phoned the two men, both of whom had since left the army. One was a security guard for a nightclub and the other drove a black cab, and spent more time moaning about increased competition from *Uber* than revealing any useful info about James Butler.

It was from these two that Brody had unearthed useful details such as Butler's nickname, 'Wild Jim', which had been no great surprise given that Brody had already uncovered Butler's reference to 'Wild Bill' Hickok. It was also how he'd elicited that someone called Big Dave had been the best man at Butler's wedding. Jonas, the cabby, had let slip that they'd all gone into the intelligence corps together. Brody assumed that this was either because Butler was already computer literate or that this was where he later learned his trade as a hacker.

After the conversations, Brody felt that he had enough personal titbits to construct a fake friend, Richie 'Rhino' Williams. Even the timing of them being in army training together had been chosen deliberately, Brody having ferreted out that Butler had met his future wife four years later, after passing out, the military term for graduating.

The inside of the house was expensively decorated. The hallway displayed antique oak furniture pieces on original parquet flooring. The kitchen was modern, marble and granite with polished white fitted cupboards and hidden appliances. Brody had glimpsed the living room and had avoided a natural inclination to pass comment on the ostentatious bearskin rug which still had its head and teeth attached.

"You have a beautiful home," commented Brody. "Jim certainly did well for himself after the army. Much different to when you both lived in army married quarters?"

"Yeah, that's true I suppose. But we were as happy then as we are now." Helen caught herself and then shrugged. "I mean, as we were."

"What did he do for a living?"

"He traded stocks and shares."

"A stock trader? Impressive. Did he work for an investment bank?"

"No, nothing like that. He was what you'd call a day trader. Every day he'd disappear into his office," she pointed downwards through the kitchen floor, indicating that his office was in the basement, "and he wouldn't come out until the London Stock Exchange closed at 4:30 p.m. He was very regimented."

"Good old army discipline, eh? How did he get into trading?" Brody then quickly added, "I only ask because I'm a few years off retirement and I need to come up with a good plan myself."

"It was a case of having to, I guess. After he lost his legs, he was wheelchair bound for years. And I was pregnant with Gemma at the time. She's nine now."

"Yeah, I remember when he was injured. It was terrible news. How did he cope? How did you both cope, I mean?"

"In some ways, I think he was more devastated to have been forced to retire from service than he was at the loss of his legs. He loved army life. Even when he was home on leave he was pining to go back. The best period was when we were based in Germany. It meant he was doing the job but we lived a normal married life. Together. And then came Afghanistan ..." She trailed off, remembering.

"Jim was always so dedicated," reflected Brody, casually. "When we trained together, he was probably the most hard-working cadet out of all of us. I guess it must have carried through his career." This part Brody made up on the spot, but with no visible reaction, he felt he'd got away with it.

Suddenly interested, Helen then leaned forward eagerly. "Tell me more about what he was like when you knew him? That was a good four or five years before I met him. I'd love to hear."

"Blimey, what would you like to know?" Brody stalled, rapidly concocting a believable white lie. An image formed. He hoped all those Eighties movies containing army-training segments would make his bluff realistic. He began improvising, "He once saved one of the cadets from drowning during an assault course. He'd stupidly got his leg trapped on the climbing net and ended up upside down with his head in the massive puddle beneath, knocked out. Jim spotted it and went back for him, despite being in the running for the best course record at the time. And, I will always be in his debt because of what he did that day." Brody finished with a deadpan flourish, "It was me that he saved."

"That's amazing," said Helen, wistfully. "He never told me that story."

Brody wasn't sure if she had sensed any untruths. "Well, I think it probably meant more to me than it did to him. He was just doing his job, after all."

"Maybe."

He needed to get Helen back on track. "So how did you both cope when he came back from Afghanistan?"

"Not very well to begin with. He was so angry, his life having been stolen from him. You're right, Richie, he did cut himself off from everyone in the army. That's why you, Dave and Jonas never heard from him after. I think the only thing that got us through that period was having Gemma. He doted on her. Being a child, she accepted him as he was. Without her, I'm not convinced he'd have made it through."

"Sounds tough." Brody was beginning to seriously hate himself.

"It was. He became self-sufficient despite being confined to the damn wheelchair. He tried normal prosthetic limbs, but never really got on with them. He said if he's going to look like he's got a fake leg then he may as well go all the way and remain sitting in the bloody wheelchair." She shook her head at the memory. "And so, each day he'd wheel himself into his office, searching for a way to earn an income online. Fortunately, he was good with computers. I think he did a lot with them back in the army. That's when he discovered day trading. He said he did tons of research to make the right investments, those that were on the way up or down within a single day. He said he always exited all his trades on the same day, no matter whether he was shorting or going long. Soon enough, he was doing so well we moved into a new apartment, the two main criteria being wheelchair access and the speed of the broadband."

Brody sipped his tea.

"Eventually he was making good money. Really good money. After buying this house, he put enough by to pay for the most advanced myoelectric prosthetic legs. They were fantastic. They gave him a completely natural walking gait. He was entirely mobile, even able to climb up and down stairs. It was like having my old James back, the one from before the mortar bomb. His whole attitude to life changed with it. These last few years have been so wonderful for the three of us." Tears were flowing freely now. "I can't believe he's gone."

Brody wanted to reach out to comfort her but knew that was

inappropriate. Instead he pulled a tissue from the box on the table and handed it to her. She took it, dabbed her eyes and took a deep breath. After she composed herself she looked up at him and offered a forlorn smile.

Brody looked around for a change of subject. "Did he cook?" He had spotted a shelf full of cookery books. Jamie Oliver, Gordon Ramsay, Michel Roux.

"Yeah, he was pretty good too." She laughed fondly. "He really got into it once he could walk again. He watched *MasterChef* all the time and was forever experimenting in the kitchen, with me and Gemma as his guinea pigs."

"Sounds great."

"He was really upset when that celebrity chef died recently. Went on about it for ages. Irish guy. What was his name?"

Brody vaguely remembered hearing something in the news from around a month before. He scanned the cookery books and the name popped out. "Do you mean David Dougan?"

"That's him. James always watched his live cookalong show on a Saturday morning. We were watching it together when the poor bloke keeled over live on air. Did you know he was only in his forties?"

Brody held back from stating the obvious. But he could see from her hurt expression that Helen had made the same connection. James Butler had also been in his forties.

A high-pitched scream pierced the air. It emanated from one of the floors above. Brody flinched and stared questioningly at Helen.

She stood quickly. "It's Gemma." She headed for the door. "She was asleep when you came. Excuse me a moment, Richie."

He called out after her. "Sorry to ask, do you mind if I use your loo?"

"There's one in the hallway, under the stairs," her voice said, retreating.

Brody listened to her footsteps rapidly disappearing upstairs. A small pause on the landing and then he heard her ascending to the top floor. It was a timely distraction. Hopefully it would give him enough time.

Brody exited to the hallway. He could see the door to the toilet, but to its left another set of stairs led downwards. He quickly took them, careful to step lightly to avoid any of the steps creaking.

The basement hallway had two doors, both ajar. Through one, he could see a well-equipped home gym, with a complex multi-gym in the centre, angled benches and racks of weights along a mirrored wall. A faint smell of sweat permeated the air. Through the other was Butler's home office. Brody pushed open the door and snuck in.

It was well appointed. Pride of place in the room's centre and facing the door was a large wooden executive desk. Three monitors were mounted side by side on a sturdy stand, their backs to Brody. Floor to ceiling bookcases covered the wall on the left, containing a selection of hardback books and ornaments. The bookshelves were not stuffed full. Two large flat-screen TVs were mounted either side of the doorway. Although it was a basement, natural light streamed in through a thin, horizontal opaque window mounted high on the outside wall immediately behind the desk.

Other than the bookcase ornaments, the only personal touch came from five full size movie posters, framed and mounted underneath the window. One was centred above the remaining four all in an even line beneath. The film buff in Brody noted the strange collection. The one on top on its own was for *Jonah Hex*. Brody recalled the movie about a scarred bounty hunter during the American Civil War, but remembered it had been panned by the critics and was a huge box office failure. Brody wondered if the scarred hero seeking revenge was how Butler perceived himself. Beneath and mounted to the left was *Zero Dark Thirty*, the poster's collage of American soldiers at war only visible within the large letters of the film's title. He wondered if Butler's time in Afghanistan had anything to do with the hunt for Bin Laden, the main subject of the Oscar-nominated movie. Next to it was absolute proof that Brody had the right man. It was the iconic image of Lee Majors, the original bionic man from the *Six Million Dollar Man* TV series, running towards the camera in his red, wide-collared Seventies track suit. The fourth poster was for another TV series, but much more modern. It was the brooding face of Kiefer Sutherland from *24*, the number cleverly written in the style of an old LED watch. Although *24* featured lots of computer hacking, Brody was surprised by its inclusion. All of the CrackerHack forum members regularly slated the show for its implausible Hollywood-style approach to hacking, as if anything with an IP address could be compromised in mere moments. All the same, for the first four posters, Brody could at least infer some level of relevance to Butler or his online persona as BionicM@n. The last, however, was a truly odd choice. It was the poster for the original *Fantastic 4* superhero movie, one of the least successful Marvel Studio comic book adaptions. Perhaps, like Brody, Butler had enjoyed the comics when he was a kid and wasn't too bothered by the inferior movie version.

Brody tiptoed around to the other side of the desk. He needed to access Butler's computer. If he could break into it quickly, he'd install a neat piece of malware that would allow him to connect back in at his leisure. But if he couldn't gain access, he'd simply drop the computer into his bag, analyse it at home, and return it later, hoping it wouldn't be missed. Brody scanned the desk, but where the laptop should have been was a yellow crime scene marker, with the number four printed on it. Damn, the police had seized Butler's computer for evidence. Brody quickly checked the drawers and under the desk, but there wasn't anything of note.

With one final glance around the room, he gave up and headed back up the stairs. For the sake of his cover story, he popped into the toilet and flushed it. A few minutes later, he was sitting back at the table in the kitchen, alone.

Everything Helen Butler had told him about Butler spelled a far cry from your typical computer hacker. Either Brody had completely the wrong person or Butler's day trader livelihood was a total fabrication. But the fact that he'd made his wife believe it was interesting. From his own experience, Brody appreciated the fervent desire to keep the hacker side of his own life under wraps. Jenny was the first woman he'd dated who knew his true profession and, even then, he'd originally attempted to keep it secret, almost derailing their relationship before it had got started. Partly it was because most people found it hard to trust hackers and partly because what he did was dangerous and therefore he wanted to protect those close to him. Perhaps Butler had made a similar choice.

The fact was that Butler disappeared every day into his home office to work on his computer. Judging by their surroundings, whatever he did on it was incredibly lucrative. But it wasn't stock trading, despite the triple-display configuration on his desk favoured by many investment bankers. Butler would never have had the time to research and select profitable investments and simultaneously stay as up-to-date and current on the hacker forums as he was. Which meant he had to be a hacker.

The question was whether he was white or black?

As a white hat hacker, Brody knew it paid fairly well. But even he would struggle to fund a home like Butler's based purely on paid penetration tests and other ethical hacking projects. Brody presumed Butler's lifestyle also came with all the other expensive middle class trappings — expensive cars, private schools, foreign homes and five-star family holidays. It was unlikely that Butler could have afforded all of this purely from ethical hacking projects. He must have ventured into black hat territory, illegally hacking into sites and corporate networks to either steal money or swipe information that could be sold on or used for ransom. These projects were dangerous and highly illegal. But, they had one advantage. They were incredibly lucrative.

In Brody's case, his main income came from running a completely legal, automated statistical betting system on the main online sports betting exchanges. He'd developed it back in university, using mathematical trending to select appropriate bets. Via the exchange, he acted like a bookmaker, offering odds to other anonymous gamblers who were speculating based on an event's outcome. He'd based the system's decision-making capability on years of historical trend data, and the result was that it won far more than it lost. It was by no means one hundred per cent perfect, but over time his betting bank increased steadily, giving him a sizeable, tax-free income for very little effort. With his online betting system running happily in the background, Brody was free to pick and choose the pentest projects he wanted, always focusing on those that were interesting, challenging or would give him information he could then share as Fingal on the CrackerHack forums to further his elite status.

Brody heard steps from above. After a few moments, Helen returned. She smiled weakly and sat back down. "I'm so sorry, Richard. Gemma's taken her dad's death hard."

"It must be incredibly hard for you both. Look, I'll not disturb you anymore. Why don't I head off?"

"No, stay. It's been good talking to you. More tea?"

"If you're sure …"

Helen refilled his cup. She hadn't touched her own.

Brody didn't know where to restart the conversation. In fact, he really wanted to leave this poor woman to her grief. This was low, even for him. Anyway, with no computer around, he'd already confirmed everything else he needed to know. He resorted to a cliché. "I can't believe he's gone."

"Me too," said Helen. "I feel so cheated."

"In what way?"

"Well, when he came back from Afghanistan, it took us all ages to adjust to his disability. But we made it through, eventually. I guess we all thought that any family who survives something like that would go on forever. But, no. Some sicko breaks into our house and forces a snake to poison him."

"Snake?"

Brody recalled the news story saying poisoning, but nothing more than that. He'd imagined Butler had been drugged in his sleep or something dangerous had been slipped into his drink at a bar. But a snake?

"Yes, it was so horrible." Helen wrapped arms tightly around herself. "Someone broke into our home. They drugged Gemma and me. They carried her downstairs, leaving me asleep upstairs. They tied up James and, with Gemma in the same room, made a poisonous snake bite him. It was horrific. Such an awful, painful way to go."

Brody's mouth dropped open slightly. "That's…" He couldn't select a good enough adjective to portray his shock. "Who? Why?"

It made no sense to Brody. Why on earth would Vorovskoy Mir resort to poisoning people with snakes? Especially after recently deploying the more traditional hitman-with-a-gun approach on him not so long ago. Maybe the loss of the hitman during the police raid on his flat had forced them to resort to other measures.

"I've honestly no idea. I've racked my brains senseless. The best I can come up with is if someone took revenge for some horrible thing he may have once done abroad back in the army. That's what I told DCI Da Silva and he said he'd look into it."

"Da Silva?" Brody was so shocked to hear the familiar name; it was out his mouth before he could stop it.

Helen narrowed her eyes.

Brody added quickly, "The name rings a bell. I used to know a Da Silva in the RMP. Always wondered what happened to him."

Da Silva was Jenny's boss, the ineffective one she passionately despised. Brody had actually met him six weeks before when he'd lent his skills to Da Silva's investigation team in their hunt for a serial killer. Highgate wasn't that far from Holborn Station, where Jenny and Da Silva were based. He should have considered that this murder would have been on their patch. Well, at least Jenny wasn't involved.

Boy, would that have been trouble.

"I can explain, sir," said Jenny calmly, looking up at a furious Da Silva. She placed her hands on her hips.

"As far as I'm concerned, DI Price, there is no explanation you can give that warrants you abandoning your current assignment to stick your nose into *my* case."

His face was inches from hers and she could feel spittle land on her skin from his shouting. She held her ground, conscious of everyone in the room staring at them, each one sensing the bloodbath to come.

"Rajesh Gowda's murder *is* currently my case. I believe you are leading the investigation of the murder of one James Butler."

He looked at the whiteboard behind her. Fiona Jones stood legs apart and folded her arms defiantly. Jenny appreciated her support.

"It's the same MO, guv," stated DI Knight, standing right behind Da Silva.

"Is it now?" said Da Silva, scanning the whiteboard, trying to catch up. "Well, in that case, DI Price, you can hand it over and go back to what you were doing."

"No," said Jenny. It was only one word, but she felt her voice catch. Out of the corner of her eye, she could see people whispering to each other. Tension filled the room like the charge left in the air after lightning.

"No?" repeated Da Silva, his tone full of exaggerated incredulity.

Alan Coombs stood and spoke. "Jenny's SIO on Gowda, sir. She's led the investigation all day. Wouldn't be right to replace the SIO in the first forty-eight hours."

"It's a linked series," stated Da Silva. "There's only room for one SIO."

Someone coughed loudly, masking his voice. But the phrase, "Then fuck off," could still be made out.

Da Silva whirled towards the seated investigation team. "Who said that?"

Nobody answered. Jenny felt as if she was back in secondary school with Mr Ponulak, her maths teacher who could never control his unruly class.

Coombs, who had remained standing, spoke reasonably. "Sir, you have two good officers and two murders." Jenny presumed he meant DI Knight for the other. "Why don't you appoint them as Deputy SIOs, reporting in to you as the lead?"

Jenny wasn't sure she liked that idea, but realised it was probably the best outcome from this embarrassing confrontation. At least she wouldn't be stuck behind a desk processing evidence. She'd have Alan, Fiona and Karim as her core team on Gowda. Knight would form his own team to handle Butler.

Behind his boss, DI Knight shrugged acceptance, but Da Silva hadn't noticed. He was too busy staring dumbfounded at Coombs, his expression boiling over.

"If I want advice from a junior officer, *DS* Coombs, I'll ask for it. Now," he turned back to Jenny and enunciated each word slowly, "I'm ordering you to stand down, DI Price."

Jenny shook her head in exasperation.

"I'm ordering you to finish the *important* job of preparing the CPS case file for the webcam murderer." He smiled, but his eyes held no mirth. "After all, you caught him. So you can see it through to the bitter end."

Jenny couldn't believe it. He was severely breaking protocol here. All to put her in her place. He was placing his own bruised ego ahead of the needs of the investigation.

She wanted to slap him hard across the face. But she contained herself. Just. She had no options left. A direct order was an order, especially in front of the whole squad.

Jenny raised her head high and, with every eye on her back, stormed out of the murder investigation room.

CHAPTER 5

THE DOOR OPENED AND YACOV KAPINSKY EMERGED with shoulders slumped. He looked at Klara and shook his head forlornly as he walked past her. His idea had not been strong enough and his job was now forfeit. She touched him on the arm as he passed. She would miss her friend.

But now it was her turn to survive.

Taking a deep breath, Klara Ivanov flicked back her long blonde locks and pushed open the meeting room door. It was her third and last chance to impress the steering committee. Failure today and, like Yacov and everyone else before, she knew she would lose her place on this special project.

She had dressed more provocatively than normal, playing up to the male dominated panel. Her blouse was open necked and she wore a tight-fitting cerise suit and, unusually for her, heels instead of flats, although not too high as she was taller than most men already. In the mirror earlier, she'd tested a black choker necklace but discarded it, thinking it was heading in the direction of lap dancer. Anyway, she wanted to win them over with her intelligence and ideas, not her body. Although, having presented in each of the two previous months, she knew that she was about to face off to an abundance of high-powered testosterone. Most Russian men found her attractive, blatantly telling her so, and two of the three panel members had done little to hide their lascivious thoughts during her previous two presentations. If they'd been able to keep up with her technical ideas then maybe they would have risen above their Stone Age programming.

The same panel of middle-aged men sat behind the antique oak table. On the left was Dr Grigori Klinkov, her ultimate boss and the operations director of MOESK, Moscow's electric power transmission and distribution company. They were in its headquarters located in the northwestern district just inside the MKAD, Moscow's automobile ring road. Klinkov looked up and pushed away a stray strand of thinning grey hair. His bored expression turned to one of interest and he unsubtly licked his lips. Inwardly, Klara groaned. Why did men equate power with sex?

On the right, dressed in a sharp black suit, sat Alexander Sokolov, the representative from the Ministry of Energy. Busy reading papers on the table in front of him, he glanced up and, feigning disinterest, pretended to continue reading. But she could see that his eyes were raised upwards, studying her long legs. If the last two times were anything to go by, he would soon get bored and actually read his paperwork. The conversation was just gobbledegook to him.

But it was the strange man in the centre that she had to impress today. He had been introduced to her two months ago as Dmitry Alexeyevich Zakharin, an external advisor to the project. He seemed impervious to her beauty, and was the only one with the intelligence to hold a conversation with her on the inner workings of firmware design. But he was certainly the odd one out in the room. He wore faded denim jeans, a yellow designer T-shirt revealing muscly tattooed arms, and had a thick gold chain around his neck. She'd guessed he was some kind of Russian mafia type, but what the hell he was doing mixing with the heads of MOESK, she had no idea. But then, in Russia, everyone knew that state and mafia were close bedfellows.

"Ah, Miss Ivanov, take a seat." Klinkov smiled, looking her up and down. "Welcome back. I hope you are able to impress us today."

Absently, she wondered if all she needed to do was strip naked for them. But she'd vowed never to return to that line of work after graduating top of her Computer Science class in Lomonosov Moscow State University five years ago. Working only three hours a week as a stripper had been the equivalent of working full time in her parents' bookstore, and so had given her the free time to devote to her studies. Also, her parents couldn't really afford to pay her a full salary anyway.

Klara said hello, sat in the chair opposite and folded her legs demurely.

Klinkov reminded her of the purpose of the meeting. "Today is your last chance to present an unbreakable method for …" He looked at his notepad for the right words. " … Firmware integrity verification during its execution."

The project had been assembled following the unprecedented attack of Ukraine's power grid last year. It was the first successful attack on public infrastructure anywhere in the world and had crossed the line from hacking normal computers into hacking SCADA-based industrial control systems, the systems that are used to manage everything from factory production, to oil and gas pipelines, to nuclear reactors. Although the Ukraine hack had only caused a blackout, it was clear the attackers could easily have caused far greater damage. It was believed to have been orchestrated to send a message to the Ukrainian government and, so rumour had it, Klara's own Russian government was responsible. Which made it ironic that the same government was now running projects like this to create defences against similar attacks from others.

"Yes, I have a new proposal for you," she said, wishing her voice had sounded more confident.

"Good, then please begin."

She stood and walked to the side wall, where there was a whiteboard. She was conscious of the three pairs of eyes following her. She picked up a blue marker and pen and turned to her audience.

"We know that load-time integrity can be checked using a cryptographic chip present on the motherboard. Through Dynamic Root of Trusts techniques we can guarantee the correct version is loaded. But with network interfaces available to hackers, the problem is ensuring the firmware is running untampered while executing, not just at load time."

On the right, Sokolov had given up already and was reading his paperwork. She had not even started yet. She was only framing the problem.

"Two months ago, I presented an approach based on remote device attestation using a challenge-response protocol. But Mr Zakharin," she nodded at the out-of-place man in the middle, "pointed out that malware could be designed to keep legitimate firmware code in memory and redirect memory reads to compute the correct checksum."

She had been floored at the time. She'd worked hard to develop the idea of remote attestation, and he had nonchalantly dismissed it with a wave of his hand. But coming up with the idea behind his objection during only the time she'd had to present her proposal was most impressive. He really knew his stuff. And, he'd been right. It wasn't tamper-proof. Not for the first time she wondered if Zakharin was the architect of the Ukrainian blackout hack.

"Last month I proposed an integrity check procedure which analysed memory areas for anything that looked like executable code. At the initialisation phase for the device, we recorded a golden model of the firmware and then checked the instruction to be run was the same as the golden model."

"Yes, I remember." Zakharin spoke for the first time. "It was a good idea, but the technique was limited to code that was not self-modifying. And the serial to ethernet converters deployed at the substations all over the Moscow grid are."

When he had said those same words a month ago, she had felt like such a fool. It was so obvious she should have considered it and had spent the week after chastising herself for it.

She nodded gracefully and shrugged. "Today, I would like to propose what I call a Shadow Call Stack." She wrote the words on the board. "The idea is to keep a reconstructed copy of the call stack of the firmware on the host. Each time we identify a CALL-like instruction, we push the corresponding return address on the shadow stack …"

Zakharin folded his arms, cocked his head to one side and stared upwards, considering her idea. This time she was confident she'd cracked the problem. If he found a way to undermine this idea she'd be totally crestfallen.

And out of work.

"Each time," she continued, "we identify a RET-like instruction, we check that the address where the firmware is trying to return meets the one saved on the stack. If it's not, then something is definitely wrong."

This time it was she who folded her arms. She waited.

Both of the bureaucrats on the end of the table turned to see how Zakharin would react. After a brief pause, he leaned forward and said, "Interesting."

It was the best response she'd had in all three presentations.

He began to ask questions, each time digging down to deeper and deeper levels of detail. She answered promptly, illustrating her answers with stack diagrams on the board and arrows pointing to a diagram of the general purpose registers available in RISC based chips.

At one point, she could see that he thought he'd spotted a flaw by raising the subject of hardware interrupts, pointing out that they can cancel instructions. But she was prepared for that and proposed a solution via the register that handled return jumps. He considered this and said again, "Interesting."

The only negative comment he was able to make was related to performance. But that would need to be tested in the lab.

She was sure she'd cracked the problem.

The meeting came to a close. Klinkov dismissed her from the meeting and she returned to her desk in the main lab area, a little disappointed that she'd not been acknowledged as having solved the problem there and then. Zakharin had said he needed to give it some thought, which was the nearest she'd got to a compliment.

Klara looked around and noticed that Yacov's desk had been cleared already. She wondered what he would do now.

The door opened and Klinkov entered.

She stood and waited for the verdict. He explained that

Zakharin had concluded that the performance degradation was too much of an issue for her proposal to be of practical use. Unfortunately, he had to formally inform her that she had failed to meet the requirements of her position. He would be sad to see her leave.

The whole thing was complete horseshit. Klara had solved the problem, fair and square. This was a farce and she brimmed with indignation.

But, five minutes later, Klara calmed down and began clearing her desk.

She had lost her job.

Jenny sat at her desk, mulling over the humiliating confrontation with Da Silva. Absently, she picked split ends out of her chestnut locks, taking meagre pleasure each time she broke off one of the offending hairs.

She'd worked for many DCIs over the years, each with different management styles. At various times, they'd all ordered her to do something she didn't want to, but in most cases it was for the benefit of the investigation and someone had to do it. In some, it was a deliberate ploy to broaden her experience, forcing her to undertake tasks she would have otherwise avoided. Even though she hated receiving direct orders, she understood there was usually some logic or merit in her superiors' decisions.

But every directive Da Silva handed out seemed to be about himself. His focus was all about making sure he was perceived positively by the senior ranks, particularly DCS McLintock, his immediate superior. Anything, or anyone, who was a threat to that was sidelined. Jenny had never experienced workplace politics like it. She'd never considered herself a threat to anyone. She was a team player and, in her mind, the team collaborated towards a shared objective: to apprehend criminals. There should be no room for personal egos.

But rather than fill his team with the most experienced officers to hunt down the perpetrator, here was Da Silva using the two snake poison cases as a means to further his own career. Jenny was confident she wasn't over-egging her own record.

DCI Da Silva and DI Knight only had a few months of murder investigation experience between them. She had two years as Detective Inspector within the Camden Borough Murder Investigation Team and many years before that as Detective Sergeant in the same team.

But, for the first time in her career, she'd had enough.

Jenny released the clump of hair she'd been pulling at and dragged the computer mouse towards her. She clicked through to the police staff vacancies system. Maybe her skills would be of value somewhere else in the service?

After a good deal of searching, a vacancy in Greater Manchester Police caught her attention. They were putting together a new murder investigation team and were seeking a DCI. She even knew the DCS in charge, having briefly worked with her six years ago. Jenny felt she was a perfect fit. And it was a promotion.

Briefly, she wondered how she'd feel about leaving everything behind. She'd miss her team for sure. But Alan, Fiona and Karim would do well with or without her. Jenny had grown up in nearby Kent. Her two brothers and her sister still lived in and around the family home in Maidstone, where their parents still resided. But as time went on, Jenny had found herself becoming distanced from her family, blaming the job for preventing her from going down the last three Christmases in a row. She was very close to her sixteen-year-old nephew Damien, her sister's son, their shared hobby of online gaming keeping them in touch over the internet. Two or three nights a week, Jenny would fire up *Call of Duty* on her Xbox and play team-based tournaments into the small hours, with Damien mostly joining in on the weekend; weekdays being off limits due to his upcoming school exams. None of her work colleagues, friends, or even Brody knew about her secret addiction to first person shooter gaming. While plotting with Damien how to take out a rival team's sniper without being killed, they would also chat amiably about his life in Kent. But, Jenny reasoned, online gaming in Manchester was no different to online gaming from her flat in Richmond.

That left Brody.

Although only six weeks old, their relationship was starting to get interesting. He was so different to everyone else she'd ever been out with. He was intelligent without being condescending, witty without ever telling a joke, attractive without seeming too aware of it and he shared her passion for good quality coffee, the two of them regularly seeking out independent coffee shops in and around London. The sex was pretty damn hot too, and getting better by the day. Unless work got in the way, they saw each other most evenings, one of them typically staying over at the other's place. While apart, they texted each other a few times a day, often inserting clever little innuendos that could be taken either way, but which kept their thoughts of each other sexually charged.

But it had only been six weeks. She'd always told herself that she should never allow a boyfriend to hold her career back. As much as she liked Brody, she was determined not to allow her feelings for him to get in the way of the job. Anyway, if he liked her that much, he could always follow her up to Manchester. After all, his job — if you could call it that — could be done from anywhere. Maybe it was the test their relationship needed?

Jenny hovered her mouse over the 'Apply' button below the job advert.

She heard a noise and looked up to see Da Silva stepping out of his office and walking over to Kevin Knight. They chatted and sniggered like thieves.

Jenny pressed the button.

Once the waiter had disappeared with their order, Jenny reached across the table to take Brody's hand. Inspired by the decor surrounding them, she mimicked a Fifties housewife.

"How was your day, dear?"

They were sitting in red leather bench seats opposite each other in *Electric Diner*, a retro restaurant adjacent to the *Electric Cinema* on Portobello Road, which they'd be visiting after their meal. Jenny was surprised at how busy the place was for a Monday night. The booths along the exposed brick walls were all full, as were the stools by the long bar.

Brody smiled to acknowledge her quip and then said in all seriousness, "Actually, I've had the weirdest day."

"Well, that makes two of us."

"Oh, really? In that case, you go first."

"No, dear. A good housewife always listens to the man of the house before prattling on about household chores."

A confused expression settled across his features. Perhaps he'd picked up on the 'wife' in housewife and thought she was pushing their relationship too far, too quickly. Damn, she'd only meant to continue the Fifties joke.

He squeezed her hand gently. "I can't picture you in the role of stay-at-home wife."

"Neither can I," said Jenny. "But these days, I'd probably achieve more than I seem to at work."

"Dickhead Da Silva's still got you assigned to the paperwork from the last case, then?"

The waiter arrived with their cocktails. Both of them had chosen the same rum-based concoction from the menu, entitled Smuggler's Cove. Greedily, she swigged half down, hardly tasting it. Brody sipped at his, savouring the flavour.

"Yup, although I had a break from all that today when a new case came in while Da Silva was out of town."

"That's fantastic, Jenny." Brody's beam then turned serious. "Although when you have a new case that usually means it's a bad day for someone else."

"I guess," she acknowledged. "Anyway, it only kept me occupied for a while. When he got back to the ranch later on he ordered me off the case and back to the paperwork. In front of the whole squad."

"That's awful."

"It was so belittling. I'm not sure I can take his victimisation much more." She wasn't going to tell Brody she'd applied for the role in Manchester. Well, not yet anyway. No point raising it if they didn't like her CV. She resolved only to tell him after an interview.

"Come on. This is not like you." This time Brody reached across for her hands, concern etched across his face. She loved his unwavering focus on her. "You're a fighter. Probably the strongest woman I've ever met. You can handle bullies like Da Silva in your sleep."

She sipped her cocktail. It was nearly empty. She should have ordered a longer drink. "Maybe …"

"Don't let him get to you, Jenny. You can ride this out."

It was probably true, but it was too late. She'd already set the wheels in motion. "What about your weird day, then?" she asked.

Brody sat back, as if to get a better look at her. He was probably determining whether to let her get away with changing the subject. The decision was made for them when the waiter arrived with their meals. She'd ordered the salmon and Brody the duck confit hash. There was only enough time for a main course before the movie began next door. As the waiter stood by their table, Jenny took the opportunity to order another drink, but this time a large craft ale. At least this one would last a bit longer.

Sidestepping her question, Brody asked her if she'd seen any other movies by the director. She admitted not knowing his name, betraying mild annoyance at being found out.

"Okay, Google," he said, his tone suddenly deepening.

"What?" she asked, but he was looking down at the table, where his phone had suddenly lit up and beeped.

"List all films by Pedro Almodóvar."

Jenny looked at his phone, which she noticed was facing towards her, and watched it flip into another app, search for the director's name and list a series of films. She wondered if he had planned this.

"Sometimes," she shook her head, "you are such a geek, Brody Taylor. Why couldn't you just use your fingers like normal people?"

"It's a feature of the phone. Pretty much anything you can do by hand you can also do by voice command. You can do the same with your iPhone. If you want, I can set it up for you so that Siri recognises your voice."

Who the hell was Siri? "Uh, no thanks. I think I'll stick to being all fingers and thumbs."

Brody shrugged, picked up his phone and took her through the director's more popular movies. She'd even heard of a couple although was pretty sure she'd never seen them. Brody kept the conversation centred on movies while they ate. He was incredibly knowledgeable, but then she recalled that his degree had been in film studies.

After they settled the tab, paying half each, she allowed Brody to lead her into the cinema next door. The art deco auditorium was luxurious, nothing like the usual modern day functional affair. There were five rows of red leather armchairs, each with footstools and a table for drinks. After ordering some drinks at the bar, Brody led them towards the front.

"You've got to be joking," she whispered in his ear. "Beds in a cinema?"

"Don't you like it?"

She was staring at the front row where, instead of chairs, was a line of six huge red velvet double beds. Other couples were already cuddled up, staring up at the curtains, waiting for the lights to go off.

"You'd better not have an ulterior motive here," she stated, glancing around. "Everyone can see us."

"Don't worry, this is a *PG* night out." He winked at her. "Well, *15* if you're lucky."

They climbed onto the bed, wrapped arms and legs around each other under the supplied cashmere blanket and waited for the curtains to draw back. Jenny immediately became self-conscious, knowing that the rows of people behind could see them while the lights remained on.

"So, tell me about your weird day then. Didn't you have a pentest job this morning in Cheltenham? How did it go?"

Brody shifted a little in the bed. "Not too bad," he said. "I got in and found the information I was looking for. I'll follow up with them in a few days. But that's not the weird part. First of all, Leroy's dad showed up at Bruno's."

Jenny raised herself up onto one elbow so that she could look at him. Since Danny's funeral, Brody had talked quite a bit about Leroy. She sensed that their continued estrangement was eating him up. "How did he know you live there now?"

"He didn't. He just showed up on the off-chance I still went there to feed my coffee addiction. He told me that I should make an effort to talk to Leroy. Go up to the farm in Wales. He said that Leroy would appreciate it. But I'm not so sure about that."

"He is Leroy's dad. He ought to know."

"Hmm."

"Will you go?"

"I don't know. Anyway, it turns out Leroy's in London right now."

"Great. Then see him tomorrow."

"I don't know where he's staying."

It was a feeble excuse.

"Brody, you're a professional social engineer. I'm sure you could find that out in seconds."

"Maybe. We'll see."

Jenny held back from pushing harder. Innately, she felt that Brody needed his best friend back in his life. But she didn't know Leroy well, only having met him in the aftermath of Danny's killing and at the funeral, when he was full of rage and despair. She could only go by the stories Brody had told her about their times together back in university and their professional lives afterwards. But she had noticed that Brody smiled less guardedly when talking about Leroy, even when moaning about his crazy antics. "What was the second thing?" she said.

"Eh?"

"You said, 'First of all', implying that there was a second weird experience."

"Can't get anything past a detective, can I?"

She poked him in the ribs, repeatedly.

"Okay, okay, I give in. I'll talk." This time Brody propped himself up onto one elbow to be able to see her face. He took a sip of his drink, buying time. Jenny knew this wasn't going to be good.

"I think I've wandered into one of your murder investigations."

"What?"

"Well, not yours. Your boss's."

Jenny sat up straight, crossing her legs on the bed, withdrawing from him. "This better not be some kind of joke."

"No, I'm serious."

"Go on." Jenny folded her arms and waited.

"Do you know a James Butler?"

At that moment the curtains opened and the lights dimmed. Music began playing and she saw light reflected from the cinema screen onto Brody's face. The pre-movie adverts were rolling. Jenny held his gaze in absolute shock. "You know James Butler?" she blurted, far too loudly.

"Shh," said two or three voices from behind.

Jenny turned around, annoyed at the interruption. Automatically, she was about to reach for her warrant card and point out she was on police business, but then realised how ridiculous she'd look lying on the double bed.

"Let's go back to the diner."

"Can't it wait? This really is a great movie, Jenny."

"Shh."

"Now," she whispered. "I'm not waiting two hours before I hear this." Jenny grabbed her coat and left. He'd better follow.

A few minutes later, she was sitting back at the same table of the diner next door. A begrudging Brody dragged his feet over towards the red leather bench opposite her.

"Took two months to get tickets for the double bed," he moaned.

"Two months!" she said, her voice an octave higher than normal. "So you'd booked them before you even met me?"

"Uh no," he stammered. "I was just exaggerating. I meant a month."

For once, Jenny could tell Brody was lying. But she let it go.

When she had first met Brody, he had duped her with a convoluted series of lies in order to involve himself in her last murder investigation. He'd done this to achieve his own objectives, maintaining a straight face throughout. At no point did it become obvious that he was deceiving her, so masterful was he at duplicity. As their objectives coalesced, Brody became instrumental in helping solve the case and he even saved her life. It was these two redeeming factors that had compelled Jenny to give him one chance to come completely clean and finally base their budding relationship on a truthful foundation. He had told her everything, holding nothing back. It had been enough for her.

"Tell me about James Butler," she demanded.

"I don't actually know him."

"Brody, don't make me take you down the station."

"You wouldn't!"

Jenny folded her arms. "I'm serious."

"Okay. Okay. Butler's a professional hacker and penetration tester like me. He's been active on the hacker forums for years. Online, he goes by the name BionicM@n." He spelled out the name for her.

This was all new. The investigation team believed Butler was a day-trader. But the reference to a bionic man made some sense, given his use of advanced prosthetics.

"How do you know all this? I thought all you hackers were precious about keeping your real world identities secret."

"We are. We have to be. I only found out his real identity after he was killed."

"Hold on. I'm missing something here. Which way round do you mean? You heard about Butler's death and tracked him back to the internet? Or …"

"No, the other way around. I heard that BionicM@n had been killed and then I found out he was really Butler."

"How can you even tell if someone online has died, especially if you didn't already know them for real? Surely their profile just goes on forever. Like dead people on Facebook."

"They do. But Butler contacted me *after* he died."

"You must have the wrong person, Brody. How could he contact you if he's already dead?" Why wouldn't he just explain himself sensibly? It was like getting blood out of a stone.

"He sent me a death letter."

"A what?"

"A prewritten message addressed to me that was sent automatically when he hadn't checked in after a few days."

It sounded strange. "Why you? Especially if he didn't know you in real life."

"Because he knew who killed him and he knew I'd gone up against them once already and survived. Butler's on the Vorovskoy Mir Most Wanted list. In third place, two behind me."

Jenny couldn't believe men sometimes. Here was Brody practically bragging that he was higher on a list of hackers targeted for execution. She forcibly avoided shaking her head and processed the facts he'd shared. If what he said was true, it meant they finally had a motive. Maybe Brody had just given her a way back onto the investigation team after all.

"That's everything I know. Can we head back into the movie now?" asked Brody. "I reckon the adverts are just finishing."

"No bloody way," she said sternly. "I haven't finished with you yet."

Brody raised an eyebrow suggestively. "I hadn't finished with you either."

Brody woke and glanced at his Android Wear smartwatch. It was four in the morning. Light from the streetlamp outside bathed the bedroom in a garish yellow glow. In their lustful rush to have sex, they'd forgotten to close the curtains after the *Uber* taxi had dropped them back to Jenny's flat in Richmond earlier.

After another twenty minutes' grilling over James Butler, he'd managed to convince Jenny to return to the cinema just as the opening credits rolled. But halfway through the movie, their attention was only partly on the screen. Underneath the cashmere blanket, their slow, wandering hands diverted their attention, even though their eyes stared fixedly at the screen, portraying the illusion to the audience behind them that they were just as interested in the movie as everyone else. In the back of the taxi, they managed to restrict themselves to holding hands, although anticipation mounted with every mile.

The clothes they had been wearing earlier were now strewn all around the bedroom. Brody searched for his boxers and found them hanging over the dressing table mirror. He climbed into them and went in search of the toilet.

It was only as he reached for the flush lever that it dawned on him through the haze of his mounting hangover that the other side of Jenny's double bed was empty. Where was she? He decided not to flush and tiptoed out in search of her.

His gaze was drawn to a crack of light from the living room doorway further up the hallway. As he neared the living room, he could hear muted machine gunfire and voices shouting to each other. Maybe she'd awoken and decided to watch another movie, although he was surprised she'd chosen a war film. As he was about to push the door open he heard Jenny speak.

"Okay, Damien, cover me. I'm going in through the window."

Gently, Brody pushed open the door.

Wrapped in her thick, comfy dressing gown, Jenny lay sideways on the armchair, her legs draped over the side, facing away from him. She held an Xbox controller and was rapidly moving the thumbsticks and pressing buttons. She wore a headset, the microphone reaching around her face.

"Good shooting, Jackal. Right, Hank, I'll flush them out the back door and you pick them off."

Jenny's full attention was on the television screen and so she didn't notice the door swinging open. Brody felt his jaw slowly drop as he observed the onscreen Jenny rush through a building, shoot everything that moved, effortlessly reload while diving to the side behind cover, and then shoot again, her adversaries either dropping dead or retreating. As her enemies rushed out the back door of the large shed, Jenny's sniper teammate shot them from some unknown vantage point off screen.

Jenny smiled grimly at their handiwork. "Yeah, thanks, Hank. It was a good move. We'll have to remember that one when we take on Arctic Dragons next week."

Brody folded his arms and leaned on the doorframe. He watched Jenny absorbed in the game for a good ten minutes, his disbelief growing as he registered just how incredibly skilful Jenny was at *Call of Duty: Black Ops III*. It wasn't just the way she manoeuvred around onscreen, but her leadership over her three other teammates, issuing instructions and calling plays as they faced off wave after wave of attack, effortlessly dispatching other online gaming teams and computer-controlled zombies.

Brody rarely played online games, although when he did it was on a PC rather than a gaming console like Jenny's Xbox. And that thought reminded him of a conversation they'd had on the day they'd first met when he got her talking about her nephew, Damien, whom Brody realised she was playing with right now even though it was a school night. At the time, she'd vigorously defended console gaming against Brody's assertion that the PC was at the top of the gaming platform hierarchy, Jenny pretending to relay her nephew's point of view. Later, when Brody had first commented on the Xbox in her living room, she had told him that she'd bought it for Damien. Brody had bought both lines at the time and, as he got to know Jenny, with her deep technophobia, it had never occurred to him that she was the real ardent gamer.

Silently, Brody retreated down the hallway and climbed back into the bed. He stared at the ceiling, mulling over the fact that Jenny had never once mentioned her hobby. To be as good as she was, probably at professional gamer level, she must play an awful lot. Yet, during six weeks of dating, she'd never mentioned it. Not once. He didn't know whether to be annoyed or impressed.

Brody had always pretended to be someone he wasn't in his relationships with women, putting on a front to hide his true profession. In his experience, it was hard for someone to trust a computer hacker and, if they found out his real profession, any relationship usually dwindled and died.

Until Jenny.

She had forced him to tell the truth as a condition of continuing their affair. It had been difficult, but they had worked through it. For the first time in his life, Brody was in a relationship based entirely on truth and he was loving it. Except here was Jenny with a secret. And if she had one, then how many more was she hiding?

Brody then considered his own position. For someone who'd promised her he'd always tell the truth, he was currently skating on very thin ice. He'd lied to her about where he'd been the previous morning, pretending it was a social engineering job rather than divulging his job interview with GCHQ. He saw it as a little white lie. Of course, he'd come clean if he was offered the job, reasoning that there was no point disrupting things if he didn't get it and wouldn't then have to spend his midweeks living far away from London and Jenny.

He'd also avoided mentioning his visit to Butler's home earlier. He wasn't particularly proud of social engineering a grieving widow, and there was nothing important he'd learned from the visit except that Jenny's boss was leading the murder investigation. He'd searched the news sites afterwards and verified Da Silva's involvement from a press interview, pretending to Jenny that was how he'd learned the case was being run out of Holborn. Either way, Brody's revelation about Butler's real profession as a hacker and pentester would give the case a whole new line of enquiry.

As he'd hoped, Jenny had asked him to come into the station on Tuesday. He'd readily agreed. After all, that was where Butler's PC was located and he needed access to it if he was going to uncover the information about Vorovskoy Mir that Butler had promised in his letter. Not that Jenny or the rest of the police needed to know about that. But there was one more deception he had been forced to employ. To avoid linkage between his online persona as Fingal, he'd doctored the death letter he'd shown Jenny so that it read as if Butler had sent it to everyone on the CrackerHack forum, removing all references to Fingal and his offer of information about Vorovskoy Mir. While Jenny knew Brody was Fingal when online, there was no need for her colleagues to be informed. Being a policewoman, he knew there was no way she would condone tampering with evidence, so he'd only shown her his amended version.

So, despite their blossoming affair, it seemed they both had their little secrets and reasons behind them. Brody wondered if all relationships operated like this. He knew he was no expert.

Just as he was drifting off, he heard Jenny tiptoe down the hallway, open the bedroom door and slide back under the covers. He didn't move, forcing his breathing to remain constant. Jenny nuzzled up next to him and he lazily turned towards her, gently wrapping his arms around her and pulling her close. She kissed him on his chest and, while wriggling downwards, she continued kissing his naked body.

As he became aroused, Brody chose not to mention that he knew why her skin was so cold.

TUESDAY

CHAPTER 6

JENNY FELT STRANGE WALKING INTO HOLBORN STATION with her boyfriend in tow. Except for Fiona, Alan and Karim, none of her colleagues knew that Brody and she were an item. Brody had first met Jenny in full detective mode and had experienced how focused, determined and, well, *bossy* she was when on the job. As a female DI, she had little choice. But since they'd become a couple, she had enjoyed just being herself with him without having to put on an act.

Today, mixing her personal and professional lives, she had to expose Brody to that 'other her' once again. There was no avoiding it. He'd stumbled across a lead that was potentially critical to the Butler investigation. Even though it wasn't her case — her boss had made sure of that — she had a professional duty to bring this to Da Silva's attention. And that meant treating Brody as a witness.

Formally.

She led Brody to Interview Room 3. Speaking loudly for the benefit of the desk sergeant at the end of corridor, she said, "If you can just wait here, Mr Taylor, someone will be down to take your statement soon." Jenny held the door open for him.

"Sure." Brody glanced sideways at her, raising his eyebrows in mock surprise at her sudden detachment. "No problem, *DI Price*."

Out of sight, she mouthed, "Sorry." He shrugged to let her

know it was okay. She shut the door and headed upstairs to the murder investigation suite.

Although it was only 8:00 a.m., it was already busy. The second killing had reinvigorated the squad, which was now busy, carrying out the lines of enquiry she and Fiona had captured on the whiteboard yesterday. She grabbed an espresso from the Nespresso machine she'd installed on her desk and headed over to Da Silva's office. She knocked on the door and entered, not waiting for permission.

Da Silva was on the phone, leaning back in his chair with his feet up on the desk. He frowned at her presence and dropped his feet to the floor, swinging forward in the chair.

"Yes sir, the press conference is set for 11:00 a.m. … Okay, sir, see you there." He hung up and said to Jenny, "This better be important, DI Price. I'm in the middle of a double murder investigation."

As she opened her mouth to speak, DI Knight waltzed in. He must have spotted her heading into the boss's office and didn't want to miss out on any further fireworks after yesterday's confrontation.

Jenny spoke calmly, not allowing any excitement to break through. "I've got a new lead on the Butler case, guv."

"You have, have you?" Da Silva folded his arms. "And how would that even come to pass, DI Price, when you are supposed to be working on something else?"

"Been disobeying the guvnor's orders again?" asked DI Knight with a smirk. "You'll never make DCI that way."

She turned towards him and, unable to bite back a retort, said, "Ah, so the correct way to make DCI is to follow every order blindly, without applying any intelligence or using any detective skills, is it? In that case, you'll go far, Kevin."

"Why you —"

"Enough, you two," cut in Da Silva. "What have you got, Price?"

"I have a witness downstairs who has evidence that James Butler was targeted by the Russian mafia." She too folded her arms and waited.

"That's a bit left field," said Da Silva after a few moments.

"Who's this witness?" asked Knight.

Jenny ignored him and answered Da Silva, as if he'd asked the question. "Do you remember the computer expert who helped us on the last case?"

"You mean the so-called 'expert' who came up with the wrong name and caused me to arrest an innocent man in front of the press?"

Damn, she'd forgotten Da Silva would focus on the negatives.

"And," she continued his sentence, "who then saw through the killer's deception and enabled us to arrest the right perpetrator."

"Yes, I remember Mr Taylor. But I'm not sure how he could possibly fit into the Butler case."

"Well, he's downstairs. Why don't you ask him?"

Da Silva stood from behind his desk and issued a warning. "This better not be a waste of my time, DI Price."

"Or mine," added Knight, trailing out after Da Silva.

Jenny started to follow, but realised she'd been dismissed. She shook her head in disbelief and then remembered the miniature cup of coffee in her hands. She swigged it back in one go and grimaced. It had gone cold.

Heading back to her own desk, she flopped into her chair. What did she have to do to make Da Silva see sense? His petty behaviour was becoming tiresome. Wanting to do something positive, she checked on her application for the vacancy in Manchester, but there was no update. She'd check again tomorrow.

Unable to focus on anything else, Jenny thought about Brody helping out downstairs and wondered if there was a way she could repay him. She considered something he'd told her the night before and picked up her phone. A minute later she ended the call and grinned with relief. It had gone relatively smoothly. Oh well, the wheels were set in motion, one way or the other. She wasn't actually sure whether Brody would appreciate what she'd just done, but she was convinced it needed doing.

With no other distractions available, she reluctantly picked up the CPS case file. She probably had another day's work left on it, so the sooner she dealt with it, the sooner Da Silva would have to admit her back into the fold.

"You're wanted in Interview Room 3," said Knight, appearing suddenly at her desk.

She looked up at him, confused. "What for?" Jenny allowed her disdain to be heard. "Don't tell me you can't even interview a witness who's come forward of his own volition?"

"Your witness won't talk unless you're in the room."

Ah, Brody! She wanted to kiss him.

A few minutes later, she was sitting opposite Brody in the interview room. Da Silva sat on her left and Knight perched on a chair at the back of the room behind them. On her request, Brody had just repeated his story about the death letter. Silence descended as Da Silva and Knight considered the implications. Da Silva was studying a printout of Butler's letter that Brody had brought in with him.

"But you have no actual proof that Butler and BionicM@n are the same person?" said Da Silva.

"Three points of convergence." Brody counted off on his fingers. "One, he said he's British. Two, the cowboy reference and James Butler being the first names of 'Wild Bill' Hickok. Three, the fact that he has advanced prosthetic legs, similar to the bionic man in the TV show."

"And four," added Jenny, "he's dead."

"But no actual proof," persevered Knight from behind.

Brody sat back and laughed. "I'm sure there'll be proof on his computer that he's BionicM@n on the hacker forums."

"Yes, these hacker forums … you're on there too, I suppose."

"Yes, but only for research when I'm carrying out a penetration test for one of my clients."

"So why did he pick you?"

"He didn't. As you can see in the letter, he's sent it to hundreds of the forum members. I'm just one of many around the world who received it."

"And being an upstanding citizen," Knight sneered, "you brought it in to the very team investigating the murder."

"Well, if you don't want my help, I can be *upstanding* somewhere else …" Brody made to stand up.

"Sit down, Mr Taylor," ordered Da Silva. Brody slowly sat back down. "But DI Knight does have a point. How come you've come straight to us, rather than — say — pop into your local station?"

"In my research, I saw you were quoted on the case in the news. During the last case, I got to know Jenny — I mean DI Price — and I know she works for you. Plus we did meet briefly last time."

"Let's work on the assumption that what Mr Taylor has told us is true for a moment," said Jenny. "What are the implications for the case?"

She had directed the question at Da Silva but Brody stepped in. "Depends on whether you guys already knew whether Vorovskoy Mir was involved."

"Who is this Vorovskoy Mir?" asked Da Silva.

"They're a Russian mafia cybergang behind many online scams on the internet. They make their money trafficking in stolen credit cards, identities, prostitution, child pornography. Anything illegal that can be traded or facilitated online and they're usually involved. They make millions and go to great lengths to protect their revenue streams."

"Why would they want to kill James Butler?"

"Let me show you," offered Brody. He reached into his man bag and pulled out his tablet. After a few swipes he turned the tablet around and placed it in front of Da Silva and Jenny, who leaned forward to see. Knight stood up and peered over their shoulders.

"This is their infamous Most Wanted list of people who've crossed them online. They put you on this list if you double cross them or help vendors plug software weaknesses they've been secretly exploiting to make their scams work. BionicM@n is listed on there with a reward of over $500,000 for information on his real world identity. I presume that James Butler did something pretty serious to be worth that much."

"So you're saying that they somehow found out his identity

and sent someone round with a snake to poison him to death," stated Knight from above Jenny and Da Silva's heads, still staring down at the Vorovskoy Mir website.

Da Silva turned around to give Knight an evil stare. Knight shrugged an apology. While they were distracted, Jenny made a separating motion with her hands to remind Brody of what they'd discussed. He was not to reveal that she had told him about the snake, as that information was not yet in the public domain.

Brody ignored her signal but stuck to the script. "The papers said it was some kind of suspicious poisoning, but nothing about snakes. What's the story, DI Knight?"

"Uh, forget it."

"If this mafia connection is true, we'll have to inform the National Crime Agency," said Jenny, knowing full well that Da Silva would, more than anything, hate handing over his double murder investigation to another department.

"Let's not get too hasty," said Da Silva, predictably. "All we have so far is circumstantial evidence. We'll need evidential proof before bothering them."

"And anyway," added Knight, sitting back down in his chair at the back of the room and folding his arms. "This is all about Butler. We've not heard anything about Gowda, have we?"

Almost imperceptibly, Da Silva shook his head in despair.

"Who's Gowda?" asked Brody, on cue. Jenny looked down to hide her smile. Brody knew full well who Gowda was. She'd already told him.

"Never mind," said Da Silva, not bothering to hide his exasperation.

"If you like," said Brody, laying his hands out flat on the table, "I can take a look at Butler's computer and see if I can find any links back to Vorovskoy Mir. Or to whoever this Gowda is."

Jenny stared at him. She hadn't expected him to make such an offer. What the hell was he up to?

"Thank you, Mr Taylor, but we have our own computer experts," said Jenny.

"I hope you don't mean O'Reilly," said Brody, full of disdain.

"I do indeed mean DS O'Reilly."

Brody clasped his hands together and raised his eyebrows in mock incredulity. "O'Reilly's an amateur when it comes to cybercrime. He's good at gathering evidence from computers using packaged forensic software. That's all." Brody leaned towards Da Silva. "You saw what I'm capable of a few weeks ago, when I narrowed down on the perpetrator's identity from the hundreds of thousands in the database. O'Reilly could never have done that in a thousand years. It's just not his bag. I'm offering my skills to help you move your case forward. If there's a link to Vorovskoy Mir, I'll find it. And if there's a link to this Gowda person, I'll find that too."

Brody sat back.

Jenny had no idea he was going to make such a pitch and she wasn't happy. She figured he was trying to become involved so that he could help her with her situation with Da Silva. But she fought her own battles. She didn't need his help. She was about to decline his offer, when Da Silva spoke.

"We don't have budget for a paid consultant, Mr Taylor."

"That's okay. I'm happy to help you out free of charge." He looked past them directly at Knight. "After all, I'm an *upstanding* citizen."

"No way." DS O'Reilly folded his arms. "Not before hell freezes over will I work with the likes of him again."

Brody, standing slightly behind Da Silva and Knight, made sure only O'Reilly could see his grin.

"That's not nice, Harry," said Knight.

"I mean it."

Around the Murder Investigation Room, heads turned to see the commotion. Brody nodded subtly to the meticulously stunning Fiona Jones and foul-mouthed Karim Malik from Jenny's team, who were leaning on the back wall by the water cooler. Fiona graced him with a warm smile and Karim nodded back. He then whispered something to Fiona, who glanced sideways at him, shocked at whatever he'd said.

Harry O'Reilly's desk looked as if a rack of PCs had been

dropped on it from a great height, their innards splayed everywhere. Brody spotted PCI circuit boards, hard disk drives, memory cards and even a case of prehistoric 3.5-inch floppy disks. God knows what use Harry had for those. Desktop PCs were piled on the floor as high as the desk, wiring leading to different LCD monitors and network hubs. It was an uncoordinated mess and Brody could see little point to it all. He suspected that O'Reilly deliberately left it all on show to maintain some level of mystique as the squad's resident techie.

"It's not a request, DS O'Reilly," said Da Silva, firmly.

O'Reilly held Da Silva's stare for a few moments and then looked away, his shoulders slumping in defeat.

"Right, we'll leave you two lovebirds to it, shall we?" said Knight. "Let us know the minute you find something."

Da Silva and Knight retreated to Da Silva's office in the windowed corner. Once inside, the blinds flipped closed and the door swung shut.

Brody gabbed a chair from a nearby empty desk, wheeled it over beside O'Reilly and sat himself down. "I'll make myself at home, shall I?"

O'Reilly grumbled under his breath.

Brody waited. He wasn't going to ask O'Reilly for anything. Especially permission. His boss had given him his orders and he would crack soon enough. Patiently, Brody looked around the squad room.

Across the far side, he could see Jenny behind a computer, intently focused. She looked up every few seconds to verify the screen showed exactly what her fingers had ploddingly picked out on the keyboard beneath. He'd never seen anyone type so slowly. For some time, he'd secretly suspected that Jenny was an utter technophobe, but hadn't wanted to embarrass her by bringing it up, especially as computers were his main area of expertise. But watching her now, he could see he'd been right. But then he recalled last night, when he had spied on her playing *Call of Duty*, where her mastery of the computer-generated warzone probably surpassed anything he could do.

Brody knew Jenny was suspicious about his sudden offer of

help to Da Silva. He hoped she would come round. He'd tried to make it look spur-of-the-moment, especially to her. As he'd half expected, she had said no. Still, he wondered why. Limiting how much she mixed her private life with work would certainly have been a factor. And, he supposed, doing anything to help Da Silva would have been difficult for her to swallow, especially considering the way Da Silva was treating her right now. Fortunately, Da Silva had overruled her negative reaction and Brody was now on the inside.

He doubted whether Jenny would have supported his need to gain access to Butler's computer if he had divulged the full truth and told her about Butler's promise of information on Vorovskoy Mir. She would have put the case's integrity first, even though she wasn't directly involved in it. Brody secretly searching for non-case related information on a computer seized as evidence from a murder crime scene was certainly dishonest, and probably illegal. She would never have supported that, even if Brody were able to also uncover new leads for the case. No, he'd had no choice but to deceive his girlfriend. He just hoped Jenny never discovered what he was really up to. He was confident she wouldn't forgive him.

"Two ground rules."

Brody turned to O'Reilly, who held up two fingers. He'd finally caved in.

"One, you never touch the original computer. We work on duplicated images only."

"Okay." Brody understood the logic of that. The minute you turned on the original computer, anything running on it could make changes, potentially nullifying chain of evidence procedures, which require evidence to be maintained exactly as recovered. That way, any claim made by the defence of the police doctoring or manufacturing evidence, especially of the digital kind, could be defended against, as the original source had never been touched.

"And two. You don't do anything without me watching."

"Sure, Harry."

O'Reilly squinted at him, trying to work out if Brody was

teasing.

"So where's your image, then?"

"Here." Harry turned his screen around. Using his mouse, he brought up an application called EnCase. From a quick scan, Brody determined it was a police forensic application and that O'Reilly had used it to copy a full image of Butler's PC, allowing him to examine the duplicate safely. "Not much on here, to be honest. Nothing in his My Documents folder. He doesn't use an email client so no offline mail to search through. Not much browser history or cached data. Looks like he had it locked down tight."

"But you're just scanning the image copy as if it's one large data file," said Brody.

"True enough. But EnCase is fiercely sophisticated. It gets right inside the file system structure and lets me see everything I need."

Brody shook his head.

"What?" demanded O'Reilly, insulted.

"I'm sure that approach works fine for your day job of searching for paedo porn. But we're not looking for images. In fact, we don't really know what we're looking for. For instance, how do you read his email if he hasn't got an offline email store?"

"Well," O'Reilly hesitated, "we don't."

"What about Butler's smartphone, have you got that? His email will be on there."

"Yes, it's in evidence."

"Well, why don't you just log into that?"

"It's an iPhone." O'Reilly folded his arms, defeated. "The NSA still haven't revealed the backdoor they're using, so no one other than them can break in."

O'Reilly was referring to the case of the San Bernardino shooters where *Apple* refused to provide the FBI with a master key into the iPhone. Undeterred, the NSA came to the rescue with a backdoor hack that only they knew about.

"Did Butler set it up for a fingerprint passcode?"

"We checked. Otherwise we would have swiped it on his

finger at the morgue."

"Okay, so we can't use his phone. Back to his computer, then. Why don't you just boot up the image, log on and look around properly?"

"That's impossible. First of all, I'd need an exact replica of the hardware on which to install the copied image. Otherwise it won't boot as all the hardware drivers will be wrong. And even if we somehow got past that, we hardly have access to Butler's passwords to log on."

"Why don't you just extract the SAM and the system registry hive and then use a password-cracking tool with rainbow tables loaded and try and obtain the password? It's only Windows, after all."

O'Reilly stared at him as if he'd just revealed the meaning of life. "You can do that?"

"Probably. Never done it from an image, though. But I'm sure it'll be straightforward enough." Brody reached for the mouse. "Do you mind?"

"Uh, sure." O'Reilly took his hand off his mouse and pushed the keyboard towards Brody.

"Okay, first of all I need to export the image to a clean drive. Then we'll crack the passwords."

"Physical or on a network server?"

"Don't mind. Physical would probably be faster."

"Okay, I've got one here."

O'Reilly rummaged around under his desk. While O'Reilly wasn't looking, Brody quickly clicked around the EnCase application, familiarising himself with its layout, menus and concepts. O'Reilly surfaced with an external hard drive which he then connected to his computer's USB port.

"Thanks."

Brody clicked his way through the EnCase export menu and selected the new drive. A percentage bar appeared as it copied the data. "You okay if I download John the Ripper onto your computer? It's my favourite password-cracking tool."

O'Reilly scanned left and right, checking to see if anyone was paying them any attention. He nodded. "Go on, then."

Brody brought up a browser and connected to one of his own online servers, typing in the native IP address from memory. He clicked through a list of application installation files and then hesitated, trying to determine which version of John the Ripper to download. By habit, he'd almost clicked on the version which also installed Poison Ivy, a remote access Trojan that would give Brody secret remote access to O'Reilly's computer long after today. Brody was severely tempted, his mouse hovering between the doctored version and the clean one, but then he looked around and recalled that he was in the middle of a police station. Installing malware on a police network was probably pushing things too far.

He hovered the mouse pointer over the clean version.

Although, having a back door into the Met Police would certainly give him bragging rights on CrackerHack.

He moved the mouse back to the doctored version.

And having secret access to police systems could come in useful.

His finger slowly began to add pressure to the mouse clicker.

"What's the difference between the two?"

O'Reilly's question cut through the temptation. Brody mentally shook himself. What the hell was he doing? This was the Met Police. He was seriously asking for trouble. He clicked on the clean version.

His bluff was instinctive. "Couldn't remember which one was for Windows and which one for Linux."

Fifteen minutes later the image had exported to the hard drive and John the Ripper had finished its work.

"Fair play to you," said O'Reilly, full of admiration. He was looking down the list of usernames and passwords displayed on his screen.

Brody was pleased it had worked.

"But what use is it? You can hardly boot the image from the external drive."

"We can if we P2V it."

"Pee-what it?"

"Make a virtualised image of the system which we can then

load on a hypervisor somewhere. You got any spare VMware servers lying around?"

O'Reilly shook his head slowly. Brody suspected that not speaking enabled him to avoid admitting he had no idea what Brody was talking about.

"Ah well, don't worry, there's loads of them in the cloud we can use."

"There is, is there?"

Brody downloaded another program, pointed it at the extracted image and then at an address of one of his own servers on the internet. He explained himself to O'Reilly. "I'm just firing up a VMware converter tool to virtualise the image." He saw O'Reilly's confusion and went for simplicity. "Remember when you said you couldn't boot it up unless the hardware matches?"

O'Reilly nodded.

"Well, this program copies the PC image to a virtual server in the cloud and, during the transfer, replaces all the hardware drivers with virtual ones. That will allow the image to boot up without crashing on the virtual server, which we can then connect to remotely."

O'Reilly nodded as if he knew what Brody was talking about.

"It'll take a while. Anywhere to get coffee around here?"

Jenny finished indexing the last witness statement and sat back, relieved. She was on the home stretch now. Probably only another day's work and she'd be free of the laborious task of preparing the CPS file.

It was a good time for coffee. Well, it was always a good time for coffee. She grabbed her espresso cup and headed for the kitchenette to wash it. Fiona Jones immediately appeared, a mug of tea in her hand that she emptied down the sink.

"Need to make a fresh one. I stupidly let that one get cold."

But Jenny had spotted faint tendrils of steam rising from the plughole and knew Fiona was only here to fish for gossip. She scanned the main room and saw Karim Malik behind his desk, staring in their direction. Fiona had clearly been sent as the advance party.

The DC dropped a teabag into her mug. "Nice to see Brody again."

Predictable. "Is it?"

She added boiling water from the kettle. "Never thought I'd see him and Harry working side by side again."

"Me neither."

Fiona squeezed out the teabag with a spoon and threw it in the bin. "He knew one of the victims, then?"

"What makes you ask that?"

She reached around Jenny to open the fridge and grabbed the milk. "Well, why else would he be here?"

After being on the outside for so long, Jenny was actually relishing the experience of knowing more than someone else. She embellished, "Maybe because he's an expert snake handler."

"Really?" Fiona stopped pouring milk and turned to face Jenny, searching her face for any deceit. Jenny remained blank and Fiona's shoulders slumped in defeat. "Damn. That's what Karim guessed. It just didn't seem at all likely."

"Does that mean you'll have to pay up?"

"Yeah," she admitted begrudgingly. "A tenner. He gave me two to one on that."

Jenny laughed. "Don't worry, your money's safe. Brody knows nothing about snakes. He was contacted by Butler."

"Phew. You had me there." Fiona popped in a sweetener and stirred her tea. "But why did Butler contact him? When? How?"

"You'll have to wait for Da Silva on that one."

"So what's the deal with him working with Harry?"

"That," stated Jenny ominously, "is what I want to know."

"Fair enough, Jen.' She picked up her mug. "Right, I'm off to collect my winnings. Thanks, boss."

As Fiona made a beeline for Karim, Jenny shook her head, amused. Noticing that Da Silva's office was empty and that he and Knight were nowhere to be seen, she washed up her espresso cup and then grabbed a paper cup from a cupboard. Back at her desk she made two espressos using her personal *Nespresso* machine. Double-checking Da Silva and Knight were still missing in action, she crossed the room towards Brody and

Harry, each huddled behind computer monitors. As she reached Harry's desk, she saw Brody grimacing as he absently sipped at a plastic cup containing instant coffee from the vending machine.

"Thought you might prefer this," said Jenny, holding out the paper cup.

Brody leaned out beyond the monitor and beamed. He stood, accepted the cup and sniffed the pleasant aroma. "Aw, thanks Jen. I think Harry was trying to poison me with that other stuff."

Harry piped up without looking up. "Coffee snobs! Why can't you lot just drink tea like normal people?"

Jenny indicated for Brody to follow her. She entered a glass-walled internal meeting room and shut the door behind them. "What's going on, Brody?"

"What do you mean?" He sipped at his coffee, eyeing her over the top of the paper cup.

"What's with you offering to help? You were only supposed to show Da Silva the letter."

"It just came out."

"Nothing you do ever just *comes out*, Brody."

"I just wanted to help."

"Help who? You? Me?"

"Come on, Jen. If there's a digital link between Butler and Gowda, I'll find it and then let you know about it."

"You'll let *me* know about it, will you? I'm not even on the case."

"But you should be. Even Da Silva must realise that this case is too big for him and Knight."

"Is that why you refused to be interviewed by them unless I was in the room? As an effort to force them to involve me in the case?"

Brody shrugged.

"And instead of that, now *you're* on the bloody case. How do you think that makes me feel?"

Brody looked completely confused.

"I don't need you inserting yourself into my battles. This is my fucking career, Brody, not one of your social engineering projects. How I deal with Da Silva is down to me."

"I was only trying to help, Jen."

"Well don't."

Jenny turned and stormed out of the room. She felt his hurt eyes bore into her back as she headed for the stairs. She was also conscious of Harry, Fiona, Karim and others staring at her. Her raised voice must have carried through the glass walls of the internal meeting room. After being the centre of station gossip while dating her immediate superior some years ago, she'd vowed never to get romantically involved with other coppers and entangle her love life with the job. She thought she'd achieved that with Brody, yet here he was, right in the middle of her place of work, working on a double murder even she was excluded from. It was as if everything she had worked years to achieve had all come to nothing. It was so damn frustrating.

Jenny stomped down the stairs, not sure where she was heading. She'd never felt this isolated before. She wondered if anyone in Manchester had reviewed her application yet. It was a long way to Manchester, definitely not commutable. She'd have to leave everything — and everyone — behind. But the way she felt right now, she was relishing the thought of starting afresh.

On the ground floor, she burst through the secure door into a pack of journalists heading in the direction of the media briefing room. That explained why Da Silva and Knight were missing from upstairs. Throwing caution to the wind, she allowed herself to be dragged along with the crowd and took a seat at the back of the room. If she was being forced to sit on the sidelines, she may as well do it literally.

DCS McLintock stood behind a podium at the front on a raised stage, waiting patiently for the rabble to take their seats. He was dressed formally in full dress uniform, peaked cap perched on his head hiding his baldness, exuding control and authority. He scanned the room and Jenny noticed his swivelling head pause for a microsecond as he clocked her at the back.

DCI Da Silva stood behind and to the right of his boss on the stage. Jenny scanned the room for DI Knight, knowing full well Da Silva's pet wouldn't be far from the chain of command. She spotted him standing with his back to the wall at the side of the room, talking quietly on his mobile phone.

McLintock called the room to order, his West Country accent softening any order he gave. The room hushed expectantly.

"Yesterday morning at nine o'clock, the body of a twenty-nine-year-old man was found in his own home in North London. The victim has been identified as Rajesh Gowda. We believe that an unknown assailant broke into his home and forced him to ingest a deadly poison, causing his death. We are treating this as murder. His pregnant girlfriend, who discovered his body, has been taken into the hospital under observation. Given certain similarities to the James Butler investigation from the week before, we are treating this as a linked series. Any questions?"

Jenny was impressed. It was a succinct summary and the DCS had not looked at any notes while reciting. She particularly liked his choice of the verb 'ingest', which didn't give away the fact that Gowda had been bitten by a snake. But when that came out later, as it inevitably would, McLintock hadn't actually lied. Snake poison was certainly ingested into Gowda's blood stream. The fact that it got there via a snakebite would be irrelevant later. And then there was the way he'd positioned Gwenda Bevan being in hospital. He'd implied it was because she was a pregnant lady who'd discovered her partner's body. But he'd actually avoided revealing the whole GHB angle. Very impressive.

The journalists threw questions at him and he fielded them well, without giving much more away. Had they arrested anyone yet? No. Did Butler and Gowda know each other? Police were exploring that. What type of poison? The lab tests had yet to confirm type of poison. Did the assailant take anything? No.

And so on.

A journalist to Jenny's left spoke up. "Given it's a serial killer —"

"We have no proof of a serial killer, James," interrupted McLintock. "We are treating the two murders as linked, but it's too early to start throwing terms like that around."

"Okay. Given they are linked, do you have the manpower to handle such a complex double murder investigation?"

McLintock paused briefly, his only hesitation so far, and then answered. "Yes. We have resourced this appropriately. DCI Da Silva here …" he indicated Da Silva behind him, who held one palm up as if being introduced as a movie star, " … is the Senior Investigating Officer. He has two independent teams under him, so that we can work both cases in parallel. The Butler case is being led by DI Knight …" McLintock pointed at Knight, who rapidly took his phone away from his ear, having been chatting quietly into it all along, and looked around, dazed. "The Gowda case is being led by DI Price. You may remember that she recently apprehended the so-called meeting room killer." McLintock pointed in her direction.

As Jenny stared open-mouthed at McLintock, all the journalists turned to get a good look at her. She saw Da Silva and Knight both glance in confusion at her presence in their midst and then turn their attention back to DCS McLintock. Da Silva even stepped forward to whisper in his ear, but McLintock gently pushed him back with one hand. Jenny snapped her jaw shut and sat bolt upright. She nodded at McLintock and smiled grimly.

Jenny barely heard another word of the press conference after that.

CHAPTER 7

BRODY HAD FINALLY LOGGED ONTO THE VIRTUALISED copy of Butler's PC a couple of hours ago. Using standard browser history as a guide to sites Butler had visited, Brody had methodically worked his way through Butler's online life. Well, at least the life that he allowed to be recorded in cookies within a standard browser. Shopping sites like Amazon and John Lewis were listed, as well as his online bank, email provider and social media sites.

But Brody knew there was far more to Butler than he was seeing here. In fact, it was increasingly looking like the PC the police had seized was used for nothing more than Butler's day-to-day life. The phone was locked and useless. And there were no USB sticks logged as evidence either. The computer held nothing that linked to his online persona as BionicM@n.

"Right, here's Butler's PayPal account," said Brody.

O'Reilly looked across at his screen. "Any suspicious online payments?"

Brody paged through the history. Lots of internet purchases from familiar websites. He filtered the history to only show payments received.

"Now that's far more interesting," said O'Reilly, looking at a list of high value transactions. "They're mostly from the same place. Who do you reckon cryptoX is?"

"Looks like he's been selling bitcoins in an online exchange. I imagine he gets paid in bitcoins for the jobs he takes on anonymously, and then he sells them online for cash into his PayPal account."

Brody was fairly certain this was what was going on because it was a form of what he himself did to convert the crypto currency payments into normal cash. Although Brody preferred using gift card exchange schemes to guarantee remaining untraceable.

"But most of these are over £10,000 a time." O'Reilly slid his finger down the screen, quickly totting up. "That's well over a million in just five years."

"Which means he's definitely a black hat. White hat hacking is nowhere near as lucrative."

That was a true statement. Brody charged a daily rate for penetration testing projects, occasionally meriting a bonus on top for exposing a particularly serious flaw in his client's security. He saw it as a fair exchange of his time and skills. However, the culture of the illicit trading marketplaces on the deep web was to pay black hat hackers based on the risk associated with the hacking job being advertised. If someone just wanted a batch of ten thousand identities with credit card details, it would have a certain price. But if someone wanted a copy of their competitor's customer contact database and sales pipeline, it would have a much higher price, factored by the expected complexity and risk.

"Look at this," said Brody, "his payments seem to have trailed off over the last couple of years. Wonder what's going on there?"

"Maybe his conscience got the better of him. He's got a young daughter, after all."

Brody thought for a moment. "Or maybe his employer used to be Vorovskoy Mir. In his letter he said something about screwing them over a couple of years ago. Maybe he did that and then went straight."

"Or maybe having the daughter made him go straight, and so he went out with a bang. Wonder what he did to them?"

"I don't know for sure, but there was talk in the CrackerHack community a couple of years ago about an anonymous donation of $10 million worth of bitcoins to The Tor Project." Brody spotted the unsure look on O'Reilly's face and explained. "The non-profit organisation behind Tor, the browser which lets you hide your identity when accessing the internet. Useful for people in oppressive countries like China or anyone who wants to avoid being tracked by the NSA or GCHQ."

"I know what Tor is. It's the bane of my life. Paedophiles use it all the time to browse child porn. Makes it much harder to make a case."

"Fair enough. Like most things, you can use it for good or bad."

"Does he have a Tor browser installed?" asked O'Reilly.

"Yup." It was one of the first things Brody had checked a couple of hours before. "But Tor discards all cookies at the end of the browsing session, so we can't see where he's been."

"So all we've got so far are the suspicious payments into his PayPal account. We haven't actually proved that Butler and the hacker who sent that letter to you are one and the same. However —" O'Reilly stopped and stared into the middle distance. He sat forward and reached for the keyboard. "We've been logging as Butler onto websites that we have cookies stored for, knowing he's been there before."

"Yes …" said Brody, suddenly fearing that O'Reilly was brighter than he'd seemed so far.

"Why don't we log into CrackerHack with his credentials? If we get in with one of the passwords you cracked earlier, we'll know for sure it's him."

Damn. Brody had planned to do exactly that, but later, in the privacy of his home. Brody was concerned that Butler's CrackerHack account might reveal something about Brody's own online life as Fingal, especially if there was a copy of the original death letter there somewhere. Although he didn't expect that to be the case, he couldn't be sure. If Butler had discussed the death letter online with anyone else, it would be recorded on the CrackerHack forums.

But there was no avoiding it now.

"I'll do it," said Brody, grabbing back the keyboard. "I know my way around CrackerHack."

O'Reilly let go.

Brody typed in the URL for CrackerHack and typed *BionicM@n* into the username field. From the sites they'd visited so far, they knew that Butler had employed five main password variations. It needed to be one of them.

Brody typed Butler's most commonly used password and pressed enter.

An error message appeared.

He repeated twice with the same result. "Shit."

"Did you type them correctly?"

"Of course. And we're only allowed one more attempt. If we get it wrong this time, the account will be locked."

"Can't we just reset the password?"

"We could, but it will go to Butler's email address."

"We have that. We were in it earlier."

"We have his public Gmail one. No hacker in his right mind would register on CrackerHack with a traceable Gmail address. And we don't know the email address he registered with, so we can't log into it to reset the password."

"Ah."

"There are two passwords left. Which one, Harry?"

Harry reached into his pocket and pulled out a coin. "Heads it's that one." He pointed at the fourth password. "Tails it's that one." He moved his finger to the fifth option, then flipped the coin into the air, caught it in his right hand and smacked it onto the back of his left. "It's tails. Let's go for the last one."

Brody began typing the password. His finger hovered over the Enter key. But Butler had only used that password for accessing his social media accounts. Brody recalled that the fourth one had been used for accessing an amputee support website community of which he was an active member. Perhaps he thought of anything to do with his disability as being a bionic man … Brody deleted the password and began typing the fourth one.

O'Reilly reached across to stop him. "What are you doing?"

Brody pressed Enter.

The familiar CrackerHack front page popped up.

"You jammy sod."

"Born lucky, me."

Brody searched for Butler's most recent post as BionicM@n and found it on a discussion forum to do with firmware programming, a subject Brody had never had reason to explore. The conversation was with a small number of other forum members and seemed to be about swapping ideas on low-level assembler code. Out of context, it was hard to determine what was being coded. Brody wondered whether Butler was learning more about the embedded software typically installed on the microchips within his myoelectric prosthetic legs.

"Look, it's dated the day before his body was discovered," announced O'Reilly. "Is that his last post?"

"Yeah. Strange subject, though."

"Not very hackery."

Brody began searching through everything Butler had done. He scrolled back through his private messages. BionicM@n was an active forum member, probably even more so than Brody. He was certainly knowledgeable about hacking and programming.

But the further back in time Brody searched, the more arrogant and angry the tone of Butler's messages became. It certainly appeared as if he'd had a change of heart around two years ago. And then Brody spotted a two-year-old conversation with Contag10n, the leader of Vorovskoy Mir and orchestrator of Danny's death six weeks ago. The person Brody wanted to bring down more than anything.

"Who's Contagion?" asked O'Reilly.

"No one in particular." Brody scrolled up, determined to revisit later when he was back at his apartment.

Half an hour later, Brody and O'Reilly summarised their findings to DCI Da Silva and DI Knight in Da Silva's office.

"If I've got this straight," said Da Silva, "You've proved what you said earlier. That Butler was a computer hacker. But that's about it."

"What do you mean?"

"You haven't proved that — what was the name of that Russian mafia gang?"

"Vorovskoy Mir."

"You haven't proved that Vorovskoy Mir was behind the

attack."

Brody nodded. Da Silva was right, and it was concerning. The only communication Brody had discovered was the message with Contag10n from two years before. He would look more deeply later. But on the surface, Da Silva was correct.

Da Silva picked up his phone to emphasise the point he was about to make. "So there's no need for me to call the National Crime Agency at this stage."

Brody shrugged, not wanting to get drawn into station politics. The geek in him noticed that Da Silva had the latest Samsung Galaxy, even newer than Brody's own.

"And you've not found any link between Butler and Gowda."

O'Reilly spoke up. "Analysis of Butler's computer certainly shows no connection. I'm also halfway through checking the other way. I've got Gowda's home computer in evidence but, so far, forensic analysis shows no linkage to Butler."

O'Reilly hadn't asked Brody for help with Gowda's PC and Brody certainly hadn't offered to help. He was here to find a trail to Vorovskoy Mir, which could only have been found on the hacker's computer. However, Brody suspected that after he left, O'Reilly would use his newfound knowledge to virtualise the image of Gowda's PC and continue his investigation that way.

"So this whole death letter might be completely irrelevant."

"A red herring," added Knight, who clearly wanted to say something intelligent and failed dismally.

"I guess it's possible," admitted Brody. It was a worrying possibility. Butler couldn't predict the manner of his own ending. Given his history with Vorovskoy Mir, he'd assumed that any untimely death would most likely be attributed to them. But if he'd died for some other reason, then the same death letter would have gone out anyway, wrongly pointing towards Vorovskoy Mir.

It was concerning, but, Brody reasoned, it didn't change anything. The death letter promised Brody access to some key information that he could use against Vorovskoy Mir. That information was still out there somewhere, regardless of whether Vorovskoy Mir were involved in Butler's death or not. Brody still had work to do.

Da Silva clasped his hands together.

"I want to say thank you, Mr Taylor. DS O'Reilly told me a few minutes ago that the progress you'd both made today would have taken weeks under normal computer investigative processes."

Brody glanced at O'Reilly, surprised he'd said anything. O'Reilly's startled expression revealed that he hadn't said anything of the sort.

"You're welcome," said Brody, warily.

"If you don't mind, Mr Taylor, I'd like to put you forward for formal inclusion on the Met's database of authorised third party advisors and consultants. Your skills would be very helpful to the police service. With the rise of computer-related crime, it could even become a lucrative sideline for you."

Brody was surprised. It wasn't something he'd ever thought of before and he quite liked the idea of it. Although he wasn't sure how that would play alongside his job at GCHQ, assuming they made him an offer.

"That would be very kind of you. I'll drop you an email with my details."

Da Silva reached into his inside jacket pocket and handed Brody a business card. "My email's there."

Brody took the card. He then grabbed his phone, brought up the business card app, snapped a picture of it and handed the card back to Da Silva. The app read the characters on the business card and automatically added the contact to his phone's database.

Da Silva shook his head good-naturedly. "You techies." He pocketed the card, stood and offered his hand. "I'll leave DS O'Reilly to escort you downstairs. Thank you once again for coming forward."

As Brody shook his hand, he asked, "Is Jenny around? I'd just like to say goodbye before I head off."

Da Silva whipped his hand back as if electrocuted. "No," he said through gritted teeth. "I believe DI Price is currently out on an enquiry."

"I feel like I've escaped from Alcatraz," said Jenny, accelerating as the lights changed.

Fiona leaned over and made a show of studying Jenny's legs within the footwell of the car.

"What are you up to?" asked Jenny.

"Just checking to see if Da Silva's put an ankle bracelet on you for your unexpected parole."

Jenny laughed. "I reckon he would if he could."

"After yesterday's showdown, I thought he was determined to keep you stuck on the CPS prep for another week. How'd you manage to escape?"

Jenny picked up speed as the road signs turned blue for the M4 motorway. She was heading in the direction of Heathrow, knowing that Stockley Park was just north of the airport, near Uxbridge.

"I don't actually know. I was sitting in the media briefing for the two cases and McLintock suddenly announces that Knight is leading Butler and that I'm leading the Gowda investigation. I could tell from Da Silva's reaction that he had no idea that was coming either."

"What prompted McLintock to override Da Silva?"

"No idea. Maybe it was the pressure of the media and the DCS wanted to demonstrate we've got everyone assigned. A DI per case."

"Or maybe he's starting to hear the station rumours about Da Silva and Knight's incompetence and he's deliberately brought his best officer out of retirement."

Jenny briefly glanced sideways to acknowledge the compliment with a smile. "I'd love that to be true. But McLintock's so detached from the troops, he's unlikely to hear much about what goes on at the coalface."

"I don't know. You know he and Alan are old mates. Rumour has it they even went through Hendon together back in the day."

"Really?" Which made Jenny wonder why she'd never known that. Alan Coombs had been her DS for two years, yet she had never really talked to him about his career in the service before working together. Yet here was Fiona, who'd only been on her team for three months, and she already knew more about everyone than Jenny. Her lower rank certainly made it easier to be accepted but it was Fiona's easy-going style that enabled her to be accepted as one of the lads, something Jenny had never achieved. But then, Jenny knew she could be quite intense and focused, which made her less approachable. She needed to work on that.

"So, how did Da Silva behave towards you after the media briefing?"

"Would you believe he tried to take credit for it, saying it was his idea?"

"He never!"

"But back in his office, dishing out who does what was a different matter. Knight tried to palm me off with a bunch of uniforms, but I demanded you, Karim and Alan. We're a proven team, after all. All I had to do was remind Da Silva that he'd fail the thirty-day audit if I didn't have a full complement of two DSs and at least one DC.

"So how come we're heading to Gowda's employer? Surely, there are better leads for us to follow up on?"

"True. I wanted to track down potential sources for obtaining GHB, but Da Silva assigned any line of enquiry common to both cases to Knight's team. That only left background checks on Gowda. But it needs to be done, so we'll do it."

"What about Alan and Karim?"

"They're traipsing around London visiting every pet shop selling snakes and every registered black mamba owner. Even though the snake is common to both cases, Da Silva made it clear that he didn't want to do that. Personally, I think he's scared of snakes."

"Aren't you?" asked Fiona.

Jenny exited the M4 and pulled up as cars backed up at the roundabout underneath the motorway. "Not really. My uncle kept a python when I was a kid. He let me hold it quite a few times. I quite liked it."

"What's it feel like?"

"Not slimy, like you'd expect. And heavy. I remember it being heavy, especially when he put it round my neck. But you had to be careful in case it tried to constrict you. He always made sure it had eaten recently before letting it near me!"

"Yeah, well, a python and a black mamba are worlds apart," said Fiona. "I've been reading up on them. Did you know that mambas are the fastest snakes in the world and that a single bite contains enough neurotoxin to kill fifteen adults?"

Jenny shook her head, trying to imagine how a snake moved quickly. Her uncle's python had been a slow, ponderous beast and barely slithered. Once, when he dropped a live mouse into the cage, she remembered being fascinated by the way the snake ignored its prey for ages, the mouse walking all over the snake, oblivious to its impending death. But when the python finally got round to it, the strike was fast.

"And," Fiona continued, "when a mamba strikes, it hits multiple times just to make damn sure it kills you."

"Yeah, I saw multiple bites on Gowda's arm."

"Why would anyone want to keep a dangerous snake like that as a pet? It's so stupid. What if it got out? You'd be killed!"

"Doesn't bear thinking about."

As cars pulled away onto the roundabout, Jenny took notice of her surroundings. Black cabs laden with suitcases and holidaymakers turned left towards the airport. A double-deck aircraft took off nearby. This close up it truly was massive, no doubt hundreds of people on board. Jenny wondered where everyone was going. It would be so much simpler for her to turn left, book a flight somewhere far away and not bother coming back. If only her passport was in her bag, then she could leave all the crap with Da Silva behind.

But that would mean giving up. Something she would never do. She'd fought hard over the years to get to where she was, despite idiots like DCI Da Silva and DI Knight. She wondered where her application for Greater Manchester ranked on the scale of giving in. But if she got promoted, everyone would interpret it as her moving onwards and upwards. Not throwing in the towel.

Not the truth.

A car behind beeped. She'd missed at least three gaps that would have enabled her to join the traffic flowing around the roundabout.

"Are you okay, Jen?"

"Yeah, sorry. Just thinking about snakes."

A few minutes later, Jenny turned off the A408, following the signs into the business park and drove down the road past large large, ostentatious, glass-walled head office buildings, each surrounded by enough greenery to make them appear standalone.

She pulled up outside MedDev Labs' head office, parked and entered the reception. Fiona showed her warrant card to the receptionist and asked for the Head of the IT department.

A few minutes later, they were greeted by the IT Director's assistant and escorted to the boardroom on the first floor, which contained an ornate oval table with twelve chairs. As the assistant offered them refreshments, a gaunt-looking man entered. He had saggy eyes behind heavy-framed black spectacles, wore an ill-fitting grey suit with tie open at the collar and introduced himself as Jerome Richards. They reciprocated and he shook their hands in turn. Fiona accepted a glass of water from the assistant. Jenny regarded the takeaway coffee that Richards had brought with him, and also chose a glass of water, rather than gamble on the coffee in the flask. If Richards had paid for his own rather than drink the free stuff, then it was probably stewed to death. They settled into chairs at one end of the table, Fiona pulling out a notebook. The assistant left, pulling the door behind her quietly.

"Are you here about Rajesh, then?" he asked. "Everyone here is so shocked about what happened."

"How do you know about Mr Gowda's death?" Fiona asked.

"Well, Gwenda … his other half. She used to work on reception. That's how they met … anyway, her brother works here. Gwenda told him the awful news. It sounds dreadful. I can't believe it. Why would someone want to poison him like that?"

"That's why we're here, Mr Richards," said Jenny.

He turned to her, shock on his face. "You can't believe someone from MedDev did that?"

"We have to cover every possibility," said Fiona. "If you don't mind, let's start with some background. What was Mr Gowda's job here, Mr Richards?"

"He was one of our DBAs." Fiona wrote 'DBA' in her notebook. Richards spotted Jenny's raised eyebrow and explained, "A database administrator. He made sure that the databases for all our business applications worked optimally. Enough storage, optimised indexes, backups, that kind of thing."

Hearing the geek-speak, Jenny decided to stay silent.

"What business is MedDev Labs in?" Fiona asked.

"We're one of the world's largest independent medical device manufacturers. We have offices and factories all over the world. This is our UK head office, but our main UK research laboratory is just outside Cambridge." He leaned forward conspiratorially. "We based ourselves there to lap up all of the best medical science graduates from the University." He sat back. "Our manufacturing and distribution facilities are spread across the world."

"What kind of devices does MedDev Labs make?"

"We specialise in cardiovascular and cardiac rhythm disease management."

Medical jargon. Now it was Fiona's turn to be stumped. "Which is what in English?" she asked with a gentle smile.

"Sorry, force of habit. Amongst other things we make heart valves, pacemakers and defibrillators. These are devices which help alleviate pain, extend life and restore health for millions of people around the world."

"Millions? Wow. How big is the company, then?" asked Jenny.

"We have more than 70,000 employees around the world and turned over $20 billion last year."

Jenny was impressed. It was much larger than she would have guessed. From watching the news, she was anecdotally aware that the pharmaceutical industry was immense, but she'd never given any thought to companies like MedDev Labs, which conducted business in the same industry, but making medical devices instead of drugs.

"My niece had a pacemaker fitted last year," commented Fiona. "Apparently it's a new type. Really small with no wires. Goes right inside the heart."

Jenny was surprised. Fiona gave so little of herself away at work and suddenly here she was talking with a stranger about a niece that Jenny hadn't known even existed.

"Sounds like one of ours," said Richards. "We launched the world's smallest pacemaker two years ago. It's about the size of a pill and can be fitted into the right ventricle of the heart through a vein in the leg. Leaves no bump under the skin or chest scar, and the battery lasts just as long as traditional ones. Being so small, it's perfect for kids. How old is your niece?"

"Uh, nine." Fiona seemed to realise that she'd just given away some personal information and switched topics. "So, how many of those 70,000 employees are based here?"

"About four hundred. This building is mostly back office operations departments." He began ticking off with his fingers as he spoke. "HR, Finance, IT, Supply Chain, Procurement and Marketing."

Fiona dutifully noted down the list of names.

Jenny asked, "How long have you worked here, Mr Richards?"

"Me?" He was surprised to be the focus of any question. But then he shrugged. "I've been here six years. Originally I ran the IT help desk, but now I run all of IT."

"Okay. Let's focus on Mr Gowda," suggested Jenny. "Was he well liked?"

"Rajesh is …" he shrugged again, helplessly this time. "Rajesh *was* a popular guy, that's why so many people are upset. We run quite a lot of events to raise money for charity: cycling trips, walking weekends, that kind of thing. He always took part. Originally, I think it was so that he could make friends outside of work. But then he just kept doing them. Actually, he was organising the next one, an overnight sleepover on the streets of London to raise money for the homeless." He made a mental note. "I guess I'll need to ask someone else to take over."

"Did you hire Mr Gowda?"

"It's fair to say I signed it off. He works for my Head of Applications, Yvonne Fuller. She actually hired him. It was about two years ago."

"I understand he's originally from Sri Lanka. How did he come to be working here?"

Richards looked up at the ceiling, making a show of remembering. "He was already here in the UK on secondment from our Sri Lankan office. He was part of the supply chain team and was an expert on the component suppliers in India and the Far East. If I remember rightly, we were implementing a new supply chain system and he was part of the project team. When the project finished, he asked to stay here in the UK and by then we all knew how bright he was and how hard he worked. His degree had been in Computer Science and he was a pretty decent programmer. Seemed like a shame to send him back to Colombo when we had an opening here for a DBA."

"So he was here on a work visa?" asked Jenny.

"Yes, of course."

"For the specialist supply chain project?"

He nodded.

"And you reapplied when he switched roles to become a DBA?"

Richards hesitated. "I'm sure Yvonne would have taken care of all that."

Sensing there might be something behind his hesitation, Jenny added, "Because you would need to have carried out a resident labour market test to prove that the DBA job couldn't be filled by someone here in the UK. You did that, did you?"

Richards shifted uncomfortably. "I'm sure we would have because we do it regularly. We have quite a lot of overseas workers here on sponsored visas. But you'll need to double check with Yvonne."

"We will," stated Fiona, making a show of circling some text in her notebook.

"Would it be possible to get a list of the employees based

here, Mr Richards?" asked Jenny.

"Why would you need that?"

"Just for elimination purposes, really."

In truth Jenny wanted to cross-reference the employees with the list of registered snake owners in the country, as well as check for anyone with a previous criminal conviction.

"Uh, sure. I can ask someone in HR to pull it off the system and email it to you."

"Thanks," said Fiona. "Did Mr Gowda ever have any run-ins with anyone?"

Richards looked confused.

"I mean, was there anyone who didn't get on with him?"

He turned his hands palm upwards. "Not to my knowledge."

"Does the name James Butler mean anything to you?" Fiona asked.

"Who?"

"James Butler."

As he shook his head, Jenny had a thought. "As the head of IT, do you ever run any penetration tests on your systems?"

Fiona glanced at Jenny, unable to hide her surprise at Jenny's left field question.

"What's this got to do with Rajesh?"

"Please just answer the question, Mr Richards."

"In a way, I suppose. I use a specialist security provider to manage and maintain all the firewalls. Once a year, they run a remote pentest as part of the service."

"Do you know who specifically carries out the test?"

"No idea. But it will be someone in the USA. It's an American firm."

Damn. That eliminated that line of enquiry. Brody had told her that Butler had been a hacker and a penetration tester. If Butler had carried out a pentest on MedDev Labs, then that would have been something that would have connected him and Gowda, albeit tenuously. But like most theories without evidence, it had come to nothing.

But thinking about Butler she came up with another possible connection. "Does MedDev have anything to do with manufacturing prosthetic legs?"

"No, not our field at all. Why?"

"Just one of our lines of enquiry."

She should know better than to shoot in the dark like this. She needed to let the evidence speak for itself and not guess at connections that didn't exist. But she knew there must be some link between the two victims. The alternative was they were chosen randomly and that made no sense, especially given how they'd been killed.

"Snakes," stated Fiona. Richards made a 'now what?' expression, demonstrating his disbelief that the strange line of questioning was continuing.

"Does MedDev or any of your employees have anything to do with snakes?"

He folded his arms. "No."

No elaboration.

He looked pointedly at his watch. "I'm late for a meeting. If there's nothing else?"

Brody concluded that James Butler's day-to-day life had been innocuous enough. His public-facing Gmail account was full of routine email and the obligatory spam. There were regular online shopping orders with Ocado. He owned an Amazon Kindle and liked to read modern military thrillers, Andy McNab and Chris Ryan being his favourite authors. He shopped at well-known high street shops and had everything delivered, which made sense given he was disabled. He banked with NatWest. He had a financial advisor in the City who looked after his pension and ensured his savings were invested in the most tax-efficient way. There was no mortgage on his house in Highgate.

Brody sat back from his computer and rejoined the real world, taking in his surroundings for the first time in an hour.

Bruno's had become busy. Most of the tables were in use. A young couple that Brody hadn't noticed before were cuddled up on the battered leather sofa on the other side of his table, drinking caffè lattes and whispering in each other's ears and laughing. He vaguely remembered someone asking if it was okay

to sit there but he had just carried on working through Butler's email history, ignoring what was going on around him.

Stefan was taking an order from a noisy group of women on the far side of the room, huddled around the coffee shop's largest table. Brody spotted multiple copies of the same book on the table and presumed it was a book club. Not being a reader of novels, it wasn't something Brody would ever do. A film club, however … now that would be interesting. Brody was a member of quite a few online film clubs and occasionally wrote reviews for movie magazines.

Stefan delivered the large order to Lorenzo, his promising protégé barista of two weeks, a suave Italian student making ends meet while studying a Masters in Fashion Design at Central Saint Martins College. Lorenzo had come to Bruno's from a Starbucks franchise in nearby King's Cross and Brody had watched, amused, as Stefan invested copious amounts of time and energy in undoing the coffee giant's 'cookie cutter' training, frustrated that a fellow Italian had been brainwashed by an inferior American ideal of how coffee should be prepared.

Brody caught Stefan's eye and he headed over.

"Ah, Mr Brody, is nice to see you taking a break. You must be careful spending so much time looking at computers. Is not good for the eyes. No?"

"My mum's been saying that for years, Stefan," Brody replied with a smile. "And so far, I've still got 20:20 vision."

"Yes, but is because you are young man still. Mark my words, in a few years if you carry on like this …" He seemed to catch himself, as if concerned he'd stepped over a line. "Anyway, can I get you something, Mr Brody?"

"Thanks, Stefan. I think I'd like a cappuccino."

"Good choice. Although …" He covered one side of his mouth with his hand and lowered his voice, preventing the young couple on the sofa hearing what he said. " … I'll make it myself, Mr Brody. Lorenzo is improving but he still pours the froth without using a spoon."

"Sacrilege!" said Brody, only playing along, having no real idea of the pros and cons of spoons.

Stefan shook his head sadly. "I know, I know. But in time, he will learn the true ways of Italian coffee."

"Well, he is learning from the Jedi master."

Stefan beamed and skipped over to the counter to prepare Brody's cappuccino. Brody returned his focus to his computer screen.

He was logged in remotely to the virtualised image of Butler's PC that he'd copied earlier to a VMware server in the cloud, while O'Reilly had watched in awe. Brody couldn't believe that the IT specialist had known so little about virtualisation that he had allowed Brody to transfer the copy to a location outside the police network. But he'd been so eager to learn this new technique, he'd been happy to bend a rule or two. Maybe there was hope for O'Reilly after all?

Although Brody now had unfettered access to Butler's computer — rather, the digital image in the cloud — he may as well have not bothered. Brody had searched it exhaustively for clues to Butler's activities as a hacker but had come up empty so far. It was almost as if the minute Butler did anything as BionicM@n, he switched to another computer altogether. But this was the only PC recovered from Butler's home, which was also his place of work. His wife talked of him only working in the basement office. There was unlikely to be a computer elsewhere.

Butler must have been exceptionally careful, covering every track. Brody thought about his own computer. While he used TOR and other proxies to anonymise his tracks online to ensure he couldn't be tracked down in the physical world, the computer on the table in front of him would no doubt have small traces of his online persona as Fingal. As much as he was diligent, there might be cookies and registry entries that would give him away. If anyone gained access to his computer, they may not find much information, but they could at least conclude from analysing it that its user was the hacker known online as Fingal. Either Butler was a better hacker — something Brody had trouble accepting — or he never used this computer when working as BionicM@n. All of which led to the troubling conclusion that

Butler's death letter promise of providing Brody with information leading to Vorovskoy Mir would be harder to track down than Brody had first anticipated.

The two-year-old private conversation on CrackerHack he'd skipped past between Contag10n and BionicM@n earlier, when O'Reilly had been watching, had been interesting. When he'd first arrived at Bruno's, he'd logged back into CrackerHack using Butler's BionicM@n username and password and had read it in full.

Contag10n: You are a dead man if you don't return the $10m within 24 hours.

BionicM@n: Tut! Tut! You shouldn't have screwed me over on the ransomware malware I wrote for you. Our deal was 5% commission on all ransoms paid. You reneged. Guess what? Now you lose it all.

Contag10n: We would have paid.

BionicM@n: I'm not stupid. I had a little extra piece of code in the malware that called home to one of my servers and told me how much you were collecting. It also gave me the key to every bitcoin blockchain collected as ransom. Your boys told me you were going to pay me 5% of $200K, saying that's all you'd collected. You are just a bunch of lying, greedy fuckers. Well, now you pay the price. As I happened to have all the blockchain keys, I've only gone and donated all $10m of your ransomware revenue to the Tor Project. That'll teach you to not fuck over the little guy.

Contag10n: Like I said, you are a dead man.

BionicM@n: Who said I'm a man? And anyway, I'm only dead if you can find me. And that, my little friend, is impossible. Fuck you :-)

Brody smiled at Butler's audacity and cleverness.

So, Butler had secretly been the author of a particularly nasty ransomware kit that had done the rounds a few years back. Brody remembered the scam well. It had even made headline

news in the UK, as victim after victim came forward, their data completely lost unless they paid up. When installed, it encrypted the data on the host PC and then demanded payment in bitcoins to be given the decryption key. Interpol and the FBI had tracked the authors to Russia but the trail had gone cold there. Brody had assumed that Vorovskoy Mir had been behind it; they were behind most Russian malware scams. But the author actually being a Brit had never leaked. And while Brody now knew that the rumour of the Tor Project donation was true, no one had realised it was linked to the ransomware scam. Vorovskoy Mir had stayed quiet on the whole thing, playing it down so as not to lose credibility in the deep web.

While all this had given Brody a sense of how good Butler was, he still had nothing specific to follow up on. The CrackerHack conversation with Contag10n gave no clues other than to confirm that Butler had had dealings with them, which meant that his offer of information on Vorovskoy Mir was probably genuine. But his PC had revealed no leads whatsoever.

Brody leaned back in his high-back leather chair, folded his arms, lowered his head, shut his eyes and began to ponder.

A few minutes later, with no obvious route forward, Brody heard a light forced cough. He opened his eyes and saw Stefan standing there, his hand retracting from having placed a cappuccino beside Brody's computer. All that was left of the young couple was their empty latte glasses, which surprised Brody. He hadn't heard them leave.

"I thought you had fallen asleep, Mr Brody."

"Sorry, Stefan, I was just thinking." Brody caught Stefan's raised eyebrows and grinned. "Yes, I know, dangerous."

Stefan smiled sheepishly, not daring to say anything that might cause offence, even though he'd clearly been thinking along the same lines. It gave Brody hope that maybe, over time, their relationship might rise above their defined roles of barista and customer, or landlord and tenant.

"Mr Brody, may I explain you something?"

"Sure." Brody sat forward to give his full attention.

"Tomorrow, my nephew is over from Milan and I have

appointment to take him to Clerkenwell."

"What's in Clerkenwell?" Brody knew the area near Farringdon, just under a mile away, but couldn't think of a touristy reason to go there.

"Is the place where my grandfather, my nephew's great-grandfather, first settled in London. Is often called 'Little Italy'. I want to show him St Peter's church and the restaurants that our family used to own. Also, I will take him to Terroni for lunch. Is the best Italian delicatessen in London. Almost like being in Milan."

Brody had been to Terroni's for coffee with Jenny and they had been impressed, appreciating its Italian pedigree. He didn't really understand why Stefan was telling him all this, although he could feel that something Stefan had said was percolating in his thoughts about Butler. "Sounds great, Stefan." It was also the longest conversation they'd had since Brody convinced Stefan to rent him the apartment two floors above.

"So tomorrow, I am leaving Bruno's in the hands of Lorenzo. He will lock up at eight o'clock. I won't be back until much later as I will be taking my nephew to the theatre. I wanted to let you know as you will need to let yourself in and out to get into your apartment."

"Ah, fair enough." Since Brody had moved in, there hadn't been an evening when Stefan hadn't been around to let him in. Whenever Brody arrived home late and fished out his keys to open the coffee shop's front door, Stefan whipped it open with a welcoming smile on his face.

"Do you remember the alarm code, Mr Brody?"

Ah, that was Stefan's real concern. "Yes, Stefan, I do. I'm good with numbers."

"This is good, then."

Stefan gathered the empty latte glasses and joined Lorenzo behind the counter.

Brody sat back. What was it about what Stefan had said that was trying to bubble up? Brody knew better than to force it. He picked up the cappuccino and sipped it, and tried to work out how using a spoon could possibly affect the quality of the milk froth.

Appointment.

Brody reached for the computer, almost sloshing his coffee over it in his rush to place it back on the table. Stefan had said he had an 'appointment' with his nephew. Brody had been through Butler's email on his Gmail account, but he hadn't checked the calendar at all. Butler's *appointments.*

Like many people, Brody also used commonly available services like Gmail for his day-to-day activities. As well as its email capability, he also used its calendar features, mainly because it synced to his phone, allowing him to have his up-to-date schedule in his pocket. Now that he thought about it, this was one of the few areas where his two lives overlapped, as he only used a single online calendar. Stored there were personal appointments, like the cinema booking that he took Jenny to the night before. But it also contained his other activities, including his meeting at GCHQ yesterday morning and a fake interview next week, which he was using to gather background information on a target company before launching a social engineering attack as part of a penetration test he'd been hired to carry out.

Brody scrolled through Butler's calendar. It was full of appointments and went back years. After an hour, Brody closed his tablet and sat back, defeated. There was absolutely nothing that referred to his life as BionicM@n. Perhaps Butler was smarter than Brody and used more than one calendar.

But there had been something that might help Jenny. An appointment had stood out, scheduled the day after his death. And maybe, just maybe, it would help deflect her annoyance with him for getting involved in the case, when she hadn't been able to. He remembered her storming out earlier and hoped she'd calmed down.

He picked up his phone and speed-dialled her number, gritting his teeth.

"Hi, Brody." From the background noise he could tell she was on hands-free in her car. But strangely, she sounded cheerful.

"I heard you were out on an enquiry. What changed?"

"McLintock overruled Da Silva. I'm just heading back into London with Fiona. We've been out doing real police work."

"Oh, hi Fiona."

"Hi Brody."

"You on the Butler case, Jen?"

"No, the Gowda one."

"Oh well, I guess I'll phone Da Silva with what I've got, then?" He knew she wouldn't be able to resist that.

"Not so fast. What've you got, Brody? You still at the station?"

"I left a couple of hours ago."

"So, if you've left, why do you even have anything?"

Blimey, you could never slip anything past Jenny. "Just been following up on a few things since. Do you want this or not?"

"Go on."

"A week ago today, the day after he was killed, Butler had a strange-sounding appointment in his diary. It was for 10:00 a.m."

"Who with?"

"Someone called Benjamin Shepard. The address for the appointment was in Elstree."

"Whereabouts?"

"I'll text it to you. But I've checked it out and you won't believe this."

"What?"

"It's a church. And this Benjamin Shepard is its First Reader. I think that's the equivalent of a priest or a vicar."

"What religion?"

"Christian Science."

"I think I've heard of that."

"Really? I hadn't. But, more importantly, are you aware of any religious ties that Butler may have had?"

"Fiona?" asked Jenny.

"Nothing's come up so far. Doesn't seem likely, but you never know, I suppose."

"Fiona, what do you reckon? Elstree's not too far out of our way. It would just be a waste of expensive police resources sending out other officers from Holborn when we're nearly there."

"I couldn't agree more," said Fiona.

"Thanks, Brody."

"Be careful, you two."

"What, of a church?" Jenny laughed.

"No, of Da Silva when he finds out."

CHAPTER 8

HE COULD SPOT THEY WERE POLICEMEN A mile off.

It was something about the haughty confidence they exuded. Even though there were only two, they had the power of knowing the whole police force was only minutes away. Just like prison wardens. Although Mullins knew from experience that you could still put the fear of death into them during those moments before the cavalry arrived; when you had them in a vice-like grip, squeezing harder and harder, their veins pulsing and eyes beginning to roll.

One was old, near retirement probably. He had grey hair and deeply lined eyes, and wore a crumpled black suit, white shirt and a loosely tied flowery tie with a wide base, its style out-of-step with the skinnier fashion of today. The other man was foreign, probably some kind of Muslim. Young and hip, wearing skinny jeans, boots and a funky T-shirt under his unzipped puffer jacket.

Out of the corner of his eye, he watched them approach the till and talk with Vaughn, the reptile store manager. As Vaughn answered questions, he gesticulated avidly to emphasise his points, showing off his tattoos of Jesus on the cross on one arm and Mary Mother of God on the other. Mullins turned his back on them, listening avidly, and busied himself cleaning out the cage that was used to contain the bearded dragons. He had been sad to see the lizards sold. He always liked watching them morph colour when they were stressed or cold.

The older one introduced himself as DS Coombs. Subtly watching their actions reflected in the convex security mirror above the front door, Mullins observed Coombs flip out a wallet with a card to prove his identity. The other was also a DS, called Malik. Definitely Muslim, then.

"Do you sell black mambas?" asked Coombs.

Mullins froze in the middle of removing the sterilised branch from the enclosure, almost dropping it. He forced himself to continue, placing it on the floor mat where he could wipe the lizard shit from it before putting it back, ready for the next batch of lizards arriving tomorrow.

"Rarely," answered Vaughn. "And only as a special order for people with the right licence to keep one. They're incredibly dangerous."

"Yes, we know."

"Do you have a register of everyone you've sold one to?"

"Yes, of course. I'm required to keep one by law."

Mullins automatically tensed, even though he was fully aware that the purchases of the animals he looked after hadn't been recorded.

So, the police were trying to track down the snake that had killed Butler and Gowda. Why would they bother? Didn't they realise their deaths were self-inflicted and the snake was only reacting instinctively? It wasn't as if anyone had forced Butler or Gowda to place their hands in the box. They'd done it of their own free will. He knew that. And he knew there was no evidence to suggest they had been forced. After all, he had been there, trying to help them survive.

But while all that was true, Mullins knew the police would twist what he'd done and turn it into something it wasn't. They'd try to turn suicide into murder and set him up to take the rap.

Mullins finished wiping down the branch and lifted it back into the enclosure. When he turned back the younger copper was standing right in front of him, his arms folded, head cocked to one side.

"Aw right, mate?"

Mullins wasn't surprised at the officer's cockney accent. He'd met plenty of Muslim Londoners on the inside. "Hello?"

"You work here?"

A sarcastic retort almost popped out of his mouth, but he caught it. He didn't need trouble. "Yes, can I help you?" It was the phrase he'd been told to say to all new customers through the door.

The man glanced surreptitiously to his right at the older copper, who was still engaged in conversation with Vaughn while noting down names and addresses from their sales register. He spoke quietly. "I'm after a snake. A particular kind of snake. But off the books, if you know what I mean."

Mullins did know what he meant, but kept his face impassive. There was a whole basement full of them downstairs that Vaughn and his friends traded off the books. "I just clean out cages and look after the animals. I don't sell nothing."

"But you might know someone, who knows someone, who could help me. Eh?"

Mullins slowly shook his head from side to side and pursed his lower lip out. He had mastered this dumb look on the inside. He knew he wasn't as bright as most people, but he wasn't a complete idiot. "Not me. I just work here. You'll need to ask Vaughn over there."

"Why Vaughn? Ah, does he know someone who knows someone, then?"

Mullins sensed he was trying to trick him. Some kind of word game. He didn't want to get Vaughn in trouble. In fact, he wanted the police to move on from here. Leave him alone so he could look after his snakes.

"I dunno." Mullins added a big shrug for effect.

"What's your name, then?"

Automatically, Mullins almost gave his six-digit prison number from when he was inside. But then he remembered he was back in the outside world. "Mullins. Ralph Mullins. I work —"

"Yes, you work here, I got that, mate." DS Malik wrote the name in his notebook. "Where do you live?"

Mullins gave his address on Allerton Road.

"How long have you worked here?"

"I dunno." He thought for a moment. "Three years, I guess."

"You good with snakes and lizards, then?"

It was a stupid question for a policeman. Of course he was good with animals. How else would he get a job in a reptile store? Mullins shrugged. "I s'pose."

"Aren't they dangerous?"

"Only if you don't treat them properly."

"Why would someone want a snake as a pet?"

Mullins could have gone on for hours about why snakes made great pets, not that he ever talked that much. He could have said how snakes are not aggressive and are more scared of humans than everyone realises. About how they should be respected. About how they live on instinct. How they never toy with their prey. Unlike the evil domestic cats that people have as pets, snakes just strike and eat. Well, that's if they're warm and hungry. When they're cold or too full, they'll happily ignore their prey, leaving it to run around in the cage with them, not stirring when it walks over their long body, confident that it'll still be there when they eventually become hungry. Mullins loved watching mice in the same cage as a snake, oblivious to their impending demise.

"I dunno. They just do, I s'pose."

"Mine of information, you are, eh?"

Mullins shrugged, not sure how to respond.

The copper seemed to tire of the conversation and turned away. Mullins almost let out an audible sigh of relief but managed to contain it … just as Malik turned back.

"One last question."

Mullins waited impassively, imagining stuffing this little brown, trendily clothed policeman into the python enclosure. He might wriggle and scream, but Mullins was strong and could hold him down while the shop's fourteen-foot python spotted its new prey and began to uncoil …

The policeman was clicking a finger and thumb repeatedly in front of Mullins face. Mullins blinked and the image cleared. DS Malik was standing in front of him, hands on hips, studying him with quizzical eyes.

Mullins said he was sorry.

"I asked, where were you two nights ago?"

Mullins knew exactly where he was two nights ago but knew he couldn't tell the truth, even though lying was bad. "I dunno. At home, I s'pose."

"Anyone verify that?"

"No."

"Thought not." DS Malik wrote some more notes in his book. "Okay. Thanks for *all* your help." He sauntered off towards his colleague, who was just wrapping up with Vaughn. After a few minutes of looking around the shop, the two policemen left.

Mullins returned his attention to cleaning out the reptile cage. There was nothing to be worried about.

It wasn't as if he'd done anything wrong.

Klara wheeled the latest batch of books out from the delivery area and headed for the Computing section of the bookstore. Ever since she was a teenager, her parents had allowed her to manage that section of their shop, where she'd spent more time reading the books than organising them into order for the customers.

She'd calmed down since losing her job yesterday. Her parents had been supportive and she'd even stayed up late with her father drinking vodka to commiserate. Like most good Russians, he believed vodka was the answer to every calamity. He claimed that it helped to see things more clearly. Halfway through he told her that she should get out of this corrupt country before it corrupted her. She told him she'd never leave him and Mama behind, but he reminded her of her mother's plan for them to retire to her family's apartment in Italy in a few years. Klara pointed out with a fond smile that he was already past retirement age and that Mama had given up waiting for him to move to Italy years ago. He shrugged. Towards the bottom of the bottle, he'd promised to sell the bookstore next week and finally make her mother happy. But she knew in the morning he'd conveniently forget. It was his way. By the bottom of the bottle, they were singing songs together and, when Klara couldn't recall the words, she gave up and headed for her bed, where she had plummeted into a drunken stupor.

Klara noticed a new book on Embedded Software Development and began flicking through absently. Firmware programming jobs were hard to find in Moscow, especially for a woman. This last one had been interesting and challenging. She hoped she could find a worthy replacement in the near future. Her first job after graduating had been working at the Bilibino nuclear power station, on the eastern side of Russia, 100 miles inside the Arctic Circle. She had lasted three years before the cold had worn her down and she had resigned, blotting her employment copybook. After, she took jobs doing general programming for commercial banks, which paid well, but she found far less intellectually challenging than writing assembler level firmware.

A year ago, she took a risk and began accepting freelance work over the internet. Thanks to her mother's Italian heritage, she had dual citizenship with Italy and a euro bank account in the country, although she had not disclosed the second passport to the authorities despite the laws demanding she do so. She was able to bid for the freelance projects over the internet and be paid in euros. It was far more lucrative than working for roubles. However, there were two problems. The first was all the money she'd earned was sitting untouched in a bank account in Italy. There was no obvious way of bringing it back to Moscow without raising suspicion. And secondly, most decent firmware programming jobs had to be done onsite, as the systems were often air-gapped from the public network. Air-gapping was a security technique of having no physical connection between the SCADA-based industrial control systems and any public-facing network. It ensured that no hacker could jump from one to the other as had happened in Ukraine.

There was a job she could take, however. Ten days ago, she'd been contacted by an electricity supply company based in London, England. The positive feedback on her profile on the freelance job site had brought her to their attention, as well as her specific expertise in working with the control systems developed by RPA, Russia's most successful component manufacturer, which were in use at the English company. They wanted her to come to England urgently to work on a specific project, all expenses paid. They estimated two months of her time were required and were offering an extortionate daily rate.

She'd ignored the request at the time, as her attention was buried deep in solving the runtime integrity verification project for MOESK. Nothing was going to distract her from solving that problem, even that much money. But now she was suddenly and unexpectedly free, the job was hers if she wanted it. Only yesterday, after having received no response from their initial communication, they'd approached her once again, increasing the offer. They explained it was an emergency situation, having come under malware attack, and they needed her onsite, that week if at all possible.

Klara finished placing the books onto the shelves and surveyed the bookstore. Her father was behind the till, serving a tourist. His glasses were perched on top of his head and he punched each button on the till slowly, trying not to get it wrong again. Her mother was outside, cleaning the windows with soapy water. She did that once a week, regardless of the weather outside, claiming that if people couldn't see inside they'd never enter. Fortunately, today was bright and sunny, unusual for early June. She smiled fondly at them.

She decided to make her hard-working parents some coffee and headed for the kitchen area. Could she really leave them and work in England for a month or two? They wouldn't want to see her go of course, but they always wanted the best for her. And the money she earned would be impossible to smuggle back into Russia, so it would be next to useless. So what was the point? She had no intention of leaving her motherland permanently, even with her secret European passport. Not unless her father finally acquiesced to her mother's wishes and retired to Italy.

She had heard about a way of transferring money anonymously via bitcoins. Maybe she should research what was involved. If she could get the money back into Russia, maybe it was a project worth taking on. Her English was good enough as well and, if she was honest, she would love to see the Houses of Parliament and St Paul's Cathedral and drink a pint of warm ale. Ever since the London Olympics in 2012, she had hankered to visit England. And two months all expenses paid was tempting.

She placed the coffees on a tray and carried them into the main shop. Just as she reached the till she gasped in shock, almost dropping the tray.

There, standing in front with his head cocked as he studied her, was Dmitry Zakharin. The same man whose verdict had caused her to lose her job yesterday.

She folded her arms and narrowed her eyes to slits.

Jenny pulled up outside the modern, redbrick, pitched-roof building, set back from the road in a residential neighbourhood just outside the village centre of Elstree. The only clue they were in the right place was the prominent sign declaring *Church of Christ, Scientist* and the front window showcasing religious leaflets.

"Looks nothing like the old church in the village where I grew up," commented Fiona.

"What do you suppose the 'science' part of Christian Science means? Most religions don't get along too well with science."

"Give me a mo." Fiona tapped on her phone and then thumbed up and down. "According to the internet, it's a branch of the Christian church … founded in 1879 in Boston, Massachusetts by a lady called Mary Baker Eddy … publishes a Pulitzer Prize winning newspaper called the *Christian Science Monitor* … I think the science part is something to do with being metaphysical …" Fiona began quoting word for word: "'We are perfect spiritual ideas of one divine Mind', capital M, 'and manifest Spirit', capital S, 'not material body' … Oh for God's sake, I give up."

"Don't blame you," agreed Jenny. "But why on earth would Butler have come here?"

"Maybe after returning from Afghanistan he found God. Many soldiers do."

"Perhaps." But Jenny was doubtful. She opened the car door. "Shall we ask?"

Fiona caught up with Jenny as she reached the side door. It was a small single-storey building almost completely obscured by trees, as if the owners were trying to hide it from passers-by. The door was closed.

"Do we knock?" asked Fiona. "Or just walk in like any normal church?"

Just then, the door swung open revealing a stooped old woman, who whispered delightedly when she saw them. "Ooh, what have we here? Come in, ladies. Come in."

The woman shuffled back and Jenny and Fiona stepped in.

"We're here to see —"

The old woman's eyes popped at the sound of Jenny's voice and she flicked a forefinger in front of her lips, ordering them to silence. Satisfied, she ushered Jenny and Fiona into the nearest row of seats and then sat on the end of the aisle, preventing them from escaping. Heads in front swivelled round briefly at the disturbance and the man standing behind a lectern at the front, who had been reading aloud, paused, took them in and then resumed his reading.

"Thus it was that I beheld, as never before, the awful unreality called evil. The equipollence of God brought to light another glorious proposition — man's perfectibility and the establishment of the kingdom of heaven on earth ..."

Jenny tuned out from the unintelligible arcane language and studied her surroundings. Instead of customary wooden pews, they were each sitting on individual padded chairs lined up in neat rows, facing a plain raised podium at the front where the man stood. The walls and high-pitched ceiling were cream with no paintings or pictures; the only decorations were two quotes in large black italic script on the front walls facing them. On the left: *We shall know the truth and the truth shall make you free. Christ Jesus.* On the right: *Divine love always has met and always will meet every human need. Mary Baker Eddy.*

The man reading was tall, middle-aged and dressed conservatively in a plain grey suit, white shirt and thin black tie.

He had piercing green eyes that occasionally searched the congregation during momentary pauses for breath, as if to check that his audience was absorbing the importance of his words. Although there was a hi-tech-looking microphone mounted on the lectern, the imposing speakers mounted on stands in the front corners didn't seem to be turned on. But then, they didn't need to be: his voice was loud and confident, never once stumbling over the archaic phrasings. He was obviously very familiar with the reading.

"Jesus demonstrated the power of Christian Science to heal mortal minds and bodies. But this power was lost sight of and must again be spiritually discerned, taught and demonstrated according to Christ's command …"

Jenny hadn't been in a church since her nephew's Holy Communion seven years before. Although she and her sister had not been brought up in a religious environment, April had married a devout Catholic who demanded his family observe all of the traditions. At least, that was, up until the day fourteen-year-old Damien stubbornly refused to go to confession and, in response to the escalating threats of eternal damnation made by his father and the parish priest, stopped going to church altogether. Jenny suspected that April was secretly proud of her son's defiance but she would never say anything negative against her husband.

Jenny refocused on the service and immediately wondered how long it would continue. She certainly couldn't stay here all day.

" … the Science of God and man is no more supernatural than is the science of numbers …"

Just as she was building up the courage to face the wrath of the old woman by standing and leaving, the sermon thankfully came to an end with the congregation all exclaiming together, "Amen!"

Everyone stood and the old woman shuffled off, engaging in conversation with a man two rows in front. As they exited to the aisle, Fiona whispered in Jenny's ear, "Shall we make a run for it?"

Jenny thought it was a sensible idea, but then noticed the reader striding towards them with a beaming smile on his face.

He splayed his arms out wide. "Welcome to our humble church. It's always a pleasure to welcome new members. Are you already members of our faith or …" His arms dropped to his sides as Jenny flashed her warrant card.

"We just have a few questions."

"Ah, such a shame." His green eyes twinkled. "But perhaps you can take just a moment to trust in the Lord our God and allow me to reveal some of His wonders of the universe."

"Sorry, we're here on official business," stated Jenny. "We're looking for Benjamin Shepard?"

"You are?" He splayed his arms out again, palms upwards and beamed again. "Well, it seems God has seen fit to lead you to him."

"Is there somewhere private we can talk, Mr Shepard?"

"There is nothing that can be hidden from Lord God above," he said. But after catching Jenny's frosty look, added, "The reading room is free. Let's go in there."

He led them to a door at the back of the church, which led into a small antechamber. One wall was covered in shelves, full to the brim with books, spines on display. Most of them appeared well thumbed, in contrast to the selection of brand new books displayed face outwards on another wall. A magazine rack contained numerous copies of *The Christian Science Journal* and *Christian Science Sentinel*. Proudly featured on the table in the centre were two books. One was an expensive-looking leather-bound edition of *The Bible*. The other was called *Science and Health with Keys to the Scriptures* and was by Mary Baker Eddy. The room contained only two chairs, so they remained standing.

Shepard shut the door behind them and asked, "How may I help you, officers?"

"Are you the … leader of this church?" Jenny couldn't recall the term Brody had used.

"Yes, I'm the First Reader, if that's what you mean."

"Is that like a vicar or a priest?"

"Not really, no. The Christian Science Church was established as a lay church. That means we have no clergy. Our sermons are centred around passages from *The Bible* and *Science and Health.*" He indicated the two books on the table. "Readers are elected by the congregation. As the First Reader I'm responsible for selecting the hymns and specific elements of our main services on Wednesdays and Sundays."

"Today is Tuesday," pointed out Fiona, her way of asking why everyone was here today.

"We have a very active community here in Elstree. So much so, we've decided to hold additional readings on Tuesdays and Fridays for those that wish to make the time."

"How long have you been the First Reader?"

"Three years already, would you believe? Before that, Jacob, my older brother, was First Reader here for five years. He's now in the States at the Mother Church in Boston."

"Is this your full-time occupation?"

"Occupation?" He laughed gently. "No, this is more of a vocation than an occupation. But I do have a day job, if that's what you mean. I run a website called newchurchgoer.com, which employs big data and social media marketing techniques to target and reach out to potential new churchgoers. I provide it as a service to other churches around the world of all denominations who need to increase the size of their congregation."

Jenny immediately thought of Jehovah's Witnesses who knocked blindly on doors and wondered if this was the modern-day digital replacement. She decided to get to the point. "Is there a James Butler in your community, Mr Shepard?"

He made a show of thinking about it and then spoke. "We've been growing enormously in the last few years, which is partly because of my other job. So much so, our congregation now numbers in the hundreds." He was obviously proud of this achievement. "I make a point of knowing everyone by name but I don't recall a James Butler."

"What about outside the congregation? Do you know anyone by that name?"

"I don't have many dealings outside of the church these days."

He shrugged. "Sorry, no, I can't think of anyone who goes by that name. Who is he?"

"He's the victim in a murder investigation."

"Murder, you say? Devil's work indeed." He folded his arms, as if that sealed the matter.

"Are you not interested as to why we are asking you about him, Mr Shepard?"

"God works in mysterious ways, DI Price. It's not for me to fathom His intentions."

"Where were you last Tuesday at 10:00 a.m.?"

"I would most likely have been here in this very room, preparing for the day's reading. I'm here most mornings."

"But last Tuesday, specifically," insisted Fiona.

Shepard reached into the inside pocket of his jacket and withdrew an iPhone. He thumbed around confidently and said, "I was definitely here last Tuesday. Yes, the responsive reading was from John Chapter 17. I remember sitting here, preparing it."

"Is there anyone who can verify this?"

"Norma — she's our librarian — is usually here by then each day. I can't remember last Tuesday specifically. But you can ask her yourself. She's just outside. Would you like me to ask her to join us?"

"Thanks. We'll talk to her in a few minutes."

"The reason for asking all this is that Mr Butler had an appointment scheduled in his diary with you, Mr Shepard. Here, at 10:00 a.m. Can you explain that?"

"A meeting with me?" He stroked his chin. "Here? That's strange. I don't have anything like that in my diary." He held out his iPhone. "You can check here."

Jenny and Fiona looked at the phone. It displayed the date in question. The only appointment was the service scheduled to start at 1:00 p.m.

"Maybe he was planning on walking in. We do get them occasionally. Last one I had demanded an explanation about God's plans for us all. But he was really seeking guidance following the sudden death of his wife. He left with a handful of leaflets and he's now an active member of the church. That was three months ago."

Jenny studied Shepard as he spoke. He was completely earnest in his desire to help and seemed as mystified as them as to Butler's diary entry. It really didn't make any sense. They would need to talk to Butler's widow to determine if he had any religious inclinations or dealings with the Christian Science Church. In fact, they probably ought to have done that first before showing up here. But in Jenny's desire to take advantage of the new lead, she had cut a corner. She would make a point of calling Helen Butler on the way back to Holborn.

Before leaving, they verified Shepard's alibi with Norma, the librarian. But that entailed wading into the huddle of church members all enjoying after-service chitchat. Cups of tea were thrust into Jenny and Fiona's hands and, before they knew it, they were embroiled in their conversations, which ranged from passing comment on Shepard's earlier reading to the football results from the previous weekend.

The old woman who had hushed them earlier learned their first names and took it upon herself to introduce Jenny and Fiona to each member of the community. It was another thirty minutes before they flopped wearily back into Jenny's car.

"Next time Brody comes up with a lead, let's give it to DI Knight, eh?" suggested Fiona. "I don't think I could go through that again."

"I suppose it could have gone either way. But, don't worry, I've arranged something that could go one way or the other for Brody later."

CHAPTER 9

"CALL ME DMITRY," HE SAID, HANDING HER a Lavender Raf.

"What do you want?" Klara wasn't about to be civil with Zakharin. He was the reason she'd lost her job. Just because he happened to order her favourite beverage, espresso mixed with cream and vanilla sugar, without asking her what she wanted didn't buy him any leeway.

They were in the Double B on Milyutinskiy Pereulok, just round the corner from her parents' bookstore. It was one of the new wave of independent coffee shops beginning to appear in central Moscow. She'd followed him past Kofe Khauz, one of Russia's local chains, so he obviously knew his coffee. She sipped at her Lavender Raf and nearly melted; it was that good.

"You are an impressive woman, Miss Ivanov."

"And you cost me my job, Mr Zakharin."

He gave a pained look, having already asked her to call him by his forename. "If it's any consolation, your concept was brilliant and met the brief."

"So why am I out of work?"

"Because I want to offer you a better job with better pay. Someone with your experience is wasted working for the state electricity company."

She wasn't going to let him off that easily. "But I would have preferred to make that choice myself. Your action is forcing the issue."

"Well, you'd better get used to it. That's how my employer works, Klara."

The use of her first name did not pass her by. She decided not to challenge it. She already suspected him of working for the Russian mafia and referring to 'his employer' pretty much confirmed it. She wasn't going to cause herself or her parents trouble with the gangs. Her parents already owed money to them from purchasing a "krisha", which they couldn't afford but had to have. Known also as a "roof", it was organised crime's way of helping her parents buy protection. All shopkeepers in Moscow needed a krisha. They protected the shop from crime and bribed officials from fining them too much every time they ran a state inspection. Given her father stocked quite a few Western books, he needed the officials to overlook them.

"And who is your employer?"

"Hopefully you've worked out that I was behind the Ukrainian power grid hack."

She nodded carefully. There was no gloating. Just matter-of-fact, as if he did that kind of thing every day.

She was impressed with the skill required to pull off such a feat, although not by its impact to the working people of Ukraine. The hack had been impressive and daring. With hackers now targeting the physical infrastructure of countries, it wouldn't be long before the first human death was caused by a remote computer hack. With cars, thermostats and power grids increasingly being connected to the internet, it was unavoidable.

"My organisation was hired by the Government. I find it interesting that one minute my organisation is being hunted by police agencies, and the next minute it's helping them. Don't you?"

"The enemy of my enemy is my friend," she quoted.

"Indeed. The point is that my organisation works for profit, without worrying too much about who hires us. Your talents could be put to good use."

"And if I wanted to apply, how would I go about it?"

"You already have. The whole project at MOESK was designed to find you. We have an interesting venture in the pipeline and I cannot do it alone."

Despite herself, she was flattered. Dmitry Zakharin was an impressive individual. His knowledge of firmware rivalled her own, perhaps even surpassed it. Away from MOESK, he was personable, and, she noticed, good looking, with incredibly sharp grey eyes. The idea of working alongside him certainly had its appeal.

"What is the job?"

"We're going to take down a nuclear power station in the West."

She was surprised both by the answer and that he'd answered at all. Again, matter-of-factly, as if it was of no consequence.

"But thousands could die!" Klara wasn't comfortable associating herself with this. "Look at Chernobyl. We're still paying the price now, thirty years later."

"Exactly." He folded his arms. "That's what our customer is paying for."

"And who is the customer?"

"You don't want to know that."

She sipped at her coffee. It was already lukewarm.

"Will you take the job?"

"Can I think about it?"

"No. You must decide now. Time is of the essence."

There was a hard look in his eyes. They'd turned steely as he went in for the kill. She wasn't sure he was so nice after all.

But Klara didn't need to give the matter further thought. She already knew the answer; she just wanted to buy some time. There was no way she would have any blood on her hands. "Then I'm afraid I have to politely decline."

He pulled his phone out of his inside jacket pocket. He placed it down on the table. She could see that it was connected to someone who had been listening in on their whole conversation. He pressed the button for loudspeaker.

"Contagion," Zakharin said.

Klara flinched. She knew that name. She also knew she was now swimming in murky and dangerous waters.

"Did you get all that? Anything to add?" And then to her, he explained, "He's my boss." Zakharin turned back to the phone. "Yes, a very unfortunate outcome. Let me ask you one more time, Miss Ivanov. Are you sure you want to turn down Vorovskoy Mir?"

Klara wasn't so sure now.

Brody ordered a fruit-based 'mocktail' from the cocktail menu. He'd had way too much coffee today already and didn't want to start drinking alcohol before Jenny arrived. He'd already established that she could hold her drink better than him.

She'd phoned earlier and told him to meet her at Brompton's, the speakeasy in Mayfair that he'd been a member of for years and where they'd had their first date six weeks before. He had no idea what she had in store for them after Brompton's, but she had made it clear she had something lined up to make amends for ruining their previous night's cinema date with her work.

He looked at his watch. She was late.

As if on cue, his phone buzzed. It was a message from Jenny, apologising. She was running thirty minutes late. She'd added a sad face emoji and two x's to soften the blow.

The waiter brought his colourful drink and left.

Brody looked around. He was sitting at a table in one of the booths, surrounded by shiny curtains rising up to the high ceiling above. It gave privacy to each table of diners, who could only make out the general shapes of their neighbours through the opaque veils. Jazz music piped through a high-end sound system, perfectly pitched to be loud enough to notice but not so noisy you were forced to shout. But, more importantly, it prevented anyone overhearing conversations from nearby tables.

Brompton's took the privacy of its guests to a new level, which was why so many celebrities and politicians were members of the expensive club. Brody occasionally noticed someone famous seated at the bar, although outside of movies, he was hardly an expert on celebrity culture. For all he knew, the four attractive young women at the table next to him, whom he'd observed as they were shown to their table, were daytime TV megastars. The fact that Brompton's was also a speakeasy, with no signage outside, just a single unobtrusive door, meant you had to know it existed to even attempt to make it past the bouncer in the reception area.

Brody savoured the sweet taste of his refreshing cocktail and decided he could put the time to good use. He fished his tablet out of his man bag, connected to the internet via his mobile phone, ignoring the option of using Brompton's public Wi-Fi, and then logged in via two proxies and Tor.

He had spent the rest of the day inspecting and analysing the virtualised image of Butler's computer but had gleaned nothing of note. Any trail to Butler's information on Vorovskoy Mir was ice cold. He had no idea if the 'Benjamin Shepard' meeting was of any significance to the murder inquiry, but it certainly had nothing to do with Vorovskoy Mir. Still, he'd been happy to pass on the lead to Jenny. Hopefully, it had helped the case in some way.

Still, there was a nagging doubt that he was missing something. The most obvious thing was Butler's email address for his hacker activity as BionicM@n. He had Butler's public-facing email address, but there must be others. Brody had many, so it stood to reason that Butler did too. Brody logged into Butler's public Gmail account and scanned through one more time, analysing every email address that Butler had received email from and sent email to. But nothing popped out. He'd clearly done a great job of keeping his lives separate, never sending an email from one account to the other. Brody wondered if he himself had ever left an email trail between his real world self and Fingal, and resolved to check. You could never be too careful, especially when you were number one on Vorovskoy Mir's Most Wanted list.

Brody considered the CrackerHack forum, for which he had Butler's username and password. However, he was fully aware that the account area of the system never displayed a member's email address. He supposed it was just another way that the CrackerHack forum ensured anonymity. But, Brody realised, the system must store the email address somewhere in its database, because a password reset was sent to the email the user had registered with. Perhaps he should have a go at hacking CrackerHack itself? This had been tried many times, with members discussing it ironically in the forums. However, the administrators behind CrackerHack were also hackers and thus ensured that the site was incredibly well defended. This was the reason why the hacker community had gravitated to it above all other available forums. They knew that their anonymity was guaranteed.

Brody thought about Butler's PayPal account, which had recorded Butler's financial transactions from selling bitcoins via the online exchange. It was the only place he'd found so far that linked Butler's two lives. What the hell! Brody decided to check it again.

After ten minutes of scrolling through Butler's PayPal history, line by line, and Googling each payee name, he sat bolt upright. There, on the screen, was a small payment of a few euros to *ContactOffice Group*, which in itself was innocuous enough. But Googling the payee name revealed that the brand name of the service they proved was called *Mailfence*, an encrypted, secure and private email service aimed at people who absolutely don't want to be tracked online. Brody used a similar service himself.

Brody clicked through to the *Mailfence* login screen and was presented with a form requesting a username and password. His only hope was that Butler, like Brody himself, used the same credentials as his CrackerHack account. It was hard work for any normal person to remember all their different account names and passwords, and hackers, who typically subscribed to many more online services than the average person, experienced the same problem, but magnified.

Brody typed in Butler's details, reached for his cocktail, took a sip and pressed enter at the same time. Immediately, he screwed up his face in disgust. The liquid had warmed up way too much and was now just a sweet morass rather than the refreshing thirst quencher he'd enjoyed when it had first arrived. He returned his attention to his computer screen and realised, with relief, that he was logged in.

Brody began inspecting the email account.

Butler had linked a private domain name called bionicman43.com to the service and had only set up one email address: anonymous@bionicman43.com. There was no email in the inbox. Either it had been emptied or he'd never received any emails. However, Brody found a handful of emails in the 'sent items' folder.

After he read them, he whistled in disbelief. Jenny would be pleased. There was a link between Butler and Gowda after all. And something much bigger going on, although it was hard to tell what.

He'd tell her when she arrived.

"Hello, Brody."

Brody looked up and the colour drained from his face. Standing by his table was the one person he'd concluded he'd probably never see again in his life.

His ex-flatmate and ex-best mate.

Leroy Bishop.

Klara sat in the coffee shop for a full thirty minutes after Zakharin left, running the conversation over and over in her mind, trying to process its implications.

Vorovskoy Mir had come calling. That had been unexpected. Of course she knew of them and their infamous leader, Contag10n. Who didn't in the Russian IT community? They were a group of black hats behind some of the world's most audacious cybercrimes. Affiliated with, but independent of the Russian mafia, they were a force to be reckoned with. And Contag10n himself! She couldn't believe that she'd talked to him over the phone, never mind turned him down.

It hadn't occurred to her that Dmitry Zakharin worked for Vorovskoy Mir, but it made sense with the benefit of hindsight. Who else would have had the resources to take on the Ukrainian power grid hack last year? And with state sponsorship backing? It didn't bear thinking about.

But as she'd calmed down and recovered from the meeting, she began to think more clearly. And then she realised why Zakharin had Contag10n listening into their conversation on the phone. There was an implied threat she had missed. If she said no, which she had done in the end, then there would be consequences. That's how Vorovskoy Mir worked.

With sudden premonitory clarity, Klara knew what they would do. She bounded out of Double B, running desperately through the streets towards her parents' bookstore.

A screaming ambulance shot up the road past her and turned right into her street. Klara dug deeper and ran faster, berating herself with every breath. She had been stupid and arrogant to think she could turn down Vorovskoy Mir without consequence. She just hadn't thought. If anything had happened to her parents because of her, she would never forgive herself.

As she turned the corner, she pulled up in shock. Even though she'd known there would be flashing blue lights outside the bookstore, actually seeing them there knocked her for six. It was chaos. Smoke and flames rose above the shop. A fire engine was shooting water from a hose into the blaze, a second screaming up the street from the other direction. The ambulance had halted and paramedics rushed into the crowd outside. Police were pushing back the onlookers to safety.

She cried out in anguish and bolted towards the burning store.

Please no, not her parents. Anything but that.

One of the uniformed police officers cordoning off the area tried to stop her entering, but she pushed him out of the way, her unexpected strength shocking her. She jumped inside the cordon, but was blocked by a wall of heat emanating from the premises. The windows had all smashed outwards and flames raged within the aisles of books inside. The firemen were hosing two streams of water onto the fire, but the thousands of books provided too much fuel for them to combat it successfully. She heard a second fire truck arriving and hoped it would be enough.

"Klara!"

Klara wheeled around and saw her mother to one side, kneeling on the floor by a group of paramedics, one of whom was checking her over. She waved Klara over. Although tattered and covered in soot, she looked unhurt. But the paramedics then lifted a body onto a stretcher in unison. With a gasp, Klara realised it was her father. She rushed over, but was held back by a policeman, shouting to her to let the paramedics do their job. She fought for a moment but then realised he was right. Her father was out cold, an oxygen mask stuck to his face. He was completely covered in soot and ash and his clothes were burnt and ragged. What little hair he'd had left had burnt away. But it was his hands that shocked her. It was as if his skin had melted off. They were raw, blistered and bleeding all over.

Klara felt the soft touch of her mother and she turned away from the horrific sight of her father's burnt body and fell into her embrace, leaning down to cry into her shoulder. "I'm so sorry, Mama. It's all my fault."

But her mother just patted her head and shushed her gently.

The paramedics lifted the stretcher into the back of the ambulance. They came back for her mother, who was able to walk with Klara's support. They climbed into the back of the same ambulance.

Before the doors were closed, Klara took one more look at the bookstore, the place she had grown up in. There were four jets of water now and the firemen seemed to be winning the battle. But the damage was total. Her parents' livelihood was destroyed.

The doors closed and the ambulance took off, the siren screaming. She watched the paramedics tend to her father, connecting him up to equipment. She spotted the machine that monitored his pulse and saw that it was weak.

Frustration and rage coursed through her body and she began to shake. She wanted to scream the roof off the ambulance, scream louder than the siren. But it would do no good.

Instead, she cried hot tears.

"My round." Jenny drained her mojito and asked, "Same again?"

Without waiting for a response, she headed towards the bar. Alan Coombs offered to give her a hand and climbed off his stool, a little unsteadily. He followed behind.

Fiona shouted to them, "I'll have a Vodka Red Bull this time."

"Actually, I'll have one of those, minus the vodka," called

Karim. "I'm fucking sick of Coke."

Jenny jumped into a recently vacated space at The Dolphin Tavern's crowded bar and caught the attention of one of the servers. She ordered herself a fourth mojito and turned to Alan for the rest. His was another pint of bitter, the two drinks for Fiona and Karim, and a Jameson whiskey for O'Reilly. Between them, they carefully carried the drinks back to the table, Alan spilling some of his pint as he manoeuvred through groups of people.

"Sláinte," said Harry O'Reilly, raising his glass.

"Cheers," said the others in return.

Jenny's phone buzzed and she attempted to focus on the small screen. It was a text from Brody.

You were never coming out tonight, were you?

She grinned. Leroy had arrived, then. She wondered how they were getting on. With no kisses on the text, though, it didn't sound promising. Oh well, she had tried her best. She'd phoned Leroy earlier and arranged for him to meet her and Brody that evening. He wasn't convinced it was a good idea so she'd laid it on a bit thick about Brody. Eventually, he'd acquiesced.

"Nice to have you back in the saddle, Jen," said Karim. "That prick Knight was driving me nuts."

"Now, now," cautioned Fiona. "Be nice about the senior officers."

"Go on, then," retorted Karim. "Say something nice about DCI Da Silva."

Fiona looked at the ceiling for inspiration and then around the room. She shrugged, giving up. The others laughed.

"It is good to be back, but I'm still not sure what made the DCS overrule Da Silva." Jenny turned to Alan and asked, pointedly, "Any ideas?"

Everyone stared at Alan Coombs, who supped at his pint, deliberately slowly. Finally, he asked, "Are you trying to imply something, Jen?"

"Just asking if you knew anything, is all. Given you and McLintock go way back."

"Well, I might have bumped into McLintock in the car park

this morning on the way in," said Alan, all innocence. "And I might have got into a general conversation about the way the caseload of a double murder investigation was being distributed. Nothing specific, mind."

"Nice one, Alan. McLintock's no fool," said Karim. "Thinking about it, I clocked McLintock dragging Da Silva into one of the interview rooms about five minutes before all the journalists arrived. I'm sure I heard raised voices."

"Good work, Alan," said Fiona, raising her glass.

As the others raised their drinks in support, Jenny leaned into Alan's earshot and whispered, "Thanks, Alan. I owe you one."

He shrugged and supped at his pint.

Their conversation turned to the case. Jenny relayed their meeting with Jerome Richards at MedDev Labs in Stockley Park and then Fiona recounted their visit to the Christian Science church in Elstree. Fiona embellished the story, gaining lots of laughs at them being trapped twice, once during the church service and once during the tea meeting afterwards.

"How'd you get on today, Karim?" asked Jenny.

"Me and Alan have been all over London visiting stupid people who keep black mambas as pets. If you ask me, every single one of them is fucking nuts. Why the fuck would you keep deadly snakes inside your own home?"

"The weird thing is," continued Alan, "at least half of them were family homes, where the dad kept the snakes as pets in the same house or flat as young kids." He shook his head in disbelief.

"One of them offered to get one out of the cage and show us up close what they're like. I wasn't going anywhere near it, I tell you." Karim was getting into his stride. "But he opened the glass cage anyway and, using some special snake tongs, just lifted it out. A fucking black mamba, no less! I was out of there, pronto."

"And then he grabbed it with his hand just behind the head," continued Alan. "Completely crazy. One slip and he's dead."

"What're they like up close?" asked O'Reilly.

"A lot smaller than I thought," replied Alan. "Given they're one of the most deadly snakes in the world, I thought they'd be huge, like a python. But the ones we saw were mostly a couple of metres and seemed quite thin in comparison. Dark brown skin on top and light underneath. But those little black eyes; they know you're there."

"Yeah, I thought that too. It's like they could see we were food or something," said Karim, who shivered in repulsion.

"Any of the snake owners show up as suspicious?" asked Jenny.

"Only one, where the owner had a criminal record for burglary, which he managed to omit from his dangerous pet licence application, knowing full well it would be rejected. Anyway, his alibis have checked out. But we'll keep an eye on him, just in case."

"We've still got about ten addresses where no one answered," added Karim. "We're heading back to them tomorrow."

"Fat lot of good you'll be if you keep running away from the snakes," pointed out Fiona with a smile.

"Tell you what," said Karim. "I'll swap with you tomorrow and you can go snake hunting with Alan. How about that?"

"Nah, you're alright, Karim."

"Anyone know how Knight got on tracking down GHB suppliers?" asked Jenny.

"Sure, I have an inkling," said O'Reilly, and sipped his whiskey before continuing. "Knight reported back to Da Silva earlier. Apparently, doctors prescribe it for narcolepsy. So it could have been obtained that way. Or, you can order it illegally on the deep web. Or, if you're inclined to, you can even make it in the comfort of your own home. Apparently, the core ingredients are easy to obtain and if you follow one of the videos on YouTube, you can manufacture your own."

"That doesn't sound good. Has toxicology come back yet? I presume that would tell us if it's homemade or not."

O'Reilly shrugged. "Not a clue. You'll have to ask Knight."

"Oh, I will."

There was a long silence while they each took a sip of their drinks, wondering if there would ever be a break in either of the two cases.

In the end Jenny said, "I really hate this kind of case. There's just no obvious motive and nothing to point towards the killer." She took another sip and realised her glass was empty. "There simply must be a link between the two victims. Nothing makes sense otherwise. If we find that, I bet you we'll be able to move this case forward."

The others murmured their agreement.

Alan downed the rest of his pint and declared, "Right, my round."

"Where's your better half?" asked Leroy, sitting down opposite Brody.

"I've honestly no idea." Brody shook his head in disbelief. He couldn't believe his old friend was here and, even more unbelievably, was even deigning to be in the same room as him. To sit down opposite. To talk to him, even.

"I see what's going on. She arranged to meet me here, but …" Leroy made an overt show of looking under the table, " … no Jenny. You know what, Brody, I think your girlfriend is playing Cupid."

"Ah."

It made sense. He wondered if Jenny would still show up. He glanced at his phone and did the calculation. It was already an hour since her text saying she would be there in thirty minutes. He hadn't realised the time had flown by so quickly. She probably wasn't coming. In fact, now that he thought about it, she probably never intended to.

"I'll need a drink to get through this." Leroy began browsing the cocktail menu.

While Leroy's attention was diverted, Brody studied his friend.

On the surface, he was the same old Leroy. There was the trademark tight-fitting designer white shirt, open at the collar just one button too many, deliberately exposing his dark brown skin and offering more than a hint of the well-toned muscular frame underneath. Leroy had always looked after himself, going to gym most days, working the weights until it hurt too much. His hair had lost its style, though. Before, it was carefully groomed, shaven at the side and squared on top. Now it had grown out and was more relaxed. The more natural Afro look suited him better.

But despite the window dressing, there were signs that he'd been through a rough time. Brody had seen Leroy many times the morning after a heavy night on the town, and it was always his eyes that gave him away. Well, that and his bad mood. But this was more pronounced. Now, his eyes were sunken and lined beyond anything Brody had witnessed before. It was almost as if Leroy had aged six years in the last six weeks. But the main sign was the absence of his toothy smile. Even when he'd jokingly looked for Jenny under the table a moment ago, it had been Leroy putting on a jovial front. His lips hadn't parted or deviated from their straight line.

"Okay, I've seen the perfect cocktail. What about you?"

Warily, Brody said. "I'll have whatever you're having."

A waiter appeared as if by magic.

As Leroy ordered two Long Island Iced Teas, Brody quickly thumbed a text on his phone under the table. Within seconds, he'd sent a text to Jenny.

You were never coming out tonight, were you?

"Coming right up, sir," said the waiter.

"Thanks, darling."

"Just because he called you sir?"

"No, because he has a tight arse. Look."

Brody found himself following Leroy's gaze and then caught himself staring at the retreating waiter's bum.

"How are things going with Jenny, then?"

"Pretty good, I suppose." Brody didn't want to talk about his other half, not when the elephant in the room was Leroy's recently murdered lover.

"She must think a lot of you to try getting us back together."

"Did you talk to her?"

"Yes, she rang me this morning. Funny thing is that she knew I was in London. Now I wonder how she knew that?"

"She's a police detective, Leroy."

But Brody knew the real reason. Last night, he had told Jenny about his meeting with Vernon Bishop on Monday morning, who had let on that his son was in town for an audition.

"Funny. That's what she said."

"What did she say when you spoke to her?"

"She said how sorry she was about Danny, but she said that at the funeral too." Leroy paused. It was the first time either of them had mentioned Danny's name and it deserved a respectful moment. After a few seconds, he nodded acknowledgment and carried on. "She said how cut up you were over everything. She said that the Brody she had got to know in the few days before Danny's death was a lot more happy-go-lucky than the one she'd been seeing ever since. She said that you've been pining for my company, reminiscing over the good old days anytime you get the chance. She said that despite what happened, you needed me in your life. She said she wanted us to build bridges so that she could have the old Brody back. She acknowledged that she was being selfish." Leroy shook his head in disbelief. "Somehow she made it all about her rather than about you and me. She also said she'd be here."

"She said all that?" Brody was shocked. He had no idea if Jenny believed all that or had just said it to get Leroy to meet with him. He doubted Leroy would have made any of it up given how easy it would be for Brody to check.

The waiter returned and placed their drinks on the table.

"Two more, darling," said Leroy to the waiter. "Me and my old friend here are going to get incredibly drunk tonight and I need you to keep shuffling your tight little butt back and forth to the bar keeping us topped up. That okay with you?"

"Uh, sure." The waiter retreated, acutely conscious that his behind had attracted Leroy's attention.

"Down the hatch!" said Leroy, leaning forward to sup through the straw. Half of the cocktail immediately disappeared. Catching Brody gaping and not drinking he said, "Come on, Brody, keep up!"

Somehow, they made it through the next hour and four more rounds of cocktails without incident.

"Let's get out of here and go somewhere with a bit of life," suggested Leroy.

"Sounds good to me."

Thirty minutes later they were in The Yard Bar in Soho, the taxi driver shaking his head as the two men stumbled out of the black cab, laughing at every little thing. Leroy ordered them both dry martinis and they sat on stools next to each other at the bar.

Within minutes, they were reminiscing about their early days together at university, when they went out on the pull in character. Pilots, policemen, firemen, lawyers and other professions, forcing themselves to stay in character all night, no matter how much they tried to trip each other up. Their issue, of course, had been the sex of their targets, with Leroy chasing men and Brody women. And so they had taken it in turns, going to gay pubs and clubs one night and straight bars the next, each supporting the other until they had struck out or pulled.

"Those were crazy days, darling," acknowledged Leroy.

Brody had noticed that Leroy had began referring to Brody as 'darling' after the third cocktail, and was secretly pleased to hear it, even though it used to drive him nuts when they lived together.

"Yeah, do you remember that time when you ended up in the Thames?"

"I do." He shook his head at the memory. "I was chatting up this tall drag queen on that nightclub boat moored by Embankment. Only he took offence when I asked his real name. Turned out he was actually a she. And then her boyfriend came back from the bar and punched me over the side when his girlfriend told him what I'd said."

They laughed at the memory and drank some more.

"Although, I must admit, her boyfriend was good looking. No idea what he saw in her."

"Let's do it again tonight."

"What, go swimming in the Thames?"

"No, you fool. Pick a profession and head out on the town."

Suddenly Leroy became serious and Brody realised he'd tripped up.

"Those days are behind me, Brody."

Brody, not darling.

"What do you mean?"

"I'm living the rest of my days in memory of Danny."

"In what way?"

"I'm not sleeping with anyone else ever again. I'm now officially celibate."

Brody didn't know what to say, but he didn't believe a word of it. He may be on tenterhooks, but this statement couldn't go unchallenged.

"You're saying that even if Brad Pitt walked in here and proclaimed, 'Leroy, come back to my hotel room,' you'd say no?"

"Don't be stupid. That would never happen. He's not even gay."

"Well …" Brody cast about for another name. "Rupert Everett, then."

"He's too old."

"Leroy, you know what I mean."

"Okay. Even if Zachary Quinto showed up and said that," Leroy folded his arms. "I'd say thank you, but no, darling. No point being rude when someone makes a nice compliment like that."

"Blimey. If you were going to be celibate for the rest of your life you could have avoided coming out to your parents."

Leroy turned sharply. "How do you—" but his elbow slipped on the bar, causing him to knock over his glass. He held a wavering finger in front of Brody as if to say, 'Bear with me, I'll come back to this.' He caught the barman's attention and ordered a replacement drink.

It gave Brody a moment to gather his thoughts. Damn, he was drunker than he realised to have slipped up like that. He only knew about it because Leroy's dad had told him, but Vernon Bishop had made it clear Leroy had no idea of his visit. Ah well, too late now.

The barman delivered the replacement drink. Leroy took a sip and then returned his full attention to Brody.

"Damn it, I knew Dad was up to something yesterday after his check-up. I wondered why he didn't want me to take him back to Euston. What did he say to you?"

Brody attempted distraction, while admitting to Vernon's visit. "The most shocking thing he said was that you've been going fishing with him."

"Yeah, I have," said Leroy fondly. "We go sea fishing in a boat Dad owns a share of. Every Friday — that's his day for the boat — we rock up just down from Beaumaris at some unearthly hour and head out in the bay between Bangor and Llandudno. Can't quite believe it, but I really enjoy it. Catching pollock, cod and mackerel. And the occasional conger eel. Who'd have thought, eh?"

"Good bonding time with your dad, then?"

"Yeah, wish I hadn't been so hard on him when I was younger … Hold on a sec." Leroy poked Brody in the chest. "You changed the subject. Why did my dad come and see you?"

"He was worried about you, that's all. Wanted me to contact you. Come up to the farm, even."

"What did you say to the old codger?"

"I told him you'd probably kill me."

"You were right."

Brody decided to risk confronting the elephant in the room. "Yet somehow we're sitting here, talking with no violence. Well, not yet anyway."

"Part of me wants to make you pay, Brody. I've had dreams where I forced you to your knees at gunpoint and shot you in the head. Just like Danny. And you know what?"

The smirk disappeared from Brody's face. He'd noted Leroy had not called them nightmares. Guardedly, he asked, "What?"

"In my dreams I even took satisfaction in it."

Brody took a slow sip of his cocktail, opting for silence. His drunken haziness dispersed rapidly as he sensed the precipice ahead. The wrong response would plummet them both over the side, never to recover.

Leroy emptied his glass. "That's why I think I accepted Jenny's meeting."

"I don't get what you mean."

"I've been blaming you for Danny's death, with good reason, mind …"

"Leroy —"

"Let me finish."

Brody sat back, dreading what was to come.

"Despite it all, I know that nothing I do or don't do to you will bring Danny back."

Brody wasn't sure he got that and his furrowed brows made that clear.

"Let me try again." Leroy's voice slurred and his eyes glistened. "There's no point me throwing out all our history when doing that won't change the fact that Danny's gone, even if you were indirectly involved." Brody tried to interrupt, but Leroy raised his hand and continued, tears dropping freely now. "I know I need to accept that he's never coming back and that I've no choice but to live my miserable life without him. The way I see it, I can do that with or without you. My choice. And even though I fucking hate you for what you did, I can't lose both of you. One loss is enough."

"Leroy." Brody threw his arms around his friend and hugged him close, conveniently hiding his own tears. "I'm so sorry."

"I know, darling."

"Oi, get a room you two," shouted the barman.

"Fuck off," said Leroy. "We're having a moment and you're ruining it."

Brody laughed into Leroy's shoulder, stood back, wiped his eyes, and said, "Right, my round."

Leroy wiped his own. "Too fucking right."

WEDNESDAY

CHAPTER 10

KLARA WOKE WITH A START, WONDERING WHAT had disturbed her sleep. She was in her childhood bed above the bookstore. Light drifted in through the curtains. She was surprised her mother hadn't woken her, but perhaps she'd allowed her to sleep in after losing her job at MOESK.

She would go down and surprise them with a coffee. They worked so hard and deserved …

Reality rushed in with a bang and Klara felt tears well in her eyes. She was in the chair in the corner of her father's hospital room, in clothes that smelled of smoke. Her father lay in the bed, his head and hands bandaged. Although he looked bad, he was alive and breathing without the aid of an oxygen mask. He was being kept in a private room to prevent any risk of infection. Her mother, whose injuries were less severe, was in a public ward on the floor below.

Klara stretched and stood by her father's side for a while, just watching him breathe. After a while she decided it was time to do something. After popping in to check on her mother, who was also asleep, Klara left the hospital and took the metro back to the bookstore.

The windows of the shop had been boarded up. The sign above the store had fallen down. Mr Merkulov from the hardware store next door came out to greet her sombrely. He explained that he and the other neighbouring shopkeepers had gathered together and organised the boarding up of the shop to prevent looters. He handed her a key to a padlock that was looped through a makeshift wooden front door.

Touched by the shopkeepers' kindness, Klara unlocked the padlock, pulled back the door and entered, leaving it open to allow enough light to see by. The bonfire smell was overpowering. There was sodden soot everywhere. The place was such a mess. She picked her way through the burnt-out aisles, occasionally recognising a book cover that had somehow survived. But as she got to halfway through the store, the damage was much less. She turned on the light on her smartphone to see more clearly. It seemed that the fire hadn't spread to the back of the shop. However, the water damage was still significant.

Whether there was anything left to salvage she had no idea. It would be months of work, that was for sure. But it would require money. Klara had no idea of her parents' financial situation. Would their insurance cover this? Did they even have insurance? She had no idea. Her own financial situation was weak, at least within Russia's border.

She made her way behind the till into the backroom kitchen area. Nothing in here had been damaged at all. The power was off, but the light from her phone revealed the old stove with its gas bottle to the side, from the days when power cuts were much more frequent. She decided to make coffee and put on a pan of water. She found a sturdy old torch on the shelf above. It worked, allowing her to conserve battery on her phone.

Halfway through carefully filtering the boiled water through the ground coffee into a jug, she heard a noise from out front.

"Hello?"

Perhaps it was Mr Merkulov from next door. The aroma from the coffee was overpowering, especially on an empty stomach. She finished pouring. He could wait a minute.

"Hello? Klara?"

But the voice wasn't Mr Merkulov's. She couldn't quite place it. Or maybe she didn't want to.

With trepidation, she reached for the torch and carefully

picked her way towards the front. Halfway there, she saw a shadowy figure and the pinpoint of light from a phone torch. It was a man. She shone the torch into his face and revealed the last person in the world she'd ever want to lay eyes on.

Zakharin. Dmitry Zakharin.

Suddenly she was frightened.

He held up his phone to see her, but it was no match for the powerful torch she held. "Klara, is that you?"

"Yes. What do you want?" She deliberately shone the torch in his eyes.

Holding his free hand up to cover them, he said, "I offer you my deepest condolences on this dark day."

It was rehearsed and almost enough to make her slap him across his smug face. Maybe using the torch.

Instead she shrugged, not wanting to betray her emotions.

"May I come in?"

Did she even have a choice? He was halfway through already.

"Is that coffee I can smell?"

Klara spoke, her voice cracking. "Yes, I made a jug."

Without asking permission, he used the light of his phone to pick his way to the kitchen area, following the aroma. "Leave it to me, I'll pour us both a cup."

He'd somehow made out that everything was normal, failing to acknowledge the burnt out shambles of the bookstore. He should get a Nika Award for his acting performance.

Further back in the store, and almost untouched by fire or water, was her favourite armchair in the Computing area. Zakharin found her a minute later and handed her a cup of the black liquid. His phone was held between his teeth to give him light. While sipping his own, he thumbed through the shelves by the light of his phone, pulling out books here and there.

"I remember this one," he said, smiling fondly. "We were taught it in sixth grade but I'd already devoured it two years before. I bet you were the same."

She took a sip of her coffee rather than answer. She felt the hot liquid pass down her throat but there was no taste. When there was no answer, he got to the point.

"Contagion wasn't too pleased with me after you turned him down. As you might imagine, he's used to getting his own way."

She put the cup down and folded her arms. How was she supposed to respond? Her parents had paid such a high price for Contag10n's displeasure.

"So I thought I'd give you one more chance to change your mind. We really need you on this project. I know you've got a lot to deal with right now." He pointed towards the burnt-out aisles behind. "But we need you to start Friday at the latest."

She couldn't believe his cheek.

He added, "It should only take a few weeks. Once complete, you'll be free to help put this place back together."

"Oh, that's generous," she said, not hiding the sarcasm.

"What's that supposed to mean?"

"You know full well."

"Look, it was only as I was driving over this morning to offer you a second chance — something I rarely do, by the way — that I heard about the blaze on the news. I know the timing's bad, but we have serious deadlines and urgently need your firmware programming skills."

"You expect me to believe that you've only just heard about this?"

"It's the truth. First I knew of the fire was this morning."

"Don't play dumb, Dmitry. You know full well what your organisation has just done. And why."

"Are you insinuating something?"

"No insinuations required. Let me spell it out for you. Your boss ordered the bookstore to be set on fire because I turned him down. There, is that clear enough?"

"I very much doubt that." His words had no feeling. It was clear he knew it was the truth.

"And when I say no again?"

Zakharin shrugged, all pretence dropped. "Your parents survived this time, didn't they?"

Klara felt the floor drop away from her and she fell back on the armchair as if punched. The lives of her parents?

Zakharin finished his coffee and placed a card down on the

arm of the chair. "Be at this address on Friday morning at 9:00 a.m."

He left. His message, with its accompanying threat, had been delivered successfully.

Klara clicked off the torch and sat in the darkness for a long time.

"Nooooooooooo!"

Leroy's scream jolted Brody out of sleep. He jumped out of bed, eyes darting in every direction. But then sharp ice picks of pain stabbed his temples, accompanied by a hot flush and wave of nausea. Whatever Leroy's problem was, it could wait. He fell back on his bed and allowed his head to hit the pillow. The ceiling above began to spin, so he closed his eyes tight. The nausea passed slowly and the sharp pain downgraded itself to a background throb.

"Brody, you bastard!" It was Leroy shouting from the other room again. "What the fuck is that?"

Steeling himself, Brody climbed gingerly off the bed. He was still in the same clothes as last night, all crumpled and skew-whiff. Treading lightly to avoid jarring his frail body, he shuffled out into the hallway, holding his forehead with his left hand in a vain effort to stall the pounding in his head. Leroy's voice had come from behind the door of the spare room at the end of the corridor, the first time it had been used since Brody had rented the apartment from Stefan. Flicking open the door to the spare room, he leaned on the doorframe. He was in no way ready to confront whatever had got Leroy so riled up.

His friend stood in the centre of the room, clutching a bed sheet to his stomach with one hand, in an attempt to cover his private parts, but leaving his arse and muscular upper body completely exposed. Mirroring Brody, Leroy also held his forehead in one hand, except he was forlornly shaking his head.

"What?" croaked Brody, allowing his head to rest on the doorframe as well.

"That!" Leroy pointed to the double bed. "What the fuck is that?"

All Brody could see was a tumble of bedclothes. But then his rational brain slowly processed other evidence. Strewn on the floor around the room were Leroy's clothes, the white shirt, the tight trousers, the brown boots. But then Brody spotted a second pair of trousers and a pair of green suede shoes. And then a bright yellow T-shirt he didn't recognise.

From the vicinity of the bed a voice groaned, "Jesus, Leroy, stop with the noise, eh?"

A figure sat up, bedclothes falling away from his face and bare chest. The first thing Brody noticed was his tattoos. A treble clef and a set of notes across a musical stave reached from left to right across his pale, scrawny chest. Surrounding his belly button was an intricate flame in the shape of a star. His head was shaven closely and only the styled beard revealed he was blond. He looked vaguely familiar, but Brody didn't have the faculties available to remember.

"See," pleaded Leroy. "That!"

"Fuck off. I'm a person, not a thing, you prick."

"What the fuck have I done?" lamented Leroy, theatrically dropping to the floor.

"That's rich, that is." The young man glared at Leroy. "Last night it was, 'Ooh, Aaron, you're the best fuck of my life,' and now you can't even remember my name."

Brody had a flashback. Aaron was the bass guitarist of the live band they'd watched in a gay nightclub after drinks at The Yard Bar. He'd been giving Leroy the eye all the way through his band's set, while Leroy danced obliviously on the floor below, a space forming around him as his moves became freer and more abandoned the faster the band played. Brody had watched on from the relative safety of the bar.

"But I made a promise to Danny!" wailed Leroy.

"Yeah, who the hell is this Danny? You went on about him for ages last night, saying he wouldn't mind."

Leroy looked up, horrified. "I said that?"

"You said he was never coming back, so what the hell."

"I never." But his voice betrayed him. He must have remembered saying it.

"And you," Aaron turned his attention to Brody. "You owe me big time, Brody."

"Me? I owe you nothing." But as Brody said it, a dawning realisation of dread came over him.

"You lost the bet."

Fuck. Brody remembered now. This could turn bad. He needed to —

"What bet?" demanded Leroy, looking from one to the other.

"Time for you to go," said Brody, stepping forward.

"Five hundred quid." Aaron held his hand out. "Come on. Pay up."

"What the fuck is going on?"

"Shut up, Aaron," warned Brody, only halfway across the room, but with no idea how to stop him.

"He bet me five hundred quid I couldn't bed you, Leroy."

"He did?" Leroy's voice had dropped an octave.

"If it's any consolation, pretty boy, I would have fucked you for free. But five hundred quid is five hundred quid."

Leroy growled and pounced off the floor, launching himself at Brody. For someone who must have been as hungover as Brody, he moved quickly. Brody twisted to avoid the threat, but Leroy collided with him, making him fall backwards on the bed, Leroy's naked body on top.

"Ooh, a threesome," laughed Aaron, wriggling suggestively underneath Brody.

Quickly, Leroy reared up to gain space and threw a punch at Brody. All Brody could do was lift his hands, but the fist burst through and caught Brody on the cheekbone, shocking him into action. As a second one rained down, Brody bucked and Leroy flipped to one side, his punch missing Brody's head and connecting with Aaron's nose instead.

Blood burst out in all directions, and the sight of it halted Leroy in his tracks.

"What the fuck?" cried Aaron nasally, cupping his nose with his hand. "Get off."

Brody wriggled out from underneath the prone Leroy. Aaron followed suit and fled the room in search of the bathroom, blood dripping through his fingers onto the wooden floor.

Leroy just sat there, kneeling on the bed. A keening sound came from the pit of his stomach and turned into a loud groan of utter despair. He collapsed to one side, and curled up into a foetal position. His groan turned to a wail and eventually became his voice, repeating, "Oh Danny, what have I done? What have I done?"

Brody stood there helplessly, wishing he hadn't been so stupid. Aaron and Leroy would probably have got together anyway last night. After the set, Aaron had made a beeline for Leroy and they had been chatting each other up next to Brody at the bar. It was pretty obvious something was likely to happen. But, when Leroy staggered to the toilet, Brody and Aaron had got talking and somehow, in his inebriated state, Brody resolved to make sure it did. He didn't buy Leroy's vow of celibacy one bit: it was just Leroy being melodramatic as usual. But, rather than let it play itself out, Brody had foolishly decided to make the bet. When Leroy had returned, bouncing from one wall to another, it had taken Aaron less than five minutes for them to have their tongues down each other's throats, with Aaron signalling to Brody to call a cab.

Leroy picked himself up off the bed.

"I didn't mean anything …" Brody's voice trailed off. There was nothing he could say.

Leroy stood next to Brody, side on, still completely naked. He spoke into Brody's ear, quietly but full of threat. "If I ever see you again, Brody, I promise you I will make my dream a reality. I will make you kneel on the floor and I *will* shoot you in the back of the head." He picked his clothes up off the floor, working his way around Brody's inert body. Once he had everything, he walked haughtily out of the room.

Brody heard shuffling from the hallway as Leroy got dressed. A minute later, he heard the front door slam shut. Rubbing his bruised cheek, Brody whispered, "But you would have done it anyway." After a few minutes, he stood and walked out of the room.

Aaron stepped out of the bathroom just as Brody was about

to pass. He had tissue protruding from his nose.

"I want my money." His voice was still nasal.

Not even knowing he was going to do it, Brody punched the naked idiot in the stomach and watched impassively as he doubled over in a howl of pain. It was the first time in his life that Brody had ever struck anyone.

It felt good.

"Now get out."

Caravan was yet another cool and hip eatery in Brody's broad repertoire of cool and hip places to visit in London. Jenny wondered absently if he'd ever run out of places like this, but then admonished herself, blaming her pounding hangover for the unkind thought. This one was located on the bottom end of Exmouth Market, a pedestrianised street full of trendy bars and restaurants. Merchants were setting up their street food stalls ahead of the lunchtime rush from the surrounding City of London. The pungent aromas in the air were diverse and her mouth began to water. She really needed to eat.

Jenny surveyed the breakfasters perched on wooden tables and benches under an awning stretching out above the open-fronted windowless side of the building, but didn't spot Brody. She looked inside and glimpsed him sitting at a table at the back of the restaurant, his head in his computer. Of course, rather than enjoy the pleasant June weather, he'd chosen a table within reach of a power supply.

"Morning, Brody," Jenny said as cheerfully as her dry mouth allowed. She sat down opposite him and then noticed that his left cheek was bruised and swollen. She reached across the table to touch his face gently. She knew the cause could only be one thing, but had no choice but to whisper, "What happened?"

"Leroy happened."

"I'm so sorry, I thought I …"

"It's not your fault, Jenny. Although I probably would have preferred to know in advance that Leroy was going to show up. What you set out to achieve did actually work out well and, as a result, I'm nursing the worst hangover I've had in years."

He did look paler than normal. And his swept back blond hair was unusually messy. She'd never seen him like this.

"Me too," she offered.

"Why? What did you get up to?"

"Just a few drinks in The Dolphin after work with the team. I felt like celebrating after getting back in the action yesterday."

"Sounds like we both need to soak up the alcohol this morning." Brody picked up the menu. "Although I'm not sure I'll be able to keep anything down."

Jenny chose organic salmon with scrambled egg. Brody went for the full fry up. Both ordered orange juice and cappuccinos. Brody added a large bottle of still water.

While they waited, Jenny grilled Brody on what happened with Leroy. In a slow monotone, he told her how it had been icy to begin with, but copious amounts of cocktails had helped to paper over the cracks. They had ended up in Soho and finally confronted the issue of Danny's death, with Leroy confirming that he wanted to rekindle their friendship. Jenny was delighted that her intervention had gone so well, but then caught sight of Brody's bruised face again and knew she hadn't heard the end of the story. It turned out that, in his drunken state, Leroy had succumbed to having a one-night stand.

"But surely that's a good thing? To help him start to move on and all that?"

"That's exactly what I thought. But you don't know Leroy. He was all righteous about staying forever celibate in memory of Danny."

"So why is that your problem?"

"He thinks I forced it to happen …" he looked sheepish, " … which I sort of did."

Jenny folded her arms and waited for his explanation.

"I bet this guy, who was clearly interested in Leroy, £500 that he couldn't pull him. And next morning, after sleeping with him, it all came out." Brody pointed at his bruised cheek. "Which is when Leroy went apoplectic."

"Men!" Jenny shook her head. "Why on earth would you do that?"

"Because although nature would probably have taken its course anyway, I just wanted to give it a helping hand. Like you said, sleeping with someone else might help him start to move on."

"Yes, but only if it was of his own accord."

"It was."

"Not in his eyes." She sighed. "Jesus, Brody. Danny only died six weeks ago."

He dropped his head in shame. "Yeah, I know."

"What will you do?"

"Nothing. He'll need a few days to calm down no matter what, so I'll leave him to it. Maybe next week I'll try again."

Jenny was conscious that Brody didn't always choose the best course of action where other people were concerned, but this time she felt that doing nothing was probably the right thing.

Their breakfasts arrived. Jenny discovered she was ravenous and wolfed it down quickly, soon beginning to feel better. Brody, on the other hand, picked at his, but polished off the juice, coffee and a whole litre of water in quick succession, asking for a refill when the waiter passed by.

As they ate, Jenny told him about her strange encounter at the Christian Science church, following the lead Brody had provided. Brody laughed a couple of times at her misfortune in getting trapped in the church, but each time stopped immediately and rubbed his temples. He was in a bad way. She'd never seen him this rough before.

She told him about her meeting with Jerome Richards at the medical device manufacturer in Stockley Park and her suspicion that MedDev Labs hadn't kept up with the paperwork around Rajesh Gowda's visa, although she couldn't see how a visa issue had anything to do with what had happened to him.

"Two dead ends in one day. Back on the case, but none the wiser. If only there was a link between the two victims."

Brody sat back and made a show of folding his arms, smirking suspiciously. "Well …"

"What?"

"There is a connection."

"Really? What kind of connection?"

"Butler emailed Gowda about two weeks before he was killed."

"I thought you and Harry checked his email?"

"Turns out he has other email addresses. The one he contacted Gowda on was a secure one set up just for that purpose."

"What did it say?"

Brody picked up his tablet and placed it in front of her. As she took in what was displayed on the screen, Brody added ominously, "There's definitely something much bigger going on."

It was an email from someone called anonymous@bionicman43.com. Jenny recalled that Butler's online handle was BionicM@n.

"Hold on," said Jenny, trying to understand. "Gowda's just one of three people this is sent to. Who are the others?"

"I don't know yet, but I'm working on it."

Jenny returned her attention to the body of the message.

You don't know me and I don't know you, but all four of us have unwittingly got caught up in some kind of terrorist plot, and now tens of thousands of people are going to be killed because of our actions.

At least twenty people have already died because of what each of us has done for Saul.

I've tried to reverse it. But everything I've attempted so far has failed.

We all had our roles to play in setting these events in motion. I believe the only way to stop it is if we work together.

<u>DO NOT</u> *contact Saul. If he discovers we're communicating with each other, then our lives are in danger. I got your addresses by hacking his email account, but unfortunately that's the only contact details I have for you.*

I've set up a secure chatroom so that we can talk privately. Email is too open. The link is below. Do not share it with anyone.

I need your help to stop this. I can't fix it alone. We need to work together.

Please help.

We haven't got long.

BionicM@n

Jenny let out a deep breath, not realising she'd been holding it in while she read.

"What the hell …"

Brody agreed. "I know. It sounds ominous."

"What kind of terrorist plot? Vorovskoy Mir are tricky customers, but they aren't exactly terrorists, are they?"

"No, not to my knowledge. They're part of the Russian mafia. They're out to make money, not destroy the world."

"Who's this Saul?"

"No idea."

"Which terrorists, then?"

"No idea. ISIS? Boko Haram?"

Jenny shook her head. Saul could be linked to any one of hundreds of terrorist groups. This was serious. She felt a chill go down her back.

"What happens when you click on the link to the chatroom?"

"Why don't you take a look?" suggested Brody.

Jenny regarded the tablet warily. There was no mouse attached. She decided it was just a large version of her smartphone and hesitantly pressed a finger on the link. A fresh window opened and she was pleased not to have shown herself up. It displayed some kind of private chatroom, with a short conversation history.

The first message was dated the same day as the email.

BionicM@n: Thanks for clicking through on the email. Please reply to this once you're in and we can talk safely and privately. The only people who know about this chatroom are the three people on the email I sent.

The next message was also from BionicM@n, sent a week later.

BionicM@n: Look, if you're concerned about this chatroom, ring me on this number. It is imperative we talk.

A UK mobile phone number was listed. But this time there was a response:

Gowda: Been off the grid, only just seen this. You've got my attention. I've just left you a voicemail. Ring me back. I've left you my number.

Then two days later:

Gowda: James, are you there? Please return my calls. We need to talk again. I've got an idea, but I'm not back in London until the 31st.

Gowda: James?

These last two messages were dated a week ago, almost two weeks after the first message, but there was no response from Butler. Jenny calculated there couldn't be. Butler had been killed the day before. She also noticed that Gowda addressed Butler by his real forename rather than his online handle. They had definitely talked. She looked up at Brody and blew through her cheeks. "What the hell is this about?"

"I honestly don't know."

"They talked and then Butler was killed the day after."

"And Gowda was killed the day after returning to London. Where had he been?"

"He was with his pregnant girlfriend on holiday in a cottage in the Brecon Beacons."

"Presumably far away from a mobile phone signal or broadband. Hence being 'off the grid'."

"I guess so, but we can check."

"And no responses from the other two. So far, anyway."

"Who are they?"

"No idea. I've tried tracing their email address, but no luck so far. From their email address, one is called Klara with a surname beginning with I. The other is called Raz, but the rest of the email name is numbers. Klara's email is at yandex.ru, which is a popular email service in Russia. Raz has a unique domain name, but its DNS ownership is hidden so I can't trace it."

Brody seemed to have put a lot of work in, which was surprising given his hungover state.

"Have you only just found out about all this?"

He looked sheepish. "I found the link yesterday afternoon."

"Jesus, Brody, why didn't you tell me then? I could have had the team all over this."

"Well, if you remember, I thought I was seeing you for dinner, which was when I was going to let you know. Instead, I was stood up and Leroy showed up instead."

"Ah." The overnight delay was down to her. "Fair point."

Brody smiled weakly.

"I need to call this in. A link between the two victims gives us something to work with, although God only knows what the hell is going on. How the hell will we find out?"

Brody lifted his head and said. "I've already made a start on that."

"What have you done?" Jenny's question was uttered as a warning.

Brody took the tablet, thumbed and swiped and then handed it back her. She was looking at a recently sent email. It was from anonymous@bionicman43.com and was sent to all recipients of the original email with a new message added above. As she read what Brody had written, she shook her head in disbelief.

Gowda and I have now talked. This is serious: thousands of people will die very soon because of what we've done. But we can't stop Saul without your help. Please reply to this email or respond in the secure chatroom. (Same link as below.) Or you can contact me on the following number: +44 7769 …

Jenny glanced up at her boyfriend with ferocity. "You stupid fool."

"What?" He was all innocence.

"Two people may have been killed because of the first email. Either one of the other two recipients is the killer or the killer is somehow tracking everyone's movements."

"Exactly."

"But Saul knows who he's killed. If he's monitoring this conversation, he'll know someone else is impersonating Butler."

"Correct. And so he'll attempt to track down who it is."

"What phone number is that?"

"It's this one right here. Untraceable." Brody lifted a cheap-looking mobile phone out of his pocket. "If someone replies to the email, I'll track them down. There's always a digital trail."

"That's too dangerous, Brody. Why can't you just leave this kind of thing to us?"

"Because if a black hat hacker like Butler's involved, then this terrorist conspiracy is technology-related. And all you've got is Harry O'Reilly, who'd struggle to spot a phishing scam. Also, you're the police and you'd never do what I've just done. We're up against the clock with thousands of lives on the line and I've just social engineered the killer or one of the other conspirators into coming out in the open."

"You've just made yourself a target, is what you've done."

"I can look after myself."

"You may think you're some kind of digital superman online, Brody. But out here in the real world, you're just Clark Kent."

At that moment, the cheap phone in Brody's hand beeped.

They both looked at it and then at each other in shock.

"Who is this?" said a male voice on the phone pressed to Brody's ear.

"My name is James," lied Brody. "Who is this?"

Opposite him, Jenny buried her forehead in the palms of her hands and shook her head in disbelief.

"Guess."

"Well, you're not Gowda, I'd recognise his voice." At that, Jenny looked up at the ceiling as if for divine inspiration. "And I would think Klara is female. So, in that case, it's good to meet you, Raz."

"Yeah, right man. I got your message. What's going on?"

"Why didn't you respond to my original messages two weeks ago?"

"To be honest mate, it went into my spam folder. I only spotted it yesterday and I've been mulling it over. Then your latest message came through this morning. So what's going on?"

Given he'd said it was morning, Brody immediately deduced that Raz was in the UK, or at least in the Western Europe time zone. From the strong Mancunian accent, he was going with British.

"I'm in a public place right now, so it's a bit difficult to speak." Brody was conscious Raz could hear the hubbub of the restaurant surrounding him. "Let's just say that what we did could put us all inside for life."

"Seriously? Shit man, it was just a job on the side."

"I know. Broken up into pieces, it seemed innocuous enough. But when you put it all together, people are going to die."

"That is well bad. I never meant no harm to no one."

"What was your role in it, Raz?"

Suspicion permeated his voice. "You don't know?"

"Well, I know my part in it," countered Brody, "but it took all four of us to pull it off."

"But if you don't know what I did, the dibble aren't gonna figure it out, are they, man?"

Brody couldn't help himself. "The police are closer than you think."

Unimpressed, Jenny sat back, folded her arms and glared at Brody.

"So what's your plan?"

"If you, me and Gowda get together, we can swap notes, work out the full sequence of events, turn this around and save the lives of all those people."

"I dunno, man. It sounds well risky to me."

"But we've got to stop it. And we need to move quickly. Time is against us." Brody paused and added for effect. "Think of the children."

In front of him, Jenny laid out both her hands palms upwards and rolled her eyes in a show of abject disbelief at his gall.

"Nah, not kids as well? That's well bad." A slight pause as Raz made up his mind. "Alright, where?"

Brody clenched his fist in victory. He had him.

"Gowda and I are both in London. Are you anywhere near here?"

"I suppose I can get to you in two or three hours."

"Let's meet in …" Brody struggled for ideas. Jenny grabbed a paper napkin, scrawled on it and turned it around. Brody read it out. " … Halfway across Blackfriars Bridge. Two o'clock okay?"

"Nah, man. That's well exposed." Brody shrugged to let Jenny know it wasn't going to happen there. Raz continued. "How about right next to the luggage trolley that's halfway through the wall on Platform 9¾ in King's Cross?"

He was referring to the attraction put in place for the tourists following the success of the *Harry Potter* movie franchise. Brody thought it sounded as good a place as any.

"Sure. Two o'clock?"

"Yeah. I'll ring you on this number and, as long as you're alone, I'll come forward."

The phone clicked off. Brody wasn't sure if that had gone as well as he'd hoped. But at least he'd found a way to track down one of the conspirators while he was still alive.

"You are an absolute liability, Brody Taylor," said Jenny. But it wasn't spoken harshly. "Where's the meet?"

"King's Cross, next to the Harry Potter luggage trolley."

Jenny thought about it. "Clever bastard. A public place with lots of people legitimately standing around. You'll be a sitting duck."

"It's okay, he wants to help fix this. I'll be fine."

"No, Brody. We've no idea who was on the end of that line or what this terrorist plot is. Better to be safe than sorry. I'll make sure we have the place staked out with police backup."

Brody thought she was exaggerating. But he had a greater concern. "Your lot might scare him off."

"We're trained professionals. Unlike you, we know what we're doing."

Brody bristled at that. As far as he was concerned he'd just done what he was a professional at: using limited information to social engineer someone into taking an action they wouldn't have normally done. Usually, it was divulging privileged information. This time it was getting them to reveal themselves.

"Hmm. Well, we'll see about that."

CHAPTER 11

"THIS, LADIES AND GENTLEMEN, IS BRODY TAYLOR." Da Silva looked around the incident room at the gathered rank and file. "He is an external advisor on the Butler and Gowda cases, with a specialism in IT. I want you to treat him just like any member of the squad."

"Does that mean I can get him to fill in HOLMES for me?" joked Karim. Jenny smiled inwardly at his cheek.

"You're walking a very thin line, DS Malik," warned Da Silva.

But, Jenny mused, apparently not as thin as the line Jenny was walking. When she'd returned to the station earlier and brought Da Silva up to speed, he'd practically exploded. Despite the break in the case, he was spitting feathers that Jenny would be credited with finding the link between the two victims, and not him or his lapdog, DI Knight. He masked his behaviour as anger at her encouraging Brody to continue working on evidence related to Butler when she was supposed to be working the Gowda case. But she wasn't stupid.

She had briefed him in his office, the blinds down as usual. Kevin Knight stood to his right, also as usual. After Da Silva's initial tirade, he'd finally calmed down as he absorbed the broader story.

"Terrorist plot? Thousands of lives at stake?" Suddenly, he was grinning at his good fortune to be SIO on such an important case. He rubbed his hands together. "This is huge."

"But which terrorist organisation?" asked Knight. "And what's their target?"

"No idea." Jenny shook her head. "Hopefully, when this Raz person shows up we can figure it out." It was the only hope they had. Brody had been unable to find out anything else since, despite trying.

"You bringing in SO15, guv?"

Jenny was surprised that Knight had asked that. Of course Da Silva wouldn't bring in the Met's Counter Terrorism Command. He'd defer involving anyone that took credit away from him.

Da Silva answered reasonably. "Not yet, Kevin. Until we talk to this Raz and get some definitive facts, there's no real evidence of any terrorist threat."

"Right, let's hear all the details straight from the horse's mouth. DI Price, please be so good as to bring Mr Taylor in." He'd said it as if accusing Jenny of lying. She chose to bite her tongue.

Jenny headed for the same interview room as where they'd interviewed Brody yesterday morning. She'd left him there earlier while bringing Da Silva up to speed, expecting Da Silva to head downstairs and interview him as a witness once again. Instead, she signed Brody in and escorted him back up to the inquiry room where Da Silva treated him as any other member of the investigation team. Some colour had returned to Brody's cheeks although the dark bags under his green eyes were still clues to his night on the town. To Da Silva and the others, however, he probably looked as though he'd been working on the evidence all night.

Over the next twenty minutes, Brody repeated the same story he'd told her an hour before and walked Da Silva and Knight through the email and chatroom conversations between Butler and Gowda. Brody then explained how he'd duped Raz into meeting up that afternoon but, rather than tell him how foolish he'd been, Da Silva thanked him for taking the initiative.

Now, out in the main open plan office area, here was Da Silva briefing everyone and instructing them to treat Brody as a member of the team. As much as Jenny loved Brody being an intimate part of her private life, his repeated involvement in her professional life was starting to become irksome. But even as the thought passed through her mind, she admonished herself for being unkind. Without Brody's help, they'd never have discovered the link between the two victims. She needed to put the case ahead of her personal issues.

"Mr Taylor has arranged to meet this Raz at 2:00 p.m. this afternoon at King's Cross. We will be there on stakeout. We believe Raz to be another player in whatever conspiracy Butler and Gowda were involved in. Therefore, we have to assume he's a potential target for the people behind it. That, or he's the killer."

"What's he look like, guv?" asked one of the DCs from DI Knight's team.

"We don't know yet."

"He had a Manchester accent," said Brody.

At Brody's interruption, Jenny spotted a flicker of annoyance cross Da Silva's face, but it was gone before it took hold.

"Can't we track him from the phone he called Brody from?"

"It's an unregistered pay-as-you-go and the phone company says it's currently turned off." The answer came from DI Knight.

Da Silva waited for silence to descend and resumed. He assigned vantage points to the two teams. Knight's team would be dotted around inside the station. Knight would be on the skywalk above. Another officer would be in the *Harry Potter* shop next to the luggage trolley embedded in the wall. Another would join the tourist queue for the attraction. And the last would be seated at one of the mezzanine cafés overlooking the station concourse and the meeting point. Da Silva, who obviously wanted to be in the centre of whatever went down, would stand nearby as if waiting for his train to be displayed on the departure boards. Jenny and her team would cover the exits, which was almost an impossible task. Between the egress points to Euston Road, the various Underground entrances and the departing trains, there were too many for just four officers.

"The plan is to wait for him to make contact with Mr Taylor, at which point we'll swoop in and invite him back here for a little chat."

King's Cross station used to be a dark, dingy Victorian monstrosity. But since it had been renovated, with its architectural centrepiece roof — a white, geometric lattice radiating upwards and outwards from a central tree-trunk, curving above the western concourse — it had become an iconic London landmark. The only trouble was that is was completely open. Brody realised he would be visible from almost any point in the station and that the stakeout teams had no hope of spotting who Raz was unless he actually came forward.

Self-consciously, he strolled through the station in the direction of the *Harry Potter* shop, careful to avoid bumping into the pockets of travellers huddled in front of the departure boards mounted high above. His head pounded and his mouth was dry, but he couldn't decide whether it was because of last night's excess or apprehension about meeting Raz in ten minutes' time. Either way, he decided to do something about his symptoms and rerouted to the Caffè Nero stand, one of the bland coffee chains he normally eschewed. It was situated directly opposite the *Harry Potter* shop.

Just as he placed his order, his phoned buzzed in his pocket. He withdrew it, expecting to see Raz calling. But it was a text from Jenny, remonstrating with him for deviating from their carefully worked-out script. With one fast moving thumb, he typed his reply.

Hangover cure urgent too. Caffeine and water. xx

Brody warranted his health was just as important and, anyway, he would look more natural this way.

With five minutes to go, Brody made his way to the appointed meeting place and stood with his back to the wall, facing the busy station. He was to the right of a cordoned-off area around the rear end of a trolley packed high with brown luggage cases and a birdcage under a black sign proclaiming: *Platform 9¾*. The whole thing had been cleverly cut in half, presenting the illusion that it was disappearing into the wall. A long queue of tourists gathered behind the cordon. For each person that went up to hold onto the trolley, their friends dutifully took pictures on their smartphones.

Brody sipped his coffee, surprised it was as good as it was, and, while affecting a bored demeanour, scanned the station. He tried spotting members of the stakeout team. He could see Da Silva twenty yards away, staring up at the departure boards. The DCI had switched his business suit for a white and gold tracksuit and had donned trainers, a woollen hat and headphones to which he was nodding his head in time with imaginary music. Brody knew the headphones were connected to his police radio. Surprisingly, Da Silva looked gangsta cool, which was impressive for someone whose default mode was officious, stilted and dictatorial. He recognised DI Knight queuing for the tourist attraction, now nearing the head of the queue. Brody was intrigued to see how he'd handle reaching the front and then watched him fake taking a call, drift out of the line, finish the call and then rejoin at the back. Brody knew there was another detective above him on a walkway, but the angle made it impossible for him to spot. Jenny was the only other officer he could see from his vantage point. She had chosen the nearest exit to Brody's location, hovering by the escalators leading to the Underground station beneath.

Brody finished his espresso and saw a bin a few yards away. He left his spot, dropped the empty cup in it and returned. With his free hand, he brought out the phone in his pocket, checked that it had a signal, saw there was a minute to go and placed it back in his pocket. He expected Raz to phone him first and then come forward if all seemed above board.

Brody wondered about Raz and his role in the conspiracy, whatever it was. Someone behind the scenes, the person Butler had referred to as Saul, had pulled together a team of four, two of which were an ex-black hat hacker and a database administrator — James Butler and Rajesh Gowda. The roles of Raz and Klara were unclear, but once he'd talked with Raz he was pretty sure he could piece the whole thing together, then they'd know the target and the police could take preventative steps.

Brody glanced at his watch. It was now 2:01 p.m. No phone call. He searched the faces of the people nearby, but no one was looking at him. Any of them could be Raz.

A man walked directly towards him. Brody felt his pulse quicken. But, just as he neared, he veered up the nearby steps in the direction of the station pub. Brody let out a breath.

His phone buzzed in his pocket. He grabbed it clumsily, almost dropping it, but then answered placing it against his ear. "Yes?"

"You definitely alone, mate?" It was the same voice as earlier.

"I am."

"You better be. I'm trusting you on this."

Brody saw Da Silva, Jenny and Knight subtly staring at him on the phone.

"Look, let's grab a coffee and talk about this mess we're in."

"You can drink more coffee, can you?"

Brody looked around furtively, checking for other people on the phone near enough to have observed him ditch the empty coffee cup. But the problem was too many people held mobile phones to their ears around the busy station. It could be any of them. "I guess I could always switch to decaf."

"Fair enough. Right, I'm heading over to you now."

Brody scanned the station, left to right. Still no one obvious. "I can't see you yet."

"Patience, my friend."

An overweight man wearing a cap, beige T-shirt, brown corduroys and white trainers waddled directly towards Brody from the direction of the main exit that led onto Pancras Road. Most importantly, he had a phone to his ear.

"Is that you with the cap on?"

In his ear, the voice said, "Yeah."

Brody squinted to get a better look at the approaching man, trying to reconcile the voice with the look. His arm dropped from holding the phone by his ear.

Out of the corner of his eyes, Brody saw Da Silva, Jenny and Knight focus on the man, who was now only five yards away. The man dropped his own phone from his ear and held it out towards Brody.

Something wasn't right, but Brody couldn't understand what.

The man stopped in front of Brody, confusion now forming across his features, but still holding out the phone hopefully.

"Raz?"

"You're not Mr Butler," he replied.

Suddenly, Da Silva, Knight and the others flew out of nowhere. Da Silva got there first and bundled the man to the floor.

But Brody was staring at Jenny, shaking his head.

"It's not him."

So this was what it was like inside a beehive, was it? There was the latticework roof above and down below thousands of worker drones milled around, most with purpose. A group of bees over in the far corner suddenly became active, the loud buzzing noise in his ears increasing in line with their agitation. Many stopped to watch. But all the time there was a steady flow of new bees in and out via the various entrances and exits to the nest. Some routes in and out were even downwards. He didn't know bees burrowed into the ground. He'd thought that was wasps. And with that realisation, the illusion was broken and Ralph Mullins was staring down onto King's Cross station concourse.

He gathered himself and saw that his phone was in his hand. The call he'd last made had ended, but he couldn't remember who had terminated it. He supposed it didn't matter now. He looked out at the commotion over by the *Harry Potter* stand. Some of the people from the queue screamed and scattered as police manhandled the fat man to the floor. Others resolutely recorded the event with their mobile phones, soon to post the hoo-ha on social media.

Mullins hadn't known there was a *Harry Potter* attraction here. He liked the idea of holding onto the trolley and having a picture taken. He'd enjoyed those movies although, to be honest, he'd lost track of who was who by the end. He particularly liked it when the bad guy changed into a massive snake. He wished he could do that. He began to imagine what it would be like to be a snake. He'd spent so much time with them it should be easy. And then, just as another lucid dream began to form, he deliberately shook his head to clear it. He needed to stay focused.

Mullins was on the mezzanine, quite happily enjoying a pizza. The waitress hadn't paused for a second when he kept his hood up while ordering and eating. He guessed she dealt with all sorts in London. But he knew there was CCTV everywhere in King's Cross and so he'd kept it up ever since piling out of his taxi earlier. He'd managed to snag a seat right by the metal railing and was able to get a good look at the man using Butler's name. He'd watched him for a while and had taken a couple of photos on his phone, although the man was very small in them, being so far away.

The fat man was hoisted to his feet and taken away. Mullins guessed those people were police, which was interesting. There were seven or eight policemen and policewomen mulling around there now. One of them, an older man, had even sat at the next table, but with his back to Mullins. When the fat man in the cap had shown up with his phone held out in front, he had jumped up and raced down the escalators to join his police friends in the arrest. Mullins was disappointed with himself, though. He'd always thought he could smell nearby policemen at anytime, but the old man hadn't given off any whiff at all. It was only when he'd rushed downstairs that he had revealed his identity. He wondered if undercover police sprayed something on themselves to hide their police smell?

Mullins took the final mouthful of his pizza cheerfully. Just as the commotion began to settle down, a truckload of uniformed transport police arrived. They all rushed up to the *Harry Potter* stand and began arguing and gesticulating with the plain-clothes policemen. The animated body language of the two groups suggested they were shouting at each other, but Mullins couldn't make out what the issue was from this far away. It was just white noise, like the bees buzzing in his brief daydream a couple of moments earlier.

The man calling himself Butler — Mullins knew that couldn't be his real name, having sat opposite the real James Butler when he passed away in abject agony just over a week ago — was ignoring the argument and scanning the crowds. There was a pretty dark-haired woman standing beside him doing the same thing. But they wouldn't be able to spot Mullins. After all, virtually everyone in the station had stopped to watch what was going on.

Mullins laughed to himself and called for the bill.

"This is a total cock-up." DCS McLintock slammed his palm down on the table to emphasise the point. Still standing, he continued, "Do you realise you are on the front page of the online gutter press for manhandling an innocent man to the ground? We work bloody hard to maintain the reputation of the service."

Da Silva looked sheepishly at his feet. Jenny had never seen him shrink into himself like this before. She almost wanted to enjoy it, but knew that McLintock's wrath could soon be directed at her or Kevin Knight at any moment. The three of them had been summoned to McLintock's office on the top floor of Holborn Station the minute they had returned from the King's Cross fiasco.

Knight spoke up. "We had good evidence that the person approaching Brody Taylor was a suspect involved in a terrorist conspiracy."

McLintock exploded. "Terrorist conspiracy! What fucking terrorist conspiracy?"

"We don't know the details yet, sir," said Jenny. "We were hoping to learn more from the person who'd arranged to meet Brody."

"And who the fuck is this Brody?" His voice was hard as nails.

Jenny chose not to answer. This would be much worse if her personal relationship with Brody came out.

"He's an IT specialist who came forward after being contacted by James Butler, the first victim," Da Silva explained. "He discovered an email conversation between the two victims, which discusses a terrorist conspiracy, but gives no details. The conversation was with two others. Brody tracked down one of the two, called Raz, and arranged to meet him in King's Cross."

"Did you contact Counter Terrorism?"

"We wanted to find out from this Raz what we were dealing with first."

"We? Who the fuck is we? You are the SIO are you not, DCI Da Silva? You know full well that any hint of terrorist activity is to be reported to SO15. Immediately."

"But —"

"Did you liaise with Transport Police for this stakeout?"

"It happened so quickly, there was no time —"

"Bullshit. One phone call is all it would have taken. I've just taken an earful from their Chief Superintendent over this. And you know what's worse, *DCI* Da Silva?"

Da Silva stared mutely.

"I had no fucking idea that this operation was going down. By keeping me out of the loop you made me look like a complete fuckwit."

"As I said, sir, it moved too quickly."

He'd just lied. Jenny wanted to throw Da Silva under the bus there and then. All she had to do was tell McLintock that they'd known about the meeting for over three hours, destroying Da Silva's claim instantly. It would be retribution for wasting weeks of her time dedicating her to the CPS preparation for their last case.

She wanted to, she really did. But she wasn't going to stoop to his level. Jenny kept her mouth shut.

"DI Knight, what time was the King's Cross meeting scheduled for?"

"Two o'clock, sir."

Maybe McLintock already knew they'd had plenty of prep time for the stakeout.

"And what time did you know this?"

Knight shuffled, knowing he'd been trapped. "Um, I dunno, sir. A bit before the meeting."

"A bit? Call yourself a policeman?" McLintock roared. "I want an accurate time, DI Knight."

Jenny was glad she'd kept her mouth shut.

Knight glanced at Da Silva, seeking inspiration. Da Silva gave the slightest of nods.

"Just after 11:00 a.m., sir."

"Just after 11:00 a.m.," repeated the DCS. "By my reckoning, that's about three hours." He turned back to Da Silva. "I'll ask again. As SIO, why didn't you alert SO15 to a possible terrorist conspiracy and why didn't you contact British Transport Police to let them know of a police operation at a major transport hub?"

"I … I was … there was just so much going on … I had to prioritise." Da Silva shrugged in defeat.

"I'll tell you what's been going on, shall I?"

Da Silva sat rock solid, shoulders slumped. Knight to his left had folded his arms tightly. Jenny was on cloud nine, but composed herself. She couldn't believe that she was here to witness this dressing down.

"Glory hunter."

"Sir?" asked Da Silva, unwisely as far as Jenny was concerned.

"The worst kind of trait one should ever have in an SIO. You are a fucking glory hunter looking to find any advantage to take the spotlight. I've seen you court the press. I've watched you cut corners to put yourself in the front line at the right moment. Like this afternoon. I've seen you take credit for the hard work by other members of your team. You are a snivelling little glory hunter."

"Sir, that's outrageous. I would never do that."

"Shut up, Da Silva. You disgust me."

"But —"

McLintock held up his hand and turned his attention to Jenny, staring at her.

She braced herself.

"Why Manchester?"

Jenny had no idea what he was talking about. Her first thought was that he was referring to where they thought Raz came from, based on Brody hearing his accent. But then it dawned on her.

"Ah," she said. He knew about her application to Greater

Manchester Police.

"Why?"

Jenny thought through her reasons. It was obvious that McLintock was gunning for Da Silva, so she didn't need to hide her real motivation. But admitting it in front of the perpetrator was difficult. "Because I want to work somewhere where I feel like a valued member of the team."

"And you don't feel that here?"

"No."

"So it's not the promotion to DCI, then?"

"Well," she shrugged, "that's important, but not the be all and end all." Jenny couldn't believe she was even having this conversation. And in front of Da Silva, who had just glanced at her with slighted eyes that said 'traitor.'

McLintock turned. "So, *DCI* Da Silva. You bring the service into disrepute in the press. You ignore protocol by choosing not to liaise with two other departments. You chase the limelight and make your most competent senior officer feel undervalued, so much so that she applies to Greater Manchester to get away from you. Have I missed anything?"

Da Silva stared at his feet. Knight folded his arms even more tightly. Jenny was still processing the hidden compliment. *Most competent officer.*

"Right, you two," he pointed at Jenny and Knight. "Out of here. I need to have a private chat with the DCI."

They hurried out of the office.

"Klara."

Klara lifted her head from her father's hospital bed and looked up at her father's bandaged face. His voice had been hoarse and cracked, but she rejoiced to hear it. His eyes were open.

"Papa!"

He brushed his lips with his tongue. There was a cup of water by his bed. She lifted the straw to his lips and waited for him to suck in some of the liquid.

"Are you in pain, Papa?"

"On these drugs? Not possible."

Klara couldn't believe he was making jokes in his condition. She put the cup on the side table, pleased to have been able to help him.

"What is wrong, my little angel?" He hadn't called her that for years.

"I'm worried about you."

"I'm only a little singed; I'll be back to normal soon. The doctors said so."

"I hope so. I really do."

"Klara, talk to your father. I can see behind those bright blue eyes that there's something else going on. Tell me."

She told him everything, slowly at first and then in a rush to get it all out. Dmitry Zakharin, MOESK's project to find and recruit her, Contag10n, Vorovskoy Mir, the nuclear power station sabotage job. All of it.

"When I said no, they burnt down the shop. I'm so sorry, Papa, I didn't think it through. I should have known better. I should have said yes."

"You did the right thing, little one."

"But —"

"No. If it hadn't been Vorovskoy Mir, it would have been the krisha or one of the rival mafia gangs trying to move in on their turf. People like us are always pawns in someone else's chess game. The only way to beat them is to remove yourself from the board."

"But I'm not going anywhere, Papa. We've got to get the shop back up and running. And you and Mama will need my help. Especially while you recover."

"Listen to me. You have to leave, my angel."

"But if I don't turn up on Friday, they will come back and this time it will be …" She didn't want to say it would be their lives. "It will be much worse."

"Don't you worry about us. The krisha owes me dearly after failing to protect us yesterday. I will call in proper protection. A twenty-four-hour bodyguard, even."

"But you can't live like that forever. They'll just bide their time."

"But it won't be forever. There's nothing left for us here now. We're leaving too. We're finally going to Italy. Mama and I agreed on this earlier. Once I'm up and about and out of these bandages, she'll have sold the shop to that property developer who wants to turn it into flats. And, more importantly, my visa will have come through."

"But you can't sell the bookstore, Papa. It's your whole life."

"It was holding me back. I should have sold up and taken your mother back to Italy years ago. The shop burning down is just a message from above. And, for the first time, I've heard it loud and clear."

Klara couldn't believe it. He was serious. It was the best news ever. Unexpected tears of joy sprung from her eyes. She wanted to hug him but couldn't work out a way to do it without hurting him. Instead she placed her hand gently on his bandaged face.

"But you must leave straight away, angel. We can meet you in Italy. Or you could take that job in London you told me about and then come and join us in Italy after. But get out now while you still can. Straight away. Don't be a pawn in their game. Remember what I said: remove yourself from the board."

CHAPTER 12

JENNY STOOD FACING THE ASSEMBLED TROOPS. IMMEDIATELY after coming downstairs she had issued a ten-minute warning for everyone involved in the stakeout to gather for a debriefing. Kevin Knight, his tail between his legs without his master present, had neither objected nor attempted to take charge, and had chosen a seat off to one side.

Fiona stood behind her, capturing key points and actions on the whiteboard, already full to the brim with their notes from the briefing she had led two days ago. The one that had ended abruptly with Da Silva arriving back and commanding her to stand down in front of everyone.

Well, that was unlikely to happen this time.

She presumed Da Silva was still upstairs with McLintock. Or, as she secretly hoped, maybe he'd been suspended and escorted off the premises. McLintock's nickname around the station was Tick-Tock. Before today, she had never experienced the reason for the moniker, but after witnessing his short fuse detonate in the direction of Da Silva, she fully appreciated it was well chosen.

In front of her, DI Knight's team and her own sat amongst each other instead of forming two distinct factions. She supposed that her leading the debriefing with Da Silva absent and Knight playing along provided enough clues for the detectives to sense something had changed and adapt their behaviour. Neither she nor Knight had spoken a word about the meeting with McLintock and Da Silva. Without knowing the outcome, it would be premature to comment. If there was something to say, that was McLintock's prerogative.

To her right, Brody sat next to O'Reilly, computer on his lap as usual. She watched O'Reilly casually whisper something into Brody's ear. As if they were best friends, Brody whispered back and they both chuckled quietly. She knew Brody looked down on O'Reilly as an amateur and was surprised to see them so companionable.

"Right," she announced, "let's start with the taxi driver. Alan, can you bring everyone up to speed from your interview with him."

"Sure," he said, pulling out his notebook and flicking back a couple of pages. "About twenty minutes before two, Mr Tarrant — that's the cabby's name — picked up a fare from Farringdon and dropped him at King's Cross, roughly ten minutes later. The fare was about £7 and the man gave him £20, waving away the change, much to Tarrant's delight. As for a description, the passenger was about six foot five, brown hair, and built 'like a brick shithouse'. The cabby's words, not mine. He was wearing blue jeans, a plain white T-shirt stretched taut across his chest, a light-green fleece hoody and black Lycra-style gloves, which was the only thing the cabby had thought odd up until that point. Obviously, we are now processing the £20 note for prints, but we're not expecting a result given the gloves."

"Did the cabby notice what accent the suspect had when he picked him up?" This was Brody. Jenny actually felt a little self-conscious standing at the front with him in the room. But she needed to ignore her confused feelings and get on with the show. Anyway, he'd asked a smart question.

"Not at that point. Yes, on the phone later. But at time of pickup the only two words the passenger said were 'King's Cross'."

"Not 'King's Cross, mate'?" persisted Brody, putting on a Mancunian accent for effect.

Coombs glanced at his notebook. "Nope. I did ask, knowing

our suspect has a Manc accent." His slightly exasperated tone indicated he was letting Brody know he was the real policeman out of the two of them.

"Odd," concluded Brody absently, but then resumed poking and swiping on his computer as if he'd lost interest in the meeting.

Coombs turned over a page in his notebook for effect and continued. "A couple of minutes before two, while the cabby was queuing outside the station for his next fare, he heard a phone ringing from the back seat of the cab. He got out, retrieved it and answered it. It was an expensive-looking smartphone."

"I've got it here," interrupted O'Reilly, holding up an evidence bag containing the phone. "It's an android, pay-as-you-go and clean as a whistle. No email address or any data on it. GPS was turned off, so there's no tracking history on the phone. Yer man left no fingerprints or anything."

Alan Coombs turned to O'Reilly. "I'm sure we would have got to the phone later, Harry. Okay with you if I continue with Mr Tarrant's statement?"

O'Reilly blushed and said, "For sure."

Coombs continued. "The voice on the other end explained he had just been in his cab, had accidentally left his work phone in it and was now calling from his personal one. He was in a rush for his train and didn't have time to come out and make it back before it left. He asked if the driver could bring it to him, saying there was a fifty in it for him, at which point the cabby dropped everything and headed into the station." Coombs turned to Brody and added, "And yes, all of that was in a Manchester accent."

"No doubt the previous generous tip helped convince the taxi driver that the promise of fifty quid was a genuine offer," commented Jenny. There were nods of agreement.

"While listening to the phone, the voice on the other end directed him through the station. He first sent him in the direction of Platform 11, and then instructed that he was standing just beside the *Harry Potter* trolley with his back to the wall. At which point Tarrant turned towards Brody, saw him on the phone looking for him and headed in his direction. As he neared he held out the phone, which was when, as he put it, all hell broke loose."

"Didn't he think it odd that the man he was handing the phone to looked different to the earlier customer?" It was Fiona from behind Jenny, who had been dutifully capturing the key points on the whiteboard.

"Only as he neared Brody. At the time he was following instructions and the promise of fifty quid pretty much blinded him until it was too late."

"Very clever," summarised Jenny. "Raz sprung our trap with such ease."

"And was probably watching everything from a safe distance."

Brody pulled his own phone from his pocket and looked at it quizzically. He then began typing. It was frustrating that he didn't behave like the rest of the team and give the debriefing his full attention. She'd be glad when he was out of the picture once again. Work-wise, that was.

"Presumably if nothing had happened to the cabby when he approached Brody, Raz would have realised Brody was on his own and then come forward." This was Karim Malik.

More sounds of agreement.

"Did anyone notice someone in the station fitting the cabby's description of the suspect?"

Everyone murmured negatively or shook their heads, turning to look at each other in case someone had been more observant.

Coombs added, "Right after this meeting, I'm off back to King's Cross with the cabby to review CCTV. Hopefully, Mr Tarrant will pick Raz out and we'll have something to work with."

"But why go to all this trouble?" This question was from Sandra Lipton, a DS from Knight's team. Jenny didn't know her well, but was pleased to see someone outside of her core team had contributed.

"Maybe Raz is above board but he was scared by all the talk of terrorists and wanted to be sure he wasn't being duped by one," said Coombs.

Some shrugs. Fiona wrote it up.

"Or maybe," Kevin Knight spoke up for the first time, generating raised eyebrows that he had chosen to contribute, "Raz already knew Butler and Gowda had been killed and wanted to find out who was pretending to be one of them."

There were some surprised nods at that.

Jenny had one more idea but wanted to see if anyone else raised it. She gave it a moment, then reluctantly voiced it. "Or perhaps Raz is actually the killer and wanted to find out who was impersonating someone he'd already killed."

A hushed silence as the team processed this alternative.

"Doesn't seem likely," commented Brody, still working on his computer, immediately annoying Jenny for contradicting her in front of her team. She folded her arms and waited. Sensing that the room was waiting for him to continue, he looked up. "James Butler was a black hat hacker who said he'd secretly obtained their email addresses from someone called Saul. That probably means he hacked Saul's computer to get the email addresses of the other three. *Ergo*, Raz and Saul are two different people."

Ergo? Jenny couldn't believe he used such an archaic word.

"Assuming Saul and the killer are the same person," countered Fiona Jones. "If this is a terrorist conspiracy then it could be a whole terrorist cell working together."

"Even if they are different people, I don't see Butler making a mistake like that. Anyway, I chatted with Raz on the phone. He sounded scared more than anything."

"Right now, its all specula —" Just as Jenny decided to calm things down, the door to the meeting room swung open. The others turned around to see who had interrupted Jenny mid-flow.

In walked DCI Raul Da Silva. With his head held high, he marched to the front. His blank expression was impossible to decode.

Jenny couldn't believe it. It was going to be a repeat of yesterday. Just when she thought she'd had a break. Her shoulders slumped in defeat.

Da Silva reached the front, walked past her and Fiona, and sat down next to DI Knight, who looked just as shocked as Jenny.

"Don't let me interrupt," said Da Silva to the room, cheerfully. He looked up at Jenny. "Please, DI Price, carry on."

"Uh, sure, guv." Jenny gathered herself. "Where were we?"

"We were speculating on why Raz sprung the trap the way he did," offered DI Knight, trying to assert some authority from beside his boss.

"Why don't we ask him?" said Brody nonchalantly.

Silence descended upon the room.

Jenny asked the obvious question. "How?"

"Well …" Brody indicated his tablet computer. "He's online with me right here."

The sound of chairs scraping back filled the room as officers stood and bustled around behind Brody, trying to view his computer screen. Da Silva and Knight stayed where they were. Jenny and Fiona watched from the front.

"What's he say?" asked Karim.

"I'll put it on the big screen."

Brody stood and walked to the table by the front. The others returned to their seats, while Brody fished about in his man bag for a connector. After a moment, his computer screen was duplicated onto the large television monitor, mounted on the wall next to the whiteboard.

Jenny read the conversation so far. It was from the chatroom that Brody had shown her that morning. Brody was still masquerading as James Butler.

BionicM@n: Nice trick with the cab driver, Raz.

Raz: I knew something smelt wrong. So are you a cop then?

BionicM@n: No.

Raz: Well what the fuck was that at King's Cross? The Salvation Army?

BionicM@n: Yes, they were cops. But not me, I'm on your side.

Raz: Yeah, right. How come, if you're working with them?

BionicM@n: I'm trying to save the people who are going to die soon. That's why I went to the police.

Raz: All that crap about terrorists and people dying. It's all bullshit.

BionicM@n: It's not. It's all true. People are going to die 'cause of what we did.

Raz: But you don't even know what I did.

BionicM@n: True. But that's why we need to work together. Then we can figure out the whole story.

"What the hell, Brody?" demanded Jenny, her voice full to the brim with exasperation. She couldn't believe that he'd been chatting away to their prime suspect during the debriefing and not told anyone. Sometimes, he really pushed his luck. "You can't do this …" She allowed her voice to trail off as a response appeared.

Raz: So tell me. How are all these people going to die?

Brody began typing. Jenny wanted to stop him, but didn't know how to advise responding to the question.

BionicM@n: I'm trying to figure that out. That's why we need to talk.

Raz: When are they going to die?

BionicM@n: Soon.

Raz: But when?

Brody began typing a response, but Jenny cut in. "Stop, Brody. Can't you see? He's trying to determine what you know."

Brody stopped and reread the conversation so far.

"You might be right."

Another line appeared on the screen.

Raz: You don't even know, do you?

"Is he goading you?" asked Fiona.

"Not sure. But either way, I'm losing him here."

Raz: I'm outta here.

Brody looked at the assembled officers. "Any suggestions?"

"Tell him to wait," said Da Silva from the side of the room, where he'd observed quietly until now.

"Tell him his life is in danger," said Jenny.

Brody typed it quickly.

BionicM@n: Your life is in danger.

No response. Brody added to it.

BionicM@n: That's the real reason I wanted to meet you.

Still nothing.

"Tell him that he's next," said Jenny.

"But that's admitting someone's already been killed," countered Knight.

But Brody typed quickly, silencing Knight's objection.

BionicM@n: If you don't get police protection, you're next.

The room waited. Still nothing.

"Tell him Gowda's already been killed," suggested Jenny.

"You just told me I'm giving away too much."

"I know, but we need to talk to this guy. How else are we going to find out what the hell is going on?"

"I agree," said Da Silva

BionicM@n: Gowda's already been killed. One of us is next.

Nothing.

Brody said, "Hold on, I've got an idea." He switched screens to a browser, Googled the phrase, *Gowda snake death*, clicked on the first news story and copied the website address. He pasted it into the chat box and pressed enter.

"That's a URL to the news story. Hopefully, he'll see it as proof."

"Good idea," said Da Silva.

"Can you see if he clicks on it?" asked Sandra Lipton.

"Not from here," replied O'Reilly.

They waited. Finally, a new message appeared.

Raz: So if Gowda's dead, who the fuck are you? I didn't know ghosts could use the internet.

"What's he mean?" asked Karim.

Jenny figured it out. "All the news stories mention that Gowda was the second snake death in a week. Now he knows that Butler's dead too."

BionicM@n: I'm a close friend of Butler's. I'm working with the police to save you from the same grizzly fate he and Gowda suffered. And to stop the terrorists.

Raz: Who are you?

BionicM@n: Let's just meet. I'll explain everything.

"Nice work, Brody," said Karim.

They waited an eternity. Eventually two messages appeared, within seconds of each other.

Raz: Fuck you. I can look after myself.

Raz: Bye.

With his shoulders slumped and his hands thrust deep into the pockets of his jeans, Brody exited Holborn Police Station and turned into Theobalds Road. It was a thirty-minute trudge back to Bruno's on Upper Street and probably the same changing tubes on the Underground. Sometimes, he really missed his nimble little, park-anywhere Smart car. He pulled out his mobile phone, intent on using the *Uber* app to get him home by minicab, but then clocked an old school black cab coming towards him with its light on. Automatically, he raised his hand.

While the cab dodged through the back streets, avoiding the congestion leading up to Angel Station, Brody reflected on the day's events.

Mostly, he was annoyed with himself. He should never have let Jenny talk him into turning the meeting with Raz into a stakeout. If there had been no trap to spring, he was sure Raz would have come forward after finding out it was safe to do so. Then they could have sat down over coffee and Brody would have discovered what the hell was going on.

He told himself that he ought not to care. The terrorist plot was Jenny's business as a police officer, not his. After all, his objective in all this was to track down what Butler knew about Vorovskoy Mir so that he could take revenge for Danny's death. Nothing else. However, as it became evident that Butler was involved in something much larger, he hadn't been able to stop himself becoming more embroiled in the investigation. He was beginning to appreciate that he enjoyed using his skills to help the police. They were clueless when it came to technology and it was so easy to make a difference.

He wondered if there really was a place for someone with his skills on the side of the law. He doubted it, despite the steps forward he had helped them make. Every time he provided assistance, he ended up telling half-truths to cover his methods, which were completely at odds with their by-the-books investigative approach.

And then there was Jenny. He felt that his involvement in the case might prove difficult for her. While some of her team knew they were an item, Da Silva and Knight certainly didn't. But it wasn't just about who knew what, it was more to do with maintaining boundaries in their relationship. While he was able to switch characters, just as he did whenever he assumed a new identity in a social engineering hack, he felt that Jenny had difficulty separating her personal and professional lives when he was around. It was as if she didn't know how to behave with him there and it was confusing her.

They had agreed that she would come over tonight, making up for her deliberately standing him up last night in favour of the failed Leroy experiment. But, for the first time, he wasn't looking forward to seeing her. He was pretty sure it would involve a lot of relationship analysis. Something he had no interest in. He liked Jenny. Probably much more than *liked*, if he was being honest. And that was enough for him. The murder investigation case was just noise as far as he was concerned. Why couldn't she act the same?

Perhaps if he distracted her when she came over? And with that thought, he recalled her playing *Call of Duty* on her Xbox two nights before and a plan began to crystallise.

Fifteen minutes later, carrying an Argos branded shopping bag containing a large box, Brody entered a crowded Bruno's just as two people exited the shop, tutting and moaning. Unusually, there was a queue of people at the counter. Stefan always provided table service, memorising orders of any size and effortlessly balancing making the drinks with taking and delivering them. But Brody couldn't see him anywhere. Instead young Lorenzo was behind the counter, mopping sweat from his brow with his sleeve as he frantically made coffees for the impatient customers, some of whom were hissing to each other.

Lorenzo caught Brody's inquisitive eye and offered up a forlorn, helpless look. Brody wanted to head upstairs and put his Jenny distraction plan into effect, but instead he lifted the counter flap and stepped behind. He'd never been here before; this was Stefan's domain. But Stefan wasn't here.

"How can I help?"

"Thanks, Mr Brody," said Lorenzo with relief. "Can you work the till if I make the coffees?"

Brody looked at the cash register. It was no complex EPOS system, that was for sure. "I reckon I can handle it." He turned to the customer at the front of the queue and said jovially, "Hello, Madam, how are you?"

"You cheeky git. I've been waiting fifteen minutes just because you're late for your own job. How bloody unprofessional." She placed both fists on the counter. "Now, I want two large skinny lattes, one small mochaccino and a medium caramel iced latte. Oh, and we'll have two slices of that chocolate cake and one of those almond croissants."

Brody nearly informed her where the nearest Starbucks was, but Lorenzo replied, "Coming right up," and went to work like a madman.

Muttering under his breath, Brody plated the cakes and croissant, entered the order into the till and took payment via credit card, rapidly working out each step as he went. Satisfied, she shuffled along to await the delivery of her order.

The next person rolled up and the process was repeated.

Twenty minutes later the queue had disappeared and peace and calm had returned to Bruno's. Lorenzo was still making coffee while Brody collected empties from the tables out front. He had directed new customers to free tables where he took their orders, Stefan-style.

While Brody filled the commercial dishwasher, Lorenzo explained what had happened. Stefan was out being a tourist with his Italian nephew, which Brody then recalled Stefan telling him the day before. Lorenzo went on to explain that the girl who was supposed to waitress today had phoned in sick ten minutes after Stefan had left.

For all Brody's love of quality coffee, he decided it was too much like hard work to make it all day long for others. In some ways, he had quite enjoyed the experience, but Lorenzo looked completely knackered and flustered. Being a good barista was a skilled job, but there was no career in it as far as Brody could see. To be fair to Lorenzo, he only did it part-time to fund his master's degree. But for the absent Stefan, it was much more than a profession. It was his vocation.

After another quarter of an hour, the front-of-house had emptied significantly and everything was under control. Lorenzo thanked him profusely and told him he could handle it from there. After all, there was only an hour to go before the sign hanging on the door could be turned round.

Almost reluctantly, Brody grabbed his shopping bag and headed for the door marked private, which led to the stairs to his flat two floors above. Halfway up, Brody glanced at the object in the bag and then took the remaining steps two at a time.

He had hardly any time left to prepare for Jenny.

The last time he'd had a coffee was four years ago. Back then, it had made his heart beat way too fast and made his daydream so real that he had fooled himself into believing he was a flying squirrel able to soar from one prison walkway to the other, above all the ant-like prisoners milling about in the atrium below. It was only thanks to four other inmates holding him down that he'd been prevented from jumping over the balcony and plummeting to his death. From that day onwards, Mullins had avoided coffee like the plague, although he did sometimes miss the more powerful caffeine-fuelled visions.

So, when he'd finally reached the front of the queue in Bruno's, he'd ordered an English breakfast tea from the man who had pretended to be James Butler. The Butler-not-Butler man with his slicked back white blond hair didn't even look up when Mullins ordered his tea, so focused was he on getting through the queue of customers, which still had four or five people to go. Mullins handed over a twenty and waited for his change. No eye contact.

Now, twenty minutes later and sitting in a large, comfortable high-back chair by the front window sipping tea, the coffee shop no longer busy, Mullins observed Butler-not-Butler pull a key from his pocket and disappear into a door marked Private. He could hear footsteps disappearing upwards from behind the wall beside him. He waited a while, but Butler-not-Butler didn't return.

Back at King's Cross, Mullins had casually watched all the commotion with the police from his seat in the pizza restaurant on the mezzanine level. He'd originally arrived at station on his black Vespa, but then took the Tube one stop to Farringdon so that he could return in the black cab, conveniently leaving the mobile phone on the rear seat. Like a lemming, the cabby had fallen for the promised reward and unwittingly sprung the police trap enabling Mullins to single out Butler-not-Butler. After all, he was the one who had tried to make contact.

When they police had eventually dispersed, Mullins had followed Butler-not-Butler. He left with a pretty-looking woman with shoulder-length brown hair, the same length as his mother used to wear when he was small, before she gassed herself in the oven to get away from his violent father one last time.

They had got into a Vauxhall Astra, which they'd parked outside the station on York Way on the double red lines. Well, they were police so he supposed they could break the law. Mullins had parked his scooter up against some railings just around the corner, so had been able to follow them easily down Gray's Inn Road as they headed south. Just over a mile later, they turned right and then right again, pulling to a stop outside Holborn Police Station. Mullins had panicked at being so close to a cop shop and immediately turned left to get away from it. His imagination automatically filled in the smell of a pig farm. And then he began visualising all the police inside standing side-by-side, eating slop and waiting to be slaughtered. He shook his head to clear the image and pulled up outside a pub called The Dolphin Tavern, which gave him a good view of the station's exit and their parked car. He waited patiently for over an hour, managing to stay lucid throughout.

Eventually, Butler-not-Butler had exited the building. He'd stood outside, looking at his mobile phone and, after a minute, hailed a passing black cab and jumped in. Back on his Vespa, Mullins caught up with the cab within a few hundred yards. Another mile and a half later, Butler-not-Butler was dropped outside a coffee shop on Upper Street. He got out and entered the busy coffee shop. Mullins parked his Vespa right outside and followed him in.

It seemed Butler-non-Butler was some kind of coffee barista and that his surname was Brody. He'd heard the Latin-looking boy call him 'Mr Brody', while making Mullins' tea. What the hell this Brody was doing working with the police one minute and then serving coffee the next, he had no idea. It made no sense. But he was the one who'd initiated contact and so needed to be dealt with.

After a while, Mullins walked up to the counter and ordered another cup of tea. As Latin-boy steamed water into a cup, Mullins asked innocently. "Is Mr Brody around? He said he'd meet me here."

"Mr Brody? No, he is upstairs in his flat."

"Oh, that explains it. I thought he meant down here in the coffee shop."

The barista handed Mullins his tea. "Would you like me to call him down?"

"That's okay. I'll give him a ring myself." Mullins waved his own phone to emphasise the point.

The barista shrugged before another customer diverted his attention.

Mr Brody, eh? Mullins was sure they'd be on first name terms soon enough. He transferred his tea from the crockery cup to a paper cup, squashed a lid on top and left the coffee shop.

Mission accomplished.

Brody's phone beeped.

She was here. Sure enough, her text said she was outside.

Brody flew down the stairs and exited into the empty coffee shop. Lorenzo had closed up over an hour ago and left. Stefan was still out with his nephew, at the theatre if Brody remembered correctly. He wondered what show they were seeing.

He could see Jenny through the glass door, waiting in the porch, leaning on the side window looking back out on to Upper Street. He unlocked the door and held it back for her to enter. She strode straight past him.

No kiss. No eye contact.

Ah well, he hadn't expected much else. Thank God he'd prepared his Jenny distraction plan.

"Evening," he said as he locked the door back up.

It was quieter than normal in Upper Street. Jenny's Astra was parked in a spot right outside, with two more spaces still unclaimed. A black cab carried out an impossible U-turn as someone hailed it down on the opposite side of the road. A black scooter pulled up and parked opposite. A woman was being dragged along by two massive Great Danes who had spotted a cat.

"Hi," she finally answered.

He knew better than to ask her how she was. That would be like inviting a vampire to cross the threshold. Instead, he suggested they go upstairs to his flat. She agreed and followed him up.

In the kitchen, Brody asked, "You hungry?"

"I could eat."

"Pasta okay?"

"Sure."

She sat on a stool by the island in the centre and leaned forward onto her elbows, resting her chin in her hands. Brody opened the fridge door, pulled out a bowl of fresh gnocchi and a bottle of Pinot Grigio. He poured them both a large glass.

Jenny took a big gulp while he sipped tentatively at his, watching her over the rim of the glass. He'd only just recovered from last night's excesses with Leroy and here he was drinking again. But the cold wine did taste good.

"What happened after I left?"

There, he'd broached the main topic of the day.

"Not much."

Brody placed a big bunch of fresh basil into a blender with a clove of garlic, some pine nuts and salt. After pulsing, he emptied the green mush into a bowl and stirred in some Parmesan. As he drizzled olive oil into the mixture, he tried again. "What's the story with Da Silva? I was surprised to see him."

"Me too."

A pause. Brody decided to stay silent and carried on preparing their meal. He poured water into a large pot and set it to boil, adding salt. Just as the silence became unbearable and he almost gave in, she sat back in her stool and stared at him.

"I can't work with you anymore." She took a sip of her wine, not letting her gaze drop.

"As in … you and me don't *work* anymore, or you don't want me involved in your *job* anymore?"

"The latter. But if we don't deal with that then it will become the former too."

"Is it some kind of professional conduct thing?"

"Partly."

"But lots of cops form relationships through work. Didn't you tell me you once went out with a senior officer?"

"It's not the same. Anyway, you don't work for the police."

"There you go, then. No problem."

"But it is a problem, Brody. You're not a trained detective so you cut corners and take risks and —"

"But —"

He held his tongue at her raised finger.

" … and you undermine my authority in front of the team."

"I do?"

Brody was genuinely surprised at that. He knew the first count was true, but the second was something he hadn't expected. He poured the little balls of gnocchi into the pan. As he watched them sink to the bottom he tried to recollect when he would have done such a thing.

"Yes, you do." Jenny sipped at her wine. "At least twice during the debriefing today."

Twice? He couldn't even come up with one example. "When?" His tone was enquiring rather than defensive. He really wanted to know.

"First you contradicted me on the idea that Raz was Saul —"

"But I thought we were brainstorming?"

"We were, but you abruptly dismissed the idea, based on your *assumption* that Butler is such an amazing hacker that he wouldn't make a mistake. In a murder investigation, we never close down a line of enquiry based on an assumption. We have to cover every base until the facts or evidence proves otherwise. You dismissed an idea there and then based on an assumption. That's cutting corners and undermining me in the process."

The gnocchi balls began floating to the surface. He reached for a slotted spoon and transferred them to a draining bowl, repeating the process as others surfaced.

"And the second time?"

"You held back the fact that you were online with our prime suspect for a good five minutes. You had a whole team of experienced detectives there and yet you took it upon yourself to have a private little chat rather than benefit from the experience in the room, making me look a fool in the process. Half the room know about our relationship and those that don't know I was the one who brought you in to help. Either way, you made me look stupid in front of the team and my boss."

Brody had realised he'd pushed his luck from the way Jenny had reacted at the time, although he'd never translated it into cutting corners or undermining her authority. But as he thought it through, he realised that was exactly what he'd done.

"I'm so sorry." He transferred the gnocchi into the pesto sauce and tossed it about. "I really didn't mean to make you look stupid. I thought we were making progress."

"You're a maverick, Brody. You don't play nicely with other people and you have no respect for authority."

Brody spooned the pesto-covered gnocchi onto two plates and handed one to Jenny. He didn't know what to say.

Jenny accepted the plate, picked up a fork and added with finality. "If you want whatever it is that we have to continue, then you can't be involved in this case anymore." She held her fork above the pasta and waited for him to reply.

"Understood. I'll keep out of it. For what it's worth, I really am sorry."

She accepted the apology and speared a couple of gnocchi balls with her fork. But before placing them in her mouth she said, "Oh, and one more thing …"

He waited. No point trying to guess. He'd got everything else wrong so far.

"If you take up Da Silva on his offer to work as a regular advisor to the murder squad on future cases, you and I are over."

That was an easy one. While Da Silva's offer flattered his ego and he enjoyed getting involved in their cases, Jenny had a point about his maverick style. He'd worked so long on his own as a social engineer, manipulating others, that he really didn't know how to work well in a team. But, if he accepted that about himself, then there was another worrying implication. The interview panel at GCHQ had stressed the amount of teamwork involved in working there. If his style caused this much trouble for the good old Met Police, then it would be considerably amplified working for the central government agency. He resolved to give that some thought.

He raised his wine glass and held it towards her. Jenny lifted hers and they clinked. "You have a deal."

"Glad you agree."

They sipped their wine. Jenny finally popped the gnocchi on her fork into her mouth, savoured the texture and flavour and shook her head in amazement. "This is bloody gorgeous! Did you make the gnocchi?"

He had and told her so, and their conversation turned lighter, avoiding any talk of the case. When they finished the meal, Brody reached across the table and took her hands in his and apologised again. She leaned forward and they kissed for a long time.

After emptying the rest of the wine bottle into their glasses, Brody led her into the living room. Just as he pushed open the door, Brody remembered that his no-longer-necessary Jenny-distraction plan was fully on display.

She spotted the frozen image on the television screen and turned to Brody, her voice full of accusation. "What the fuck are you up to?"

CHAPTER 13

"WHAT?" ASKED BRODY.

JENNY STARED AT THE imposing television screen standing upright in the centre of the room and then stared at Brody, studying him to determine if butter would or wouldn't melt in his mouth.

Did he know or was it just a coincidence? And then she remembered that she was going out with one of the most manipulative people on the planet and concluded it was no coincidence.

"Since when do you play video games?"

Displayed on the screen was a frozen in-game image from *Call of Duty: Black Ops III.* She recognised the screen layout immediately, as well as the Cairo-based backdrop from the Breach multiplayer map. Then she looked below the television and spotted the source and another question superseded the first. "And an Xbox too? You hate console gaming. You're always going on about PCs being the best gaming platform."

"For some games, maybe. *Call of Duty* is good on both but the console version ensures everyone has the exact same configuration, which makes it fairer."

"Hmm," she said and then looked again, this time realising there was more to the setup than she first realised. It wasn't just one TV, but two mounted back to back. And there were two Xboxes. Brody had set it up for two players to compete online from within the same room.

"How long have you known?" she demanded.

"For definite? Only a couple of days. But right from the day we met I knew there was more to your knowledge of gaming than third-hand titbits from Damien."

Damn, he must have seen her playing two nights ago when she'd woken in the middle of the night, her mind playing on Da Silva's latest rant. She'd not noticed him see her gaming, but then she had been completely wrapped up in the campaign with the headphones on high volume, busy ordering her teammates about, one of whom was her nephew, Damien. Despite it being a school night, Damien had begged her to let him play as a brief respite from all his exams. Why hadn't Brody said anything at the time?

"Well, now you know."

"Why is being a pro-level gamer such a big secret, Jen? I thought we agreed to tell each other everything."

"No, what we agreed was that you would never lie to me again."

"Even so."

She thought about it. There had been tons of times she could have steered the conversation to her hobby. But she had chosen to hold it back. Was that because she didn't trust him? Or was it just habit? Or was it really something else? She decided to tell the truth for once.

"You know I'm uncomfortable around technology, right?" She'd never confessed that to him and it had taken serious effort to get the admission past her lips.

He smiled.

She decided it was a patronising smile. That was unfortunate. "See," she hissed, her finger poking him in the chest. Determined not to lose her temper, she took a breath and tried to speak calmly. "You have such a superior attitude whenever there's anything going on with technology. How is anyone supposed to compete with that?"

"Compete?" He paused, confused. "What competition?"

"With you, everything's a fucking competition. Just look at

today."

"Hold on a sec." Brody furrowed his brows and thumbed in the direction of the kitchen behind him. "We just dealt with that. Why is that coming up again?"

"Because the reason you don't play nicely with other people is that you want to win at every single thing you do. You hold back information — like that live chat with Raz — so that you can show off and win and be ever so fucking superior. You could have just admitted you know about my gaming. But no, that's not enough for Brody Taylor, elite fucking hacker." She realised that her voice had risen in direct proportion to the amount of swear words she had interspersed for emphasis, but she didn't care. "Instead, you create a fucking elaborate Xbox set-up to challenge me and try and put me back in my place on the techie hierarchy!"

"But, that's not —"

She wasn't finished. "When I told you just now that I hate technology, you gave me such a condescending grin." She put on a high-pitched voice to emphasise the point. "Ooh, poor little Jenny doesn't understand technology.' Well fuck you, Brody."

To her disgust, her voice caught. She pushed past him and headed for the stairs, flying down two steps at a time. She burst into the empty coffee shop below, making straight for the front door and rattled it in frustration, failing to open it. She almost smashed the glass pane to get out, but managed to regain a semblance of control and forced herself to breathe deeply. At that point she noticed it was only a Yale lock and that a quick flick of the knob would free her, but now that she was more composed, she thought more logically. Her coat and purse containing her car keys were still upstairs. Not that she should be considering driving after the amount of wine she'd consumed over dinner.

Jenny decided to sober up and headed over to the main counter with the massive professional espresso machine sitting on it. She needed coffee but had no idea where to start on this metal monster. It had way too many dials and buttons.

She heard him step up behind her. She refused to turn around in case he saw the tears she could feel brimming at the edge of her eyes.

He reached around her and pulled her close, nuzzling in close from behind. At first she stayed rigid as a plank, but as Brody whispered he was sorry over and over into her ear, she felt herself slowly collapse into him. She turned around, reached up behind his neck and drew him forward. She kissed him deeply and urgently.

After a minute, she drew back her head and added her own apology. He pulled her close and hugged her tightly, almost crushing her.

Eventually he spoke into her neck. "Coffee?"

Smart move. It was their safe ground.

She pulled back and nodded. "Double espresso, I think."

"Perfect," he said, all smiles. "Okay, I'll teach you how to make this thing work …"

— What a damned idiot! Jenny's eyes widened and she took a deep breath, ready to unleash all hell for implying she was —

He held his hand up to stall her. " … if you teach me how to play *COD* in return."

She looked at him in utter disbelief and then all the wind dropped from her sails. She'd had him so wrong all along. He hadn't been about to challenge her earlier just to prove he was better at technology. He'd already conceded to her expertise and wanted to learn from her. Give them something else in common other than coffee. Sometimes, she was such a fool.

Jenny closed her eyes and shook her head gently to let him know that she had acknowledged her foolish behaviour of the last ten minutes. But rather than discuss it, she grinned and simply said, "Okay, sounds like a deal."

"First things first, then," said Brody. "We need proper coffee shop muzak."

He docked his phone into a cradle connected to a piece of hi-fi equipment. After a few moments of swiping, piano music began playing from speakers around the shop. He upped the volume on the amplifier so that it was way too loud. It was the desperate backing music you heard in hotel lifts around the world.

"Brody!" Jenny laughed. "Turn it down."

He did. And then changed the music to Dean Martin singing 'Mambo Italiano'.

"Much better," she agreed.

And everything was.

Outside Bruno's, in the shadows of an alley across the road, Ralph Mullins watched Mr Brody and the woman from King's Cross Station make coffee on the massive machine. Mullins was sure there was a faint whiff of cop emanating from her, even this far away.

About ten minutes earlier, he had finally decided everything was quiet. The coffee shop was dark, although there was still a light on upstairs. He had figured it was too conspicuous to carry everything he needed, so he hid half of his possessions behind some wheelie bins in the alley. He could come back for those later when he needed them. With his trusty break-in equipment contained in his backpack, he headed across the road to carry out the first part of his plan.

Halfway across the road, a light appeared inside the coffee shop as the internal door from the stairway to the flat above opened and the dark-haired woman came flying into the café area. She made a beeline for the door and began rattling it in an attempt to open it. But it seemed to be locked and she obviously didn't have a key.

Mullins immediately diverted towards the darkness of the neighbouring designer clothes shop. It would have drawn attention if he'd stopped and turned back. He was reasonably sure she hadn't noticed him despite the yellow glow from the streetlights.

Standing in the darkness of the shop's porch, he wondered what the hell was going on next door. Maybe Brody was trying to kill the woman and was chasing her around the building with a huge dagger, just like Jack Nicholson in that Stephen King movie. What was it called?

The thought of the dagger made him unbuckle his own knife

from its leather sheath under his coat. It was a decent-sized hunting knife with a wooden handle and an incredibly sharp blade about the width of the woman's neck. He loved gripping it tightly in his hand and wanted to slash it around from side to side, but remembered he mustn't attract attention. Even this late into the evening, Upper Street was full of pubs and bars and there were lots of people wandering about. Reluctantly, he reholstered the knife and stepped back out onto the pavement, moving away from Bruno's. Once out of sight, he crossed the road and made his way back to his original hiding place in the alleyway directly opposite.

He checked the items he'd hidden behind the wheelie bins and nothing had been touched. Everything was still okay. He just needed to be patient.

He stole frequent glances across the road. The two of them stood drinking their coffees either side of the counter, chatting and laughing. Then, a few minutes later, they stepped out into the centre of the coffee shop, wrapped their arms around each other together and began swaying side to side. Was that music he could hear? Were they dancing? Why would they dance? A few minutes earlier, he'd been trying to kill her, hadn't he? Mullins blew his cheeks out. Sometimes other people really didn't make sense. In fact, he corrected himself, it wasn't just sometimes: it was most times.

After a few minutes they stopped dancing. Brody took the woman by the hand and guided her to the door that led back upstairs. She followed willingly. As the door closed behind them, the downstairs lights went off again, plunging the coffee shop into blackness. A few minutes later, he was pleased to see that the light upstairs went out as well.

He checked his watch and decided to give it half an hour.

In the darkness of his bedroom, Brody grinned from ear to ear. He almost wished he smoked, because if this was an old Seventies movie, he'd be taking a huge post-coital drag right now. He and Jenny were spooned together in the bed, she in front, her head resting on his arm, but with her arm draped back across his thigh. She was breathing deeply and he was pretty sure she'd dropped off.

He'd heard of the term 'make-up sex' before but this was the first time in his life he'd personally experienced it. The physicality and abandonment of their actions had taken them to new levels of intimacy. He guessed it was because both of them were overcompensating for their earlier argument. But Jenny had also been a far more aggressive lover than ever before and, if he was honest, it had been a major turn-on.

He wasn't clear about how they'd survived tonight intact, ending up sleeping together. Nothing had gone to plan. At all.

In his mind, he'd calculated that him cooking a meal for the first time might have deflected whatever argument was coming his way. He'd actually expected the first accusation. Yes, he took risks and he would have held his ground on that if he'd been given a chance. But Jenny had moved quickly to his next crime: undermining her authority. He'd had no idea that his actions or behaviour gave out that impression and he was genuine in his desire to make an effort to improve on this. It was why he'd apologised.

Apology accepted and arguments out of the way, his double-Xbox powered Jenny-distraction-plan had then come into play when it was no longer necessary, backfiring completely and inciting whole new levels of anger. It seemed she'd been trying to hide her technophobia mainly because his primary expertise was the very thing she was fearful of: technology. He understood that, until he considered her pro-gamer skills. It was hard to reconcile, almost like holding two opposing thoughts in your brain at the same time. But her admission had somehow been turned into a brand new accusation of him acting superior all the time; wanting to win in every personal interaction he had with anyone. Including Jenny.

He suspected there was some truth in that accusation, as uncomfortable as it was to admit. When it came to the likes of O'Reilly and most of the members of the CrackerHack forums, it was deliberate. Status in the hacker community was everything and behaving as if you were the best was part of the deal. But he'd never meant for that attitude to spill over into his personal life. Especially to Jenny.

The worrying part, however, was that she'd actually had him banged to rights when it came to his reasons for setting up the two Xboxes. He had indeed planned to challenge her at the one technology-related thing she was good at. And he would have done his best to win, having managed to practise for an hour before Jenny arrived. He wasn't sure whether he would have beaten her, but he would definitely have given it his best shot. He'd not really considered his own motivations before she'd pointed them out. He'd fooled himself into buying the two games consoles as a way to distract her and then sold it to himself that it would be good if they had shared hobbies and no more secrets. But now, with their argument still visible in his rear-view mirror, he realised she was right about his need to win and be the best in the room at all times.

Even with her.

He decided it was a personality flaw he needed to work on, but only with those close to him. O'Reilly and the CrackerHack members would have to put up with the old Brody.

But before the row had deteriorated to the point of no return, he'd improvised with a masterstroke: declaring that he'd only set up the two Xboxes so that *she* could teach *him* how to play, which made him appear subordinate to her, completely deflating her argument that he was so damn superior. It had been the natural manipulation of a master social engineer. Even though he'd strayed away from the truth, he was delighted with the outcome. The little white lie had saved their relationship and improved the way she thought about him. He was pretty sure he could live with that.

Hence the satisfied grin plastered on his face.

Over shots of espresso downstairs in the coffee shop they had talked through everything again, much more calmly and rationally. He'd plugged his phone into Stefan's music dock, popped on Spotify and before Brody knew what had happened, they were behaving like it was the last dance in an old-school nightclub, arms wrapped around each other, snogging like teenage kids fearful of the lights coming on and bursting their bubble. He didn't think Stefan would mind but maybe it was best not to say anything. But then he should have washed up the cups. And, now that he thought about it, he'd left his phone downstairs on the dock. Hopefully, he'd wake up early enough to grab it before Stefan started work—

A noise came from downstairs. It sounded like something thudding on the floorboards. After a moment of straining to hear more, Brody relaxed when he recalled that Stefan was due back from taking his teenage nephew to the theatre. He wondered if the barista had had a few drinks, causing him to drop something. Brody realised he'd never seen Stefan drink alcohol. Maybe he had a drink problem. Or maybe …

Brody realised his mind was drifting aimlessly. Over Jenny's shoulder he could see the alarm clock declaring in large digits that it was just before midnight. He pulled her tight, enjoying the feeling of her naked skin, and relaxed his body.

Within a couple of minutes he was fast asleep.

Getting through the coffee shop front door had been a breeze. His backpack contained an old brass glasscutter. He'd bought it years ago in a DIY shop, which had ostensibly marketed the tool as perfect for installing bathroom extractor fans. But he was pretty sure most sales were to professional burglars like himself. The suction pad had stuck to the glass pane first time and, after a quick circuit with the scoring wheel, Ralph Mullins was reaching his hand through and unlocking the door from the inside. It was only a Yale lock, after all. Although, if the mortise lock had been thrown, he had other tools in his backpack. He'd come prepared for all eventualities, fully informed by his earlier reconnaissance.

It was much later now and Upper Street was quieter, although not devoid of life. Mullins supposed that nowhere in inner London ever stopped completely.

Illuminated only by the lamplight outside, he made his way across the room, taking great care to avoid the mismatched tables and chairs. In that he was successful, but he hadn't accounted for the age of the glass cutting tool in his hand, which still held the glass to it. The rubber suction cup must have degraded, for the round piece of glass unexpectedly fell off, landing on the wooden floor with a loud thump. Fortunately, it landed side on and then toppled to the floor, spinning in circles like a larger than life coin. He snapped it up before it reached the final, slower, noisier circles.

Mullins listened for movement upstairs or outside. When he was sure no one had stirred, he bent and picked up the piece of glass with gloved hands.

He arrived at the door to the stairs and gently pulled it open, revealing the wooden steps leading upwards. He gave himself a mental pat on the back.

He had a decision to make. The rest of his belongings were hidden in the alley across the road behind the wheelie bins. Either he went back now and got them or he did it after he'd dealt with Mr Brody and the brunette. He decided that once they were immobilised he would have plenty of time.

Mullins took off his shoes and quietly headed up the stairs.

"Jen."

Brody's voice was quiet but insistent. However, there was an urgency in his tone. She squeezed her eyes open, forcing herself out of the pleasant dream state she'd been in.

"Jen."

Something was wrong. His tone was insistent, but somehow resigned. And then it came to her. She could hear someone else breathing.

Jenny flipped around, pulling the sheet over her naked body. Brody, also still naked, was sitting rigid on the wooden chair from the dressing table, facing her. He caught her eye and briefly turned his hands outwards by way of apology. A huge mountain of a man was standing behind Brody, holding a large knife to his throat.

"Don't move or I slice your boyfriend's jugular open. Understand?"

"What do you want?"

"Shut up, copper."

Jenny shut up. The intruder knew she was police but it didn't faze him at all. This was bad.

"Drink." The huge man nodded towards a glass of water on the bedside table. Jenny's head was a little fuzzy from earlier, but she didn't recall bringing a glass of water to bed. They had been far too preoccupied. So where did it come from?

And then she knew who the man was. God, she was slow.

She shook her head defiantly. "No way, Raz. It's drugged."

He raised an eyebrow at that. She wasn't sure if he was surprised by her knowing his name or the fact she knew there was GHB in the water. Raz really was tall, well over six feet. But he was wide without being fat, an immense barrel chest and tree trunks for arms. He was dressed head to toe in black: shoes, jeans, T-shirt, bomber jacket and Lycra gloves. All black. His hair and bushy eyebrows were dark. The only colour was a glint from a gold tooth.

"Your choice." He spoke reasonably. "Mr Brody will lose his head if you don't." And he pressed the knife in harder, drawing blood.

"Stop," she pleaded desperately, scrabbling around for ideas. Her bag with her phone was in the kitchen from earlier. Her clothes were strewn across the room. There was nothing to hand.

"Tell you what, I'll count back from five. If you've not drunk the water by then, I'll slice his throat wide open. And God will never forgive you."

His pauses between words were clipped, almost as if he wasn't used to speaking much. His voice was deep with not much of an accent other than to say he wasn't from the north of England. And then it hit her, wasn't Raz supposed to have a Mancunian accent?

"Five."

She decided to mull over the accent issue later. Jenny spotted the alarm clock. Maybe she could grab it and hurl it at him.

"After I slice open his neck, I'm coming for you next. Four."

Jenny thought about hurling herself at Raz, but realised she was caught up in the sheets. She loosened her grip on them, allowing them to drop. She couldn't afford to trip when she launched herself.

"Nice tits." His eyes had dropped down as her breasts were revealed, but then snapped back up to her eyes. "But you won't distract me, *police whore*. Three." He leaned in closer to Brody, blood oozing out more freely from Brody's neck. There was no way she could make it across the room before he finished garrotting his prisoner.

If this played out along the same lines as the two previous murders, then she might survive this, but she would awaken to find that Brody had suffered a slow, horrible death. She couldn't allow that to happen. However, if she consumed the water then she would be totally incapacitated and unable to help Brody. He would be at the killer's mercy and the two previous murders, as well as his cold dark eyes, proved he would show none. Jenny was immobilised with indecision. She couldn't just let Brody die. But if she refused to drink the water, then he would be killed immediately.

She had no choice. Her shoulders slumped in defeat.

"That's better. This way he has a chance of surviving. I did once. And he can too, if the good Lord chooses."

She had no idea what Raz meant, but it offered her irrational hope. She reached for the glass.

"No, Jenny, don't." It was Brody, fear etched in his eyes. For her or for him, she wasn't sure. Not that it mattered.

"Shut up, you." The man yanked Brody upwards by the head, almost lifting his body from the chair, and opened up his neck even more. The knife was pressed hard against the carotid artery. She could see the veins in the side of his neck pulsing rapidly.

Jenny lifted the glass and brought it towards her mouth.

"Don't even think of throwing it. Two."

She had just thought of exactly that, but he was one step ahead of her. She lifted it to her lips.

"Jen, no —" But Raz yanked him higher, lifting him right out of the chair. Completely naked and exposed, Brody looked feeble in the arms of the huge man.

Resignedly, she tipped the glass back and began swallowing

the liquid.

"Noooo!" The gargled cry was Brody's final attempt to stop her.

She gulped the poisoned water. Ironically, she was dehydrated from the wine earlier and would have greedily drunk it under normal circumstances. As she wiped her mouth with her forearm, the glass empty, Raz dropped Brody back into his chair.

"Good choice."

He waited.

Jenny watched the killer, wondering what would happen. But nothing did. Maybe it was just plain water after all.

After a minute, Raz spoke. She was sure he had, as his mouth moved, the gold tooth bobbing up and down to the rhythm of the words. But whatever he said wasn't clear. She could hear his words, but couldn't process them.

Brody was sitting, naked. His penis hung limply between his legs. She decided it was worth a joke and said with a giggle, "Normally you'd be pleased to see me." But the words that left her mouth sounded blurred and incoherent. She screwed up her eyes, searching Brody's face to see if he'd got the joke, but it was hard to focus. He looked sad and angry. She hadn't meant to upset him. God, men were so sensitive about their penises.

She felt horny and realised with surprise that she was already naked. She lay back on the bed and, as seductively as she could, threw off the sheets and told Brody to come over and join her. But there were two Brodys. The naked one and another one pumped up like a balloon and dressed in black. She was sure there should only be one of him.

Before either version of him made it over, she drifted off, the empty glass falling out of her hands and smashing on the bedroom floor.

The killer let go and Brody slumped down into his chair. He checked his neck with his hands. It felt wet but not painful. He wiped his hands across his legs, leaving bloody streaks. The huge man moved across to the bed and placed his knife against Jenny's mouth.

"Make any sudden move and I'll give her a permanent smile."

Brody stared forlornly at Jenny on the bed. She was completely naked. Her legs and arms were splayed freely in all directions. Sickeningly, the killer cast his eyes over Jenny as well, drinking in her beauty. He licked his lips. Disgusted, Brody scanned her chest for breathing. Her chest rose on cue.

"Who are you? You're obviously not Raz. Are you Saul?"

The man glanced at him with a confused expression, as if suddenly realising Brody was there. It was almost as if he'd drifted off somewhere else. Brody had an inkling that he was a few fuses short of a full circuit.

Although missing the massive sideburns, the huge man reminded Brody of a professional French wrestler from the Eighties known as André the Giant, whom Brody had first discovered in the movie *The Princess Bride*. He had the same hulking top-heavy build and bulbous face.

Brody had noticed the lack of Manchester twang and, although accents could be faked, it was much harder to disguise your voice. Brody felt certain that the voice on the phone and André the Giant, as Brody had decided to think of him, were two different people. But if André wasn't Raz, who was he? Which then automatically led to, who the hell was Raz? And which of them was Saul?

"Pick her up. We're all going downstairs."

Brody stood and pointed to the pile of clothes on the floor. "Can I at least put my jeans on?"

André considered for a second, cocking his head as he stared unashamedly at Brody's manhood. "Yes. But empty the pockets on the floor first."

Brody did as he was told, his wallet and some coins dropping out, and then climbed into his jeans. He reached for his T-shirt.

"That's enough. Now pick up the bitch."

Brody made his way around the bed to get a decent angle. The man-mountain stepped back but held out his knife menacingly. Brody wasn't about to take any chances, not with Jenny so unprotected. He took the opportunity to wrap the bed sheet around her body, causing her eyes to flicker open. He heaved her up and lifted her into a fireman's lift across his shoulder, her head dropped down behind him. She giggled like a little girl and smacked him on the bum.

"Downstairs."

Brody made his way to the stairs, pulling open the bedroom door. He could feel André a step or two behind. Halfway down his legs began to tire with the effort of carrying Jenny and he paused briefly. Just as he moved off, she grabbed hold of the bannister, the unexpected movement almost sending them tumbling down the stairs.

"Let go, Jen," he commanded gently.

"Oops!" She laughed, but followed his order.

It was only as he entered the coffee shop, minus the insistent beeping of the alarm code warning, that Brody realised he'd not set the alarm as per Stefan's instructions. When he and Jenny had drifted upstairs earlier he'd only had one thing on his mind.

He was really struggling with Jenny's weight now and looked around for somewhere to drop her. André propped open the door to upstairs, which allowed some light to cast across the large room.

"That couch, there," said André, still brandishing the knife.

Brody carefully placed Jenny onto the sofa, making sure she was still covered up. She curled her body up but her eyes remained open, watching vacantly. The giant removed his backpack and placed it on a nearby table.

"That chair. Put it there."

He had pointed to a sturdy wooden chair with arms. Brody lifted it to the position directly opposite the sofa.

"Sit."

Brody did as he was told. Beyond the sofa Brody could see the world outside. It was quiet. Even so, this was Upper Street, full of bars and restaurants. Surely someone would walk past and see what was going on, even in the dim light? There was a hole cut in the glass part of the door, which Brody deduced was how André had broken in. Maybe someone would notice that and conclude a burglary was underway and call the police.

At that moment a young couple did walk by, right outside,

arm in arm, chatting and laughing. But neither of them glanced inwards and, before he knew it, they had passed beyond the shop front.

He was about to holler after them, but André placed the knife against Jenny's throat. Brody kept his mouth shut. André reached into his pocket, pulled out a handkerchief, balled it up and threw it at Brody. Instinctively, he caught it.

"Put it in your mouth."

It dawned on Brody that André had prepared for this and now would be his last chance to talk his way out of this.

The words tumbled out. "Why are you doing this? We've done nothing wrong. We don't even know what the terrorist plot is, you have to believe me. That's why we were trying to contact Raz. To find out more. The police haven't got a clue what's going on. Please —"

Ignoring Brody's pleas, André the Giant simply applied a little more pressure to the knife he was holding against Jenny's throat.

Brody shook his head in despair and squashed the rolled up handkerchief into his mouth. Adrenalin was coursing through his body now.

"Hands on the chair arms."

Brody did as he was told. André reached into his backpack, pulled out some rope and walked over to Brody. He threw a piece of rope at Brody and ordered him to tie one of his wrists to the arm of the chair. Brody picked it up and slowly dropped the length over his wrist, taking one end and looping it through the other. His free hand shook from the adrenalin and he fumbled a few times but eventually he was able to pull a knot tight.

"Put your free hand back on the arm."

Brody did, his body beginning to convulse from the fear of what was to come. He'd not allowed himself to think about snakes until now, hoping that someone would interrupt. But as it became clearer it was really going to happen, he became paralysed by fear.

André the Giant kneeled down next to him and placed another length of rope into his teeth. Brody knew he would need both his hands to tie Brody's remaining free arm and so would need to put the knife down. Now was the time to do something. Just as he was about to lash out, André slammed his colossal hand down on Brody's free wrist and wrapped his fingers tightly around it and the wooden chair arm. Brody tried to yank his arm away, but the man had a vice-like grip. In quick succession, André placed the knife on the floor, took the rope from his mouth, looped it around Brody's arm and pulled it down, trapping Brody's wrist against the wooden arm. Only then did he release his grip and, with both hands, quickly finished tying the knot.

Brody screamed in fear and frustration, but the gag in his mouth turned it into a muffled, gurgled howl. André pulled out other pieces of rope and tied both of Brody's legs to the chair legs, wrapped a piece right around his middle and tied it to the base of the chair and then did the same to his chest with the chair's back. He even added another piece to the arm Brody had already tied to make sure it was tight.

Brody was completely immobilised. Tears escaped his eyes. Jenny had watched it all but she was in the full hold of the drug, completely unaware of what was happening.

Brody saw movement by the front door and his hopes raised instantly. André spotted Brody noticing something behind him and whirled around to see what it was.

Stefan had arrived back and was leaning against the side window while fumbling to place his key in the door. Couldn't he see the hole in the glass? But no, he carried on trying to locate the keyhole. Stefan laughed at his failure and then hushed himself for making too much noise. Was he drunk?

André the Giant flew in the direction of the front door, hurdling the sofa that Jenny lay on. Brody struggled with his bonds to no avail. He tried rocking the chair but couldn't get enough momentum to topple it over.

André ran around another table. Stefan finally pushed the key in and turned the lock.

Brody took a deep breath through his nose and blew out and at the same time, used his tongue to push against the handkerchief in his mouth. It was stuck against his upper front teeth.

André was two tables away. Stefan began pushing the door inwards and saw Brody in the centre of the room tied to the chair. His brows furrowed in confusion just as the killer reached him from the side.

"Mr Brody, what is —"

André grabbed him by the coat and yanked him inside. Stefan flew across a table and crashed onto some chairs.

Finally, the handkerchief spilled out and dropped on the floor beside Brody's foot. But it was too late. André had already got to Stefan and punched him in the jaw from the side, snapping Stefan's head back with a sickening crunch. Stefan slumped to the floor, his head bouncing off a table on the way down. He stayed there, out of Brody's sight.

Brody would have shouted but there was nothing he could do. Jenny had also heard the commotion and sat up, innocently looking over the back of the sofa, but if she understood what was going on, she gave no sign.

André stood above Stefan's still body and waited. Once satisfied the threat was dealt with, he checked outside for anyone else. Seeing no one, he came back in and closed the door behind him and headed towards Brody once more.

Brody had little freedom of movement but he managed to raise the front of his foot and cover the handkerchief. He made sure his mouth was closed.

"Now," said André the Giant, back in front of Brody, "where were we?" His smile was savage. "Ah yes, I know. It's time for taking up serpents."

Brody's eyes widened in abject fear.

CHAPTER 14

MULLINS CHECKED THE ROPES AND KNOTS HOLDING Brody. He was completely secure. The girl had sat up on the sofa, but was still tranquil in her drugged state. He told her to lie down. She followed his order. He realised she would follow any order and he considered what else he could ask her to do. Perhaps take off the sheet and expose her stunning body once more. Then he could tell her to play with herself and maybe she would do that too. Or he could unzip his flies and tell her to —

He pulled himself together.

He was here for one reason: to give Mr Brody his chance at redemption. He had to follow through with the plan. But maybe while Mullins waited for the venom to course through Mr Brody's body, he could play with the policewoman just a little. She wouldn't remember and most likely Brody wouldn't survive.

He resolved to think about that when it was time. Right now he had to go and collect the items he'd left behind the wheelie bins in the alley across the road. He hoped no one had opened the box or they'd have got a nasty surprise from the black mamba inside.

As Mullins made his way to the front door, he looked over at the man who'd nearly spoiled his plans. He was lying motionless on the floor, blood oozing from a head wound where he'd bounced off a table as he'd fallen. Mullins hoped he'd not killed him but it had been a much harder hook than he'd intended.

Sometimes he just didn't know his own strength.

He stepped out into the night air, careful to put the front door on the latch. Further up the road, he could see people milling around outside a kebab shop. In the other direction a pub was closing up, the final stragglers heading towards Angel Tube station, away from the coffee shop.

Comfortable that everything was going well, Mullins crossed the road. There was only the occasional car, so nothing to worry about. On the other side, he went straight into the alley. It seemed even darker now, but he could still make out the shape of the bins, using the light of his mobile phone to illuminate the way.

There, behind the bins, was the portable box containing the black mamba. It would have been too much to carry while breaking into the shop, especially if any passers-by had interrupted him.

From across the road came the shout of a male voice. It sounded something like, "Bombay poodle," which didn't really make a lot of sense. Mullins grabbed the box and made his way back to the road, but there was no one there. Strange. He shrugged and crossed over, careful not to cause any distress to the serpent in the box under his arm.

As he neared the shop, he heard the voice again, talking now, not shouting. He couldn't make out what was being said, but it was a full conversation. As he arrived at the door, he realised it had been Brody. Damn, he must have somehow spat the gag out. He wouldn't let that happen again. He shouldered the door open and burst into the coffee shop. Everything seemed just as he'd left it.

"Jen, he's back," said Brody. "Lie down, now. Go to sleep."

Mullins hurried over. Yes, there was the gag on the floor. The policewoman was lying down on the sofa. He must have been trying to get her to do something, but she was too far gone. Her eyes were still glazed from the effects of the drugs, staring into the middle distance. Perhaps he'd overdone it with the GHB in her glass of water? He had given her almost double the dose he'd given Gowda's wife a few days before. But she was a piggy policewoman so he'd needed to be extra careful. Now, instead of just being pliable and suggestible like Gowda's wife, she was almost comatose. He figured she'd come to by morning.

Mullins turned his attention back to Brody, who was eyeing the white plastic box warily.

"I see you've brought your pet black mamba to the party."

Mullins was shocked. How did he know what type of snake was inside? He checked over the box to make sure it wasn't halfway through escaping, but the lid was sealed tightly.

"Why are you doing this?" the bound man asked. His tone was reasonable, no shouting. It was almost like he didn't care anymore. "You know it's still murder, don't you? In a minute, you'll put that knife to Jenny's throat and threaten to kill her if I don't place my hand in the box with the snake. You do realise that's still inducement? Just because *you* don't physically force me, doesn't make it suicide on my part. You're still committing murder."

Mullins didn't know that. As far as it had been explained to him, it was exactly that: suicide. "But that's only if you die."

"Of course I'll die, you fool. The black mamba is one of the most lethal snakes in the world."

Mullins didn't appreciate his tone of voice. Why wasn't he scared? "But I will pray for the good Lord to lay his hands on you."

"Fat chance of that."

Mullins shrugged.

"You know what I think?" the captive persisted. "If you're trying to absolve yourself of the crime of killing me, I reckon that means you won't kill Jenny if I refuse to put my hand in the box."

Mullins squinted in confusion. Could he be right?

"And if you're not willing to commit murder, then all your threats with the knife are empty. You won't kill her. I'm calling your bluff."

Mullins cocked his head in thought. Brody did have a point and Mullins was surprised that he'd figured it out. But he had got the wrong end of the stick. Mullins grinned. "We'll see, won't we?"

Brody's expression dimmed as doubt crept in.

Mullins continued, ramming home his advantage. "You think I care about damnation? It's already far too late for me." He lifted the knife and ran his thumb down the blade. "I've broken the sixth commandment far too many times already. I'm beyond redemption, I know that. But I can help others."

"You're fucking twisted, you are. How does lethally poisoning people enable you to help others?"

For a second, Mullins considered the question. It really was the crux of the matter. But then it dawned on him what was going on. Brody was trying to distract him with conversation, trying to delay the inevitable. Instead of answering, he picked up the handkerchief from the floor, rolled it up into a ball and shoved it into Brody's mouth.

"Enough."

Brody screamed and roared, shaking as much as he could in the chair. Mullins saw the gag was being forced out again and he quickly reached into his backpack and pulled out some tape. A minute later, Brody's mouth was sealed shut and the groans and shouts had diminished in volume. The policewoman was watching brainlessly. The old man was slumped on the floor under a table.

Mullins picked up the white plastic box and smiled grimly at Brody.

Brody was out of options now. He'd tried his best but to no avail. Too little, too late. He knew now he was out of time. He was going to die.

Desperate, he tried throwing his weight in all directions. Maybe if he could make the chair fall over, it would break and he could get free of his bindings and attack André. Perhaps he could throw the box containing the snake back at him. If a black mamba could fell an elephant it could easily handle a man-mountain like André the Giant.

But the chair stood resolutely still no matter what he did.

André leaned forward and placed the point of the knife on

Brody's right wrist. Brody stopped throwing himself in case he caused André to slice open an artery. Instead, André flicked the blade around and ran the knife up Brody's arm and underneath the binds, slicing through the rope like butter.

Abruptly, Brody's arm was free. He waved it around to let the blood flow back through and then grimaced as pins and needles coursed through his fingers. André grabbed another chair and manoeuvred to Brody's right. He picked up the box and placed it on the chair, careful not to jolt it.

Brody eyed the box warily.

André stepped back and made his way behind the sofa that Jenny lay on. Her eyes were still glazed over and she hadn't recognised any threat. He leaned over, lifted her head by the chin revealing her vulnerable throat and placed the blade in front as he'd done before. He looked over at Brody, his eyes full of challenge…

"Take the lid off the box and place your hand inside."

Brody looked at the plastic box. The lid simply rested on top. He could easily flick it off with one hand.

"No!" The words were muffled by the gag in his mouth and the tape over his mouth.

"If you don't, I'll slice her throat wide open."

Brody considered the threat and decided to call his bluff. The idea of gambling with Jenny's life tore him apart, but if there was any truth in his earlier deduction, then André wouldn't directly kill either of them. Why else go to all the trouble of using a snake?

Brody shrugged.

Mullins laughed in disbelief. He considered Brody for a moment and said, "Are you sure?" To emphasise, he pressed the blade harder against Jenny's neck. Jenny didn't react.

Brody's eyes narrowed, weighing up the situation. After a moment, he shook his head, holding his ground.

Mullins took the knife away from Jenny's throat and released her chin. She sagged to the side and her head lolled on the arm of the sofa. Thank God for that. Brody released a long breath through his nose.

Mullins put down his knife on the nearby table and reached into his backpack. He pulled out an ominous-looking pair of tongs and, repeatedly opening and closing them, brandished them at Brody. "Plan B, then."

Brody wondered what was going on. Was he going to torture him with them? Or Jenny? But then Mullins reached over and used the tongs to lift the lid of the white box as if he didn't have a care in the world. Brody instinctively tried to shuffle away from the box, but couldn't move. From this angle, he couldn't see inside.

Mullins placed the lid down on the nearby table and stood over the box, studying the contents. A wide grin formed on his huge face and he reached in with the tongs. A flick of the wrist later, he held steady.

As he lifted his arm, he watched Brody, wanting to savour any reaction. As the tongs withdrew, the head of a dark snake appeared, and then its body, coiling underneath. It was much smaller than Brody expected, chocolate brown on top and ash-coloured underneath. The snake's body writhed. It was pissed off at being disturbed. Brody had frozen at the sight of it, but then the snake's forked tongue suddenly slid out and Brody reacted violently, throwing everything he had in the direction away from the snake. This time the heavy wooden chair began to topple. Just as he thought he was going to fall over, André the Giant placed a heavy foot on the bottom rail and countered the balance, forcing the chair to fall back in place.

Brody's face turned ashen as André brought the snake closer. Brody flicked his head back to create more distance. The tail of the snake brushed Brody's knee and he jerked in fear. André lifted the head of the snake to align with Brody's face. It was right in front of his eyes. The tongue flicked out again, almost touching Brody's nose. It had scented prey.

"Are you ready to pray with me?"

André smiled and prepared to loosen his grip on the tongs.

Mullins watched Brody's face snap from side to side as he tried to avoid the black mamba. He was shaking in his chair, but

Mullins kept one foot on the bottom rail to prevent him toppling over.

Should he simply release the snake, allowing it to fall onto Brody's lap? Or should he grab the snake behind the head with his own hand and lower it down to Brody's free arm where it would bite the bare flesh? Choices, choices. He settled for the first option. As long as he aimed properly, the snake wouldn't be harmed. That was the important thing.

Mullins began to release pressure on the tongs and —

A booming male voice shouted from behind Mullins. "This is the police! Drop the snake."

He whirled around in shock, expecting to see someone right behind him, but there was no one there. However, he'd released pressure on the handle and the snake escaped from the tongs, his momentum causing it to fly across the room in the direction of the helpless policewoman.

Almost in slow motion, it arced in the air, its body writhing, and landed with an audible slap on the policewoman's bare leg. Free from being manhandled, the snake coiled itself just above her knee and then reared its head up in a classic defensive display. The drugged woman stirred briefly at the sudden weight on her leg. She was in God's hands now.

Mullins scanned the room but couldn't see anyone else. The old man was still out cold on the floor. Brody was right behind him, still bound to the chair, his eyes bulging as he stared in horror at the serpent coiled on top of his defenceless girlfriend.

"Step away from Mr Taylor and DI Price," boomed the voice. "Police officers will enter the premises in just a moment. Lie face down on the floor. Do not resist."

The disembodied voice came from above the coffee counter. But there was no one there. And then Mullins saw it: a smartphone plugged upright into a docking station, connected to the cafe's speakers, which were located above the counter. On the phone's screen, an angry black face was staring outwards.

Mullins grabbed his knife.

"Put down the weapon and lie on the floor."

This time Mullins saw the man on the screen speaking. It was some kind of video call and, up until a moment ago, he'd been quietly watching and listening to everything.

"Police are about to enter the premises. Drop the weapon," ordered the voice.

Mullins looked over his shoulder at the exit, but couldn't see any movement. Maybe the police were still on their way. He made a beeline for the door.

Brody watched helpless as the snake hovered above Jenny, its tongue darting outwards.

"Backup is less than one minute away, Brody," said Da Silva as reassuringly as he could. But Da Silva didn't know about the damn snake.

He tried shouting at the phone, ordering Da Silva to hurry the hell up. But the gag wouldn't budge and it came out as a muffled shout. With his free hand, he clawed at the tape on his mouth. Eventually it came out and he ripped the gag out of his mouth.

He shouted at Da Silva, the words rushing out from his dry mouth. "The snake's about to bite Jenny. I can't get to it. Get someone in here now!"

On the screen, Da Silva's face came closer to the camera as if changing his angle would help him see more, but Jenny and the sofa were below the smartphone's viewpoint.

"We're coming as fast as we can. One more minute."

There was movement. The snake spotted a gap in the blanket covering Jenny's body and slithered inside. Brody watched its outline make its way up her body.

"Jenny!" Brody shouted at his girlfriend. She was oblivious to the threat, just lying there, half curled up. He raised his voice higher. "Don't move. Whatever you do, don't move. Please."

Dreamily, she looked in his direction, but without any focus.

Brody groaned in despair and then grabbed the table to his right, using it to pull himself off balance.

"What are you doing?" demanded Da Silva on the video call.

"There's no time, it's going to bite Jenny. I've got to try something."

Brody felt the chair lift and for a moment he hovered in mid-air.

From outside, he heard sirens in the distance. Damn, they were still too far away. From nearer by, he heard an engine start and accelerate away, the tinny sound of a motorbike.

The chair began to topple and Brody felt the hard wooden floor rushing towards him. He put out his right hand to break his fall, but still hit the floor with an almighty crash. His wrist and shoulder took most of the impact and he cried out in pain, but the momentum threw his head sideward and smashed his skull on the floor.

"Jesus." Da Silva again.

Brody felt the room spin and he fought to stay conscious. But the back of the chair had splintered in the crash and he realised that there was some movement. Frantically, he began pulling at the rope with his free hand. On the sofa, he could see the outline of the snake on her belly, still gliding upwards.

A crashing noise came from behind him and he heard the sound of bodies piling into the coffee shop.

"Police, don't move," someone shouted from behind as they ran to the centre of the room.

The black mamba sensed the new threat and began to rise up. The movement caused the blanket to slip away, revealing the snake lying on Jenny's naked stomach. Its tail was wrapped around the top of her left leg.

"Stop, you fools! Don't make any sudden movements."

But the bodies still piled forward, crashing through tables and chairs. Brody pulled the rope over his head and was then able to lean downwards and began grasping at the knots that held his legs in place.

He felt the presence of someone directly behind him and a shadow passed over his body. But so did the snake, which puffed out its throat in defence.

"Whoa," said the person next to Brody. It was an armed police response officer and he had spotted the snake on the half-naked Jenny and halted in his tracks.

"Stop it!" pleaded Brody, but the man didn't move, rooted to the spot.

And at that moment, Jenny reached up an arm and waved dreamily at the armed officers. “Hi guys.”

“No!” Brody shouted.

Helplessly, he watched the snake react instinctively to the movement of Jenny’s arm. Its head flew downwards and bit four or five times in rapid succession across the inside of her wrist. Jenny whipped back her arm at the sudden pain, but it was far too late.

“Ow!” she said, with annoyance.

The threat eliminated, the snake slid off the chair to the floor and slithered under the sofa.

Brody shook his head in despair, still tearing at the ropes. Tears formed around his eyes as his brain processed what had just happened.

Jenny was going to die.

CHAPTER 15

CHAOS REIGNED FOR THE NEXT HOUR. BRODY half watched, half participated from within a trance-like blur.

The armed response team secured the coffee shop, but were scuppered by having no idea how to handle the presence of the deadly wild animal. One officer, using his initiative, found a broom and used it to brush the snake away from everyone, cajoling it into the open.

Meanwhile, another officer helped Brody untie the ropes that bound him. Once free he threw his arms around Jenny, covered her body and pulled her close, burying his head in her neck and whispering sorry, over and over.

Jenny began to scratch her arm, where the bite marks had already swollen up. Soon she was clawing at random points all over her body. The venom was spreading rapidly. Brody whirled around, anger frothing from his mouth, and demanded an ambulance. There were at least six armed police officers in the room and one of them placed the radio to his mouth and demanded an update on the whereabouts of the paramedics. After a few minutes, Jenny began to sweat profusely, first on her forehead, then under her nose and then all over. Where the hell was that ambulance?

One officer grabbed the white plastic box and, working in tandem with the one with the broom, finally managed to drop it on top of the snake. The snake's tail protruded and the other officer pushed it inside with the broom head. Once done, the other officer jumped on the box and held it in place. After a minute, his colleague brought over a heavy-looking side table and placed it on top, upside down. The snake was trapped. The two officers high-fived each other.

Finally, flashing blue lights appeared outside. The ambulance had arrived and paramedics rushed in to treat Jenny and Stefan. Brody had to be prised off his girlfriend and he only released her when he saw DC Fiona Jones walk in. He looked up at her and shrugged helplessly, tears still falling.

"I couldn't stop it. I couldn't stop it."

Softly, she placed an arm on his shoulder. Together they watched the paramedics take charge.

They demanded to know what had happened and Brody explained that she'd been first drugged with GHB and then bitten by a black mamba, pointing at the swollen bite marks on her arms. The look of confusion that passed between the two paramedics didn't help and Brody shouted at them. "She's been poisoned by the most deadly snake in the world! Please, be quick." At that moment, Jenny arched herself back and moaned. She was feeling the pain of the venom despite the GHB.

The paramedics lifted her onto a stretcher and wheeled her away. Stefan, who was still unconscious but breathing, wasn't far behind.

Brody crumpled in a heap on the floor.

It was only as the ambulance sped off that it occurred to him that he should have gone with her.

"Did you catch him?" boomed a voice. It was Da Silva through the speakers.

Fiona, who was trying to comfort Brody, looked up at Da Silva's face on the phone. "No, sir. He got away."

"Damn," said Da Silva. "I thought we had him."

Brody lifted himself up, stood in front of the phone and began railing at the DCI, his frustration gushing out. "Why couldn't you have got here quicker? You saw what was going on, for fuck's sake. I can't believe how long it took. Christ, we're only round the fucking corner. What the fuck is it with you and her anyway?"

Da Silva's face retreated at the onslaught and he spluttered, "There's no need for that —"

Brody lifted his phone from the dock and disconnected the call.

He felt sick. His initiative with the phone had saved his life but the impromptu plan had backfired, costing Jenny hers. Earlier, when André the Giant had left the shop to go get the snake, Brody had spat out the gag and tried talking to Jenny, trying to get her to do something. Anything. But the GHB had dulled her senses completely and she barely acknowledged him, just lifting her head in the direction of his voice. Desperate, Brody had scanned the room and then spotted his phone still sitting in the docking station from earlier that evening when they had used it to play music.

Back when life had been normal.

Immediately, he had shouted at the phone, "Okay Google," and to his delight, it recognised his voice first time. It beeped and waited obediently for his vocal command. He thought through his options and then remembered that he'd scanned in Da Silva's business card earlier that day. He told the smartphone to call Da Silva's mobile number. The DCI answered groggily, having been awoken from his sleep. Rapidly, Brody explained their dire situation. Da Silva put him on hold briefly while he ordered a police response team to the location. Brody knew they wouldn't be quick enough and came up with a second plan.

Recalling that Da Silva had a modern android phone, he told Da Silva that he would call him back straight away using the Google Hangouts video app, which was installed by default on new phones like his. Da Silva tried to explain that he didn't know how to use it, but Brody told him to shut up and hang up. He did and Brody gave the voice instruction to his phone. Once the video call was connected to a surprised Da Silva, who marvelled at the technology in his hand, Brody told him to mute the line his end and watch. He was to only interrupt if he could see that the giant man was about to release the snake. Although nowhere near ideal, it was the best plan he'd been able to concoct at such short notice.

Unfortunately, Da Silva's timing had been a moment too late. Da Silva's shout of, "This is the police! Drop the snake," had amplified through the speakers, surprising André and caused him to wheel around instead of forcing the poisonous fangs to bite Brody on his free arm. However, André had lightened his grip on the pincers and the snake had been flung in Jenny's direction due to his rapid rotating motion.

Brody replayed the scene over and over in his mind, each time finding different ways to have saved Jenny. The most obvious was that he should have just let André kill him with the snake instead. At least then the armed response team would have arrived and captured the huge man. And Jenny would still be alive.

Brody collapsed in a heap on the sofa.

Ralph Mullins stumbled into the basement and almost fell down the steps. He caught himself at the bottom, but knocked over an empty Coke bottle he'd left on a shelf two weeks before. The bottle smashed on the floor, the noise ricocheting around the underground room. Mullins listened, but heard no stirring from above.

He bent over, resting his hands on his knees, taking massive breaths.

Eventually, he calmed down and took stock of his surroundings.

The snakes in the racks of cages all around took no notice. However, the cage in the centre on the left bank stood out accusingly. It was empty, its inhabitant left behind in the coffee shop in Islington, like a soldier caught behind enemy lines. He hoped that the black mamba hadn't been hurt. The last sight he'd had of it was when it landed on the drugged up policewoman. He supposed if that resulted in one less copper in the world, then it hadn't been such a terrible outcome.

He would have preferred to see the mamba sink its fangs into Mr Brody's arm, though. Although Mullins would have prayed hard, he was pretty confident that no one would have heard and

Mr Brody would have died. He was sure that his instant dislike of the cocky man would have got in the way of the pure thoughts he needed to attract the attention of Him upstairs.

Mullins couldn't understand how the police had come flying out of nowhere. And there was that man's face on the phone, shouting at him through the shop speakers. Maybe it was some kind of advanced CCTV system where operators monitoring the shop called in when they spotted movement. Although why they would do a video call was beyond him. And anyway, he'd checked for video cameras when he'd been in the coffee shop earlier and was convinced there were none. What had happened made no sense.

Mullins had hurtled out of the shop and made it into the pedestrian alley across the road just as the first patrol cars arrived, screeching to a stop outside the café. He jumped on his scooter, careful to wear his black helmet so as not to attract attention and to disguise his face, and made his way out the back, heading up the pedestrianised street where the police cars couldn't follow had they spotted him. Which they hadn't.

Half an hour later he had pulled up outside. He probably should have gone straight home but he felt bad about screwing up.

Mullins heard someone moving about upstairs. The door above opened, letting light stream down. Mullins saw slippered feet at the top of the stairs. They began to take steps down, revealing red tartan pyjamas and a grey sweater. Eventually, Saul stood in front of Mullins, looking up at him. His face was like thunder.

"What are you doing back here?"

"I … I …"

Saul glanced at the open cage and then scanned the room for the white plastic container used to transport the snakes.

"Ralph, where's my black mamba?"

"I had to leave it behind. The police arrived out of nowhere. I had to run. I'm so sorry."

Saul's lips thinned. "Before or after you administered God's test?"

Mullins shuffled from one foot to the other. "Before. But he said that me forcing him to put his hand in the box was inducement and that made me a murderer. I don't want to be a murderer again, Saul. I'm not, am I?"

Saul's face softened. He placed his hands on each of Mullins' shoulders, reaching up. "No, of course not. You wouldn't take the word of a stranger over the Word of the Lord would you?" His eyes bored into Mullins' soul.

Mullins was doubtful and he knew it showed.

"Remember Jesus' last words on earth, Ralph. Mark, Chapter 16, Verse 18." Saul changed his voice as he quoted, holding Mullins' frightened stare. "'In my name shall they cast out devils; they shall speak with new tongues; they shall take up serpents; and if they drink any deadly thing, it shall not hurt them; they shall lay hands on the sick, and they shall recover.'"

Mullins listened intently. Saul had explained it to him many times before. As always, he was right. Of course he was not a murderer again.

"Anyway, God has seen fit to give you one more chance to prove yourself to Him."

"He has?" Mullins smiled in relief. Maybe he could make God notice him after all. And then he said sadly, "But I lost the mamba."

Saul withdrew his hands and pointed all around. "Ask and it will be given to you; seek, and ye shall find."

Mullins knew that one and finished the proverb. "Knock, and it shall be opened up to you."

"Exactly, Ralph. Come back in the morning and choose a new serpent to carry out God's work."

"What's his name? Who does God want me to test this time?"

"The only man God is testing is you, Ralph."

That was true, Saul had told him that before. He should have remembered that.

Saul continued. "However, this test is the biggest yet and I'm sure God will hear your prayers this time."

"Really?"

"Because this time it's not a man you will pray for."

That was different. Everyone before this had been male. Well, maybe except for the policewoman earlier. But that couldn't count because he hadn't intended to kill her.

"A woman? Why?"

"God has chosen. Who are we to question Him?"

That was true.

"It will be your biggest test yet."

"I am ready, Saul."

"When the time comes tomorrow, I will also pray with you."

"Really? That would be a great help."

Saul smiled and indicated the door at the top of the steps. Mullins took the hint. It was late anyway and he needed to get some sleep. Halfway up the steps, he turned around and asked, "What is the woman called?"

"Her name is Klara Ivanov. She flies in from Russia tomorrow."

As it was her last night in Moscow, Klara treated herself to the most expensive vodka in the hotel bar, which, according to the barman, was called Stolichnaya Elit. He recommended she sip it and savour the taste.

It hadn't taken long to organise her exit from Russia. After reserving a place on the Aeroflot flight to Heathrow the following morning, she had emailed the agency in London to accept the assignment with the electricity supply company and told them she was able to fly in the next day. They replied immediately, delighted to have someone with her rare experience on the project, promising to pay her travel expenses. She confirmed her flights and, within an hour, they'd arranged for transportation to meet her at Heathrow and had booked her a room in the Landmark Hotel in London. She Googled it and was delighted to see that it was a luxury five-star hotel that even served the British classic of 'Afternoon Tea'. They would meet for breakfast in the hotel on Friday morning, brief her on the project and make further arrangements from there.

She spent the afternoon packing her suitcase. But as most of her clothes stank of smoke, she took them to the local launderette. While she waited for the tumble dryer to complete its long cycle, Klara checked her email, worried that Zakharin had chased her further. Or maybe he'd play it cool and just expect her to turn up on Friday morning? Well, wasn't he in for a surprise? She just hoped that her father's assessment of the level of protection he could obtain from his krisha was accurate and would be enough of a defence against Vorovskoy Mir. She couldn't bear it if her parents were hurt again because of her.

There had been no email from Zakharin, but there was a strange one from someone called James Butler and written in English. She vaguely recognised his name. She read the email:

Gowda and I have now talked. This is serious: thousands of people will die very soon because of what we've done. But we can't stop Saul without your help. Please reply to this email or respond in the secure chatroom. (Same link as below.) Or you can contact me on the following number: +44 7769 …

Klara recalled the first email from the same guy a couple of weeks before. Butler had said that he and the three people he'd written to had worked independently on different elements of a project and had unwittingly got caught up in some kind of terrorist plot. She remembered the project. She'd worked on it about a year ago. It had been for an American political activist and involved assembler level reprogramming of the firmware contained in a branded vending machine. She was only given the firmware source code, not the actual device, and so she did it blind. They had wanted to hardcode some settings to force the machine to fire off a specific subroutine at a certain time, which she guessed would cause the vending machine to spew out all its contents. She remembered thinking it was a pointless prank, but hacktivists were always coming up with strange subversive protests. Anyway, the money had been good and the job easy. Well, easy for her. She'd even got paid twice when they asked her a few weeks later to reprogram the hardcoded dates.

But she couldn't see how that could have anything to do with a terrorist plot and so she'd deleted the first email, thinking it was some kind of weird English prank. But here was the same guy again. Insistent.

She thought for a moment, watching the tumble dryer turn her clothes, and decided to click on the link.

She was brought to a private chatroom. She could see that Butler and Gowda, one of the other recipients of the email, had been chatting on and off over the last few weeks. And then there was a further conversation from earlier that day between Raz, the third person emailed, and Butler. It was a strange conversation. First of all they discussed a police presence at King's Cross and then moved on to the thousands of people that were going to die very soon but without anyone knowing when or how. Then, shockingly, the conversation switched to an admission that Butler and Gowda had been recently killed and that one of Butler's friends had been masquerading in the chatroom as Butler. It finished with Raz deciding to not get involved.

Klara thought it through. She still couldn't see how what she had done could cause the deaths of thousands of people. But, if what this person pretending to be Butler said had any truth in it, then whatever it was would happen in two days' time. She knew that because she was the one who had hardcoded the date and time into the firmware of the device. But they didn't know that. And they would need to know if they wanted to stop whatever was going on.

She decided to reply.

Klara: I'm not sure I can help, but if I can I will. I find it impossible to believe that what I've done could lead to people dying. But in case it's true, I do know when it will happen.

Klara pressed enter. She waited for a minute, to see if the person pretending to be this Butler was online and would respond. Nothing happened. She decided to drop in the information anyway.

Klara: Friday, 5th June at 12:36 p.m., London Time. In two days' time.

She waited a minute more, but there was no response. She decided she'd done all she could and closed her laptop. Once her clothes had dried, she packed them in her suitcase.

Klara returned to the hospital and double-checked that both her parents were still serious about moving to Italy. Despite the fact that their family home and livelihood had been destroyed and her father was covered in burns, the Ivanov family bristled with nervous excitement. Their life had been turned upside down and the future was uncertain. But at least it would be far away from Russian corruption.

She did her best not to hurt her father as she tearfully hugged him goodbye. Her mother was being kept one more night in the hospital and would then temporarily move in with her cousin, a few streets away from the shop. Klara walked her back to her ward bed and tucked her in. She waited for her to drift off to sleep and then kissed her on the forehead goodbye.

Klara headed for the airport and rented a room in a nearby hotel. The plane to London was at 10:05 the following morning.

Now sitting in the hotel bar, she studied the expensive vodka in front of her. She made a silent toast to her parents and knocked it back in one, just as her father had taught her.

Brody paced the hospital corridor.

He had never felt so helpless in his life. What was going on?

Fiona Jones sat calmly in a chair opposite the coffee vending machine. Brody had watched her drink three cups of rancid-looking hot chocolate already. She was on her phone talking with someone, telling them she was fine, despite it now being past three in the morning.

"I'll be home in a couple of hours," she said. "No, everything is fine." Looking past Brody, she spotted someone coming down the corridor and said, "Look, I've got to go."

She ended the call and Brody wheeled around at the sound of squeaking steps on the linoleum floor. It was one of the emergency doctors still in scrubs. Fiona stood and joined him by his side.

"Are you here for Mr Di Caprio?" the doctor asked.

Brody was thoroughly confused. Why would they bring up the Hollywood movie star? Fiona, sensing his confusion, helped him out by confirming, "Stefan Di Caprio?"

Brody blinked. He'd never heard Stefan's surname before. The rental contracts were in the name of an agency and so there'd never been an opportunity to learn it. It made him realise how little he really knew about his landlord and friend, and he was suddenly disgusted with himself.

"How is he, doctor?"

"He's awake but has quite severe concussion. Nothing's broken, which is good. We're going to keep him in overnight for observation." The doctor leaned in conspiratorially. "It probably helped that he'd had quite a lot to drink."

"Well, that's great news." Brody was relieved.

"You can see him if you like."

"Thanks. I will."

The doctor headed off.

Brody looked at the closed doors they were waiting outside and then up the corridor in the direction the doctor had come from. Fiona spotted Brody's torn expression and said, "You go see Stefan. If I hear anything here, I'll come get you straight away."

"Thanks. I'll be quick."

A minute later Brody was by Stefan's hospital bed. He had bandages wrapped around his head and a massive bruise had formed across his cheekbone, the swelling almost forcing his right eye shut. He was connected to a bunch of monitors and an intravenous drip fed a saltwater solution into his vein.

"Ah, Mr Brody," he said weakly.

"Hi Stefan. Can I get you anything?"

Stefan looked confused.

Brody carried on theatrically. "Let me guess. It's too late for espresso. Too early for cappuccino. And the tea in the machines here is dreadful." Stefan grinned appreciatively at Brody's initiative in swapping their normal roles. "I know, let's get you a glass of water."

Brody poured from the jug on the bedside table and lifted the plastic cup to Stefan's lips. He sipped a little. Brody was pleased to have helped him, especially after what he'd put him through.

"Are you okay, Stefan?"

"Yes, Mr Brody. I'll be back on my feet tomorrow, just you wait and see."

"I'm sure you will."

Stefan's face clouded over. "Is Bruno's okay?"

"Yes, don't you worry. Everything is fine with the shop. The police are there right now but they'll be gone by morning. Lorenzo will open up. I'll get the glass in the door fixed first thing. Everything will be back to normal."

As Brody spoke, Stefan's eyes closed and he slowly drifted off.

"I'm so sorry, Stefan. I really am."

But Stefan hadn't heard. He was fast asleep.

Brody headed back to Fiona, who was at the vending machine again. But she was no longer alone. DCI Raul Da Silva stood there.

"Any news?" Brody asked.

Fiona shook her head and handed Da Silva a coffee. She then ordered herself another hot chocolate.

"What are they doing?"

"They're doing their job, I'm sure," said Da Silva.

Brody began pacing up and down.

"Why was DI Price in the coffee shop with you so late at night?" asked Da Silva.

Brody looked at him disbelievingly. Wasn't he supposed to be a detective?

Fiona answered, "Jenny was seeing Mr Taylor in a personal capacity, guv."

To Da Silva's credit, he looked down, suddenly unable to meet Brody's eyes. "Ah, I'm sorry. I didn't realise."

Just then, the doors opened and the doctor appeared. Brody, Fiona and Da Silva turned in unison to face her. Brody had seen her once earlier, but there had been no news then.

"Is there any news, Dr Rama?" asked Fiona.

The woman looked from one to the other. It was impossible

to tell anything from her expression. "We believe we finally have her stable."

Brody nearly collapsed in relief. He felt Fiona grip his arm tightly.

"Thank God," said Da Silva.

"If it had been yesterday, we would have lost her. The black mamba antivenom arrived this morning, almost like it was preordained."

"That was me," said Da Silva, as though admitting a secret. "We've had two black mamba deaths already in London in the last week so I made some calls to ensure all the local hospitals obtained some stock proactively. I had no idea it would be to save one of my own officers."

Brody and Fiona turned to Da Silva in utter disbelief. Brody was suddenly filled with gratitude for the man's initiative and immediately forgave him everything he'd ever done against Jenny.

"Well," continued Dr Rama, "that's certainly a great example of police and medical professions working in tandem." She went on to explain that she'd administered the first slow push of antivenom the minute Jenny had arrived. It had no effect. Ten minutes later they tried a second vial, but still nothing. Despite the need to move quickly, they had to ensure that Jenny didn't drop into an anaphylactic allergic reaction. Ten minutes after the third dosage of antivenom, she began to show the first positive responses. They allowed the fourth vial to be administered by drip and she had already come to, although was quite weak. Which was a double win as they'd only received four vials of antivenom. It was prohibitively expensive stuff.

"Strange as it may sound, but the GHB she'd taken probably helped as well," the doctor continued. "Her body was in such a calm state, meaning her heart rate was low, and so the venom didn't spread as fast as it normally would."

"How long until she makes a full recovery?" asked Fiona.

"She may be weak now, but by morning, I reckon she'll be starving. By mid-afternoon, she'll be up and about, frustrated with us for keeping her in for observation."

"Really? That's amazing," said Da Silva, his relief evident as well.

"Yes. Neurotoxic venoms are incredibly fast-acting and attack the nervous system and brain. Most people die because they don't get antivenom quick enough. But, if they do, there's little in the way of residual effect. Cytotoxic venoms on the other hand …"

Brody zoned out of her explanation, dumbstruck. Jenny was fine. It was truly amazing. When he'd seen the snake rise up from under her sheet and then lunge at her arm, biting multiple times, he truly thought she would die. He'd never have forgiven himself. If she had —

"You coming, Brody?"

It was Fiona, who was halfway through the double doors with Da Silva and Dr Rama.

"Uh, yes."

Jenny was completely and utterly confused.

Her body felt groggy and weak. She attempted to lift her head, but the room began to spin. She rested it back on the pillow and waited for the room to stop.

Why did she have such a hangover? And, hold on a second, why was she in a hospital? She had IV drips stuck in her wrists and there were electronic monitors bleeping reassuringly next to her.

The last thing she remembered was arguing with Brody over the damn *Call of Duty* set-up in his flat above the coffee shop. No, wasn't there more after that? They'd gone downstairs and made coffee on the humongous machine. Hold on, had they actually slow danced in the coffee shop? No, that can't be right. She must have dreamt that. But then they'd made love, and she felt sure that was memory, not fantasy.

But that was it. Wasn't it?

How strange.

She felt like there was more, in fact was convinced there must be, based on the evidence of her lying in hospital. But she was completely blank.

She felt a shiver go down her spine. Something wasn't right.

Then, to add to the confusion, the doors in the room she was in opened and in walked the doctor who'd talked to her a few minutes earlier, accompanied by Fiona, Da Silva and, trailing behind, Brody. They were all smiles, although Brody looked upset. He never gave away his feelings, she knew that. His ability to mask his emotions was legendary, so he must be really shook up about something.

She wasn't sure she wanted to know.

An hour later, two nurses told Da Silva, Fiona and Brody they had to go. She was to be wheeled down to a standard ward and they couldn't follow, not at this time of night.

Between them, they had filled in the blanks for her. She had been horrified, unable to accept or believe what had happened. She couldn't even recall what the intruder looked like, despite Brody telling her she had talked to him prior to taking the GHB. All she had in her mind was an impression of him being very large.

Out of the whole crazy story, she particularly hated the idea that she'd drunk the water knowing it had GHB in it. Why would she knowingly disable herself and leave them both to the mercy of the killer, especially when she knew what would have happened next? But she'd seen the plaster on Brody's neck and put two and two together.

He'd certainly thought on his feet when calling Da Silva on the phone by using remote voice commands. She remembered despairing at him the other day when he showed off the capability, dismissing it as just another geek toy.

But the snake had poisoned her nonetheless. She was glad not to have any recollection of that event. It explained why she was in hospital and why Brody looked so shaken. Apparently, Da Silva was to be thanked for making sure local hospitals had black mamba antivenom on hand. She wasn't sure she wanted to be beholden to him of all people, but she guessed it was better than the alternative.

But, despite it all, they hadn't caught the killer. Although they had captured the deadly snake. She hoped it was the only one he had.

They were none the wiser as to who he was, why he did what he did, or what the terrorist attack was. The only new information seemed to be that he repeatedly used Christian-style religious phrases as justifications for his actions. Surely religion had nothing to do with a terrorist plot? Yet, as she thought about it, she realised how naive she was being. So many terrorist attacks of recent times were carried out in the name of Islam. That didn't mean that other religions like Christianity couldn't also spark extreme violence. She resolved not to let her own familiarity with Christianity cloud her judgement.

Some time later, Jenny drifted off into a fitful sleep and dreamt of snakes slithering all over her naked form. At times, nurses checking in on her noticed that she kept pushing her bedclothes away as if trying to remove something from her body.

THURSDAY

CHAPTER 16

THE ALARM WENT OFF AND BRODY ALMOST threw it across the room in frustration. He'd been so tired last night he'd neglected to cancel it, forgetting it was set to the same time as the day before, when he'd arranged to meet Jenny for breakfast in Caravan. But even then, Leroy had woken him ahead of the alarm, screaming at finding the bass guitarist in bed with him. It was only twenty-four hours ago but seemed a lifetime away.

Mournfully, Brody reflected how he had nearly been killed last night. And then, when he'd managed to distract the killer, it had almost led to Jenny's death. Either way, still a lifetime away.

Brody switched off the insistent alarm and begrudgingly shook himself awake. He stomped into the shower and set it as cold as he could bear. A few minutes underneath the powerful jet and the enormity of what had happened yesterday hit him hard. He crouched in the corner of the shower basin, grateful that his tears were hidden within the rivulets of cold water gushing down over his face.

Violence was not something he knew how to handle. That was Jenny's domain. She was trained for it and never backed away from a conflict. He was little more than a keyboard jockey. In the virtual world, violence was limited to how well you slung words or code about; nothing that could hurt you physically. Thanks to his relationship with Jenny, Brody was living far more of his life in the real world rather than the virtual one these days. But this exposure was starting to take its toll on him emotionally. He wondered if he could keep up with the rollercoaster that was real life?

Take last night. He and Jenny had quarrelled, made up, made love and nearly been killed. Even now, she was recovering in hospital having being poisoned by one of the world's deadliest snakes. Then there was Stefan. He was in the same place too, thanks to Brody imprudently provoking a serial killer. Jenny had warned him about it as well. He just hadn't considered the consequences of his actions, too busy showing off and going for glory. It had been the crux of Jenny's argument with him last night and he now understood how right she was. If he was going to make it in the real world he needed to play by its rules, not his own.

And with that undertaking made, Brody pulled himself together, finished his shower, dressed and headed into the kitchen where he breakfasted on toast with marmalade and a cappuccino from his own machine. Not as good as Stefan's, but acceptable.

He heard the door open downstairs. Lorenzo had arrived. Brody had texted him last night, asking him to come in again. Even though it had been in the middle of the night, Lorenzo had phoned back straight away, demanding to know what was wrong. Brody had explained that Stefan had been attacked in the shop, but not why. He agreed to come in first thing and help put everything back together, open up and hold the fort.

The crime scene team had left about 4:00 a.m., their evidence bags full. A specialist had been called in to capture the snake. He had brought a wire funnel trap, placing a live mouse inside. The first thing the black mamba saw when the white box was lifted off was potential prey. Within seconds, it had slithered into the trap and was captured.

Brody finished his coffee and decided to go downstairs to give Lorenzo a hand. But before leaving his flat, he reverted to habit and checked for messages on his tablet.

Brody sat down, and Lorenzo was forgotten in seconds. There was a response to his message from yesterday, when he posed as

Butler. It was from Klara, the fourth person in the conspiracy. She claimed to know when the attack was going to happen. Brody couldn't believe what he read: it was tomorrow afternoon.

He looked at his watch. It was now 8:00 a.m. If she was right, there were just over thirty hours to go. But he had no idea where the attack would take place.

Or how.

Or by whom.

Brody's head fell into his hands.

He had to think.

At every milestone through Domodedovo Airport Klara was convinced she would be stopped. At check-in, the grumpy passenger service assistant took ages to review her passport, print her ticket and tag her two cases. At security, her hand luggage containing her laptop was taken to one side and swiped for explosives and drugs. Just as she thought she was going to be dragged into a room, the customs officer handed everything back with a smile. At passport control, the step she had been most frightened of, the uniformed officer demanded to know why she was visiting London when she had an Italian passport. Breathlessly, she said, "Business". It had been enough and he had stamped the passport, allowing her to pass. Finally, as the passengers were called for boarding, the computer seemed to take longer to approve her boarding pass than anyone else's.

At long last she was on the plane.

Even now, she looked around, expecting to see Zakharin across the aisle, laughing imperiously at her foolhardy attempt to escape the clutches of Vorovskoy Mir. But it was an old granny, a *babushka*, who gave her a toothless smile.

Klara picked up her phone and texted her mother that she was on the plane and would text her again in four hours' time when she landed. Just as she was about to dutifully put the phone into flight mode, she noticed she had another message. Hesitantly, in case it was Zakharin having the last laugh, she clicked on it.

She was relieved. It was only a response to her message in the chatroom yesterday. But it wasn't from Butler or Raz, the two people who had been active in the chatroom previously. Instead, it was from someone calling himself Fingal.

Fingal: Thanks for the information. That doesn't leave us much time to stop it. Can we talk?

Klara paused, considering. She decided to reply.

Klara: No, not right now. Anyway, who are you?
Fingal: I'm Butler's friend, the one who tried to get Raz to help. But Raz chose not to. I'm assisting the Met Police. Trying to stop this thing from happening.

The stewardess was walking up the aisle. Klara noticed that others were being told to turn off their electronic devices. Her fingers flew across the keyboard.

Klara: How do I know I can trust you? You already said Butler and Gowda are dead.
Fingal: Unfortunately, they are. I was nearly killed myself last night, but I survived. Here's a link to a news story to prove what I'm saying is true.

Klara clicked on the link. While it loaded she glanced up. The stewardess was only five rows away.

She was taken to an English newspaper website. The story was about a snake attack in a coffee shop in London. She skimmed it quickly. No one had been killed, although two victims were now recovering in hospital: Stefan di Caprio, the owner of the shop, and an unnamed Metropolitan Police detective injured in the line of duty. A third witness, also not named, had survived without injury. The attack was believed to be linked to the prior murders of James Butler and Rajesh Gowda. The snake, a deadly black mamba, had been caught. Police were still hunting for the perpetrator.

Fingal: My name is Brody Taylor. I was the third person in the shop. Listen, Klara, we need to share what we know to put an end to this.

Klara: You are in London?

Fingal: Yes.

Klara: This is strange. I am on way to London now. Maybe I will contact you this afternoon.

"Please turn your device off, Madam."

Klara glanced up. The stewardess was waiting impatiently.

"Just one second, please."

Fingal: But that's too late. We need to talk now.

Klara: No choice. Stewardess is telling me I have to put phone in flight mode. I must leave.

"Please Madam. You have to turn it off now."

Klara typed one more word and, with an over-elaborate show, turned the phone off.

Klara: Bye.

Within a few minutes, the plane was taxiing towards the runway.

She thought about the strange snake story and this person called Fingal. Why should she expose herself to risk when she didn't need to? She was travelling to London to do a job and escape the clutches of Vorovskoy Mir. And, once her parents recovered and sold up, they would all meet in Italy, free from Russian corruption. She wasn't going to do anything to jeopardise that.

She realised this Fingal person, or Brody Taylor as he'd christened himself, could be just about anyone. He could even be someone from Vorovskoy Mir trying to entrap her and then he'd report back to Contag10n straight away. They would stop the plane.

But the plane accelerated up the runway unheeded and the wheels left the Russian tarmac below. Klara let out a deep breath.

Then she realised that she told him she was on the way to

London. Damn, that was stupid. But at least he didn't know where she was flying into London from.

She vowed to take no more risks and would ignore any further contact with Fingal. Or Brody Taylor. Or whatever his name was.

Recalling that Klara's email address originated from Russia, a quick Google told Brody that Klara was on the morning Aeroflot service, departing Moscow at 10:05 local time and landing in Heathrow at 12:05 London time. That was four hours from now. Four out of the thirty hours left to stop whatever atrocity was about to take place.

He needed to meet her off the plane. But he didn't know her full name or what she looked like. And after the fiasco with Raz, he had no intention of telling Jenny or her colleagues. He would do this his way.

Brody made a call. It was answered immediately.

Victor Gibb skipped any pleasantries. "I knew you couldn't be this cool, Brody. Even you had to pick the phone up sooner or later to check how your job application was progressing."

It took Brody a moment to work out what Gibb was talking about. Of course, he was referring to Brody's application to join GCHQ.

"Sorry Doc, I'm not phoning about that."

"You're not?" He sounded disappointed.

"I need your help. Got an urgent situation going down here and you can assist."

"What have you got yourself involved in this time, Brody? Not more Vorovskoy Mir shenanigans?"

"No … Yes … Maybe. Listen, Doc, I need the full name and passport picture of a woman who just took off on Aeroflot flight 2578 from Moscow and is on her way to Heathrow right now."

"Whoa, Brody. I can't just give you that kind of information."

"You have to, Doc. There's an imminent terrorist attack and she's key to cracking it open."

"What the fuck!" Gibb's voice rose at least two octaves. He recovered quickly and spoke more deeply. "Look. If there was an attack about to happen, don't you think we'd know about it?"

"Normally, yes. But this one seems low key. Even so, there's thousands of lives at stake."

"When's it supposed to happen?"

"Tomorrow at 12:36 p.m."

"That's very specific."

"I know."

"What's the target?"

"I don't know."

"Who's behind it?"

"I don't know that either."

"Fuck, Brody. You don't know a lot."

"Will you help me?"

"Maybe. Tell me everything."

Brody told him what he knew and sent over copies of Butler's email to the other conspirators as well as a link to the private chatroom.

Ten minutes later, he clicked off the phone. Brody wasn't sure if he'd just opened Pandora's box or not. But he was pretty sure his friend would come through for him.

"How are you feeling?"

Jenny looked up from her magazine at the sound of Brody's voice. She was in a bed in the corner of a ward. The five other beds were occupied by women with a range of different ailments.

"Visiting time's not until later," she said.

"I told them I was the new hospital DJ just taking song requests for this afternoon's show."

A snigger escaped Jenny's lips before she could stop it.

"You're crazy, you are." Knowing him, he probably had used the line to make it past the nurses on the desk outside.

Brody reached into his man bag and pulled out two small takeaway cups, glancing around to make sure he wasn't being observed. He handed one to her. "Thought you could do with a decent espresso. It's from *TAP Coffee* around the corner from here."

She accepted the peace offering, removing the lid and allowing the aroma to waft up her nose, briefly displacing the hospital's sterilised odour.

He reached back into his bag and pulled out her leather handbag, mobile phone and charger, which she had left behind at his place. He placed them on her bedside cabinet. He seemed nervous, unsure of his role.

"How's Stefan?" she asked, sipping the coffee. It was exceptional.

"He's okay. Bruised and concussed but they expect to let him go home later. Lorenzo's covering the coffee shop."

"That's good."

"Yes." Brody sat on the bed, put down his coffee and reached for her hand. She allowed him.

"I'm *so* very sorry," he said, full of feeling.

"For what?" But she already knew. She just wanted to hear him say it.

"For exactly what you said yesterday. I made an assumption that Raz wasn't behind what's going on. Well, he is. And the guy with the snake is working for him. It's the only explanation that fits the facts."

"And …"

He gripped her hand tighter. "I pooh-poohed the idea when you proposed it in front of your team, when it had every right to be explored. And if we had, maybe last night would never have happened. I nearly caused you to be killed."

Well, well. He had thought it all through. She'd come to similar conclusions herself, but it was good to hear them corroborated. Even better to hear it in the form of an apology.

"The accent?" she asked.

"Yup, that was the clincher. André the Giant didn't have a Mancunian accent. He and Raz are two different people."

"André?"

"He looks like the old French wrestler, André the Giant. Didn't you see the size of him?"

She had no idea who André the Giant was and she certainly couldn't form an image of the intruder. "I guess …"

"You don't remember?"

She shook her head. It was so damn frustrating. She was a police officer, trained to be observant.

"Of course, the drug." He squeezed her hand in sympathy.

"The GHB, yes. Do you know, I've interviewed rape victims who were drugged with this stuff. No recollection of anything that happened. Each time I thought that was probably a good thing for them. Who'd want to remember something horrible like that being done to you? But I tell you what — I hate not remembering what happened last night."

"Do you want me to walk you through it again?"

"Yes. In exquisite detail please. I especially want all the bits you held back last night when Fiona and Da Silva were here."

Brody did. She stopped him repeatedly, clarifying elements, making sure she understood. As he relayed the events, she found it harder and harder to believe she had been there at all. There was nothing — not even one faint memory that aligned with his story. In a way, she felt like she had been robbed.

The conversation turned to her. He couldn't believe how bright she was considering she'd been poisoned less than seven hours ago with one of the most deadly neurotoxins known to mankind.

"I know, I feel absolutely fine. That antivenom is amazing. Dr Rama says that even the slight grogginess I feel is more likely down to the GHB than the poison. "

"Not the wine then?" he said, squeezing her hand lightly to let her know he was teasing.

"I can't believe the only reason they had the antivenom is because of Da Silva's initiative. It never occurred to me to warn the hospitals that there could be more victims."

"Maybe there's hope for him yet."

"Hmm, we'll see." She wasn't convinced.

"What are the odds of your team tracking André down today and arresting him?"

"I'm pretty hopeful. Although he wore the same Lycra gloves as when he got the taxi to King's Cross yesterday, the scenes of crime team reckon there's a load of fingerprints on the white plastic box he used to transport the snake. Anyone who goes to the trouble of wearing gloves usually has a past they're trying to keep hidden."

"How come you're so on top with the forensics? I've only just brought your phone in."

"Da Silva left me with his personal phone last night." She held up the massive Galaxy phone. "His idea as well."

"Wow, something really changed his attitude."

"I know. I reckon Tick-Tock read him the riot act yesterday." When she saw his confused expression, she clarified. "Sorry, station nickname. DCS McLintock."

"Fingerprints, eh? Well, hopefully you can catch André today and he will lead you to the orchestrator. There's not much time left."

"What makes you say that?"

There was an almost imperceptible pause. "Just what Butler said in his original email. He said, 'We haven't got long.'"

Jenny studied his face. He was lying. For the first time since she'd known him she could tell. Normally his mask was impassive or he used diversionary tactics to move the focus away from him. But this time she'd spotted his eyes briefly glance upwards and to the left. A classic tell.

"There'd better not be something you're not telling me, Brody Taylor."

"What makes you say that? Anyway, yesterday I agreed to keep out of your case. I'm not doing anything else to jeopardise our relationship, Jen. I've already screwed up enough as it is." He indicated the hospital bed.

"Okay …" She let the word trail out, giving him one more chance to come clean.

"When will they let you out?"

He'd changed the subject, proving beyond any reasonable doubt that he was up to no good. Sometimes he was so damn infuriating.

"Hopefully this afternoon," she answered. "As long as all my vitals remain steady, I should be home by teatime."

"Perfect."

Which perfect did he mean? Perfect that she'd be home

tonight? Or perfect that she was out of the way today?

A nurse entered the ward and he stood up quickly, whispering, "I guess I'd better go. I'll pop back when it's official visiting time later on."

"Thanks for the coffee." It was all she could say. Anything else would be the start of another row. What the hell was he up to?

"So …" he said loudly with a cheeky wink, "'(Everything I Do) I Do It For You' by Bryan Adams. No problem, Miss Price."

She gave him a despairing look for labelling her with choosing such a naff song in front of the nurses. He left the ward with a wave and a smirk.

Despite the levity, there was definitely something going on. His behaviour wasn't right. Then she considered the song title he'd chosen.

Did he simply choose it for fun? Or was he telling her something?

The arrivals board updated. The Aeroflot flight from Moscow was now shown as having landed. Brody left his seat in the arrivals lounge café and wandered into the crowd of waiting family members and taxi drivers holding up name placards. Some had even gone hi-tech and held up iPads. As travellers pushing trolleys full of luggage exited through the double doors, there were frequent shouts, screams and hugs from reunited friends and families.

Brody looked at his phone once again. He was trying to ingrain the image of Klara Ivanov into his brain. She was certainly pretty. Sharp features, precise manicured eyebrows, straight nose and full lips.

Victor Gibb had finally come through during Brody's *Uber* ride to Heathrow Terminal 4. He had sent over her passport photo, full name, address in Moscow and an initial employment summary. It seemed she was a twenty-eight-year-old firmware programmer, with specialist experience of components and devices contained in nuclear and electricity power stations. Gibb had taken Brody's story of a terrorist threat far more seriously when he'd seen mention of nuclear power stations on her résumé. He told Brody that he had escalated the threat and that GCHQ were all over it. So far they'd found nothing. Gibb also informed him that Graham, the senior executive from Brody's interview on Monday, was demanding that Brody came in and briefed GCHQ in more detail. Brody told Gibb he was too busy and, after disconnecting, blocked Gibb's calls and texts.

Brody had no idea how he was going to play it with Klara when she walked through those doors. But then, he'd not exactly played his earlier conversation with Jenny well at all. He should never have referred to an imminent threat. He had been in two minds and had slipped up as a result. He really had wanted to tell Jenny what he had learned from Klara about the specific date and time of the attack. But he knew full well that she wouldn't be able to help herself from taking over, potentially repeating the 'Raz' stakeout from yesterday. And so, in the end, he'd chosen not to say anything. He would come clean once he'd talked to Klara and learned what the hell was going on. He just hoped that the information he gleaned from her would be enough for Jenny to overlook the fact that he had temporarily held back information. He knew it was a risky strategy, especially with Jenny, but what choice did he have?

It was imperative to learn everything there was to learn from Klara Ivanov. She had been hesitant in their chatroom conversation earlier. Untrusting. He couldn't blame her for being suspicious. So for him to show up and walk up to her as she exited from the baggage hall would no doubt be shocking.

Brody considered whether there was another way to play it. He looked around for inspiration and a mischievous thought occurred to him. And with it, a plan immediately slotted into place. He didn't have much time.

He walked around the railing and made his way from one side of the waiting crowd to the other, as if he was an arriving traveller. He scanned the crowd, reading the name placards being held up by the awaiting taxi drivers. Then he saw what he was looking for right in the centre of the crowd.

A uniformed chauffeur was holding up a tablet PC with the name 'Ms Ivanov' prominently displayed on it. In smaller writing in the corner was the name of the chauffeur company, *Thames Chauffeur Services*.

Brody moved to the edge of the crowd. Within a few seconds he had searched the internet for the chauffeur company's phone number and pressed dial on his phone. It was answered immediately.

"Thames Chauffeur Services, how can I help you?"

"Yes, hello," said Brody, effecting a deep voice and a posh accent. "I ordered a car to pick up a Miss Klara Ivanov from Terminal 4. She was landing on the 12:05 from Moscow."

"Yes, that's correct. The driver's waiting for her to come through at the moment."

"Ah, I'm too late then."

"Too late?"

"Sorry, but I've just been informed that Miss Ivanov missed her flight in Moscow and will be on the evening flight instead. It lands tonight at 9:35pm." This was accurate as he'd quickly Googled that as well. "So sorry to muck you about."

"Oh, I see." There was a little frustration in the man's voice but he recovered quickly. "No, not a problem. I'll send a car for her this evening. Obviously, we'll need to charge the call-out fee for this morning."

"Yes, I understand. That's fine."

"Are we taking her to the same hotel?"

"Hold on, let me just check." Brody paused for effect. "Damn computer, it seems to be stuck. Which hotel have you got her down for?"

"The Landmark on Marylebone Road."

"Ah yes, I think that's it. Hold on, the computer's just come back online. Yes, the Landmark."

"Okay great, that's all booked in for you, sir."

"Thanks." Brody hung up and observed the chauffeur. Sure enough, he was soon reading a text on his phone. The chauffeur swore under his breath and then abruptly turned around and stomped off, pushing people out of the way.

Brody whipped his own tablet PC out of his man bag. Within a minute, he was holding it up with Klara's name displayed prominently on it. While he waited, Brody brought up the *Uber* app on his phone. He flipped it to *UberExec*. There were six executive cars within the vicinity of the airport. He programmed in the Landmark Hotel and got ready to order a car.

Ten minutes later, Brody spotted Klara Ivanov. She was stunning in real life. Slim, tall and elegant. He looked away as she began scanning the placards for her name, and waited for her to approach him. Surreptitiously, he pressed the button on the *Uber* app and ordered a car. He was pleased to see he had been allocated a BMW 7-Series.

"I am Klara Ivanov," she said.

"Hi!" said Brody, looking up as if surprised. He pointed at her two pieces of luggage. "Here, let me take those for you."

She handed them over willingly. "Follow me," he said. "The car is this way. How was your flight?"

She told him it was fine and they made small talk. He explained that it would take under an hour to get to the Landmark Hotel, as it was the middle of the day and traffic was lighter. She said she would be shocked if traffic was worse here than in Moscow. She had a wonderful Russian accent, but spoke English beautifully. Brody slowly led the way to the Short Stay car park where the *Uber* meeting point was located. He deliberately allowed some half-full lifts to go on without them, allowing more time for the driver to arrive.

As they neared the meeting point, the black car he ordered pulled up in front of them. Subtly, Brody flashed his phone at the driver to let him know that he was the expected pickup. The driver got out and gave them a hand loading the luggage in the boot. For an impromptu plan it had worked like clockwork.

Klara climbed into the back of the car. Brody opened the other door and sat down next to her. The car pulled off before she could object.

"Hi, Klara." Brody held out his hand. "It's a pleasure to meet you in person. I'm Brody Taylor."

Her mouth dropped open in disbelief.

CHAPTER 17

"LET ME OUT," KLARA DEMANDED, IGNORING BRODY'S outstretched hand.

The car was making its way down the circular ramp from the first floor of the car park. The driver, who was sitting on the right instead of the normal left, told her he couldn't stop where he was. She was surprised to hear he had a Romanian accent.

"Listen, we really need to talk," said the man called Brody. He was late twenties, early thirties, with sparkling green eyes and swept back white blond hair. There was intelligence and intensity evident in his pleading stare. "People really are going to die unless we help each other."

The car pulled up at the exit barrier. She pulled at the handle and opened the rear door.

"Please, Klara. I need your help."

She pushed the door outwards and stuck out a leg. The driver looked in his rear view mirror, concern that he would lose his fare etched on his face.

"I know you don't know me from Adam, so I'll leave it up to your conscience." He held up his hands in a conciliatory gesture. "I won't stop you if you leave."

Who the hell was Adam? She was halfway out of the car. The fact that he'd made it her choice gave her some sense of control over the situation. In front of the car, the barrier rose. The driver monitored her movement via the side mirror. She sat back down and drew her leg back into the car, closing the door. The car pulled off.

"Thank you," said Brody.

"How did you find me?"

He shrugged. "Basic detective work. You told me in the chatroom that you were about to take off."

"But how did you know I was flying in from Moscow? I could have been anywhere in the world!"

"Your email address is yandex.ru, which is a Russian provider."

"That was it?"

"I'd say it was enough."

She supposed he was right.

On the opposite side of the road to normal, the car drove along a trunk road skirting the edge of the airport, airport hangers on the right. The left side alternated between intense green grass fields and dull housing estates.

"Who are you really, Mr Taylor?"

"I told you the truth. I'm a friend of James Butler. And please, call me Brody."

"James Butler, who was killed? Who was he?"

Brody shifted back in his seat before answering. "He was a computer hacker."

Her eyes widened in shock. Suddenly, she was back in Vorovskoy Mir territory. She thought she'd left all that behind. She took a deep breath and calmed herself down. "What did he hack into?"

"I don't know. That's what I'm trying to work out."

"I thought you said he was your friend. Didn't he tell you?"

"Not exactly. I'm trying to piece it together, which is why I was so desperate to talk to the other recipients of the email he sent. Which leaves you and Raz."

"And who is this Raz?"

"I don't know. He chose not to help."

"Maybe I will make same decision."

"Maybe you will. But I hope you won't."

The car drove down a highway ramp onto a motorway. She

knew that the M25 circled London. The traffic was light, nothing like Moscow's outer ring road at the same time of day.

She turned to face Brody, who was staring at her intently. She found his unwavering focus a little disconcerting. "Okay, what is it you want to know?"

"You're a firmware programmer by trade —"

He paused because she had moved to interrupt him. How could he possibly know that? But then she waved her hand to allow him to continue. It would wait.

"Who did you work for? Who is Saul?"

"I've no idea. He approached me online. I have a profile on freelance job website and I take on programming projects I can do remotely. Just a sideline."

"How did you communicate with him?"

"Over email."

"Do you have his email address?"

"Yes, on my laptop." She indicated her laptop bag by her feet.

"Great, would you mind showing me?"

"I can't right now." Klara grimaced guiltily. "I used up battery on plane, watching movies."

"Okay, we can look later I guess. Did he have a surname?"

"Yes, I think so. Baker, I think."

"So what did he hire you to do?"

Klara was uncomfortable admitting to the project. It was the nearest she'd ever come to doing something illegal. "He wanted me to put time bomb in assembler source code of electronic control system."

Brody leaned forward. "So that's how you know when on Friday the attack is going to happen."

"Well … yes, of course. But I'm not sure you'd call it attack exactly."

"What does the time bomb code do?"

"It calls existing subroutine elsewhere in same program over and over and over. I didn't need to change subroutine, just force it to be called repeatedly at specific date and time."

"Overriding all other inputs?"

"Yes, exactly. Normally subroutine would only be called when other events happen."

"So what's the target? A nuclear plant control system or something like that?"

She looked at him in horror for two reasons. First of all she would never do something like that. But secondly, he obviously knew far more about her background than he had disclosed so far.

"No, of course not," she hissed.

"Okay. That's good," he leaned back, visibly relieved. "Must be an electricity substation control system or something like that?"

He definitely knew her background then. She folded her arms in pure exasperation. It also served to let him know he was wrong again.

"I'd never do anything that would put peoples' lives in danger," she stated firmly, "no matter how well paid."

"How much was the job, then?"

"More than three months' salary." There was a hint of pride in her voice.

They'd turned off the M25 and had joined another motorway. Finally, she saw signs for London. There were tall buildings in the distance.

"Wow. So it must have been serious."

"Personally, I wouldn't call it serious. But you know what these hacktivists are like."

"Hacktivist?"

"Someone who hacks things to make political point."

"I know what a hacktivist is." He seemed annoyed that she would have thought he didn't know the term. "I'm just surprised this is a hacktivist agenda. What are they fighting against?"

"American corporate greed."

"Really?" He sounded unconvinced.

"Specifically, American company called *Coca-Cola*."

"Coke? You're joking."

"That's why I was paid so much. Going up against such iconic global brand. Even in Russia we drink *Coca-Cola*."

"I don't get it." He shook his head. "This makes no sense at all."

"That's why I ignored original message from James Butler. Nothing I've done could possibly hurt people. I said same thing when I replied to your message last night in chatroom."

"Yes," he agreed. "That is what you said. So what's the target then? What hardware component is the firmware on?"

"Vending machines. *Coca-Cola* vending machines."

"What?" Now he was completely incredulous. Why wouldn't he believe her? It was the truth. "All this for some *vending* machines? That makes no sense at all."

"It does if you are hacktivist."

The car sailed over a flyover in between some high-rise buildings. It was starting to become the London she'd seen on television.

"Go on."

She knew what she'd done was technically illegal. But that didn't stop her from being a little bit proud of it. "Imagine every *Coca-Cola* vending machine around world suddenly spewing out all of their contents at once. It would generate headlines everywhere, damaging company's reputation. And profits."

Brody's forehead furrowed deeply. "This really makes no sense at all. People have died for this." He turned to her in earnest. "Can you run it by me again?"

Klara repeated her story but his incredulity remained as he questioned her on the details.

The motorway turned into a standard highway, with lots of side roads and traffic lights. The car weaved in and out of lanes, picking its way eastwards. Eventually, it turned off the main road and pulled up outside a large old building. She saw the sign above the doors and realised they were at the Landmark Hotel.

"I'm sorry it's less sensational than you expected."

"It just doesn't make sense." It was at least the fourth time he'd said the same thing. He'd obviously built this whole thing up into being something a lot more dramatic. It was almost as if he was disappointed that nuclear plants weren't going to explode tomorrow. She knew men loved explosions, but that was sick.

"It is what it is. Now, if you don't mind, I'd like to check in to my hotel." She opened the door of the car. This time she stepped outside fully.

He jumped out of his side and spoke across the roof of the car. "Would you mind showing me the emails between you and this hacktivist guy?"

"I need to charge my laptop first."

"I'm sure we can find a plug inside."

"I tell you what, Mr Taylor." She smiled at him. "I'm going to check in and have a well-earned shower. Then, if you like, I'll come back down with my laptop and show you whatever you want to see."

He didn't seem impressed that he'd have to wait. "Okay."

"But only in hotel bar and only if we are drinking good Russian vodka."

"Please doctor, I really need to leave."

"I'm sorry, Miss Price, but we need to keep you under observation for a few more hours. The venom is still in your system and you could easily have a delayed reaction."

"But —"

"No." She placed a hand on Jenny's shoulder. "It's far too risky."

Jenny gave in and lay back on the bed. She knew the doctor was right. After Brody had left earlier, she had even fallen back asleep, which was unlike her. And when she'd gone to the toilet a few minutes before the doctor had arrived on her round, she had felt a little queasy and faint.

The doctor moved off to look over the patient in the neighbouring bed, an old woman called Edith who had been attacked and robbed on the doorstep of her home in Chalk Farm. As a police officer, Jenny had been exposed to so much violence over the years and, although she'd interviewed hundreds of victims in hospital beds, they were always short visits to gather facts and testimony. Lying next to Edith made Jenny better appreciate the ongoing physical and mental trauma suffered by victims of violence. Edith was in physical pain from her broken arms and ribs but it was her mental state that caused her to scream out every now and again, tears of distress streaming down her face. Jenny felt deeply sorry for her and wanted to help. She'd even made a call to Camden station to check in on the case, using her rank to increase the focus. But there were no suspects, other than the local street gangs.

Jenny's phone rang. It was Fiona Jones.

"Jenny," said Fiona, "we've got a name."

She sat up in the bed, her heart pounding. "Fantastic. Who is it?"

"His name is Ralph Mullins."

"How'd you track him down?"

"Fingerprints on the box he carried the snake in."

"Makes sense. I suppose he didn't expect to leave that behind. What do we know about him?"

"He's been out of prison for three years. Get this: he was inside for murdering a juvenile. I talked to the arresting officer from Watford about five minutes ago." Jenny was impressed that Fiona had used her initiative to get the inside story. "Apparently the kid was part of local gang that was taunting Mullins' dog. They kicked it and slashed it with a knife while he was in the post office. The story goes that he took the dog home, nursed it and then went out on the warpath. He tracked down one of the kids and beat the life out of him, literally, with his bare hands. The sentence was downgraded to manslaughter because of his mental disability and the provocation. He got sixteen, did ten."

"Where's he live?"

"What's that …" But Fiona was talking to someone else. "Hold on, Jen."

Jenny held on, annoyed she couldn't be there. She heard Fiona talking but it was muffled. She thought she also heard Karim Malik's voice. After a minute, Fiona spoke to her again.

"He's definitely our man. Karim says his description matches an assistant who he talked to in a reptile shop in Brent Cross on Tuesday. His job was cleaning out the snake cages."

"Can you text over a picture of Mullins?"

Jenny was desperate to see if his image would cut through her GHB-fogged memory of the night before.

"Will do."

Fiona clicked off.

With no other role for herself, Jenny resorted to imagining what was going on in Holborn. They'd be planning the takedown. For someone like this, armed and dangerous, the tactical response team would be called in. Jenny hated not being involved.

She decided to 'do a Brody' and used her phone to Google Mullins' name with the word 'dog' added, scanning for hits from thirteen years before. She was surprised by how quickly she tracked down the news stories. Fiona's recount matched the newspapers of the time. The only colour she could add was that the victim, unnamed, was fifteen years old with his own juvenile record for robbery, driving without a licence and anti-social behaviour. He was part of a well-known gang from the Meriden estate. There was little sympathy for the victim. Mullins had been single, lived alone and was known in the local area for being a simple-minded gentle giant who doted on his pet dog. Although he went down for manslaughter, he was portrayed in the press as the real victim.

There was only one photo of Mullins in the newspaper articles: his mug shot from his arrest, which was in black and white. It showed an unkempt man, with an uneven face, a messy mop of curly dark hair and bushy eyebrows. He had a dull look in his eyes, as if he hadn't quite focused on the camera taking the shot.

Even allowing for the thirteen years that had passed since the photo was taken, her imagination could conjure up nothing from last night. It was as if she was looking at his face for the first time.

Her phone beeped. It was Fiona texting through the picture. It was the same one that Jenny had already seen from searching the internet. She gave herself a mental pat on the back.

An hour later, after eating a surprisingly acceptable lunch, Jenny decided she'd had enough. She didn't care what Dr Rama said. There was far too much at stake. Anyway, she was sure she felt strong enough to get back in the saddle.

The ward's two nurses were dealing with a patient opposite her, the curtains drawn around the bed, leaving the nurses' station by the ward exit unattended. She climbed out of bed and carefully withdrew the IV clip from the vein on the back of her forearm, praying it wouldn't cause the heart rate monitor to beep in alarm. It stayed silent. She opened the cupboard next to the bed and found her neatly folded clothes. A moan of pain emanated from the bed opposite. She glanced around, but the nurses were still behind the curtain, issuing instructions to their unruly patient.

As Jenny bent down to retrieve her clothes, a wave of nausea caught her unawares. She held on to the bed frame and waited for it to pass. Maybe she wasn't quite ready to be back on her feet after all, but dammit, she had to join her team. She was useless here. After a minute, the queasiness passed and, soon after, Jenny was dressed and walking down the maze of corridors searching for the way out.

She finally exited the hospital, pleased not to have bumped into Dr Rama. As she scanned the surroundings for a taxi, Jenny's phone rang again.

"You there, Jenny?"

"Yes?"

"Okay, I've conferenced you in. Alan, you there?"

"Yes, I'm here, Fiona. Hi Jen, you okay?"

"Yes thanks, Al. What —"

Fiona cut across the pleasantries. "Right, Jenny, thought you'd appreciate being part of the takedown, whichever location it is."

What did that mean?

"So, I'm here in Borehamwood with Karim and DI Knight, outside the flat where Mullins lives."

"And I'm in Brent Cross," continued Alan, "outside the pet shop with Da Silva. We've each got an armed response unit. We're synchronising takedowns."

That made sense. Karim and Alan were in separate locations as they'd both recently met the target and could each spot him. Jenny really appreciated them phoning her, although wished she'd discharged herself an hour earlier. Then she would have been with them for the arrest rather than stuck on the end of a phone.

"Okay, Knight's on the phone with Da Silva. Looks like we're going in now."

Jenny didn't say anything.

She spotted a taxi and waved it down. She would go directly to whichever location Mullins was arrested in.

"Right, we're off," said Alan. Jenny could hear running steps and huffing and puffing. She presumed that was Alan, who was nowhere near as fit as Fiona.

There was the noise of a bell and lots of shouting. It was the response team commanding people to lie down on the floor. She presumed that was the pet shop.

The cab pulled up and she climbed in.

"Where to, darlin'?" asked the driver.

"Brent Cross." It was the nearest of the two locations. "Quickly." The driver pulled off.

Over the phone, she heard a loud crash and the sound of a door splintering off its hinges. More running and heavy breathing.

"Either of you got him?" she asked.

There was no reply. More shouting and deep breaths. "Clear. Bedroom clear. Bathroom clear."

"Is he here?" she heard Fiona ask someone.

"Have you got him, Fiona?" asked Alan.

No one answered.

"Fuck it," said Jenny, who had been holding her breath. "Have you got him or not?"

As the *Uber* taxi driver lifted Klara's luggage out of the boot, a uniformed porter appeared out of nowhere to take over. Brody accompanied her into the hotel and found he had to pause momentarily to take in the unexpected grandeur and opulence.

Marble and stone dominated a central atrium, the building rising eight floors on all four sides. An imposing curved glass roof crowned the indoor courtyard. Taking advantage of the protection from the British weather, palm trees had been erected within, giving the illusion of a tropical garden. The bar and restaurant area looked elegant and inviting.

Brody realised he hadn't found out why Klara had come to London in the first place. If she was on holiday, then she must be rich. If she was here for work, then she had one hell of an expenses budget.

Klara headed for the check in desk. Brody scanned the atrium for somewhere for them to sit. "Klara." He pointed towards the seats when she turned around. "Let's meet over there. There's a plug for your laptop."

"Okay. I'll be about half an hour."

Brody did his best to hide his disappointment. "Okay, I'll be waiting."

He left her to it, heading in the direction of the seats he had pointed out. He decided he could do with a caffeine boost to keep him going after the events of last night and the early start. Glancing at the drinks being consumed by guests at other tables, he decided he could do better. He had half an hour to kill anyway.

Outside the hotel was Gino's Coffee Bar. While it didn't look much more than a greasy spoon, Brody knew from experience that they served a decent espresso. And right now, he could do with a double hit.

He aimed for the northerly exit of the hotel, which would lead him out onto the road directly opposite Marylebone Station. He turned right and headed for the café. It was on the corner of the side road opposite the hotel. As he crossed the road he checked both directions to make sure he didn't get run over.

Something caught his attention but his conscious brain couldn't process what it was. He lifted his hand to push open the door of Gino's but the reflection in the glass showed a scooter in the reserved parking area for motorbikes outside Marylebone Station. Slowly he turned and stared at it.

It was a black Vespa. But it had an unusual matt finish, making it quite striking. But why was it catching his eye? Had he seen it before somewhere? And before his brain processed the answer, his legs were already sprinting in the direction of the hotel.

Yes, he had definitely seen it before. Yesterday, in fact. As he'd let Jenny into Bruno's, he remembered noticing a matt black Vespa pulling up on the other side of Upper Street. In fact, now that he thought about it, hadn't he heard the tinny sound of a motorbike accelerate away when the police arrived last night?

He supposed it could just be a coincidence. But he couldn't take that chance. Brody burst into the hotel knowing Klara was in mortal danger.

"He's not here," said Fiona. "Flat's empty. No one here at all. Not even a snake cage."

"What about you, Alan?" asked Jenny from the back of the cab, which was heading along the perimeter of Regent's Park. She switched the phone to her other ear as she'd been pressing it far too hard and her arm was tired.

"Doesn't look like it. The response team are just checking out back … No, just got the nod that it's all clear. He's not here, either."

"Where the hell is he?" asked Jenny.

It was the question they were all asking themselves. No one answered because no one had the answer.

"Jen, I'm going to need to disconnect and process this flat," said Fiona.

"Same here," said Alan. "I need to interview the store manager. See what I can find out. Sorry, Jen."

The phone clicked off. She was left listening to silence, completely frustrated. She so wanted to be part of it but she was at least half an hour away.

Where the hell could Mullins be?

Klara inserted the magnetic key card into her hotel room door. It clicked green and she withdrew the card, pushed it open and entered.

She didn't know what to make of Brody Taylor. He was utterly obsessed with the private job she'd done a year ago. She could tell he didn't believe her that it was something as simple as reprogramming the firmware of vending machines. But she hadn't lied and she'd enjoy proving him wrong later. Perhaps when he'd calmed down and drank a vodka or two, maybe he'd lighten up a bit and perhaps become good company. She could do with a charming, good-looking guide on her first night in London.

Klara took in the grandeur of her hotel room. It was huge, with a king-sized bed between two windows. She placed her handbag containing her dead laptop on the side table, kicked off her shoes and headed over to one of the windows, enjoying the feel of the plush carpet under her feet. The view out oversaw the atrium below, where lots of people were enjoying themselves eating or drinking. She'd be down there soon.

There was a knock on the door.

She headed over and pulled the door open. It was the porter with her luggage. He carried her cases in effortlessly, despite the fact that she had packed them with nearly everything she owned. He placed them on trestles next to the wardrobe and the other on the floor. Pausing for a moment, he smiled at her. She smiled back and thanked him. He told her she was welcome and then left. It was only as the door closed that it occurred to her that he had been waiting for a tip, not that she had any British money on her.

She opened one of the cases, pulled out her bag of toiletries and went into the bathroom. A few minutes later she was under the powerful, boiling hot shower, washing off the journey. It felt good and she only turned it off when she realised she must have already been ten minutes underneath. She'd told Brody thirty minutes and it was probably twenty already.

She dried off and tied one of the luxurious bathrobes around her.

She knew just what outfit to wear, but wasn't sure which of the two cases she'd packed it in. She pulled open the bathroom door and —

A huge, brown haired man stood there, brandishing a knife in his gargantuan hands. He had a gruesome smile on his face, revealing a gold tooth.

"It's time to pray, Klara," he said.

Klara reacted instinctively and threw the door shut. He blocked it with one of his big boots and shoved it open with his shoulder. Klara took the force of the opening door full on and was thrown backwards across the bathroom, slipping on the wet floor. She fell over and into the marble bathtub, bashing her head on the ornate taps.

The man entered the room, almost taking up all the space, and immediately lumbered towards her. He grabbed her by both lapels of her robe and yanked her out of the bath. She screamed and clawed at him, but stopped when she felt the point of the knife at her throat.

Klara hung limply from Mullins' fist, her feet dangling above the floor.

"Come and meet my venomous little friend."

CHAPTER 18

BRODY CURSED HIS STUPIDITY. HE SHOULD HAVE taken Klara's phone number earlier. He could have phoned or texted a warning.

Brody thought through his options.

He could approach hotel security but wasn't convinced they'd take him seriously, especially if he told them about a snake. The police would take too long to get here, but they were probably the best option. He couldn't phone Jenny, not after the promise he'd made her earlier. But what choice did he have? Her team knew what they were up against and would take the right precautions with a venomous snake in the mix. Anyone else would blunder in and risk being bitten, which was probably lethal now that one of the nearest hospitals had used up its supply of antivenom on Jenny.

Jenny answered her phone on the second ring. It sounded like she was in a car, which made no sense. She was supposed to be in hospital. "Brody, I can't talk now, I'm in the middle of —"

"Jenny, he's here. The snake guy is here."

"What! Where are you?"

"I'm in the Landmark Hotel on Marylebone Road. Whatever room Klara Ivanov is in, he's there. Get your team here straight away. But make sure they're prepared for another fucking snake."

"Who's Klara Ivano — oh!" She caught up quickly. "The

fourth person on Butler's email. Brody, you told me you were having nothing more —"

"Not now, Jenny. Her life's in danger. Get your lot over here. Now." He clicked off the phone, knowing he was in deep shit with Jenny now.

Brody paced up and down. He had to do something. He spotted the porter who had taken Klara's luggage up exiting the lift, pushing an empty trolley. Brody caught up with him before he reached his colleague.

"Hi, mate. What room is Klara Ivanov in?"

"I can't tell you —"

The porter paused when he saw the £50 note Brody had pulled out of his wallet. Greedily, he looked over his shoulder to make sure he couldn't be heard. "It's eight-oh-eight, mate." Brody thanked him and handed over the money. He headed for the lifts, still trying to come up with a plan.

He texted, *Room 808* to Jenny.

He knew he couldn't really knock on the door himself. That was pretty much committing suicide if André was in there. Brody had no skills for a physical fight, especially against someone the size and strength of André. He had to be smart.

Brody spotted the hotel shop and diverted into it, casting around for inspiration. Within twenty seconds he had the bones of a plan and within a minute had bought the items to make it work. It was a crazy ploy and probably wouldn't work anyway, but it was the best he could come up with on such short notice.

He knew he was putting his life on the line, but he had to do something to save Klara. The simple fact that André was here meant there was far more to what was going on than her bloody vending machines.

He had to try and save her.

Brody only had half a plan. It had a small chance of working if he just knocked on the door and rushed in, but his chances would be improved if he could make his way into Klara's room without announcing himself. Brody thought of the greedy porter again but realised even he wasn't likely to open the door for Brody, no matter how much he bribed him. That was a line too far for hotel staff.

He needed a key.

These days, hotels had wised up to handing out replacement keys to anyone who simply walked up to a reception desk. They needed proof of who you were or proof you were a —

Brody headed for the wide reception desk. He chose the receptionist on the far right.

"Hi, can I get a room please?"

"Sure, do you have a reservation?"

"Uh no. I'm staying over in London unexpectedly."

"That's no problem, Mr …"

"Taylor."

Two minutes later, Brody had his own credit card-sized room key. The hotel's logo was all over it but the only indication it was for Room 423 was handwritten on the paper wallet containing the key. Of course, he'd had to pay extra for an executive suite, as that was apparently the only room left. Brody didn't care. He'd achieved his objective. He left the reception area in the direction of the lifts.

Once out of sight of the front desk, he paused and caught his breath. He hoped Klara was still alive. Brody thought back to last night and calculated how long it had taken André to tie him up. He looked at his watch. It would be tight.

Brody glanced back to the front desk, choosing his moment. The receptionist on the right who'd served him was now dealing with someone else. The timing was good. He made a beeline for her colleague on the far left.

"I checked in a few minutes ago," said Brody, pulling the plastic key out of his pocket, the paper wallet left behind. He placed it on the counter. "But my key's not working."

"Oh, I'm terribly sorry, sir," said the receptionist, picking it up. "I'll program a new one for you immediately. What room number is it?"

"Number 808," said Brody, trying to stop himself sounding relieved at his impromptu plan having worked.

The receptionist withdrew a new key from the machine and handed it over with a further apology.

Now he had a way into Klara's room.

The lift to the eighth floor seemed to take ages. Brody reached into the bag from the hotel shop and started unboxing the largest item. He turned it on and configured it to work as he wanted, discarding cardboard casing on the lift floor. Littering was the least of his issues right now.

He headed down the carpeted corridor and found Room 808. Placing the largest item he'd purchased on the floor opposite the door, he dropped the other two items into each of his trouser pockets.

He was as ready as he was ever going to be.

Brody slid the key into the slot. The light turned green and there was a slight click as the lock opened. He had no idea if it was loud enough for anyone inside to hear, but he had no choice. Taking one last deep breath, Brody pushed the door open as gently as he could.

It swung inwards, revealing a short corridor that led into a large open area of the room. There was a closed door immediately on the right, which Brody presumed was the bathroom. Brody placed his man bag containing his computer on the floor to hold the door to the corridor fully open.

He listened intently, hoping that the black Vespa outside had just been a strange coincidence and he was completely wrong. But then he heard a muffled scream and a male voice, quoting.

"'And Paul shook the snake off into the fire and suffered no ill effects …'"

With utter dread, Brody recognised the voice. He stepped inside the room, the thick carpet silencing his footsteps.

"' …The people expected him to swell up or suddenly fall dead …'"

Brody reached the end of the short corridor and put his head around the corner. The room was large with a king-sized bed on the far wall in between two windows that overlooked the hotel's atrium. A small round table was in the centre of the room, a bowl of fruit on top.

André the Giant was standing to one side of the table, his back to Brody. He was holding a snake, similar in size to the one from last night, although this one was dark grey on top instead of brown. André was gripping right behind the snake's head, pressing down with his thumb, his other hand helping to take the weight of the snake's body, the tail writhing around.

Klara was tied to the dressing table chair, facing in Brody's direction. She was gagged and bound tightly, terror in her eyes. Her hair was wet and she was clothed only in a bathrobe. He must have got to her after her shower. When he saw that Klara had seen him, Brody immediately put his finger to his lips. Her eyes registered but she managed to contain any reaction. She focused back on the snake in André's hands.

André neared the end of his recital, waving the serpent in front of Klara's face, teasing her. "'But after waiting a long time and seeing nothing unusual happen to him, they changed their minds and said he was a god.'"

He lifted the snake above her, ready to drop it.

Klara wriggled in the chair but was bound too tightly. Her head snapped left to right as she fought.

Brody moved into the room and stood on the other side of the round table. He was six feet from André and as near as he wanted to get to him or the beast. He placed his hands inside his pockets.

"You need to get a new hobby, mate," said Brody with as much flippancy as he could muster given he was scared as hell.

"What the —" André wheeled around in shock. And then, when he registered who was standing there, he shouted, "YOU!"

"Yup, little ole me. I see you've got a new pet." Brody nodded at the replacement black mamba.

Holding the snake out in front of him, André took a step towards Brody. Brody stepped the other way, keeping the round table with the fruit bowl between them. But André had moved away from Klara.

"You won't be lucky a second time. How's your girlfriend?" he leered. He was pacing side to side, but Brody mirrored his moves.

"She survived the snakebite, thanks for asking."

"She did?" André stopped pacing at that, surprising Brody.

With sincerity, he then asked, "Did you pray for her?" This surprised Brody even more.

"Eh? What is it with you and all this praying bollocks, anyway?"

In his pocket Brody pressed the correct part of his phone and got ready.

A voice boomed from the hallway: "And I will strike down upon thee with great vengeance and furious anger those who attempt to poison and destroy my brothers. And you will know my name is the Lord when I lay my vengeance upon thee."

André whirled around to face the new threat, but there was no one there, only the sound of loud gunfire. While he was distracted, Brody lifted the can of deodorant out of one pocket and the lighter out of the other. He brought them out in front of him, pressed the nozzle on the spray can and flicked the lighter, which immediately flamed into life. André turned back at the noise, just as a long burst of flame reached across the table towards him. Automatically, he raised his hands to protect himself, inadvertently releasing the snake. The movement caused the mamba to drop from above onto André himself, coiling its tail around one of his arms. The flame caught on André's Lycra gloves and cotton jacket, and suddenly he was dealing with two hazards. Using the arm for leverage, the mamba raised its head and snapped forward, biting André across his exposed neck. He screamed gutturally, trying to pull the snake off him, but it bit again and again, now on his face. He dropped to his knees, his hands on fire, and the snake slithered away over his shoulder.

Brody ran around the other side of the table, careful to avoid the retreating snake, which was making for the dark space under the bed, and began untying the ropes that bound Klara. Behind him, André was frantically padding at the flame on his jacket, trying to get the fire under control. But the Lycra gloves were melting on his hands and he was making it worse.

Brody managed to free one of Klara's arms, enabling her to help him, and within a few seconds both her arms were free. While Brody worked on her leg binds, she ripped off the tape that held her gag in place with a scream.

Free at last, Klara jumped up and away from where the snake had disappeared. André was rolling about on the floor. He had laid his body on top of his hands. The flames were almost extinguished.

Brody stood and headed for the exit. “Let’s get out of here,” he said.

Klara nodded and went to follow him, but then stopped, turned back and stood over André, who was still writhing on the floor. She let fly a stream of Russian swearwords and finished by spitting on his face. André was so distracted by his melting hands that he didn’t notice and continued trying to smother the final few flames.

Klara turned and followed Brody. Before they exited the room, Brody had the foresight to unplug her laptop, which had been charging on the side table and bring it with them. As they passed the hotel room door he also grabbed his man bag and the portable Bluetooth speaker he’d placed on the floor opposite the door of Room 808 earlier. He’d singled out the *Pulp Fiction* audio sound bite from his vast mental database of movie quotes earlier, choosing it because he knew that Samuel L. Jackson had shouted it so loudly. But having heard the line once more, which itself was quoted from the Bible, Brody was now much more appreciative of the irony of the words considering the situation he’d walked into.

As they waited for the lift, Klara threw her arms around Brody and whispered, “Thank you,” burying her head in his neck. She began shaking as the adrenalin wore off. Uncertainly, he pulled her close to comfort her.

The lift doors opened.

“Brody!”

Jenny rushed out of the lift, three armed response officers behind her. She took in the sight of Brody and Klara and withdrew in shock.

“There’s no fucking way I’m going in there,” said Malik. “There’s a poisonous snake lurking in the shadows. I’m not Steve Irwin, you know.”

Jenny, Malik, Fiona and three armed response officers stood outside the hotel room door. One of the officers had propped it open, revealing a corridor leading into a room. None of them had ventured in.

"Steve Irwin's dead, you idiot," said Fiona.

"Exactly, that's my point." Malik folded his arms. "He got too near to a poisonous animal and ended up dead. I'm not doing that."

"That was a stingray, not a snake."

"No difference as far as I'm concerned."

Jenny ignored the two of them bickering and took a tentative step inside. She had no idea if having recently been administered antivenom gave her protection against further bites from the same species. Eyes peeled, she checked every inch of the corridor as she took each step.

"Mr Mullins, are you in there?" she called.

"Jenny, be careful," cautioned Fiona.

An acrid burning smell emanated from the room. She took another step forward.

"Mr Mullins?"

She reached the end and slowly peered around the corner into the open room. Although her eyes registered the massive frame of Mullins sitting cross-legged on the floor, she ignored him and scanned around for the snake, the more immediate threat. She couldn't see it anywhere. Brody had said that it slithered under the bed after biting Mullins. The bed frame was only a few centimetres above the carpet, which meant she couldn't bend down and peer underneath to verify. She hoped it was still under there, but she was taking no chances. She held back by the corridor.

"Ralph Mullins?"

He looked over at her voice, his eyebrows rising in recognition. "You really did survive." His voice was filled with a mixture of awe and relief. "I thought he lied. Perhaps there is hope for me yet."

He clasped his hands out in front of him, as if praying. Smoke rose up from his jacket, but the Lycra gloves that had covered his hands had melted and they were now blistered and bleeding, dripping a mixture of flesh and black plastic onto his knees. He seemed unaware of the pain. Beads of sweat had formed on his forehead, the first visible sign of the venom coursing through his system. She could even see the fang marks on his face.

Brody had taken a huge risk when he'd taken on Mullins. The man was physically colossal and intimidating. And that was without the black mamba, wherever it was now. Jenny had to admit, Brody's bravery surprised her. This kind of physical confrontation was not Brody's way. But he had been the only one on the scene and so he'd stood up and been counted, using his initiative to distract the killer and then improvising with a deodorant can and a lighter. She'd never have thought of that herself.

She had been shocked when she had first clocked eyes on Brody with his arms around a tall, striking blonde wearing nothing but a hotel robe. Brody went into embarrassed overdrive, explaining the crazy situation. Klara Ivanov had arrived from Moscow a couple hours before, but Mullins had been waiting for her, hidden in her hotel room. Brody had noticed a black Vespa outside, recalled seeing it the night before, and put two and two together, sounding the alarm and rushing to her rescue. The scene in the hotel room sounded gruesome when Brody had described it and, now that she could see the hulking form of Mullins, fallen, burnt and melting, it truly was. She had ordered Brody to take the girl down to the lobby and out of harm's way. There were statements to be taken and procedures to follow.

But Jenny knew there was still more to come out. He'd conveniently ignored explaining *why* he had been on the scene in the first place. She wasn't looking forward to that. She suspected that Brody had lied to her face earlier in the hospital and, if that was true, she wasn't sure how she'd handle it. She needed to be able to trust the man in her life. He couldn't just say one thing to appease her and then do the exact opposite behind her back. She'd deal with him later. Mullins needed to be her concern right now.

Jenny tried to recall him from last night. The best her brain would offer up was that his face seemed familiar. She wanted to hate him for what he'd done to her, but he looked in such a sorry state that she almost felt sympathy for him.

"We need to get you to the hospital, Ralph."

"No."

"But you'll die if you're not treated."

"That's in God's hands now. If He hears my prayers then He will intervene." He turned away and began praying quietly. He spoke insistently, over and over.

Jenny shook her head at his stupidity, but she had to do something. She couldn't just leave him to die.

"I'm pretty sure it's still under the bed." She pointed at the two uniforms behind. "Right, you two, I want you to cuff this idiot and get him to a hospital."

The two officers glanced around warily.

"We'll keep an eye out for the snake," she added.

"Yeah, we will," offered Karim, stepping back towards the corridor.

The two men looked at each other and with one more glance around the room, said, 'Yes, ma'am." They walked up behind Mullins, who was praying even more reverently. He shuddered and faltered briefly as a wave of pain surged through him. This caused the uniforms to pause briefly, seeking confirmation from Jenny, who nodded curtly.

In one practised move, they each grabbed an arm and pushed his body forward, so that he landed face down. He screamed and resisted briefly as they pulled his arms behind and expertly clipped the handcuffs around his burnt wrists. Once secured, they grabbed him under the shoulders and lifted him up off the floor.

"Let me pray," he wailed as they dragged him out of the room. "Let me pray."

All the while, Jenny, Karim and Fiona had watched the room for any movement, but there was nothing. They retreated from Room 808 and closed the door behind them. Jenny would accompany Mullins to the hospital and find out who the hell was pulling his strings.

Jenny ordered the remaining uniform to guard the door and allow no one to enter, not until after the reptile expert had arrived and captured the snake.

Her hand shaking from the adrenalin rush, Klara knocked back the vodka. She hardly tasted it but felt the familiar burning sensation make its way down her chest. It felt good.

"Another," she said to the barman.

Brody, who was sitting next to her, sipped at his vodka.

"You must drink in one go," she advised. "It will help."

"That would get me drunk. And right now I need to think."

The barman arrived with a second shot. She was conscious of other patrons staring at her in her hotel robe, barefoot with her hair still wet from the shower. She didn't care what they thought.

"It's a classic social engineering scam," Brody concluded, shaking his head in admiration. "They were expecting you."

"Who? The man with snake?"

"Yes, and the people he works for."

"But no one knows I am here."

"Except the people who arranged for you to come to England in the first place."

"But what has job with electricity supply company got to do with snake man?"

"There is no job. It was a trick to make you come to this country, where they could get to you."

"No job?" She'd come all this way for nothing? She took a sip of her second vodka, trying to figure it out. "But makes no sense. How can electric company and snake man be same persons?"

"The people Mullins works for set it up. I reckon they recruited you to work on the firmware code last year. Same as Butler and Gowda. And now he's cleaning up, covering his tracks."

"What is cleaning up?" Perhaps her English wasn't as good as she'd thought. He used lots of phrases and idioms she'd never been taught and she found she had to work them out consciously.

"The person who you worked for last year is killing everyone involved in the project, all because Butler exposed him. He got to Butler ten days ago and Gowda the other day." He turned to face her. He had such an intense stare. "When were you first contacted about the electricity supply company job?"

Klara calculated and then her voice dropped. "Ten days ago."

"Which is when Butler was killed. How did they contact you?"

"I have profile on freelance programmer website. People contact me via site when they need firmware skills. If I have time I take on extra jobs."

"And is this how you were originally recruited for the …" He made quote marks in the air … "*vending machine* project."

"Yes. Is how I get all my private work outside Russia." Klara didn't like where this was going.

"Did you reply when they first contacted you ten days ago?"

"No. I was busy on SCADA hacking project in Moscow."

Brody looked surprised. "You're a hacker too?"

"No!" She laughed. The vodka was certainly calming her down now. "I was creating real time defence mechanism to make sure of firmware code integrity." But he'd said something odd. *Too.* Did he mean as well as her normal job? Or that she was a hacker, *like him*? It would make sense, considering the way he'd met her at the airport. Perhaps there was more to this Brody Taylor than was initially apparent.

"So you just ignored it?"

"Yes."

"And they didn't follow up?"

"No."

He thought for a moment. "They were from England but knew you were from Moscow?"

"Yes, is stated on freelance profile. I can charge more." She spoke proudly. "Russian programmers are best."

"Maybe," he conceded. "But it seems they wanted to get you to England."

"Is where job is."

"I know, but that was their excuse for getting you to come here. Sounds like they threw out the bait to see if you'd nibble, just as a precaution."

Now he was talking about fishing?

"And you didn't reply, so they didn't follow up, leaving you alone. Which means the idea of Vorovskoy Mir being behind this whole thing is questionable. They could much more easily deal with you in Moscow."

"Vorovskoy Mir!"

"They're a Russian mafia backed cybergang."

He'd explained as if she'd asked clarification, but she'd just blurted out their name in shock, horrified to hear them being referenced here in London. She thought she'd left all that behind.

"You know Vorovskoy Mir?"

He turned to her, surprised. "Yeah, I'm intimately familiar with them," he said, with an unexpected note of regret in his tone. "Six weeks ago, I lost a good friend — well, two good friends — because of those bastards."

Now it was her turn to gawp at him. What would this Englishman have to do with Vorovskoy Mir? She decided to offer a little more of her own story.

"Me also. My parents are in Moscow hospital because of Vorovskoy Mir." She went to take a sip of her vodka only to realise it was already empty. "Taking this job was not only reason for me to come to England. I was escaping from mafia. They were forcing me to do job to attack nuclear power station somewhere in West."

"You're joking."

"No, I not make fun of that. They attacked my parents and burned down family bookstore to force me to join them. But I escape."

"I'm so sorry." He raised his glass to his lips and made a silent toast before sipping. "So let me get this straight. You came here to escape Vorovskoy Mir?"

She nodded.

He shook his head. "What a small world."

But it was his ominous tone that scared her more than anything.

"Come on, Mullins," demanded Jenny. "Who told you to kill Butler and Gowda?"

Mullins writhed about on the hospital bed, his arms tied to the metal frame with leather straps, which held him there no matter which way his body twisted to deal with the excruciating pain.

Jenny turned helplessly to Dr Rama. "You've got to give him something, Doctor. I need him to answer my questions."

Dr Rama shook her head sadly. "As much as I want to help, I can't. He's refused medical intervention on religious grounds. There's absolutely nothing I can do."

"But there must be something, look at him! He's in real pain."

"If he changes his mind, I've got some more antivenom being rushed over from another hospital. We used up our last vial on you." Rama turned to examine her. "How are you, by the way? You disappeared without being discharged earlier. Any side effects?"

"I'm fine. Sorry about running out." Jenny pointed at Mullins. "Now you know why."

Mullins arched his back in abject agony and then fell back on the bed. His body hung limply, but his breathing was laboured. Jenny could see that he'd drifted off.

"Damn, this is so frustrating."

"If he'd been in this state when he'd arrived, maybe I could have helped with the pain because he wouldn't have been able to make his views known. Unfortunately, he was still fully conscious and absolutely demanded not to be treated, despite his suffering. The General Medical Council's rules are clear on this situation."

"What religion is this anyway? Jehovah's Witnesses?"

"I don't know, he didn't say. Usually is them."

"Usually? You've seen this before?"

"Yes, a couple of times, although not for treating a snake poisoning. Mostly it's blood transfusions they object to. The last one I saw was for a pregnant woman seven months gone, who had been diagnosed with leukaemia. The transfusion would probably have saved them both but she point blank refused."

"That's terrible."

Mullins screamed out loud and Jenny whirled around. He was pulling at one of the leather straps so hard she thought the metal bed frame would bend. After a moment he gave up and fell back, tears falling from his eyes.

Suddenly Mullins spoke, angrily forcing words through gritted teeth. "Why hast thou forsaken me?" Jenny wasn't religious but even she knew these were the words Jesus was said to have spoken on the cross.

"Mullins, can you hear me? Did Saul tell you to kill Butler and Gowda? Who is Saul?"

He ignored her, still squirming about, although less so now.

She turned back to the short woman. "And so we just sit here and watch him die?"

Dr Rama shrugged.

Jenny couldn't understand it. Wasn't she supposed to be a doctor? Didn't she have an obligation to heal above all else?

"What about something for the pain? Just that. Maybe then he'll talk."

"I really can't. I'm so sorry, DI Price."

"Oh for fuck's sake!"

Jenny was absolutely convinced that someone else had been driving his actions. Mullins was too much of a dolt to be the person behind the terrorist conspiracy, whatever it was. He had to be carrying out someone else's orders. Why it was all dressed up in some ceremonial religious charade with a snake made no sense to her. Although, given that he'd refused medical treatment for himself, perhaps it hadn't been a charade. Perhaps he really believed that he could pray for divine intervention to overcome the bite of a black mamba.

She clenched her fists in frustration. This was going nowhere. Jenny took one more look at Mullins and then stormed out of the room.

CHAPTER 19

BRODY AND KLARA SAT AT A SIDE table by the wall in the lobby, the one he'd originally pointed out to her when she was checking in. Her laptop was plugged in and they were hunched over the screen, Klara walking him through the firmware source code. Brody had talked Karim Malik from Jenny's team into retrieving Klara's case from her hotel room and she'd disappeared into the bathroom and emerged a a few minutes later in a short, figure-hugging dress, leaving little to the imagination. She drew just as many stares from other patrons now as she did when wearing just a bathrobe.

Brody was an excellent programmer, especially with C++ and a whole host of scripting languages. But assembler language? This was way too low level for him. Assembler was perhaps the lowest form of human-readable programming code, although because it had to mirror the resulting binary machine code and device architecture, it was, to Brody, like trying to read a foreign language where you only knew a few keywords.

"So, that subroutine you forced it to call on tomorrow's date, what does it do?" asked Brody.

"I've no idea. Let's look." Klara scrolled down. "I just followed instructions. Easy money. I didn't look closely and believed what they said. That it was emptying the trays of vending machines."

"Why are there no programmer comments to help decode

what all the various subroutines do?"

"Yes, is unusual. I thought that before."

"I guess they were trying to hide what the real device was from you."

"Perhaps … Ah, here we are."

Klara read through the code quickly, scrolling up and down. Brody did his best to keep up, but it was beyond him.

"It definitely calls specific function on the device," she said, hesitantly. "Without knowing, is hard to say what it might be. Parameters are loaded into registers. Primary one allows ranges between 0 and FF. My brief was to call it with maximum, so I hardcoded FF."

Brody shook his head. Now she was talking in hexadecimal. He'd always hated that number base when he was learning programming, and was pleased that the higher order programming languages allowed him to think in normal decimal.

Klara was an exotic, enticing mixture, with strong Slavic features: high cheekbones and almond-shaped steely eyes. But it was her brain that struck Brody as particularly alluring. She was by far the most technically gifted person he'd met in some time. It was such a pleasure to talk hi-tech with someone in the flesh. Normally, that was only something he could do with strangers online. She really knew what she was doing when it came to firmware programming.

But for all her technical proficiency, she was not streetwise. The fact that she had taken on this job a year ago without understanding the impact of what she was coding was amateurish. Brody would never have done that. But then he had to correct himself. Less than two months ago, he'd foolishly trapped himself in a race to 'get root' against another hacker without doing the proper due diligence. If he had, then Danny would still be alive and Leroy would still be his friend.

Klara's connection with Vorovskoy Mir had taken him by surprise. Brody had grilled her further. It turned out that she had even been graced by the presence of none other than Contag10n himself, well at least via a phone call. Brody had noted the name of Dmitry Alexeyevich Zakharin. Perhaps Zakharin could lead him to Contag10n? It was certainly something to follow up on when all the immediate craziness was out of the way.

Before diving into the firmware, they had focused on the email communications Klara had received via the freelance website. The email address used to recruit her a year ago to carry out the firmware recoding was different to the email used to invite her to work in London. But what they both had in common was that they were untraceable. Another dead end, but a common factor to link the two events.

Brody's eyes had glazed over the assembler code. He refocused his attention. "Okay, what if we look at when the subroutine normally gets called? Maybe we can work it out from there."

"Good idea." Klara searched for all calls to the subroutine. Her face screwed up as she tried to decode what she saw. "That is odd," she said, speaking slowly as she formulated her ideas. "It seems to be some kind of continuous measurement system."

"What, like you'd find in an electricity substation? Or a nuclear power station?" Brody felt a chill go down his spine at the thought.

Klara continued scrolling and studied the other events that called the routine. "No, I do not think so. I am familiar with most components like those. This code tracks events over time and stores them in octal registers. Then there's an exit that occurs based on bit pattern." She pointed to the specific assembler mnemonics on the screen.

Brody did his best to decode what he saw. "That doesn't make any sense."

"That's because you're thinking in decimal. In hex, it's just simple matter of flipping to binary groups." Klara went on to explain the techniques of register programming, but Brody had zoned out. Something had clicked in his head when she mentioned *hex*. He'd come across that word already this week, but not in the context of being hexadecimal. It was in Butler's original death letter to him.

Brody fished out his own computer and brought up Butler's message.

"What are you doing?" asked Klara.

"I think I know another way we can find out what's going on."

Yes, there it was. Butler had said, "*If you do, I will help you place a hex on those bastards. I want them to pay for killing me.*"

Brody had thought his use of the archaic word for a spell was strange at the time, but presumed it was just some kind of affectation, not knowing anything at the time about Butler. In fact, that was back when he'd known him only as BionicM@n. And Brody had thought nothing of it since. But now that he did think about it, wasn't it some kind of clue? After all, there had been nothing else to indicate Butler was into witchcraft or spell-casting.

"The devious bastard!" Brody laughed, suddenly figuring it out. He picked up his phone and called Jenny.

"Why are we here, Brody?" asked Jenny, looking up and down the private street. They stood on the steps outside James Butler's home. Jenny hadn't been there before, having been stuck behind her desk when the team originally investigated his murder. Butler had obviously had money, as Georgian townhouses in Highgate didn't come cheap.

Brody had been waiting for her when she arrived, parking further down the street. She'd taken a moment before exiting as Fiona had sent her a text during her journey, updating her on Mullins. He'd died in terrible pain without revealing anything about who drove his actions.

Brody answered her question. "Because Butler left us a clue that might blow this whole thing open."

"He did?"

Jenny listened as Brody explained about Butler using the phrase, *I will place a hex on those bastards.* She agreed it was odd, but it still explained nothing.

"Are you sure there's something in it? I'd rather not disturb Butler's grieving widow unless I really have to." She went to press the bell.

"Hold on a sec, Jen."

She turned to Brody. "What's up?"

His sheepish expression enabled her to make the mental leap. He'd been at it again. "You've been here before, haven't you?"

"Yeah, I have." He placed his hands in his pockets. "On Monday."

"Brody, what the fuck is it with you? You can't just wander into a crime scene on a whim."

"I was checking out Butler's background. It was before I knew you were involved."

"Hold on a sec. This was before you told me about Butler being a hacker. You told me that on Monday night."

"Yes."

"So why didn't you tell me you'd been here before?"

"It slipped my mind."

"Rubbish. Nothing slips your mind. You knew I'd be pissed off."

"Yeah, you're right. I'm sorry, Jen."

She went to press the bell and then a thought struck her. "What were you doing here, anyway?"

"I was trying to verify if BionicM@n and James Butler were the same person. At that point it was just a supposition. But I didn't learn anything as his wife knew nothing about his secret life as a black hat."

"Did you tell her?"

"No, of course not."

Jenny was sure there was something he was holding back but couldn't think what it would be. She pressed the bell and waited. After a moment she heard footsteps approaching from inside. Heels clicking on a stone floor.

"One more thing," said Brody into her ear. "She thinks my name is Richie Williams."

Why could nothing be straightforward with him? The door opened, giving Jenny no time to deal with this last minute revelation.

A tall, thin woman stood there. She had deep black circles under her eyes, obviously not sleeping well since her husband's death. When she saw Brody, she smiled gently. "Hello Richie. I didn't expect to see you until the funeral. We haven't got a date yet. Would you believe the police still haven't released his body?"

"Yeah, I'm just down from Dundee, Helen. I've been helping the police with some background on Wild Jim. This is Detective Inspector Price from the Met Police."

Jenny wanted to shake her head in exasperation. Dundee? Wild Jim? But instead she pulled out her warrant card and introduced herself. "We're just following up on a lead, Mrs Butler. May we come in?"

Helen Butler led them to a well-equipped modern kitchen. Brody said, "Actually, would you mind showing us his home office?"

"Your colleagues," she explained to Jenny, "already searched it and took away most things."

"I know," Brody answered. "But we just need to check one more thing."

She didn't look convinced, but told them to follow her and led them down some stairs into a basement split into two rooms. One contained a gym. The other was Butler's office, with floor to ceiling bookcases and a large ornate desk in the centre.

"Can I offer you tea or coffee?"

"That would be fantastic, Helen. Coffee for me, please."

Jenny would normally have declined but as Brody had already accepted she asked for coffee too.

"Richie Williams?" she hissed when she was sure Helen Butler was out of earshot.

"I pretended to be an old friend of Butler's from his time in the army. It was the easiest way to get her to tell me about Butler."

"You social engineered a grieving widow, Brody. Is there any level you wouldn't stoop to?"

"It was the quickest and easiest way. Also, I didn't do any harm."

"But you could have. What if it had backfired and she found out?"

He shrugged. "It didn't." But he was looking at the floor rather than at her, a sure-fire admission that he knew he'd gone too far.

"We'll deal with this later. What are we looking for, anyway?"

"There, on the wall."

He pointed at the expanse of wall below a thin window mounted high, which gave the basement room some natural light. Beneath the window a collection of five framed TV and movie posters were mounted. She recognised a couple of them. The *Six Million Dollar Man* TV show from the Seventies and the more modern *24* starring Kiefer Sutherland. The others she'd never seen.

Jenny had no idea what Brody was going on —

And then she saw it. One poster was mounted above the other four. It was for a movie called *Jonah Hex*. From the hats worn by the characters, it appeared to be a violent Western movie.

"Hex," she stated.

"Exactly. "

"You think he's hidden something in the picture frame?" Jenny moved towards it.

"That's my guess. Probably a USB stick containing access to his black hat life. I've not found any of that part of his hacking life anywhere. The computer seized as evidence had nothing on it. He obviously kept it separate. Do you remember his email to the other conspirators?"

"Yes?" She lifted the bottom of the picture away from the wall and peered behind.

"In it, he explained that he got hold of the email addresses for Gowda, Klara and Raz from hacking an account being used by Saul. If we can find the computers he used for his hacking, I should be able to track down whoever is behind this whole thing."

"Even Raz?"

"Sort of. I think there's something in your hypothesis the other day that Raz and the killer are the same person. What if Raz is Saul?"

"Go on …" Given that he'd publicly dismissed her idea the other day, she was definitely going to make him finish this line of thought. Maybe he'd have to eat his own words.

"I think Saul might have invented 'Raz' as an extra person involved in the conspiracy. All it required was a fake email address and a few phoney email conversations between himself and 'Raz'."

"But why go to all that trouble?"

"Because he recruited BionicM@n, a well known black hat hacker. It was insurance in case Butler turned the tables on him and hacked into his private messages. Which is exactly what happened."

Jenny couldn't help herself and finished off the line of thought. "And so when Butler contacted them all, including Raz, to expose the conspiracy, he inadvertently let Saul know as well. And so Saul started picking them off, one by one, sending out Mullins to do his dirty work."

Brody nodded and folded his arms. "It seems Butler wasn't as smart as I gave him credit for."

"So that means Raz was never going to show up at King's Cross the other day."

"Saul knew Butler was dead, because he sent Mullins to kill him. Yet, apparently, there he was again, full of life. Saul knew from the beginning I was some unanticipated outside factor and needed to deal with me quickly."

"So King's Cross was all about exposing whoever was pretending to be Butler. You."

"Looks like it."

At least Brody had the good grace to look sheepish.

"So Mullins followed you from King's Cross to Holborn to Upper Street?"

"And came back that night to clean up."

The theory certainly fitted the known facts, but they would need to prove it. It still didn't shed any light on why Mullins included a whole snake-based religious ceremony when he dealt with his victims.

Jenny turned her attention back to the picture. She lifted it off its hook. "You do realise the crime scene team would have already examined this?"

"Really?" Brody's face dropped at that. "But if they didn't know what they were looking for …"

She placed it face down on the desk and began to examine it. "Let's take a look, shall we?"

Brody stood beside her as she lifted the hardboard backing away from the picture. There was only the back of the poster. She lifted it out to reveal the glass front and examined every inch of the inside of the frame with her fingers.

"There's nothing here, Brody."

"Must be. Let me take a look."

She allowed him to examine it himself. After a moment he stepped back, cocked his head towards the ceiling, thinking deeply. She could almost hear the cogs turning within his brain.

Jenny heard steps. Helen Butler was returning.

"Damn, I thought …" Brody's voice trailed off in despair.

Mrs Butler arrived carrying a tray holding cups, saucers and a cafetière containing very dark coffee. "What's going on?" she asked when she saw the disassembled picture frame lying on the desk.

"Mrs Butler, did Mr Butler use any other computers other than the laptop we've already taken down to the station?"

She looked confused. "Not to my knowledge. What's that got to do with the picture?"

"Or USB sticks?" persisted Jenny.

Mrs Butler thought. "I've no idea."

"Would the crime scene team have taken in any they found?" Brody asked Jenny.

"Yes, if there were any."

"I'm definitely missing something here," said Brody. He turned to Mrs Butler. "Do you know why James had these particular posters up, Helen? They can't be his favourite movies and TV shows. Far too obscure a collection."

"He said the bionic man one was a good reminder that he could recover from his injury and be even better than before."

Jenny recalled that Butler's online handle was BionicM@n, which made it more apparent that his wife knew nothing about his life as a hacker.

"That makes sense. But what about Jonah Hex here?" Brody lifted up the poster, which was now outside its frame. "Or the others?"

Helen shook her head. "I don't know. Should I?" Tears welled up in her eyes. "I just thought he must have liked the posters."

Jenny automatically moved towards Helen. She took the tray from her and placed it on the desk.

"Excuse me. I've got to check on Gemma," Helen said, wiping her eyes. She turned and left them to it, running up the stairs.

"That's their daughter," explained Brody.

Jenny knew full well who Gemma was. She'd been the leverage that Mullins used to force Butler to put his hand in the box with the snake.

"Why these four posters?" asked Brody to the room while pouring coffee into two cups. "And why mount them four in a row under Jonah Hex?"

Now that he said it, she did think it was odd. Most people would group them evenly, or display them as two on top of three, in a brickwork style.

Suddenly, Brody struck his forehead with his palm, grinning inanely. "Butler, you doubly devious bastard!"

"What?" demanded Jenny, not getting the joke.

Brody fished out his tablet from his man bag and sat at the desk. "It's an IP address."

Jenny looked blankly at the posters.

"Four posters. They've all got numbers. Look. *Zero Dark Thirty* is 30. *Six Million Dollar Man* is 6. Then *24*. And 4 for *Fantastic 4*. That's an IP address: 30.6.24.4. It's brilliant!"

Jenny was aware of IP addresses, but wasn't sure how this helped.

Brody typed the code into his computer and then frowned. "Hmm. Must be more to it. I did think it was too simple." He sipped at his beverage. "Not bad coffee, actually."

"What are you going on about, Brody?" She picked up the other cup and sipped it. It was strong and bitter, just how she liked it.

He looked up at her. "There never was a USB stick. The posters point to an IP address on the internet. Once we work out which one, we'll find Butler's real computers."

"But computers need a box to run in."

"Every website you connect to is a computer in a box somewhere. You don't have to physically have the box to run the computer. You can put them anywhere."

She understood that. "Okay … What about the fifth poster, *Jonah Hex*?"

"Hex. Of course! Klara would have got it straight away."

"What's Klara got to do with this?"

He looked up briefly, confused. "Klara thinks in hexadecimal. She's a firmware programmer."

That explanation did nothing for Jenny. "Hexadecimal?" She hated herself for having to ask.

"Computers work in binary. Hexadecimal makes it easier for humans to represent binary as it's shorter. The digits 0 to 9 represent values zero to nine, and the letters A, B, C, D, E, F represent values ten to fifteen. So it runs from 0 to F, which is the same as zero to fifteen in decimal."

Jenny vaguely recalled something about number bases from maths classes in school.

"The poster must refer to the hexadecimal numbers. Thirty in hex is forty-eight in decimal. Six is, well, six. Twenty-four is thirty-six. And four is four." He typed the IP address into his computer. "No, that's still not it." He looked up at the posters on the wall. "What if *Zero Dark Thirty* isn't about the number thirty but the Zero D? 0D in hex is fifteen in decimal. That makes 15.6.24.4." He typed in the new code and frowned. "Nope, that's not it."

Jenny stared at the posters. "What about F4 for *Fantastic 4*?" she suggested.

"244? Brilliant!" Brody typed the revised address into the computer and waited.

After a moment, he looked up at her, beaming like the cat that got the cream. With a flourish, he spun around his tablet on the desk for her to see.

"Welcome to BionicM@n's digital lair."

"Turn right," Brody demanded.

"Why?" said Jenny. "It's left to get back to Holborn. I told you: we need to hand over Butler's virtual computers to O'Reilly. He knows how to treat digital evidence properly."

"But I know what the target is!" declared Brody. "And put your foot down."

He was connected over the internet to Butler's virtual machines from his tablet. He tried his best to ignore the car's movement, wanting to avoid motion sickness while he flicked in and out of directories, marvelling at Butler's creativity. He had been an excellent hacker. A true member of the elite.

And incredibly dangerous.

From the chat conversation with Contag10n on CrackerHack, Brody already knew about Butler's role in authoring the ransomware malware kit with which he'd eventually screwed over Vorovskoy Mir. But that was only the tip of the iceberg. He was also behind a range of other online scams. He discovered that Butler had created the original fake antivirus software seven years ago, which pretended to find malicious software on your PC. The frightened victim then paid for the software to fix it and magically the PC was cleaned, even though there had been nothing there in the first place. There was also a rootkit for creating authentic-looking phishing scams, designed to retrieve login credentials for bank accounts and credit cards from unsuspecting victims. Butler leased out the rootkit to others via the Deep Web, taking a small percentage of the profits.

But over the last two or three years, Butler seemed to have gone legit. He'd dropped all of his scams and took on pentesting jobs, much like Brody. He was particularly adept at breaking in over networks. Brody's normal approach was to apply social engineering techniques to hack the humans using the computers, which usually gave him the privileged access he needed. But, with social engineering hacks being more effective in the flesh and Butler being disabled, it seemed he had defaulted to brute force hacks.

Brody recalled what Helen Butler had said when he'd first met her. She told him that she'd got the old James back when he received his myoelectric prosthetic legs, giving him the ability to walk again. That had been about three years ago as well. Brody wondered whether his ability to walk again had also changed his attitude about all the black hat work he'd been doing. It made some sense.

"Where are we going, Brody?"

"To Stockley Park. It's near Heathrow."

"I know where it is. I was there the other … Are we going to MedDev Labs?"

Brody glanced at her in surprise. "Yes, how'd you know that?"

"That's where Rajesh Gowda worked."

"Of course. That fits."

"Explain."

"I have here a pentest report from a year ago, created by Butler. As part of it he broke through MedDev Labs' defences. They were pretty weak by the sound of it. His target was to install a new version of some firmware code into their source code management system. Saul hired Butler to carry out the pentest and provided the code."

"So, does that mean Gowda's role in this was to retrieve the code in the first place? And give it to Saul?"

"Probably."

"So why not just get Gowda to stick it back?"

Brody thought it through for a minute. "What did you say Gowda did for them?"

"He was a DBA."

"Okay, that makes sense. Being a DBA that means Gowda had low-level access to all the databases in MedDev Labs. Which means he can easily copy them, stick them on a USB stick and give them to someone else. But installing a new version of code requires you to go in through the application on top of the database, something Gowda either didn't have access to or wouldn't know how to use."

"But why not just replace the code directly into the database? He could have done that."

"He could, but the management system takes care of any code dependencies between modules and bypassing the application means the code may not compile properly without the dependent modules."

"Okay, too much detail," said Jenny, throwing the car into a roundabout. "I believe you. So Gowda gets the code out, gives it to Saul. Saul hires Klara, who changes it. And Butler hacks in, under the guise of a pentest, and installs it back into their system."

"You got it."

Brody felt they were accelerating and looked up. They were shooting down the ramp from Hanger Lane onto the A40. Jenny had certainly made good time around the North Circular from Highgate.

"So what does the code do?"

"I've no idea. Nothing about that in the pentest report. Not even Klara knows and she's the one who changed it."

He browsed through MedDev Labs' website, looking at the types of products they manufactured. They made insulin pumps, defibrillators, neurostimulators, drug pumps, ventilators and a whole host of devices with long, unwieldy names derived from medical jargon only surgeons understood. He thought through what Klara had told him about the device's normal operation being to carry out continuous measurements and then calling the subroutine when a certain pattern occurs.

"Jenny," Brody turned to face her, a deep frown on his face. "I've got a really bad feeling."

"What is it?"

He shook his head, unable to believe what he was about to say. It was truly a nightmare scenario. It was audacious simply because it was so crazy. It was a terrorist attack that would cause deaths on a scale that dwarfed even 9-11.

And it was too late to stop it.

CHAPTER 20

"POLICE. I NEED TO SEE JEROME RICHARDS, immediately," demanded Jenny, flashing her warrant card at the receptionist. When the receptionist did nothing, Jenny shouted. "Now!'

The receptionist called the IT Director, telling him, "You'd better come down. The police are here."

Jenny consciously stopped herself from drumming her fingers on the counter. Half of the Met Police were on their way. After Brody's conclusions in the car she had phoned DCS McLintock, going straight over Da Silva's head. This was way too big for Da Silva to muck it up. McLintock had listened intently, asking pertinent questions, and said he'd escalate the case. He would meet her himself at MedDev Labs. Before hanging up, Brody added that he needed to bring Klara Ivanov with them. McLintock agreed, not bothering to ask Jenny whose voice that had been.

Brody was sitting on one of the reception chairs, his head buried in his computer as usual. He appeared not to have a care in the world, despite what they'd stumbled into. She had no idea how he compartmentalised everything so effectively. Two people in white medical overcoats passed through the turnstiles, heading for the way out. Brody jumped up and held open the door for them, half blocking their exit more than he seemed to be helping them. They squeezed through.

The lift opened and she recognised the gaunt IT director from her visit two days before. He wore the same ill-fitting grey suit, but with a different tie.

"What now?" he said, spotting Jenny. "I was in an important meeting."

"You've been hacked," stated Jenny. "And it's serious."

"Bullshit. We upgraded our cyberdefences last year. I should know, it cost a fortune."

"Really?" asked Brody. "So what if I told you that your recovery phrase for your password is Bruno, your childhood dog's name? Or that your current meeting is with …" Brody glanced at his computer. "Jasmine Shelby, your Head of Desktop Support. Or that—"

"How do you know that?" demanded Richards.

"Invite us in. Get us some nice coffee and we'll lay it all out for you."

"And," added Jenny, impressed with Brody even though she knew he'd probably just broken fifteen laws. "Get every member of the Board of Directors in front of us. Now!"

A few minutes later, after having been escorted through security, they were in the boardroom on the third floor. A huge glass window gave a view over the lake and nearby golf course. The Head of Sales was halfway through a round with the HR Director and a supplier. They were now on their way back.

The room was filling with a new MedDev Labs board member every few moments. Eventually, a middle-aged woman entered, wearing a slick black trouser suit and black blouse buttoned to the top. She naturally exuded authority and the seven or so others in the room automatically deferred to her, including Richards. She immediately sought out Jenny and introduced herself as Dr Eva Dunst, Chief Executive Officer of MedDev Labs. Despite the German-sounding name, she had an American accent.

Brody leaned over to Jenny. "There's too many people. This can't be a committee meeting."

She nodded, deciding that there would be no pussyfooting around. She would be direct.

Dr Dunst called the room to order.

Brody stood and whispered, "Back in a sec. I'm bursting."

"Brody," Jenny hissed. "Don't you dare leave me to explain all this!"

But he'd already exited the room, just as two men entered wearing golf attire.

Dr Dunst lifted her hands and the room silenced. She turned to Jenny and said, "Okay, DI Price. You have our full attention."

Brody made his way along the corridors of the MedDev Labs building.

This was likely to be the roughest, shoddiest hack he'd ever undertaken. Normally he would prepare for weeks, get in and out of a corporate facility like this without ever being discovered. Then he'd present his report and walk them through how he'd compromised their security. But, for the first time ever, it didn't matter if he was caught. It might even help.

As he walked past an empty office he noticed a white lab coat on the back of someone's chair. He popped in and put it on. It was a bit tight but would do the job.

He reached a secured door and waved a pass at it. The light turned green and he opened the door. He'd surreptitiously lifted the security pass from one of the two people he'd held open the door for in reception earlier. He was no expert pickpocket, but had been pleased to get away with it.

Butler's pentest report had given Brody all the information he'd needed to hack into MedDev Labs earlier. Butler had conveniently left himself a virtual backdoor, exactly the kind of thing that Brody did whenever he carried out a pentest for a client. And that backdoor gave him admin level rights on most systems. This was how he'd discovered Richards' secret phrase for his password and how he gained access to his online diary to see with whom he'd been meeting. It had helped cut through Richards' bluster.

Brody walked past some labs. He smiled and nodded at two lab assistants coming the other way. They nodded back. The white coat did its job. Eventually he made it to his destination.

Brody entered and headed straight for a lab worker bent over a complex-looking machine. He was in his early twenties, with shaven hair and huge ear piercings that made massive holes in each of his ear lobes.

"Are you Frederick?" asked Brody, knowing from the photo on file that he was.

"Yes?"

Brody held out his hand. They shook. "I'm Brody Taylor. I'm carrying out an emergency project for Dr Dunst and she said you'd be able to help me."

"Dr Dunst?" He lightened up immediately. "Sure, how can I help?"

"Have you got any animals with the latest implantable defibrillator fitted?" Brody studied his computer. "The 4000 range, if possible."

"Sure, pick your choice." He indicated the bank of cages along the far wall. There were mice, rats, rabbits and even rhesus monkeys.

"A rabbit should do the trick. That soppy-looking white one."

Frederick dutifully lifted the rabbit out of the cage and placed it on the table in the centre of the room. "Now what?"

"The 4000 can be programmed wirelessly, can't it?"

"Yeah, I've got a reprogrammer here. It uses a radio frequency band to —"

Brody cut him off. "Can it reprogram the time in the device?"

"Sure." Frederick hesitated. "But why would you want to? Once that's set, it's done."

"But can it do it?"

"Yes."

"Right, I'll take Flopsy here. Frederick, you take the reprogrammer. Follow me."

Brody left the room, carrying the white rabbit. The lab assistant followed right behind.

Jenny was losing them. She'd tried her best to explain, but without access to Brody's intricate level of detail, she sounded out of her depth and unclear of the specific facts.

Where the hell was he?

Approaching police sirens soon drowned out their voices in the meeting room and a few minutes later, DCS McLintock entered with Klara Ivanov in tow. She was now dressed in slim black trousers and a white, tight-fitting T-shirt. Many of the men in the room looked up in interest. A minute later, Jenny's own team arrived: Fiona Jones, Alan Coombs and Karim Malik. Just as she was about to resume, Da Silva and Knight walked in, frowns of displeasure on both their faces at having been the last to be informed.

It was standing room only now. Jenny stood and tried again.

"Right, as I was trying to explain, there is a terrorist plot scheduled for tomorrow afternoon —"

The door opened again and Jenny shook her head in exasperation until she realised it was Brody.

"Blimey, you lot multiply like rabbits," he said, taking in everyone. "But that's okay, I've brought my own."

For some reason, Brody was carrying a white rabbit, which he then placed in the centre of the boardroom table. Surrounded by so many staring faces, it sat still, twitching its nose.

"Hi everyone, I'm Brody." He looked around the room. "And this is Frederick." A young man entered the room behind Brody, carrying a strange-looking machine.

"Before we start, I just want to dial someone else in." He fished his trusty tablet out of his man bag and swiped it. After a few seconds he stood it upright on the table. A face appeared on a Skype video call. "Hi Doc, sorry to interrupt. You might want to get Graham and Edward from upstairs to join you. This is big."

Jenny recognised the man. She'd met him at Danny's funeral and he'd been introduced as Victor Gibb. She recollected that he was from GCHQ.

"Not more terrorist conspiracies, Brody," he said and then noticed the group of people assembled behind Brody. "Where are you?"

"Doc, meet the board of MedDev Labs Inc., one of the world's foremost medical device manufacturers. Only one small problem: their security is a bit lacking."

"I resent that," said Richards. "I've —"

"Jerome, I'd shut up if I were you," interrupted Brody. "When this is finished, Dr Dunst is going to be looking for a fall guy and I think you'll be a strong candidate. After all, MedDev Labs' share price is about to collapse."

Suddenly, lots of people were trying to talk at once.

Jenny had never seen Brody like this. He seemed to be really enjoying himself. Was this what he was like when he delivered his normal pentest reports?

On the computer screen, two other men joined Victor Gibb.

"Right, let's begin," said Brody. "Frederick, where did I get this rabbit from?"

Frederick looked around the room nervously, focusing mostly on Dr Dunst. "From the testing lab on the lower ground."

"How did you get down there?" demanded Richards.

Brody cocked his head and sighed theatrically. He didn't answer, focussing instead on the lab worker. "And what is special about this rabbit, Frederick? Or would you prefer Fred?"

"Fred's fine," he replied, confused at Brody's tone in front of the upper echelons of his company. "Uh, nothing's special. It's just a rabbit."

"But doesn't it have a pacemaker fitted?"

"No." Brody glanced at him, surprised.

Fred went on, "It has a defibrillator."

"You say defibrillator, I say pacemaker," Brody quipped. "Same difference as far as we're concerned right now. When was it fitted?"

Fred thought for a moment. "Last week."

"So no one could have tampered with it? As far as you know, it's just a standard, run-of-the-mill factory-produced defibrillator manufactured by MedDev Labs?"

"Well, yes."

"Okay. And what's that you're carrying?"

"It's a standard wireless reprogrammer for our pacemakers and defibrillators. Hospitals have these to check battery status, collect statistics and optimise the settings for things like the pacing mode, rate-responsiveness and so on."

"Okay. So to summarise: we have a standard, off-the-shelf defibrillator and a standard, off-the-shelf wireless reprogrammer as manufactured by MedDev Labs?"

"Yes."

If Brody pulled up his sleeves, Jenny decided she would scream. He was taking the magician act just a little too far. But he certainly had everyone's attention.

"Fred, is it possible to wirelessly change the date and time of the defibrillator?"

"Yes, but why would you want to?"

"I'm asking the questions right now, if you don't mind. So, can you wirelessly connect to the device inside Flopsy here and set the date and time to tomorrow at 12:35 p.m.? I believe it's the fifth of June tomorrow."

Fred looked behind DSC McLintock for a power socket and plugged in the reprogrammer, putting it down on the same table. After thirty seconds or so, it was ready.

Fred withdrew a peripheral from inside the machine. It looked a bit like a computer mouse. He held it by the rabbit. It was connected by cable back to the programmer main unit. Fred pressed some buttons on the programmer menu and then said, "Okay, I've just reset the date of the defibrillator within the rabbit."

"Okay, thanks Fred. Let's put Flopsy back in the centre where everyone can see." Brody pushed the white rabbit forward and stroked its ears, before stepping back. It sat there quietly, unconcerned.

Everyone stared.

Brody, who was looking at his watch, said, "I'm sorry, Flopsy."

Suddenly the rabbit flinched dramatically and gave a high-pitched squeal. But within a second it dropped down flat on the table.

Dead.

The room exploded with noise, with everyone pointing at the rabbit and asking questions. Brody had made his point.

"Right, let me explain."

The roomed hushed.

"Every pacemaker and defibrillator manufactured by MedDev Labs in the last year has a time bomb programmed into it. And every device made before last year that has since had its firmware upgraded by a programmer like this one, also has the same time bomb. It forces the pacemaker to send the maximum possible shock to the heart over and over and over until the battery runs out."

He spotted Klara standing open-mouthed towards the back of the room, caught her eye and said gently, "Sorry Klara, this was never about vending machines." He switched his attention to the firm's CEO. "How many people around the world have this type of device fitted, Dr Dunst? A rough estimate, please."

Her face had turned ashen. She licked her lips before speaking, trying to moisten them. "Well over 100,000 people, all around the world."

Brody took a deep breath and, realising the enormity, said simply, "Fuck, that's a lot."

"Are you saying that this time bomb could go off and could kill all those people?" DCS McLintock spoke for the first time.

"Not could. Will. The time bomb will go off at 12:36 tomorrow afternoon and over 100,000 unsuspecting people are going to drop down dead."

For the third time since Brody had entered the room, everyone began speaking at once.

Jenny looked at Brody and gave a thin smile. He could see that she was tired. Only this morning she had been in hospital recovering from being poisoned by one of the world's deadliest snakes. He was not aware if she'd eaten today, probably making it through on caffeine alone. He vowed to get her something to eat as soon as he had a minute to himself.

He felt fine, physically. But the enormity of the situation weighed heavily on him. On the way over from MedDev Labs' offices in the back of a blacked-out chauffeur-driven government car with Jenny, DCS McLintock and Dr Dunst, he'd quietly remonstrated with himself over taking too long to track down Butler's virtual computers. If he'd not been distracted with investigating the murders themselves, maybe he would have figured out the message in the death letter more quickly and given everyone more time to deal with the threat.

"Behave yourself in there, Brody," said Victor Gibb. The huge GCHQ agent had flown up from Cheltenham in a military helicopter, accompanied by the more senior agent Brody knew as Graham from his interview on Monday morning — a lifetime ago now.

When they'd arrived at the Cabinet Office in Whitehall, the car picking its way through scores of journalists trying to snap pictures of the dignitaries in the back, Gibb was waiting for them.

"I'm sure Mr Taylor will do fine," said DCS McLintock. "He and DI Price have got us this far and given us a fighting chance."

Gibb was referring to what was waiting for them beyond the oak-panelled door the five of them currently stood outside. It had a sign on it declaring 'Cabinet Office Briefing Room A'. Also known as COBRA.

Once news of the scale and timing of the hack had been established, events had escalated quickly. Within ten minutes, it was being treated as an impending terrorist threat and the Prime Minister had been informed. Given the global nature of the problem, with targets being in countries all around the world, the Prime Minster picked up the phone and personally informed the American President, German Chancellor and French Prime Minister. Other countries were informed by her minions. Within twenty minutes COBRA had been convened, chaired personally by the PM. This was the UK's emergency response committee, consisting of ministers, civil servants, police and intelligence officers.

The door to the COBRA meeting opened and they were ushered in.

Brody couldn't help himself and, indicating the COBRA plaque, whispered Indiana Jones' famous line from *Raiders of the Lost Ark* into Jenny's ear. "Snakes. Why'd it have to be snakes?"

She elbowed him gently in the ribs.

An expansive veneered oak table filled the room, with leather chairs all around. A bank of television and computer screens filled the wall at one end of the room, three of them displaying video conferences with faces filling the screens. The others had different news channels on mute. Seated in the centre of the room, directly opposite Brody, was the Prime Minister. She glanced up as they entered and gave them a grim smile.

Brody recognised some of the other faces from the news. Graham from his interview at GCHQ was sitting in the corner.

"Ma'am," said the man who'd ushered them in, "This is DCS McLintock and DI Price from the Met Police, Victor Gibb from GCHQ, Dr Eva Dunst from MedDev Labs and Brody Taylor."

She studied them intently and invited them to sit down. Five chairs had been made available.

"I understand we have you to thank for exposing this conspiracy, Mr Taylor?"

"Not just me. Jenny — I mean, DI Price — as well."

"Well, on behalf of the nation, thank you both. Now, as you are fully aware, this is an urgent situation and we have to move quickly."

"Klara Ivanov is working on the new firmware right now," said McLintock.

"Yes, very strange. I understand that Miss Ivanov is a Russian programmer who created the payload in the first place."

Brody immediately jumped to her defence. "Technically correct. But she had no idea what the device she was reprogramming did. She'd been led to believe that it was for a vending machine."

The PM raised an eyebrow at that. "The main thing right now is whether we can trust her or not?"

"She's absolutely distraught at the havoc she's been party to causing. She wants to help fix it."

When Brody had theatrically killed the rabbit, within a couple of minutes Klara had broken down in tears, devastated at what she'd done. Brody had tried to comfort her, pointing out she was the person best placed to fix the code.

"And anyway," added Dunst, "my firmware programmers are

working alongside her."

"Why can't they just go back to the previous version?" asked Graham.

Brody answered. "When James Butler installed the malicious version, he deleted all prior versions from the repository. They have them backed up remotely on tape, but it will take hours to get them restored. Quicker to update what's there."

"This code can really cause people to drop down dead?" asked the PM. "I find it hard to believe."

"There's already been a spate of deaths. At least fifteen," said Brody. "But no one realised they were connected."

Most members of the COBRA committee looked up. This was news. The PM said, "Go on, young man …"

"This is actually the second version of the hijacked firmware. Klara followed the brief to the letter and set the time bomb to go off as requested. However, because she was taking instructions from an American she interpreted their request for '5/6' to be sixth of May instead of what they wanted, the fifth of June. Tomorrow."

Unit conversion errors was a common enough issue in programming. The most famous example was when NASA lost a Mars orbiter when one team used metric units for a calculation and the other team used imperial.

"Last month, on the sixth, quite a few people died. From our research so far …" Brody flipped his computer round and clicked through a presentation he'd prepared. Each one was a screenshot of a local newspaper announcing someone's death, each with a photo. "A crofter called Murdo MacLeod in the Hebrides, who dropped down dead on his textile loom. Ellie-Rae Granger, a stroke victim living in a retirement home in Newcastle. A Cornish fisherman called Winston Jones. An IT salesman in Edinburgh called Darren Raymond. A Leicester postman called Surinder Patel. And the most famous of them all …"

Brody had their attention. As he'd ticked off the names, most people in the room had begun to shake their heads in disbelief, the reality of what they were dealing with sinking in.

" … David Dougan, the Irish celebrity chef who dropped down dead on live television. There's at least another ten, but I think you get the point."

"You're joking."

"No, we've verified that each of these people had a MedDev Labs heart implant. They received software upgrades based on the first version of the hacked firmware. A few weeks later, Klara was contacted again and asked to correct the error. Butler hacked in once again and loaded the new code onto MedDev Lab's systems, replacing the first doctored version. But, as you can see, it had already been deployed. It's official. The payload works on humans as well as rabbits."

Brody remembered Helen Butler telling him that James Butler had been overly angry about the death of the celebrity chef. She said that he'd gone on about it for ages. He wondered if this was the catalyst for Butler trying to stop the clock on the conspiracy. Something must have triggered Butler to challenge what was going on nearly a year after the firmware had been installed.

The PM turned to Graham. "Why didn't GCHQ or MI5 pick up on these deaths? Surely a pattern or a spike like this should mean something? If we'd worked this out last month …"

Graham shook his head sadly. "There was nothing to suggest foul play, Ma'am."

She folded her arms and let out a deep sigh of frustration. She collected herself and then said, "Okay, let's focus on what we can do now. When the new code is available, how does it get deployed to everyone with one of the affected pacemakers?"

Brody almost corrected her as Fred had corrected him earlier about the differences between pacemakers and defibrillators. But Jenny kicked him under the table, having sensed where he was going.

Dunst took up the reins. "We've narrowed down the types of devices affected. We've started contacting every hospital and clinic that buys from us or our partners; about 8,000 in total around the world. We've been asking them to get ready to receive the new firmware for the affected devices on their programmers. Being late in the evening, the issue of course is that the people who normally deal with this kind of stuff have gone home. At least here in the UK."

"But can you get the new firmware distributed first thing in the morning? Because when we break this to the press we're going to have overnight queues at every hospital and clinic in the country."

"We'll do our best."

"If you'd done your best beforehand," pointed out the PM, "then your company would have had better security defences to avoid this in the first place. But that's something we'll pick up on at a later date."

Dr Dunst sat back meekly in her chair. After seeing everyone subsuming to her natural authority back at MedDev Labs, it was quite a change around. Brody decided he wouldn't want to be in Dr Dunst's shoes when her company's behaviour in this became the focus of conversation.

"Which leads us on to the public," continued the Prime Minster. "We've got to control this because, believe me, there will be riots in the streets if it's handled badly."

"We've got a press conference scheduled in thirty minutes, Ma'am," said the man Brody recognised as the Downing Street Press Secretary. "Our angle is that this is just a programming bug that needs resolving immediately. We're trying to position it in a similar way to the approach automotive manufactures use to manage product recalls. At least the resolution doesn't require an invasive operation. It's just the wave of a wand from a wireless programmer to update the firmware in the device."

"That's not good enough, Jack," commented the PM. "Too many people will ignore the recall. There's no choice here. We have to up the urgency and admit the impact. Thousands will die if we don't."

"We can't possibly say that. There'll be civil unrest," said a man in an army uniform. Brody presumed he headed up the armed forces.

"Which is much more palatable than if we hadn't known about this whole thing in the first place, Barry."

They carried on debating the public communications strategy

for a few more minutes, but the PM's view was carried through. The public would be told people would die if the matter was not addressed, but the terrorist hack element would be kept under wraps for now.

"How will we know if we've got everyone?"

"Unfortunately we won't," said Dr Dunst. "We don't have central records of everyone who's been fitted with a device, particularly in the UK with the regionalised healthcare authorities and no central medical record system."

"Are you saying that if we miss anyone, we'll only know when they drop down dead?"

"Unfortunately, yes."

"Charles," the PM turned to a man who had remained quiet throughout the meeting. "As Health Secretary I want your team to spend tonight scouring every medical database to come up with a finite list. And I want every person on that list contacted first thing tomorrow. We're lining up the army for logistics on this. You get them the names and they'll call and get them into a hospital."

"Uh, yes, Ma'am." The Health Secretary didn't sound confident, but was clearly not going to argue with his senior when she was in this mood.

"Which leads us to our last topic," stated the PM. "Who the hell is behind this conspiracy? Has anyone come forward to take credit?"

"We don't know yet," said DCS McLintock. "We've caught the man who tried to kill all the people recruited to make the hack work in the first place. But unfortunately he died before giving up any information."

"Who was he? ISIS?"

"We don't think so. There was some form of religious motivation behind it."

"Then it must be ISIS," persisted the PM.

"Sorry, I mean Christian religious motivation."

"That makes no sense," said Graham from GCHQ. "The only radical Christian terrorist groups on our radar are in Africa, India or the USA."

"What about Ireland, Graham?" asked Barry, the military leader.

"You're thinking of some kind of splinter group from the Provisional IRA, Barry? But it doesn't really make sense. Those groups target Protestants specifically. This situation is hitting a much wider catchment than that."

Jenny spoke up for the first time. "We've still got a lot of background checking to do on Ralph Mullins, the man behind the killings this week. We only learned his name today."

The PM leaned forward and said, 'If you don't mind me saying, dear, you look like you've done enough and could do with a rest. Did I hear correctly that you were in hospital this morning recovering from snake poisoning at the hands of Mullins?"

Jenny blushed. Brody had never witnessed that before. "Yes, Ma'am. But we've got to keep going. Too much is at stake."

"Well said, my dear." The PM looked around the room. "Anything else we need to discuss before I go and wreak havoc on the public?"

The sea of blank faces provided her answer.

Brody and Jenny tucked into their Korean sharing platter of fried chicken sliders, kimchi rice, pork belly tacos and steamed dumplings. They were in the basement dining room of Jinjuu, a trendy Korean restaurant on the edge of Soho. Brody had recommended it as he knew it stayed open late. In the bar upstairs a DJ was in full swing.

"This is sooo good," declared Jenny.

"Have you tried the dumplings? They're amazing."

It had been three hours since their meeting with the Prime Minister and the COBRA committee. Since then, all hell had broken loose. The PM had briefed the media, who had gone wild with the story. It was breaking news all over the world. Every country was organising remediation plans for the people affected. In the UK, anyone with a pacemaker or defibrillator was ordered to go to their nearest hospital or clinic first thing in the morning. Of course, people started going immediately.

Just after 11:00 p.m., Brody called Klara to check on progress. She and the MedDev Labs programming team were just waiting for the final tests to complete before releasing. They needed to make sure they didn't introduce any unwarranted side effects.

Just before midnight, UK time, the new module was made available for download. By 1:00 a.m., the first people were having the firmware in their devices upgraded.

In the absence of a compelling reason, the press speculated as to why this had happened. They clearly didn't buy the programming glitch put forward by the PM. The Health Secretary had tried to compare it to the Year 2000 bug, but had got shot down quickly. The world had years to prepare for that non-event, not one day. A three-year-old story about a hacker called Barnaby Jack surfaced and fuelled the press with conspiracy theories not too far from the truth.

At black hat security conferences, Jack had made a name for himself by publicly exposing security weaknesses in networked devices ranging from ATMs to insulin pumps and pacemakers. In 2013, he was supposed to give a presentation on hacking pacemakers wirelessly. His presentation would have shown how he could remotely send an electric shock to anyone wearing a pacemaker within a fifty-foot radius. But he died the week before of a drug overdose. That hadn't stopped the hacking community from firing off conspiracy theories of big businesses assassinating him. The story was now making the rounds again.

The business news was speculating how bad the fall would be for MedDev Labs' stock the following morning. And probably the stock of every other medical device manufacturer.

Brody was pleased Jinjuu had no televisions on display. He'd had enough of it all. All week, he and Jenny had been so close to the action, almost losing their lives in the process. Now that the conspiracy had been exposed, they had been relegated to bit part players on the sidelines as the government machine and the media swung into action. He was impressed, though. Many people's lives would be saved.

"How's Stefan?" asked Jenny.

"He's home from hospital. Lorenzo texted me earlier saying

that Stefan was busy bossing him about for not cleaning up well enough after the crime scene team left."

"That's good. I'm glad he's okay."

"He'll probably kick me out of the apartment."

"Somehow, I doubt that. For whatever reason, he seems to have a soft spot for you, Brody."

They ate in companionable silence and drank sparkling water. Neither had wanted to introduce alcohol into their tired bodies.

Suddenly, something occurred to Jenny, and she leaned forward. "So what's the story with Victor Gibb? He knew about the conspiracy before you dialled him into the meeting at MedDev Labs."

Brody carried on chewing his mouthful, buying himself time. How much to say? He swallowed. "I told him what I knew early this morning. I needed his help to figure out who Klara was so that I could meet her off the plane."

"Why go to him? Is this because of our row last night? Because we agreed that you were to keep out of my cases going forward."

He grinned. "Haven't done a good job of that, have we?"

She laughed. "No, I suppose not. But thank God you stayed involved. So many people would have died tomorrow."

"They won't save everyone. It's impossible."

"Yeah, I know. But tens of thousands of people will survive."

Brody picked up another fried chicken slider.

"You didn't answer my question. Why Victor?"

"I needed Klara's full details so I could track her down. Just as I said."

"Why would a GCHQ agent help you out like that? That's confidential information. As far as I know, you don't work for them yet. Do you?"

Jenny had the nose of a bloodhound. Sometimes she was so damn frustrating.

"No. I'm still deciding."

"What's to decide? You said you want to bring down Vorovskoy Mir after Danny's death and GCHQ would give you the best platform."

"Yeah, I know. But there's more than one way to skin a cat. I'm not sure joining GCHQ is right for me. Like you said, I don't seem to play nicely with others."

"I did say that, didn't I? Maybe I was being a bit harsh."

He decided now was as good a time as any. "I'd also need to move to the Cotswolds."

"Ah."

He reached across and took her hands in his. "I don't want to turn us into a long-distance relationship. I'd be crap at it."

"Me too," she admitted. "Which might be a problem even if you don't take the job."

Brody didn't understand. "What do you mean?"

"I've applied for a DCI position in Manchester."

"Ah."

And there was him dreading bringing up the subject of moving to the Cotswolds when, all along, she was heading off to Manchester.

"It's not certain," she added. "I only applied the other day and I haven't even had an interview yet."

"Even so." He withdrew one hand from hers and picked at a dumpling. It didn't taste anywhere near as good now.

"What are we like, eh?" she joked.

"We can make this work, can't we?"

"You see, the thing is … I don't know if I want to anymore …"

He bored into her eyes, but there was a smirk peeking through. Brody relaxed, but was still wary about what was to come.

"I'm not sure I can be with a bloke who goes around killing poor, defenceless rabbits."

FRIDAY

CHAPTER 21

HOLBORN WAS A HIVE OF ACTIVITY. IT was before 8:00 a.m., yet it seemed as if every shift had been called in this morning. Jenny had never seen so many uniformed officers in the station at the same time. No wonder she'd been unable to park nearby.

They all seemed to be heading for the media briefing room. Rather than go straight upstairs to the murder investigation suite, she followed them in to see what was going on. The room was packed to the rafters with police officers. Not one journalist in sight.

DCS McLintock stood alone on stage. After a minute, he called everyone to attention and began.

"We've now received a list of every person in our borough with a heart implant. There are over 1,200 names. I need each of you to take ten names. We've got home addresses, work addresses, secret mistress addresses, local pub addresses, and any other known addresses. I need every person tracked down, contacted and, if necessary, dragged into the nearest hospital or clinic." He surveyed the room. "If you can't find someone on your list, I want it escalated back here. We'll set the Territorial Support Group onto them. If they're somewhere else in the country, we'll transfer their case to the nearby nick and they'll track them down. If they're on holiday in Mogadishu, we'll track them down. If they're at the top of Mount Everest, we'll track them down. But by God, between us all we will track everyone down before 12:36 p.m. and get their implant upgraded. No one on our patch dies today. Do you hear me?"

There was a half-hearted response.

"*Do you hear me?*"

"Yes, sir!" they all shouted as one.

Jenny felt like she'd stepped onto the set of a Hollywood action movie, with McLintock giving the rousing speech at the end just before the aliens attack.

"Okay, four queues, one in each corner of the room. Collect your ten names and go and save some lives." The officers spread to the four corners of the room. McLintock stepped down from the stage and spotted Jenny at the back. He headed over to her. "This is all thanks to you, this is. I'm proud of you."

It was the highest praise she'd ever received from McLintock and she was embarrassed.

He hadn't finished. "By the way, I've blocked your application to Manchester. You're staying here."

What the hell? That wasn't fair.

"As soon as all this is over, I'm promoting you to DCI."

He walked off, leaving her standing at the back of the room, dumbfounded.

Brody exited Angel Tube station and walked up Upper Street towards Bruno's and home.

After their late meal last night, they'd gone back to Jenny's place in Richmond. Jenny had been on her last legs by the time the cab had dropped them off. Peace had descended after they'd both admitted to the possibility of moving away from London. There was no more arguing over what Brody had or hadn't done wrong. With the future of their relationship in doubt, they had climbed silently into bed, held onto each other and slept.

Jenny was up extra early. In the kitchen making toast, Brody requested an *Uber* cab on her behalf to take her back to Stockley Park so that she could pick up her car. He ate the toast on his own, washed up the plate and left, picking up a cappuccino from Taylor St Baristas next door to Richmond Station, before jumping on the Tube back home.

The newspapers were full of the pacemaker story. Strangers opened up conversation with other strangers on the Tube about it, just in case the person they talked to had an implant and somehow hadn't heard the news. It was as if everyone had been brought together by a common purpose.

As he walked along Upper Street, Brody heard ambulance sirens in the distance and helicopters above. A police car screamed up the road and pulled up outside the building opposite Bruno's. A few minutes later, the elderly woman who'd rented his old apartment was practically dragged out and pushed into the police car. The car sped off.

He entered Bruno's, pleased to see that the window had been repaired already. Lorenzo was behind the counter and waved. Stefan, who had his back to Brody and hadn't seen him arrive, was busy taking orders from some patrons sitting in the exact sofa where Jenny had been bitten by the snake two nights ago. There was no evidence of the crime that had threatened both their lives.

Brody's favourite seat in the window alcove at the front was free and he thought, why not? He sat down and waited patiently, connecting his PC to the power socket and his personal hard-wired network point.

"Ah, Mr Brody, Mr Brody."

Brody looked up to see Stefan's beaming smile. He had a black eye and his cheek was swollen and bruised. There was a plaster on his forehead. "It's good to see you, Stefan. How are you feeling?"

"Me? I am fine. This …" He pointed to his cheek. "Is nothing, Mr Brody. I had much bigger in military service. How is Miss Jenny?"

"She's fine thanks, Stefan. Look, I'm so sorry about what happened to you. It was all my fault."

"It was no one's fault but the bad man. Now, what will Mr Brody have to drink, I wonder?"

Brody marvelled at Stefan's ability to write off everything that had happened. Unless he'd read past the front-page news stories about the pacemakers, he wouldn't even know that the man who'd attacked him was now dead.

Brody agreed to Stefan's suggestion of a cappuccino even though he'd have preferred an espresso. He owed him too much and promised he would never correct him.

Brody refocused on his computer and got back to work.

The murder investigation suite was also buzzing. Jenny pushed open the door and entered. She saw Fiona across the room and headed in her direction.

"Here she is," shouted Alan.

At that, everyone stopped what they were doing, stood, turned in her direction and began clapping. Jenny was taken aback again and fought not to blush. She offered an embarrassed smile and marched towards her desk. The applause followed her all the way. Whoops as well, started by Karim. Da Silva and Knight even stepped out of Da Silva's internal office and joined in.

"Get back to work, you lot," she ordered the room.

They laughed, but the applause petered out and everyone returned to what they had been doing.

She reached her desk and sat down. Fiona came over.

"That was embarrassing," said Jenny.

"You deserved it, Jenny. You're a real hero right now. This time yesterday you were in hospital. And yet you somehow uncovered this crazy terrorist plot. Everyone in this room has at least one person they know with a pacemaker. For me, it's my nine-year-old niece. Thank you."

"Has she had her pacemaker upgraded?"

"Yeah, I took her to the clinic myself in the middle of the night, before it got crazy today. Apart from queuing for two hours, she was in and out in a couple of minutes."

"That's great." Jenny couldn't think of anyone close to her who relied on a pacemaker. "The small meeting room looks free. Can you get the team to gather in there in five? O'Reilly as well."

"Sure."

Jenny made herself an espresso and headed into the meeting room. Alan was waiting for her and told her how proud he was to know her and that thanks to her, his sister would live beyond today. Karim and O'Reilly arrived, both naming people she'd helped save.

It made her mind reel. When it had been huge abstract numbers it hadn't really meant that much, but hearing names of people made it tangible.

Once the gushing was over, she tried refocusing the team. "Right, we've done all we can on exposing the conspiracy. Everyone else is dealing with that. I want us to focus on who the hell is behind this. Mullins, Butler, Klara or Gowda. One of them will lead us to Saul Baker."

They all nodded assent.

"Alan, what have you found out about Mullins?"

As always, he flipped open his notebook to the correct page, glanced at it once, then hardly referred to it again as he spoke. "Mullins lived in a flat on a downtrodden housing estate in Borehamwood. He'd been there since leaving —"

Alan halted abruptly as the door behind Jenny opened.

"Don't mind us," said Da Silva, entering with DI Knight behind. They took seats at the end of the table. "Carry on."

Jenny just about held it together. Although she had much to be grateful for thanks to his foresight in requesting the antivenom that had undoubtedly saved her life, she still sensed an underlying resentment. He had been on his best behaviour since being dressed down by McLintock, even showing genuine concern towards her in the hospital. But she wasn't buying it. If she'd learned anything about Da Silva, his actions were always self-serving. She had no idea what plans McLintock had for Da Silva, but once she was the same rank as him at least she'd no longer have to put up with his crap.

"As I was saying," continued Alan, "Mullins had been there since leaving Maidstone prison three years ago. He was inside for killing a teenage kid who taunted his dog. Before that, people who knew him described him as a gentle giant. In fact, his neighbours in Borehamwood use the same description, although they kept well away as they knew what he went down for. He lived alone. Only family was a brother in Australia who hasn't been in touch with him since before he went down."

"Was he religious? Before prison or in prison?" asked Jenny. She was thinking of all the Bible talk Brody said Mullins had spouted.

"The brother said not and I talked to the chaplain at Maidstone. Mullins never registered a choice of religion and never visited the prison chapel."

"And since? Did he go to church somewhere?"

"I can't find anyone who knows. He kept himself to himself where he lived and worked. Never any talk of going to church. Although he was known to quote from the Bible."

"Brody said that he didn't seem to be rowing with both oars. Anyone been able to verify that?"

"The prison doctor described him as having a dependent personality disorder coupled with …"

"Would that have made him easily led?" interrupted Fiona.

"Yes. He said Mullins had difficulty making decisions and he needed others to take responsibility for his actions."

"Good. That adds weight to the theory that someone else was pulling his strings," said Jenny.

Coombs continued. "He also said that he had suspicions that he was suffering with something called …" Coombs referred to his notes for the first time. "Maladaptive daydreaming. Apparently, he was capable of immersing himself in much more vivid worlds than the real one."

There was a pause as the room digested that.

"That sounds like a form of schizophrenia," suggested Da Silva.

Coombs was unfazed by the questions coming from all directions. He'd certainly done his homework. "Apparently the difference is that people with schizophrenia can't differentiate between their fantasies and reality. Maladaptive daydreamers are able to keep it under control."

"What about the whole black mamba side of things?" asked Jenny.

Karim spoke up. "I've been following up on that line of enquiry. Alan and I actually met Mullins when he was working in a reptile shop in Watford. But …" He folded his arms. "But we met a lot of people that day when we visited pretty much every pet shop in London and the home counties."

Jenny could see he was being defensive. "We can't all spot criminals when we first meet them, Karim. Don't beat yourself up."

"Thanks, Jen," he said, although to his right Da Silva scornfully raised his eyebrows. Fortunately, Karim didn't notice and carried on. "Seems he's worked there ever since leaving prison. Apparently he used to work there even before going inside, although the shop changed hands while he was away. When he showed up, the new owner thought he was such a natural with the animals that they didn't bother checking his background. When I told the owner he'd done ten years for manslaughter he almost shit a brick."

"Did the shop trade in black mambas?" asked O'Reilly, straying outside his domain of technology.

"No. The proprietor said they're far too dangerous for people to keep as pets. But I'm still working through a list of reptile importers. He did hint that there is a black market in exotic snakes. It's entirely possible that the mambas used in the attacks were never registered anywhere."

"So, where the hell did Mullins keep the snakes?"

Everyone looked at each other for answers. None were forthcoming.

Jenny summarised. "The dependent personality disorder. The snakes. Someone else was definitely calling the shots. Is it too far a leap to say that the snake keeper is the orchestrator?"

Lots of nodding heads.

"Okay, let's move on. O'Reilly, what have you got from Butler's virtual computers?"

"What virtual computer? The only computer I've got from Butler is the one under my desk. Unless you mean the virtual copy Brody stored in the cloud?"

Jenny was confused. Brody had told her all about them. It was Butler's 'digital lair', where Brody had discovered the pentest report on MedDev Labs. She had asked him to hand over the details to O'Reilly as evidence. Although now that she thought about it, he had conveniently changed the subject.

Bloody techies! What the hell was it with him always wanting to get one up on O'Reilly? She decided to keep it quiet for now and deal with Brody later.

"Sorry, yes, I meant that one." Although she didn't really understand what O'Reilly had meant by computers in the cloud.

"Nothing beyond what yer fella got out of it a few days back."

Jenny let it lie and instead changed tack. "Harry, can you also call Victor Gibb at GCHQ? I hear they've got all their mass surveillance assets pointing at this case right now."

"What've you got in mind, Jenny?"

"Well, I understand Mullins didn't have his own phone, credit cards or much that made him part of the modern world. But the one thing he did have was the black Vespa …"

Harry nodded and finished off for her. "You want me to see if they can track his movements over the last few days."

"Thanks, Harry."

"What about Miss Ivanov?" asked Fiona.

"Difficult one," said Jenny. "She was definitely an actor in the plot, but if her story is to be believed, she had no idea of the impact of what she'd done. She had been told that she was working on firmware for vending machines."

"What I meant is that she had communication with Saul Baker. He recruited her for the job. That's a lead worth following through."

"Great idea, Fiona. Let's have a car pick Miss Ivanov up and get her down here today and you can interview her. Harry, I want you involved in this as well. If there's an email address that needs tracing, I need you on it straight away."

"I'm yer man."

"Well, as we're dishing out actions, what other lines of enquiry have we got?"

"I think we should follow up on the reptile shop where Mullins worked," proposed Karim. "He got the black mambas from somewhere. Just because Vaughn, the proprietor, told us they didn't trade in them doesn't necessarily mean it's true. Plus, he seemed a bit dodgy to me."

"Can we get a search warrant for the premises?"

"I'd support that," said Da Silva. "Mullins killed two people with an illegal non-registered snake. He worked there. That's enough for a warrant."

"We'll need a reptile expert. None of us would know whether what we were looking at was legit or not."

"What about that reptile expert we brought in to catch the two snakes?" offered Alan.

"Perfect. Right, that's for you and Karim. You were already there the other day and can spot if anything's changed." Jenny scanned the room. "I need someone to go and ask Helen Butler about her husband's religious beliefs. He had that meeting at the Christian Science church in his diary. I meant to do it on Wednesday, but it's been chaos since King's Cross. And given that Mullins was some kind of Bible-basher as well, maybe there's a connection."

"And there's the name Saul," added Fiona. "Saul's typically a religious name, especially as a first name. Maybe it's linked somehow."

"I'll take all that," said DI Knight, speaking for the first time. "Mrs Butler will remember me from the original investigation."

"Thanks, Kevin." She was surprised that he'd offered to do anything without first clearing it with Da Silva. "Can you also check the same thing with Gowda's fiancée, Gwenda? I know Gowda's originally from Sri Lanka, but maybe there's some kind of link."

"Will do."

"On the subject of religion, I'm going to head back up to that Christian Science church where Butler had a meeting scheduled in his diary with Benjamin Shepard, the First Reader there, even though Shepard had no record of it. Mullins most probably went to church somewhere. Elstree neighbours Borehamwood. Maybe Mullins went to that church? And if he did, that would be two links to the same place." Jenny saw a couple of raised eyebrows. She commented, "Yeah, I know, clutching at straws."

That got a few laughs.

Jenny looked around. Everyone sported a purposeful gaze.

Da Silva shifted in his seat, his movement automatically infuriating Jenny. "I agree with the plan of action. Let's regroup here at midday at the latest." As usual, he'd found a way to get the last word in, as if the whole plan had been of his making. But then he said the last words Jenny ever expected but never wanted to hear. "I'll accompany DI Price."

"I can take care of myself, guv."

"I won't hear of it, especially after what you've been through during the last few days."

Jenny wanted the ground to swallow her up.

Brody picked up his coffee only to realise he'd already finished it.

He found it strange having the freedom to roam around another elite hacker's virtual world without fear of interruption or discovery. Everywhere Brody turned, he discovered something new and was ever more impressed with Butler's abilities and ambitions.

If what he'd seen so far was for real, Butler had either developed or got hold of some impressive malware exploits. And as tempting as it was to look into these in more detail, Brody had to keep focused on his immediate objective.

Butler had hacked into Saul Baker's computer via the malware he'd inserted in the pentest document. This had enabled Butler to find out about the other actors in the conspiracy and alert them. If Brody could figure out what the malware was and how it was controlled, then perhaps he could track Saul down. After all, he was the orchestrator behind the world's most destructive hack, the first one to ever cross over into the human world and kill people en masse.

It was even more important than the other seriously tempting diversion available to Brody right now. He'd already noticed a directory referencing Contag10n's name. That was, after all, the prize that Butler had offered Brody in the death letter that had started all this: information that would help him bring down Vorovskoy Mir. But that too would have to wait. Brody forced himself to stay focused.

Eventually, he tracked down an index of all of Butler's secure email accounts. There were hundreds, one for each client project he undertook. It took some time logging in and out of each one. For each, Butler had set up a new untraceable, encrypted email account to manage his communications with his client or the targets. Brody did the same thing.

The thirtieth email account turned out to be what Brody was looking for. He read the email exchanges.

Someone calling himself Saul Baker and using an equally untraceable email address had approached Butler, in his guise as BionicM@n, about thirteen months previously. He claimed to work for a security services company that had been recruited by MedDev Labs to carry out a deep penetration test on their systems. There was a bonus available if they were able to prove they could access their crown jewels, the source code management system. Saul claimed that their best consultants had tried and failed and so he was contacting him to see if he'd be interested in taking on the challenge on his company's behalf. Saul claimed to have been recommended BionicM@n by people on the CrackerHack forum, which was probably true. It was how Brody got much of his work. Saul offered a lucrative bonus and was prepared to pay BionicM@n a significant fee for his success. He wanted a full pentest report as well.

Butler accepted the job, but only after pushing Saul Baker up another twenty per cent on the fee. Saul provided the firmware and the location in the target system. Brody looked at the code and recognised what he and Klara had walked through the other day. Although, this was the first version.

It was dressed up as a pentest, but it was clear to Brody that this was all about the firmware. At the very least, Butler must have suspected some form of corporate sabotage from one of MedDev Labs' competitors. It's what Brody would have thought. Brody would have walked away, regardless of the fee offered. But Butler didn't. And that was probably the biggest difference between them.

Butler carried out the pentest and documented it all in the report that Brody had already read and used to aid him in his activities at their head office yesterday. Only Butler doctored the report, presumably suspicious of Saul Baker's real motivations. When Saul opened the report, it installed malware on his computer, which Butler exploited a year later.

There was another round of emails a few weeks later, when Saul requested Butler install an updated version of the firmware. Butler charged the same amount again and Saul paid. No discussion.

Whoever Saul Baker was, he had access to a lot of money.

When the celebrity chef died, Butler obviously figured out what was going on. He had all of Dougan's recipe books on his kitchen shelf. Helen Butler had said he often cooked along live with the Saturday morning program Dougan hosted. Brody presumed he must have known about the chef's heart condition, being such a fan. Because he also knew about the hard-coded date written into the first version of the doctored firmware, he put two and two together.

Interestingly, before Butler contacted Gowda and Klara, he approached Saul directly. His email was blunt and to the point.

Saul, I know what you've made me do. The dead chef is too much. Undo it immediately or I go public. Call me.

Butler provided a mobile number. Brody couldn't tell whether they'd ever talked. But Butler's next step was his email to Gowda, Klara and Raz. Brody knew the rest and stopped reading through the email history.

It all confirmed his theory that Vorovskoy Mir had absolutely nothing to do with Butler's death. Saul had constructed the whole plot himself, pulling Gowda, Klara and Butler into a loosely connected virtual team, patiently exploiting their skills to update the firmware in MedDev Labs' systems and launch the deadliest cyberweapon ever constructed.

During the last few hours of his life, Butler might even have realised Saul was behind Mullins' visit with the black mamba, but he was tied up and unable to update his death letter, which accused Vorovskoy Mir of killing him. It went out unchanged and Brody was grateful it had. Without it, Brody would never have become involved and the conspiracy would have remained hidden, right up until Friday, 5th June at 12:36 p.m., London Time, when tens of thousands of people would have dropped down dead.

He looked up for the first time in an hour, caught Lorenzo's eye behind the counter and called over an order for more coffee. The next step he faced required a caffeine boost.

Brody turned his attention to the malware Butler had installed. It took a while to figure out which type had been used and which of Butler's many virtual machines hosted its command and control system. Eventually, Brody tracked it all down.

The malware was a variant of Poison Ivy, a kit that Brody also used. It provided remote access and key-logging of infected computers. Butler had deployed the malware to hundreds of computers over the years and many were still calling home to Butler's command and control servers. Brody had to carefully analyse the infected pentest report to work out the name assigned to Saul's computer. But once he had this, he logged onto the command and control server and pulled up the details for Saul's infected device.

Stefan brought over fresh coffee, but didn't interrupt Brody, whose head was down and didn't look up to acknowledge his presence.

The first thing that stood out was that Saul Baker's password was Tarsus123. That might come in handy later. Butler had recovered some emails from Saul's computer and these were stored on the server. They were Saul's communications with Gowda and Klara.

Brody read through them.

Gowda had been blackmailed to carry out the work. Saul had somehow found out that Gowda's visa was not as it should be. He'd been transferred over to MedDev Labs in the UK from their Sri Lankan office to work on a supply chain project in which he was an expert. But a year later he'd changed to become a DBA and no one updated the visa, which meant he was in the country illegally. Saul pretended to be from one of MedDev Labs' competitors and threatened to report Gowda, who had a lot to lose having recently moved in with his girlfriend, Gwenda. To avoid being exposed, Gowda did as he was told and dumped all the databases, which was how Saul got hold of the firmware source code.

The email communication with Klara was much as she'd described, even down to the hacktivist agenda against *Coca-Cola*'s vending machines. It was simple and effective.

The fake communication with Raz was well constructed. It made out that Raz was being hired to carry out unit testing of the firmware to make sure it worked on the device in question and did no harm. Butler hadn't worked out that the person on the other end of that email address was Saul himself. Brody had concluded that from events since, but would make a point to prove it for real later.

Brody had wondered why Butler didn't hack back into MedDev Labs and reinstall the version of the firmware he'd originally replaced. But, from what Brody could deduce, there were two problems. Firstly, Butler had destroyed all of the previous versions, which was part of the pentest brief. But secondly, MedDev Labs had since upgraded their security systems and Butler had been unable to gain access to the source code control system. Brody recalled Richards, the MedDev Labs CIO, saying that they'd conducted a pentest a year before. Brody wondered whether that was the whole truth. Perhaps Saul had sent them the report, amended to remove the firmware replacement, so that they upgraded their security systems. Brody decided that proving that theory was something that could also wait until later.

Brody checked Butler's command and control server to see if Saul's computer was online.

It wasn't.

Disheartened but not defeated, Brody checked when it had last been connected. It was entirely possible that when Saul, pretending to be Raz, had received the original email from Butler, he had dumped the PC he'd been using. In the email Butler had mentioned he'd got their email addresses from hacking Saul's email account. While that was technically true,

Butler had got to the email via Saul's computer. The question was whether Saul had figured that step out.

Brody looked at the log and clenched his fist in triumph. The malware hidden in Saul's computer had connected to the command and control server only last night. Saul still didn't know it was there.

Now it was just a waiting game. Would Saul come online?

Brody looked at his watch.

Just over four hours to go.

Da Silva drove far too slowly for Jenny's liking. He even took the wrong turn out of the King's Cross one-way system. Instead of going up York Way and heading for the A1, he drove along Marylebone Road and then went north via the A41, a much slower route towards Elstree with loads of traffic lights. It would take them a good hour this way.

"Can't you use your blues?"

"I don't have any installed in this car. It's new."

"At least put your foot down."

"What's the rush? We both know this is a weak lead."

"Then why are you tagging along?"

"Sir." He corrected her. "Why are you tagging along, *sir*."

Jenny folded her arms. There was no way she was crediting him with that title, but was slightly amused that he'd repeated *tagging along*.

"The reason I am here supporting you is to understand more about your investigative techniques. Every time you follow a lead, it's the right move. Happened on the meeting room murder case and it's happened again this week with MedDev Labs."

"Nearly got me killed both times," she lamented.

"Either you're brilliant or you're exceptionally lucky. Or maybe it's because you're getting outside assistance."

Ah, so that was his angle. "You're referring to Brody Taylor, I take it?" Jenny managed to suppress any natural defensive tone.

"Yes, Mr Taylor, our cheeky outside security consultant who seems to have a nose for trouble."

"You're the one who was trying to recruit him the other day.

Not me."

"Yes, but that was before it became known to me that you and he are more than just friends."

"What's that got to do with anything?"

"It's unethical to have a relationship with a witness, which is how you introduced him to us this week."

"He was a witness. And then you promoted him to IT advisor."

"Either way, you should have declared your relationship."

"My private life is none of your fucking business. Sir." She only added the *sir* to piss him off.

"It is when it has the ability to negatively impact one of my cases."

"Negatively?" Incredulity oozed out. "It's done nothing but save thousands of lives so far!"

"We'll soon know if that's a true statement or not."

Jenny looked at her watch. Jesus, couldn't he put his foot down? They were only just passing the North Circular at Brent Cross.

"Is DCS McLintock aware of your special relationship with Mr Taylor?"

Her silence was enough of an admission.

"I thought not. He seems to have developed a soft spot for you even though you're cultivating your special relationship with him under false pretences. I wonder how he'll react when he finds out?"

She chose not to comment. Was he jealous of McLintock's focus on her? All he had to do was step up and do his job properly. McLintock believed in proper police work and acting your rank. He didn't suffer fools gladly.

"What's he been saying about me?" asked Da Silva.

"What did he say to you on Wednesday after Kevin and I left you in his office?" countered Jenny.

"Not much."

"Bullshit." She'd had enough of this pussyfooting around. If he wanted to make threats against her, she wasn't going to take it lying down. "Ever since you came down from his office, you've had your tail between your legs. To be honest, I was surprised you survived. If I were him, I'd have fired you long before now."

His face tightened as her words hit him full on.

"He must have you on the tightest leash imaginable. And you're going to fail. You're no DCI. You have no idea how to lead a murder investigation team." Her voice had risen to just under a shout as the tension that had built up over the last few months came to a head. "You're a disgrace to the uniform."

Da Silva casually pulled to a halt for some red lights. He turned to her and said calmly, "When we get back to Holborn later, at least I'll still have a job."

He pulled off.

Jenny fumed all the way to Elstree, replaying their conversation over and over. She wondered if any of his threats would carry weight. But she was beyond caring. At least she'd finally spoken her mind and told him to his face.

Fuck the consequences.

Eventually, they pulled up outside the modern-looking church. Jenny was struck again by how odd it looked surrounded on all sides by middle-class residential homes. She wondered how many of the neighbours went there versus the more traditional Church of England, ancient-looking stone church they'd passed a few minutes earlier.

Her phone rang. It was Karim. Despite what had just happened, she put it on loudspeaker.

"Fuck me, guv!" He sounded breathless and full of excitement. "We've uncovered a whole basement full of illegal snakes and other reptiles. Turns out this pet shop has been running an underground network, importing and supplying venomous snakes all over the country."

"So is that where Mullins was getting his snakes from?"

"Must be, he worked here. And they've got two more black mambas. They look well creepy to me. Can't believe you had one crawling all over you …" He realised he'd overstepped a boundary. "Sorry guv, I didn't mean —"

"Don't worry, Karim. We're on our way over now."

"Great. Like you said earlier, whoever is the snake keeper

must have been calling the shots with Mullins. We've arrested four of them so far. But my money's on this Vaughn character being Saul. He owns the shop and he's got mean-looking eyes and religious symbols for tattoos."

Da Silva spoke. "You and DS Coombs carry on with the scene, DS Malik. We'll complete what we came here to do and join you later."

"Uh, okay, boss. You sure?"

Da Silva reached over and clicked off her phone.

Jenny sat open-mouthed. "What the fuck? Is this some kind of reverse glory hunting?" So close to their deadline, Da Silva's decision sounded lazy, not to mention dangerous for Karim's team and risked missing vital information for the case at the hands of less experienced detectives.

"I'll get the credit anyway, DI Price. After all, I'm SIO on this overall investigation. It'll be my name on the reports. And the best part is that I won't have to write your name in any of them relating to the takedown of Saul. Then, when we get back to the station, I've got a nice little anecdote to tell McLintock."

Jenny was dumbfounded. She couldn't believe this.

"Shall we go and do our job, DI Price? While you still have one?"

CHAPTER 22

NEARLY TWO HOURS HAD PASSED AND SAUL still hadn't logged on. Brody had refused to allow himself to be tempted by the other toys in Butler's digital lair. His primary focus was to track down the people behind the terrorist plot.

In the end, he'd packed up and headed upstairs.

He set the computer to connect to his Bluetooth speaker system and configured it to ping a loud alert the second Saul came online.

While he waited, he showered, changed and prepared some breakfast. He turned on the television and was bombarded with news stories related to the pacemaker time bomb. By now, the press had figured out it was malicious and not just a coding error. Someone must have leaked it. They'd also leaked a photo of Jenny and given her full credit for exposing the conspiracy. He'd never seen a picture of her in police uniform before and smiled. He wondered if she knew her face was being bandied about everywhere. He was glad it was her and not him. That would play havoc with his other life.

Cameras were camped out in every conceivable place around the country. Outside hospitals, they captured the queues awaiting their turn. A scuffle outside a clinic in Glasgow was repeated over and over, as desperate people tried to jump the queue. Police cars were flying about in every city, collecting people and dropping them to the back of queues.

But he knew what the media really wanted was to catch someone dropping down dead live on TV at 12:36 p.m. Brody guessed that would probably happen somewhere, on CCTV at the bare minimum. There really was no way they could save everyone, despite the incredible logistical operation the government had spun up overnight.

At 10:30 a.m., Brody was twiddling his thumbs. The live news channels were repeating things over and over and bringing in a stream of supposed experts to add commentary to the reports. The speculation as to who had been behind the firmware hack ranged from ISIS to China. Journalists took to the streets, interviewing people who'd been upgraded already and asking them how they felt. 'Betrayed but relieved' was the common expression of their emotions. But all remained nervous, saying they wouldn't feel safe until the time clicked through to 12:37 p.m.

Media vans were also parked outside MedDev Labs, even though there was no more to be done by them. That said, their business was tanking spectacularly. The share price had dropped so quickly that the Stock Exchange had suspended trading on their stock. Dr Dunst was in for a rough ride over the next few months. But there was a knock-on effect to all their competitors, whose share price also dropped significantly, despite all their CEOs talking to the media about their much stronger security postures.

Brody picked up his computer and headed back downstairs to Bruno's. It was quiet compared to normal; most people probably huddled at home with friends or family who had heart implants fitted. Whether they were there for support or to be a spectator when they keeled over probably differed from family to family.

Brody took his usual seat and plugged in his computer. Stefan played his usual game and chose a macchiato and a glass of water. For once it was actually what Brody would have chosen.

Just after 11:00 a.m., Brody's computer beeped the noise he had been waiting for. He rubbed his hands together and dived in.

It took him longer than expected. The person who owned the computer on the other end was definitely technically-minded and had a good set of defences lined up, but also was careful about what data he stored where, with quite a lot being encrypted. If Brody was actually in front of the computer using the person's session, he'd be able to read any of the documents natively as they'd de-encrypt in real time. But coming in through the back door meant the encryption stood firm.

Perhaps this was what had defeated Butler from taking his actions any further directly with Saul, instead resorting to emailing the others.

In the end, it was Saul's browser history that gave him away. While his browser was set to clear the cache at the end of every session, Brody was connected live and could see the sites Saul was visiting in real time.

The first one, which was probably the site his home screen was set to display, gave him away. And Brody whistled in surprise. He did some more digging and realised it all made sense, well in a twisted world anyway.

He picked up his phone and called Jenny.

She didn't answer and it went to voicemail. He left her a message telling her Saul's true identity. And for good measure, he texted her as well.

Jenny followed Da Silva up the long path. The church was set back from the residential road and the neighbouring houses by about 100 feet of lawn on all sides.

She was still fuming, but knew she was stuck with him. If only she'd driven, she could be on her way over to Watford right now to help in the takedown. And instead, she was following up on a spurious lead with a boss who'd just told her she would be fired the minute they got back to the station.

Da Silva knocked on the side door and waited. Her phone rang. She didn't really want to hear any more from her team about the takedown, but pulled it out anyway. It was Brody. She sent the call to voicemail. She would phone him back later.

The door swung open. Jenny was relieved to see it was Benjamin Shepard, the First Reader, rather than the old woman who'd bossed her and Fiona about on Tuesday. She peeked beyond and saw that the church was empty of congregants. Thank God for that.

"Can I help you?" he asked and, noticing Jenny behind Da Silva, said, "Ah, DI Price. It's good to see you again. Are we on official capacity or have you decided to seek out the word of the Lord?"

Jenny was in no mood for anything religious right now, unless it involved the God of the Old Testament smiting Da Silva where he stood.

"May we talk to you?" asked Da Silva.

"Of course. Everyone is welcome in the house of the Lord."

As Da Silva followed Shepard inside, Jenny's phone buzzed again. She took a look and saw it was a text from Brody. The preview display on her locked screen showed the opening words of the text:

Jenny, I've worked out who Saul is. You won't believe it. It's …

But she already knew. Karim and Alan were taking him down right now. She shoved the phone back in her pocket. She would click and read the rest later.

They followed Shepard towards the altar.

"Quiet day today," he remarked. "I suspect it has something to do with what's going on in the news. I think people are staying home and caring for loved ones." He paused and surveyed the empty pews. "Shame, really. I had prepared a reading based on James 5:15 that's turned out to be quite relevant. 'And the prayer of faith shall save the sick, and the Lord shall raise him up; and if he have committed sins, they shall be forgiven him …'" He stopped, seeing that he had lost his audience.

Da Silva took the lead. "We wanted to ask you if your congregation included a Ralph Mullins."

"Ralph? Yes, he comes at least two or three times a week. Has been for a few years now. Why?"

"Have you heard about the snake poisonings in the press?"

"Yes, of course." Realisation dawned on his face. "Not Ralph, surely!"

"Yes. He died in hospital last night after being bitten by one of his own snakes."

Shepard's hand covered his mouth. "That's dreadful. He was a bit of a wayward soul, but I would never have suspected …"

Rather than dig into Shepard's intriguing description of Mullins, Da Silva blindly pursued the core line of enquiry. "He refused medical attention on religious grounds, which is why he died. I'm not familiar with your church. Is that something that Christian Science is a proponent of?"

"He died alone? Was no one praying for him?"

Da Silva looked to Jenny. It was a strange comment.

Shepard continued. "He should have contacted us. We would have gathered together and prayed for him. It might have made a difference."

"Prayer against the neurotoxins in black mamba venom?" Jenny blurted.

"You'd be surprised at the power of prayer to heal," Shepard retorted. "It's like this heart implant story all over the news right now. That's man intervening in God's natural law. In our church, if one of the congregants was diagnosed with a heart condition, for example, they would visit one of our practitioners for spiritual advice and prayer. We would also pray for them together as a whole congregation. In fact, there is one member of our community who was diagnosed years ago and resisted succumbing to medical intervention. And yet he is still alive forty years later." He paused and added with a twinkle, "That's me, by the way."

Jenny felt a shiver go up her spine. This was definitely the line of thinking that drove Mullins' behaviour. It corroborated with how Brody described his actions and words on the night in Bruno's. She still hated that she couldn't remember it herself. "It seems that your congregant took your teachings to another level," she said. "He used venomous snakes to poison his victims and then prayed for them. None of them survived."

"Like medicine, prayer is an imprecise art."

"Are you condoning his actions?" asked Jenny, unable to hide her exasperation.

"No, of course not."

Da Silva spoke. "We're trying to track down where Mullins kept his snakes. Do you know anything about that?"

That was a waste of a question as far as Jenny was concerned. They'd already got the answer from her team over in the pet shop in Watford.

"Ah, snakes." He sounded embarrassed. "Yes I know about that. Please, follow me." Shepard headed for a door in the far corner. As he walked he said, "I know about his love of snakes. He's had it since he was a small child. I probably shouldn't have encouraged it, but I had plenty of extra space in the basement. His landlord refused to allow him to keep any and he couldn't get a licence, not with his criminal record …"

Shepard opened the door and walked in, stepping downwards. Jenny and Da Silva looked at each other in shock at this sudden revelation. Cautiously, they followed him down, Da Silva first. Shepard switched on the torch on his mobile phone. "Sorry, the light bulb needs replacing. Over here."

Jenny and Da Silva followed Shepard and the main source of light, which he kept focused ahead of him. Jenny reached into her pocket to pull out her own phone. Now, could she remember the steps to turn on the torch? Wasn't there an app for that?

They reached the end of the underground room and Shepard pointed forward. "Just there." Da Silva and Jenny focused on the dark space beyond, but it was impossible to see.

Jenny gave up and focused on her phone. As the preview of Brody's message reappeared on her lock screen, she was suddenly fearful that she'd made a dreadful assumption. She clicked on the message and entered her passcode.

Jenny, I've worked out who Saul is. You won't believe it. It's Benjamin Shepard, the First Reader at that Christian Science church you visited the other day. Butler figured it out and that was why he had the meeting in his diary: to confront him about the firmware hack. Text me when you get this.

Her heart thumping, Jenny whirled around, ready to attack Shepard. But he had withdrawn from them. He was to one side of the room, his phone's torch now picking out a bank of glass cages on one side that she hadn't seen in the darkness before. Just as she was about to rush him, he pulled at the bank of cages from the top.

"I can't see anything," said Da Silva, reaching for his own phone, still oblivious to the threat.

"No!" shouted Jenny, running back. But the bank of cages began to topple. Shepard sidestepped and ran back the way he had come, just as they smashed to the floor. There was an almighty crash of glass. Suddenly the room was flooded with light. Shepard had switched on a light — obviously having lied about the broken bulb before. A pile of debris separated Jenny and Da Silva from Shepard and the exit behind him leading up the stairs. And then Jenny froze in horror.

The cages that he'd smashed had contained snakes. Lots of snakes. Against the opposite wall stood another bank of cages, untouched. If the first was a mirror of the second, then there were about thirty snakes amongst the wreckage on the floor.

Da Silva stood dumbstruck beside her, his eyes flicking from Shepard to the snakes and back again, over and over, failing to process his predicament.

Shepard grinned gleefully. He stepped over the other bank of cages. "Shall I?"

He chose not to wait for an answer and pulled at it from the top. The second bank toppled forward. Da Silva, who hadn't been paying attention, was struck by the other end of the bank of snake cages, and was knocked forward. The cages continued their descent and crashed down onto the floor, landing on top of Da Silva's legs.

He screamed. Pain or fright? Jenny wasn't sure which. She studied the broken cages, which now blocked the whole corridor back to where Shepard stood leering. Sure enough, snakes began to slither out from within the gaps.

There was no escape.

Jenny hadn't answered. There was no response to his text.

Typical.

Well, he'd done everything he could for her and the team. They'd get to Shepard in good time. Right now, the world was focused on the terrorist plot and the time bomb. Whether its culprit was caught or not paled into insignificance compared to the number of lives at stake.

Brody was now free to get on with Butler's original objective in sending Brody the death letter: exploring his digital lair to use the information against Vorovskoy Mir. Brody rubbed his hands together. It was time to go deep-sea fishing for Contag10n and any other members of his cybergang.

He began searching through Butler's directories for the folder he'd seen earlier. But as he dug deeper, the phrase he'd just used was trying to break through into his conscious thoughts.

Fishing. Deep-sea fishing.

What was his brain trying to tell him?

He paused and tried to focus. But nothing was forthcoming. Deep-sea fishing? Why the hell was that important?

He took a sip of water and tried to think of the last time he thought about fishing. And then he had it. It was here in this very seat on Monday with Vernon Bishop, Leroy's dad. Was that it? He wasn't sure. He remembered Vernon saying that he and Leroy were going fishing on Friday. He remembered how strange it was trying to imagine Leroy on a fishing boat. Come to think of it, Leroy and he had joked about it the following night.

But fishing wasn't quite it. There was something else.

Then it hit him.

When Vernon had come to London, he had been to the Harley Street specialist for his pacemaker check-up. And if he and Leroy had got up early today to go fishing, they might not have heard the news.

Brody grabbed his phone. He looked at his watch. It was just after 11:00 a.m. There was an hour and a half until the time bomb struck.

Leroy's number went straight to voicemail. That was a bad sign. If he was out of reception range on the boat in some remote part of North Wales, then it would go straight to voicemail. Brody left a message telling Leroy to watch the news and get his father down to a hospital immediately.

Next he rang the Bishop home phone. It rang but after six rings it was picked up by an old-school answering machine. Gloria, Leroy's mum, said to leave a message. He repeated what he'd already said and hung up.

North Wales was a four-and-a-half-hour drive. Brody knew because he'd been up to the farm a few times with Leroy and his sister, Hope.

He looked at his watch.

There was no time.

Jenny rushed over to Da Silva. He was desperately trying to escape but his legs were trapped. He tried lifting the cages from him, but couldn't get the leverage from where he was sitting. A brown snake slithered over his ankle and he froze.

Jenny grasped hold of the cages and lifted. She budged it an inch but no more. "Help me, dammit," she said.

Da Silva saw what she was doing and added his own strength. The cage lifted up and he was able to withdraw his foot. Jenny saw a small green snake heading up the side of the cage towards her exposed hand. She wanted to wait until he was free before letting go, but the snake would determine that. It coiled just below her hand, raised itself up on its tail and —

Jenny dropped the cage and withdrew her hands just as it struck. It missed her by less than an inch. But Da Silva had scrambled away on all fours behind her.

The lithe green snake continued towards them. Jenny looked around and saw what looked like a large pair of tongs hanging on the wall. She picked them up and brandished them in front of her — not in their intended purpose but more as a broom. The snake slid forward onto the floor beyond the debris and, using the tongs, she flicked it backwards onto the broken cages.

She scanned the nearest wreckage but nothing was coming her way at that point. Further back, she could see snakes of all sizes and colours slithering over the broken glass, taking advantage of their sudden freedom.

It was time to call for backup. Jenny put the phone to her ear, but it was silent.

"There's no phone signal down here, DI Price," stated Shepard from the other end of the long room. He had retreated onto the lower steps to get away from the snakes moving around freely at his end of the room.

She looked at the signal. The bars were empty.

Brody had tried the coastguard. It took a while to get through to the right coastguard station and convince them there was a real issue. Only when they turned on the TV station did they believe him. They tried broadcasting to Vernon's boat, but without knowing the name or registration number of the boat, they were stuck.

He wasn't ready to give up.

He called Victor Gibb over Skype. He answered immediately. The agent's huge frame filled the screen. He was wearing earphones.

"Hey, it's the hero of the —"

"Doc, did you say you came up here by helicopter yesterday?"

"Yes, why?"

"I need it. There's someone I know with a pacemaker out on a fishing boat off the North Wales coast somewhere. We need to get a programmer up there now."

"Damn, Brody, the GCHQ 'copter is back in Cheltenham. Hold on a sec, I'm putting you on the big screen."

There was shuffling as Gibb connected up his laptop. Once done, he turned it around so that the webcam on Gibb's laptop picked up the surroundings. He was still in the COBRA committee room. The PM was still in the centre.

She leaned forward and said, "Ah, Mr Taylor, the secret hero of the hour. Thanks to you we've saved thousands of lives already. We're on the home stretch now."

"That's why I was calling Doc — I mean Victor, Ma'am. A friend of mine is fishing off the coast of North Wales right now. He's out of range of a mobile phone signal and they don't know what's going on. There's no way to contact him. Even if we could divert a couple of local police, there's no guarantee they'll track him down, get him back on land and get him to a hospital."

"Okay, Mr Taylor. What did you have in mind?"

"I was after Victor's helicopter. The programmer I used in MedDev Labs is probably going spare. I was thinking we could get someone to fly it up there and …"

He hadn't really thought through the rest.

"Okay. This country owes you a lot, Mr Taylor. I've got something better than the GCHQ helicopter. I'm sending a car to pick you up and get you to RAF Northolt. Where are you?"

"A coffee shop called Bruno's in Upper Street. But that's at least a forty-minute drive."

"Not in this car with this driver. Twenty at most. He's on his way already. He'll be with you in a couple of minutes."

"Okay, thanks, Ma'am."

Brody disconnected. He was pleased to have the bones of a plan but hadn't expected to feature in it front and centre.

He jumped back into Butler's digital lair and found the pentest report on MedDev Labs. Within thirty seconds he had the phone number he wanted. It was answered straight away.

"Fred, is that you?"

"Brody? I was going to phone you. I've been promoted, thanks to you."

"Congratulations. I need you to repay the favour right now."

"Sure, how can I help?"

"Is the programmer from yesterday still going spare?"

"Yup."

"I need you to jump in your car and take it down to RAF Northolt. It's only about seven miles from where you are. As fast as you can."

Brody looked outside as a black car with tinted windows and blue flashing lights screeched to a halt. He grabbed his computer and ran out of Bruno's, just as Stefan brought over a fresh espresso to replace the one Brody had forgotten to drink.

Shepard stared at Jenny across the ruins of the snake cages.

"I see your name is being touted all over the media today, DI Price, as the heroic police detective who exposed the terrible cyberterrorist conspiracy."

It was? She had no idea her name had made it into the public domain.

"Talking about names," she countered, "I take it you are Saul Baker."

She glanced behind her to check on Da Silva. He sat on the floor behind her, wide-eyed, his back to the wall where he could watch the floor for snakes. He was rubbing his sore leg.

"Yes, a convenient pseudonym I use when dealing with people you can't trust online. Baker I borrowed from Mary Baker Eddy, the founder of the Christian Science Church. Saul is for Saul of Tarsus, known to you as Paul the Apostle. He is also the man who was bitten by a poisonous viper, but thanks to the power of prayer and God's mercy, his life was spared."

"And Raz? You hide your Manchester accent well," stated Jenny.

"Oh, I can do any accent I want, mate." He spoke with a heavy Mancunian inflection. "Or would you prefer I talk like this, darlin'?" Now it was Cockney.

Jenny glanced at the broken cages to make sure none of the inhabitants were coming her way. For now they seemed content sliding in amongst the debris. "Your plot is going to fail, Shepard. All those tens of thousands of people you targeted are going to survive."

"Yes, you've been a busy bee. I saw that in the news this morning. It's very disappointing. I even had a whole marketing campaign lined up on newchurchgoer.com to take advantage of it. I think a lot of people will now realise the power of prayer for healing over medicine, regardless of the number of deaths today."

Jenny found that hard to accept. "You planned to kill thousands of innocent people for a church recruitment campaign?"

"Come on. All those people were living on borrowed time. They should have died years ago as per God's plan for them.

Unless they prayed to him seeking his divine intervention, like Paul the Apostle."

It was disconcerting talking to him. He spoke so reasonably, like he was having a normal religious debate, as if trying to convert Jenny from an agnostic to a believer.

"And Ralph Mullins, what was he, your very own apostle?"

"Mullins was a killer, beyond God's redemption."

"But still, you made him believe that prayer could solve even a black mamba bite?"

"Well it can, and he was witness to it. He survived a mamba bite himself with just me praying for him. Never doubt the power of God." Shepard smiled as if deciding to let her into a secret. "He wasn't to know that I'd devenomed the mamba beforehand. He probably wasn't going to die anyway."

"You tricked him into doing your dirty work!"

"Mullins needed God's redemption for that kid he killed for hurting his dog. If he learned to pray hard enough and attract divine intervention on behalf of those he'd inflicted the snake bite — like I did for him — then that would be evidence that God would be merciful to him when the time came."

"That's twisted. You bent your own church laws completely out of shape, just to suit your own purposes."

"Whatever, darlin'." The Cockney accent was back. "Mullins was a killer and would always be a killer. Maybe killing was God's plan for him."

There was no reasoning with him. She changed the subject. "Why today? Why 12:36 today?"

He paused and studied her, as if measuring up how much he should say. She held up her bare hands to indicate how defenceless she was. Behind, Da Silva was still scanning left to right, panicked.

Shepard let out a deep breath. "Just over four years ago, my twelve-year-old son, Gabriel, was diagnosed with ventricular arrhythmia. Of course, the medics recommended an implantable cardioverter defibrillator, but that was out of the question. Only God can truly heal the sick!" He raised his voice an octave and began quoting the Bible from memory. "'Is any among you sick?

Let him call for the elders of the church; and let them pray over him, anointing him with oil in the name of the Lord: and the prayer of faith shall save him that is sick, and the Lord shall raise him up; and if he have committed sins, it shall be forgiven him.'" Shepard nodded as if that settled any argument. He resumed his explanation. "My brother was the First Reader here before me. And before him it was our father. Under my brother's leadership, the whole congregation prayed for my son every day." Tears dropped from his eyes. "But, a month later, on June 5th at 12:36 p.m., Gabriel suffered a cardiac arrest and passed away in my arms."

Jenny felt only anger at him for stupidly refusing the medical treatment. Despite his tears, she scoffed, "The power of prayer obviously failed you that time."

"God has different plans for us all." He wiped his eyes with his sleeve.

She heard shuffling behind her. Da Silva was scrabbling to one side. Shepard laughed, the Manchester accent back. "Don't let that python wrap itself around you, mate. She'll crush you to death with her coils."

Jenny spotted a Bible on a small table to one side. She picked it up and threw it towards the massive snake. It reared back, sensing a threat, and then veered off in the other direction, away from Jenny and Da Silva.

"This whole thing is over your dead son?"

The fact that he'd called out to help Da Silva told her there was more to his story. Despite their desperate situation, she wanted to at least try and understand this madness.

He studied her. "You'll be dead soon enough, I suppose. And although confession is not part of the Christian Science Church, it does feel good to get this all off my chest. Talking it through is a classic healing therapy we do subscribe to."

Jenny waited. He could justify it any way he wanted, but it was his ego that wanted to show off and tell the full story.

"Bravo, detective. Yes, there's more to my sob story. I have another son. His name is Thaddeus." He paused and glanced around. "You know something, I've never told anyone that before. It feels good. You should retrain as a therapist. I'll recommend you to others."

Jenny ignored him, and studied the floor for threats. He would get round to it soon enough.

"His mother is my brother Jacob's whore of a wife who slept with me."

"Jacob?" she interrupted. "He's the one you told me had moved to the States. Boston, I think you said."

"My, you have a good memory. Yes, that is what I told you and it's what I tell everyone. But in reality, he left the church in shame and has gone into hiding with his whore wife and Thaddeus. Somewhere in the States is all I know. He's being helped out by one of those ex-Christian Scientist groups."

Jenny made the mental leap. "It's genetic. You were diagnosed forty years ago and, what was it? 'Resisted succumbing to medical intervention.' You have a heart condition. Gabriel had a heart condition. Stands to reason that Thaddeus has one too. And Jacob chose to handle it differently to you by accepting medical aid. Is that it?"

"Very good. Maybe you are a better detective than you are a therapist. Yes, Jacob was the head of our church. He should have set a much better example and relied on the power of prayer as we believe. We would have all prayed and it would have been God's will one way or the other." Shepard's voice rose as he began to shout, spittle flying from his angry lips. "But no, he succumbs to the temptation of man and accepts medical aid, breaking all his vows and shaming himself and the memory of our father! And what does he do? He just walks off into the sunset. One happy little family."

"So you believe God's plan was for Thaddeus to die, was it?"

"Yes!" He was shouting at the top of his voice. "And Jacob cheated! He aligned with the devil."

"And so you conceived this whole plan. To kill the one person in the world you couldn't track down."

"God's plan," he roared, "would be returned to its original intent."

"And to kill one person, you're willing to take out tens of

thousands of innocent strangers."

"The same applies to each of them. They're all on borrowed time provided by Satan."

Jenny simply raised a circumspect eyebrow.

Shepard stopped, turned away and composed himself. When he looked back at her, he spoke reasonably once more, the debater of religion back in the room. "Illness is a form of sin. You pray for your sins to be treated. You don't go to the doctor and cheat God's plan."

Long before now, Jenny had determined that he had a few screws loose. But having listened to it all, she decided he was truly certifiable.

CHAPTER 23

BRODY TOOK ONE LOOK AT THE V-22 Osprey and said, "You've got to be joking."

It was a monster of a machine: half helicopter, half aeroplane. It had two gigantic rotors on the end of normal aeroplane wings, which enabled it to lift off and land like a helicopter. But once airborne, they rotated ninety degrees and it became a high-speed aircraft.

Brody had picked up the programmer that Fred had waiting for him on arrival. Fred had explained that he'd made sure to install the new version of the firmware on it and then gave him a quick tutorial on how to use it. The driver had driven the car like a madman, flying through every red light with lights and sirens blaring, each time narrowly avoiding a deadly collision. On the way over, Brody tried Leroy and Gloria again, but to no avail.

Once inside the belly of the aircraft, he was shown where to sit and strap in. He was given a black helmet containing a headset that was on the same frequency as the pilots up front. Then he was left alone.

He felt the aircraft lift vertically, rising into the air incredibly quickly. There was a single window in the side door and Brody focused on the clouds in the sky beyond to avoid motion sickness. After a thirty seconds or so, the engine noise changed and suddenly the plane shot forward.

"Okay, Mr Brody." A voice came over his headset. "This is

the co-pilot here. It will take us just over thirty minutes to get to North Wales. But it would help if we had a specific destination."

"Somewhere between Bangor and Llandudno."

"You'll need to be a bit more specific than that, sir."

"Uh, yeah. Give me a minute." He whipped his computer out of his man bag. "Do you have Wi-Fi on board?"

"What do you think this is? Upper Class on British Airways?"

"Fair point. Can I pick up a 3G signal from up here?"

"You can if we fly low enough." The altitude dropped immediately. "We'll follow the M40 north-west to begin with. There's plenty of mobile cell towers on that route. But once we hit the Welsh countryside, I can't guarantee you a decent signal."

"Okay, thanks."

Brody connected to Google on his tablet. He logged out of his own account and typed in Leroy Bishop's email address. Brody had always known Leroy's password but never had cause to use it before. Fortunately, like most people, he hadn't changed it in recent history.

Once logged in, he went straight to the Google Maps timeline. This was a feature of Google Maps that most users didn't realise was active on their smartphones. Google recorded an online history of exactly where the phone and its owner travelled and made the information available to view thereafter. Allegedly, the data was only available to the user and was used to improve targeted advertising. Naturally, Brody had it turned off on his phone. But, like most average users, Leroy hadn't.

Brody narrowed in on today's date and saw displayed on a map of North Wales, the route Leroy had taken earlier that morning from their house to a spot on the south coast of Anglesey, just north of Bangor. Brody zoomed in and found the name of a small fishing port.

"Okay, we need to head for somewhere called Gallows Point in Anglesey. Do you want GPS coordinates?"

"That would be helpful."

Brody read them out.

Google's tracking of Leroy's phone had stopped this morning at Gallows Point. The minute they boarded the boat and went out to sea, the signal must have dropped and the phone could no longer send its tracking data back to Google. That didn't mean the phone wasn't recording his journey, as GPS satellites could be picked up anywhere. It would automatically sync the journey later after Leroy returned to an area with a data signal.

Brody flipped the date back seven days and appraised the route plotted on the sea that they'd taken a week ago. They had headed north and had circled a small island on the south-east tip of Anglesey. He zoomed in and clicked.

Damn, it seemed to be some kind of tourist destination. With numerous boat trips travelling in and out, there would be heavy traffic in the vicinity, making it harder to work out which boat was Vernon's.

But would they go to the same place this week?

He checked the previous two Fridays. In both cases, they circled the island. It was the best bet.

"Okay, I've got a revised location for where they'll be. It's called Puffin Island."

"I'm sorry your new career as a therapist is going to get cut short." Shepard was all smiles and jokes now that he'd got the story out of his system. He backed up a few steps towards the exit. "Well, it's been nice chatting with you, but in just over twenty minutes the time bomb will go off. And as much as I'd enjoy watching you try and deal with my sixty-odd friends down there, I feel I've earned the right to watch it all unfold on the news."

Jenny watched the door close behind him. She let out a breath. At least he hadn't —

The door popped open and he poked his head back in. "Sorry, trying to save on bills."

He flicked off the light switch and closed the door behind him.

Jenny and Da Silva were plunged into absolute blackness.

Da Silva squealed behind her.

Jenny fished her phone back out of her pocket. It gave off ambient light and she used that to check whether there were any approaching threats.

None.

She worked her way through the apps and eventually found the one that turned her phone into a torch. She shone it back in the direction of the snakes. There was movement in the debris, but still nothing coming towards her.

"Guv," she called. "Turn your phone on as well."

There was no answer.

She forced herself to turn around to where she thought Da Silva might be, despite leaving herself exposed to the threat behind her. Had he gone to pieces? "Raul!" She'd never called him by his first name before. "Pull yourself together. Now!"

His dimly lit frame was to her left. She could see the whites of his eyes rolling in the darkness as he looked frantically left and right for snakes.

"Raul!"

He managed to take his eyes off the floor and focus on her for a moment.

She softened her tone. "Raul, where is your phone? We can make more light."

"It's in my bag." He pointed back to where he'd been trapped under the glass. His bag must have fallen off during the chaos. Jenny shone her torch in the area. She could see a strap poking out.

She shone her torch around further. There was a shelf above the hook where she'd picked up the tongs she was now brandishing as a weapon. There was something on there. In case a snake was hiding behind whatever it was, she used the tongs to push the item off the shelf and onto the floor. No snake. But the item split into two. A pair of specialist snake handler gloves. She grabbed them and started to put them on. But then she realised she couldn't hold her phone as a torch with the gloves on, so she settled for just one. Then she had a brainwave. She pulled a hairband out of her pocket and slid her hand inside, fixing the band above her wrist. She then slipped the phone underneath, trapping it on the outside of her forearm. Jenny was now free to don both protective gloves. She had protection for her hands and could direct the light forward.

She returned to Da Silva's bag. As far as she could tell, the coast was clear; all the same, she approached hesitantly, stepping carefully. She reached down to retrieve it, but it was stuck. Struggling slightly, she began to lift the heavy remnants of cage trapping it and a snake immediately slithered over her glove. Jenny withdrew her hand instinctively, but then reached down with the other and grabbed it. Her grip was halfway along its body and as she lifted it, the snake began to arch backwards, trying to reach the bare skin of her elbow. She quickly threw it over towards the side wall. It landed with a slap and dropped to the floor.

Jenny stood there for a moment, her heart beating wildly in her chest. She could do this, she reasoned, just as long as the snakes were unable to reach any part of her body not covered by the gloves. She returned to the bag, lifted the cage and freed it, throwing it behind her in the direction of Da Silva. She heard him shuffle towards it, the first positive movement he'd made since Shepard had released the snakes.

"Raul, are you okay? Have you got your phone?"

He grunted, but a light came on behind her. The torchlight shone all around and then settled. She sensed him rise up behind her and come forward. She kept her light focused forward, watching out for the serpents.

"That's DCI Da Silva to you, DI Price," he said from behind her. His voice was deep and determined. Briefly, she saw two bright dots of light dancing about ahead of her. She immediately recognised the configuration from her brief time in riot protection, and immediately knew what was coming. She was about to turn around, but the dots of lights disappeared and she felt him poke the weapon in her lower back. "Don't turn around. This is a Taser and it's fully charged."

"What the fuck are you doing?"

"We're going to make our way through the broken cages and escape up those steps at the other side of the room."

"Are you mad? We can't get through there. There's over sixty fucking snakes! We'll never make it."

"I will with you as my shield. Don't try anything or I'll fire. You'll drop like a lead brick on top of the slippery fuckers."

Jenny had been so busy focusing on the threats in front, she had forgotten about the one immediately behind her. She should have known Da Silva would put himself first in a life or death situation. She should have got his phone out of his bag herself. She might have seen the Taser. Maybe she could have used it against one of the larger animals.

"Right, one step at a time."

Jenny considered every self-defence move she'd ever been taught. If she was going to do something, she had to move now, before she was in amongst the wreckage. She could maybe survive one electroshock while she was still on safe ground. She knew they lasted thirty seconds, as long as he didn't pull the trigger again and send a second jolt her way. But Da Silva was much larger than her, fit and strong, and likely knew all the moves she did. As he pushed her urgently in the back with the Taser, she had no choice but to step forward onto the first cage.

Damn, there was no escape now.

Jenny shone her torch ahead of her. She held the tongs as a weapon in the same gloved hand, leaving the other free to swipe at any snakes.

The pressure in her back was insistent. She stepped forward. Glass crushed beneath her feet. But nothing moved towards her. She shone her torch about wildly each time she took a step. Da Silva did the same with his. She was weirdly glad of the light from the second phone, despite the circumstances.

As she moved, she mostly heard the snakes slither away from the approaching threat. She couldn't remember if they were scared of bright light or were pretty much blind. She knew it was one of the two.

About halfway across, her torch picked out an immense black mamba rising up nearly four feet on its tail. She'd recognised it immediately, brown on top and light grey underneath. Absently, she realised that the memory of the mamba must have permeated the GHB, the primitive nature of the encounter cutting through her memory lapse.

She couldn't back away. She watched, hypnotised, as the mamba swayed on the spot for a moment, before spreading out the narrow flaps around its neck and hissing at her, glistening white fangs standing out against the impenetrable ebony lining of its gaping maw.

"Come on, then," she shouted.

The mamba launched itself forward. It moved fast. Faster than any of the other predators she'd seen so far tonight. But Jenny was ready. She swiped across with the gloved hand and caught it square behind the head in a vice-like grip, holding on for dear life.

The mamba's tail flicked back and began to wrap itself around her arm. She lifted the tongs up with her other hand and used them as intended, grabbing the snake by the tail, removing its grip from her arm. Once she was sure she had control, she rotated to one side and then launched the snake as if she was throwing a Frisbee with two hands. She let go at the last second and it flew into the darkness to the side, crashing into the wall with an audible thud.

Adrenalin was coursing through her and everything was happening in slow motion. Da Silva was right behind her, breathing hard across her neck and shoulders. She wondered if she could have jumped out of the way when the mamba launched. Maybe then it would have bitten the human snake right behind her. But it would have been impossible to move that quickly.

Just as she reached the end of the wreckage, a massive python reared up in front of her, hissing at the threat. Jenny stopped.

"We can't go any further."

"Yes we can, DI Price."

And with that Jenny received an almighty electric shock in her back that propelled her forward into the snake. Immediately paralysed, she dropped on top of the huge animal and, through the intense pain, felt the snake begin to coil around her. But she couldn't move.

Da Silva broke for the stairs and made it. He bounded up them two at a time. For the briefest moment, light shone down from the outside world as he reached the door and opened it. Meanwhile, the python was wrapping its second coil around Jenny's midriff. She could feel it tightening. But the electroshock was still spasming through her system and her body was held completely rigid. Across the floor her torchlight from her forearm caught the side wall and she saw the mamba she'd already dealt with rise up again, searching out the threat.

Completely immobilised and with the python beginning to squeeze, Jenny watched the mamba slide in her direction.

"Brody, we're just coming up to Puffin Island now. There's lots of boats down there. What's the one we want look like?"

"It's an Intrepid 350, a thirty-five-foot motor yacht. It's white from above but has blue sides, and two black-coloured outboard motors hanging off the back. There should be two black guys on it. Is that enough?"

"Yeah, that should give us something to work with."

Brody felt the plane swoop down low and bank to the left. After a moment it banked to the right. It continued to change direction frequently as the pilots searched for the boat.

Coming up with Vernon's yacht had been easy. He'd accessed Leroy's Facebook timeline — fortunately, Leroy hadn't unfriended him — and looked through his pictures. Sure enough, there was a picture of father and son proudly holding up a huge fish with the motor yacht in the background.

Brody looked at his watch every twenty seconds or so. It was now 12:20 p.m.. Only sixteen minutes left. It was going to be tight. Ten slow minutes dragged by.

Suddenly, the plane drew to a halt in mid-air and the motor noise changed as the nacelles rotated upwards and the rotors took over.

"Think we've got them," said the co-pilot. "I'll head back to where you are now."

As the plane descended, the door up front opened and the co-pilot walked through. He wore the traditional green RAF flight uniform with a black helmet.

He walked past Brody and pressed a button. The cargo tail

started to lower and Brody could see the sea below. They were still a good fifty feet high, but getting lower every second. The co-pilot started a winch.

"So how does this work?" asked Brody. "Do we winch him up here?"

"Maybe, if we could communicate with them. But there's no response over the radio."

"Then how do we get down there? We can't just jump. We need to bring this machine with us."

"There's no 'us', sir. And you've just volunteered. Put your arms through here."

"For fuck's sake," moaned Brody, but he did as he was told, clutching the bulky medical device programmer close to his chest.

He inched towards the edge of the helicopter. The boat was immediately below. He could see Leroy and Vernon looking up, wondering what the hell was going on. Brody stepped out into thin air, holding the rope with one hand and the programmer with the other.

He heard the winch motor burst into life and he began to drop.

The wind from the rotor blades above created one hell of a downdraft, sending up spray from the waves and causing Brody to swing erratically in circles. Eventually he was down at the level of the boat. The Osprey shifted position and Brody moved towards the boat. As he neared, he shouted over the noise of the rotor blades.

"Take this!"

Leroy didn't seem to hear as Brody came flying towards him. Brody let go of the programmer as he connected with Leroy, who caught it instinctively and fell backwards into the boat.

He picked himself up, leaving the programmer on the deck.

Brody swung round towards the boat again. This time he got ready to disconnect the harness. He timed it well and landed on the side of the boat. The Osprey, job done, lifted off and hovered above. The boat rocked and Brody began to fall backwards, but Leroy caught him and held on.

"*Brody?*" Leroy registered the face hidden under the black helmet. There was disgust in his voice. Shocked, he shouted, "What the fuck?" and let go.

Brody fell backwards into the freezing cold water and began drifting away from the boat.

Treading water, Brody looked at his watch. There were four minutes to go.

Brody watched the boat get smaller. He'd come so close.

He slapped the water in anger.

CHAPTER 24

THE ELECTROSHOCK WORE OFF ABRUPTLY. NOW JENNY was able to move.

Squeezing her torso tightly, the python was heading for her neck. Across the room, the mamba moved swiftly across the debris. She had less than ten seconds.

She ripped the gloves off both hands and reached behind. Feeling for the two barbed electrodes from the Taser in her lower back, she ripped them out, screaming as the darts tore from her flesh. Making a fist of them, she searched around for the Taser gun that had fired them. Her light caught it and she reached for it, simultaneously plunging the electrodes into the python's skin and pressing the trigger to release the second of the Taser's three charges. Immediately, the snake's grip relaxed and she pulled the trigger again. She pushed the enormous, useless body away and flew towards the stairs. Just as she lifted her trailing foot the mamba struck, but missed.

She was quicker up the stairs than the snake and she flew out into the bright light of the church hall, slamming the door shut behind her.

She collapsed on the floor, breathing heavily, unable to believe she'd escaped. She could still feel the aftereffects from the Taser's electric current. Her body ached all over and the adrenalin caused her hands to shake. But she ignored it all and pushed herself up off the floor.

Jenny staggered through a row of seats facing the altar and made for the exit. She reached the door and pushed it open, grateful to see sunlight once again. She stepped outside onto the path and fell into the arms of Fiona Jones.

Not ready for Jenny's weight, they both fell backwards and landed on the grass.

"Jen, are you okay?"

"Where is Da Silva?"

"Over there."

"Help me up."

Fiona lifted Jenny and allowed her to lean on her. Jenny took in the sight ahead. Alan, Karim, O'Reilly and Knight were all there. Karim had captured Shepard and had him in cuffs, face down on the floor, his knee in Shepard's back. But he was staring up at Da Silva, his back to Jenny, who was shouting down at Karim.

"He's *my* collar, you jumped up little shit!" shouted Da Silva.

"No way," said Karim. "I caught him. He would have got away if I hadn't been here. You were ages behind him."

"He's mine!" Spit flew from Da Silva's mouth. "After what I've just been through, he's mine."

"Whatever happened to team effort?" DI Knight was clearly disgusted with his boss. "As SIO, you'll get the credit anyway. Let DS Malik take some credit too."

"Fuck you, Kevin. He's mine, I told you. He's the biggest mass-murderer in history and I'm taking him in."

Jenny and Fiona made it within a few feet before anyone noticed. The officers turned, switching their attention from the deranged Da Silva to concern for Jenny.

Jenny walked up behind him. "Hello, *sir*," she said.

Da Silva wheeled around, but halfway round she had already let fly and punched him full in the face, knocking him flat on his back. He landed on top of Shepard, Karim being smart enough to jump out of the way.

The DCI looked up at her, completely dumbfounded.

"That's been coming for a long time, you fucking prick."

Everyone's jaw dropped.

After a few seconds, the boat chugged into life and steered towards Brody. It pulled up alongside and Leroy hauled Brody out of the water.

Brody was shivering and found it hard to speak. "P-p-plug that in."

"What is it?"

"Leroy, d-don't ask questions. I'm h-here to save your dad's life. We've got less than three minutes before he dies." Brody looked up at Vernon, who waved down to him. "Vernon, get down here. It's urgent."

Leroy pulled the power cord over to the plug inside the cabin, disconnecting the microwave to make room. The programmer came to life. Brody watched it boot up.

Vernon arrived on the lower deck. "Hi Brody! That was amazing, son. But what's going on?"

"Vernon, take off your shirt. There's a problem with your pacemaker."

Vernon stood there, confused.

"Now!"

Vernon began unbuttoning his shirt.

"Oi you, don't talk to my dad like that."

"Not now, Leroy. For once in your life, this is not about you."

The machine whirred to life. Brody pulled out the wand and moved it towards the scar on Vernon's chest.

"What are you doing, Brody? You're no heart specialist."

"Fuck off, Leroy, I don't have time to explain."

"Bollocks to this." Leroy stepped forward. "You can't be trusted. First you kill Danny. Then you force me to break my vow of celibacy to him."

"Take some responsibility for your own actions, will you?"

"Right, that's it." Leroy leapt forward, knocking Brody out of the way. They fell onto the deck. Brody let go of the wand so as not to snap the cord to the machine.

"Boys!" shouted Vernon. "Please calm down."

Leroy was much stronger, fitter and more agile than Brody. He still looked like he worked out most days. Within a few seconds, Leroy had Brody in a choke hold.

Brody tried to reason with him, but couldn't form words.

He looked around for something to free him from Leroy's grip, but the deck was tidy. Fumbling with his sodden man bag, still hanging from his shoulder, he unhooked the clips, reached inside and grabbed his trusty tablet. He pulled it out and swung it towards Leroy's head. It struck side on and Leroy fell off the boat, splashing into the water, unconscious.

Brody looked at his watch. He had no choice. There were less than thirty seconds left. Seizing the wand, he passed it over Vernon's chest, pressing the correct button on the programmer to update the firmware.

"Leroy?" wailed Vernon.

"I'll get him in a minute. Stay still."

Each second was an eternity.

Brody watched Leroy's motionless body sink under the water.

Eventually, the machine beeped.

Brody dived over the side.

The seconds counted down towards 12:36 p.m. in the UK and the world waited with bated breath. Every news channel in every country was covering the story live. It had been established that the devices were time zone-aware, so the countdown was to 1:36 p.m. in Paris, 7:36 a.m. in New York and 9:36 p.m. in Sydney.

Cameras were everywhere, mainly focused on people who'd had their heart implant devices upgraded. They were officially present to capture the relief of the intended victims and their supporting families, but there were many news directors sadistically hoping they would be the one lucky enough to capture someone dying live on air.

One of the BBC's top chat show hosts was holding a live special, with ten victims being interviewed about their thoughts and feelings in front of a studio audience as the time approached. They sat on two long red sofas. Their implanted devices had all been upgraded, but that didn't stop the drama. Sweat broke out on one man's bald head, spotted by the director in the studio, and zoomed in on by the cameraman. One young mother visibly began shaking, her hands uncontrollable and her chattering teeth preventing her from articulating her feelings.

The queues outside the hospitals and clinics in Europe had abated with an hour to go. But in the USA and Canada, where the events had happened mostly overnight and the deadline was early in the morning, they were still dramatically rushing people in right up until the last minute.

In London, Big Ben struck 12:36 p.m.

Everywhere there was silence, as people waited ten or twenty seconds, before nervously looking up and giving a relieved smile. When the clock finally moved on to 12:37 p.m., champagne corks flew and the cheering started. No news director anywhere in the world caught a death occurring live on their television cameras.

But CCTV did.

On the security cameras mounted in Penn Station in Manhattan, a tramp who went by the name of Mac shuffled down an empty subway, pushing a trolley with his latest garbage heist. No one had known his real name or medical history and, despite strangers checking up on strangers everywhere, no one had bothered to ask him if he had a pacemaker. Halfway along, he arched his back in agony and dropped down, his trolley disappearing down the slight incline of the subway.

In a Bangkok whorehouse, a British taxi driver called Raymond Smith had arrived the day before on his annual pilgrimage to Asia's city of sin. The news broke on the plane journey, but he'd been listening to his second erotica audiobook and hadn't heard the captain make the announcement. After checking into his hotel, Raymond began what he planned to be a two-day binge of alcohol, drugs and sex. After that, he'd promised himself that he'd calm down and pace his hard-earned money over the next two months, before having to go back to Oxford and take fares for another nine months. In the middle of receiving a sensual massage from a nubile young ladyboy, who was naked, covered in oil and rubbing himself all over the man's back, Raymond flinched and died.

Deep in the Andes, and halfway along the Inca Trail, Rose

Forrester from Kennebunkport, Maine dropped down dead, despite a massive search and rescue operation mounted by her family. She had been out of range for two days, just her and a local guide, camping and living off the land. The helicopter found her body thirty minutes too late.

In a hotel in Brighton, Jackie Frenton, mother to four boys and wife of nineteen years to Charles, collapsed and didn't recover during sex with her secret lesbian lover of three years, also her boss. Her family thought she was away on a business trip in Blackpool, and that's where they had concentrated their search.

There were many more, mostly those who were unable to be contacted because they were off the grid, either geographically or deliberately because they were leading double lives. But for every death, over fifteen hundred people were saved. And over the following weeks, the tally mounted up to just sixty-six known medical device deaths around the world. Over one hundred thousand people had been saved.

One of those saved was a fourteen-year-old boy, living with his parents, Jacob and Isabel, in the small town of Hartwell, located on Georgia's border with South Carolina. His device had been upgraded in the middle of the night, when one of their neighbours called round having heard the news on the television. Over barbecue and beers just three weeks before, the neighbour had noticed the scar on the boy's chest while he played in the swimming pool with his son. When asked, Jacob, who had an English accent, explained patiently that the boy had been fitted with a defibrillator for ventricular arrhythmia.

The boy's name was Thaddeus Shepard.

Brody swam towards where he'd last seen Leroy, kicking off his shoes to gain momentum. The water was cold and choppy and it was hard to tell where he'd gone down.

Brody dived but there was little to see.

Underwater, he rotated fully, scanning in all directions.

Was that a dark shape? He swam downwards towards it. It took a full minute and Brody's chest was burning. But he kept pulling himself downwards. He finally reached the shape and grabbed hold of Leroy. He kicked upwards and slowly they began to rise.

When they surfaced, Brody cupped his hands around Leroy's neck and prepared to power backwards towards the boat. But he didn't have to. With relief he could see Vernon above, full of life and waving, steering the boat towards them both.

Within a minute, Brody had dragged Leroy onto the boat deck. He cleared his mouth, angled his neck properly and gave him the kiss of life. After three breaths, nothing had happened. Brody carried on, not knowing what else to do.

Still nothing on the fourth.

Then the fifth … and suddenly Leroy convulsed forward, retching seawater out of his lungs.

Brody lay down, looking up at the sky, taking huge breaths.

Vernon called down from above, cheerfully. "I know I said you two needed to kiss and make up, but I didn't expect you to do it literally."

Brody glanced over at Leroy who was staring at him, puzzled. After a second they both burst out laughing, Leroy then clutching his chest in pain as he laughed even more. He clambered over and threw his arms around Brody. "Thanks for saving our lives. I'm sorry for being such an arse, Brody."

"But Leroy, you can't apologise for your whole life."

"Oi, watch it, I'm saying sorry to you sober here. This is a once in a lifetime opportunity. Take it or leave it."

"Apology accepted. And for what it's worth, I'm sorry too."

"Now, Brody, what the fuck have you got involved in now? And before you start, I just want to say that — for a geek — that was one hell of an entrance."

"How come you lot are here?" asked Jenny of her team. She'd never been happier to see them. Too tired and bruised to stand, she was now sitting down on the grass to one side of Da Silva and Shepard. "I thought you were all dealing with the illegal snake den in Watford?"

"We were, but you can thank O'Reilly here for diverting our

attention," said Alan.

"Harry? Not Brody?"

"Not everything technical has to come through your better half, you know," grumbled O'Reilly, but with a smile. "You might recall we've been chasing the mobile operator for the location details of the phone that 'Raz' used to call Brody at King's Cross, but from when Brody was first called, when he was with you during your romantic breakfast?"

"Yes."

"Well, the details never came through. But, when I was on the phone with Victor Gibb chasing down Mullins' Vespa's recent movements, I had a brainwave. I asked Gibb to look it up on their surveillance systems. He did it straight away. The call was made from this address. And I remembered that you and dickhead Da Silva were on your way here. So I alerted everyone and here we are."

"Nice work, Harry."

"Good job and all," said Karim, who'd lifted Shepard off the floor while Harry spoke, "or this fucker would have escaped." He switched his focus to Da Silva and carried on their argument. "It was a good few minutes before you came out."

A large silver Mercedes pulled up. DCS McLintock exited and headed over to them.

Da Silva stood up at the sight of him. His nose was bleeding.

"What the hell is going on?"

They all looked to Jenny and she was grateful. "This is the man we've known previously as Saul Baker. His name is Benjamin Shepard and he is one fucked-up individual."

Shepard went to say something, but Karim lifted his arm up behind him and he winced instead.

"And Da Silva," McLintock turned to him. "Did you get that making the arrest?"

"No, sir. That was DI Price who hit me with no justifiable cause after everything had calmed down. Personally, I think she was still wound up over the fact I questioned her conduct during the case earlier."

McLintock turned to Jenny. "What's this?"

"Follow me, sir." Jenny spun on her heels in the direction of the church, not waiting for a response. She heard his footsteps behind her. She called back to the team, "Stick around guys, you might enjoy this."

Jenny stepped into church. Immediately, she checked the door at the rear to make sure the snakes hadn't got through. It was still closed.

She headed for the office behind the altar. Although she'd never been there before, she knew exactly what she'd find.

On a shelf above a large bank of impressive-looking computers — seeming oddly out of place in a religious setting — was a digital CCTV system. While Shepard had revealed his story to her in the basement, the light had been on and she'd noticed two cameras. So many expensive snakes certainly warranted twenty-four-hour surveillance.

She found the control system, selected the camera with the best view in the basement and rewound it, back to when she'd rescued Da Silva's bag containing the mobile phone and Taser from the wreckage.

McLintock watched events unfold, with an increasingly open mouth. "I can't believe what I'm seeing."

When they reached the end and Da Silva tasered Jenny on top of the python and ran, he exclaimed, "That's it! He's dead." But he stayed, intrigued to know how Jenny escaped.

Jenny found the whole thing hard to watch. Now that she could be objective, she couldn't understand some of the choices and decisions she'd made. While they had turned out to be the right ones, she realised how lucky she'd been and how close to death she'd really come.

When it was finished, McLintock said, "Let me deal with this."

She followed him outside and he stormed over towards Da Silva.

Da Silva was fuming. "I want to raise a formal complaint about DI Price's conduct, particularly her relationship with Brody Taylor."

McLintock stopped in front of him. "Really? Well you'll have to make one against me as well."

"What for, sir?"

"This." McLintock punched Da Silva in the stomach. He doubled up in agony and fell back on the grass.

"You are fired," McLintock said. "And I'll see you in prison for what you tried to do in there. DS Malik, cuff him."

Jenny and her team stared at each other in shock, not registering what they'd just seen. Then smiles broke out all around. Grinning from ear to ear, Karim cuffed Da Silva.

McLintock walked over to Shepard, who flinched, thinking he was about to get the same treatment. "So, this is our terrorist cell, our criminal mastermind is it? A preacher, even. A man of God."

"I'm just —"

"Shut up," McLintock spat the words out. "Nearly everyone survived. In fact, everyone in my borough, I'm proud to say. So far, the known casualty list is in single figures. Globally. I'm sure more will come through. But the tens of thousands you originally targeted are alive and well and will live happy lives. Your plan failed. Completely."

EPILOGUE

"RIGHT, SHALL WE TRY THIS AGAIN?" SAID Brody. "The other night was going well, but …" he paused to wink knowingly " … you seem to have forgotten what happened later."

"Maybe that's because someone spiked my drink," countered Jenny.

"So, this time, let's keep off the hard stuff, eh?"

"Good idea." Jenny looked up at the chalk-written menu above the counter. "Do you know how to make a flat white?"

"You can't go Australian in an Italian coffee house. Have some etiquette."

Jenny looked around for show. "Stefan's not here to tell us off."

"Well, in that case, if Madame wants a flat white, who am I to judge?"

"Thank you."

Brody began frothing the milk. He'd never in his life made a flat white, but how hard could it be? It was something to do with how you swirled the frothed milk around in the jug before pouring.

"How's the case wrap-up going?" he asked.

It was the first time tonight either of them had mentioned the case. They'd got through their fish and chip takeaway in Brody's kitchen upstairs just on small talk, avoiding everything important. It was also the first time they'd come back to Bruno's since

Mullins had attacked them last Wednesday night.

It had been a crazy few days since Friday's drastic events. Jenny had even been interviewed on the BBC's *Andrew Marr Show* on Sunday, sitting alongside the Prime Minister. The Met Police press department was revelling in its new, media-friendly heroine. Not that Jenny particularly enjoyed the attention. She saw it as a distraction from real police work, but understood that if she wanted to succeed as a DCI she needed to keep the media on her side. Brody's role in the case was kept under wraps. He had no intention of exposing himself publicly, not when he led a double life online and was still top of Vorovskoy Mir's Most Wanted list.

"Yeah, there's been a lot to sort out. Shepard's not talking, but his conversation with me in the snake pit was recorded on the same CCTV system as the one showing Da Silva tasering me."

"What's happened to Da Silva?"

"This afternoon was his hearing for bail. He's up for attempted manslaughter. It was negotiated down from attempted murder because of diminished responsibility. Apparently his medical record shows he's been previously diagnosed with ophidiophobia."

"Which is what, when it's at home?"

"Fear of snakes."

"You're joking?"

"Nope. Apparently as a kid he was attacked by a cobra while on holiday in India with his family. Taken to hospital, the lot."

"Maybe that's why he chose to go with you that day. To avoid going to the reptile shop where there were definitely going to be snakes."

"No, definitely not. That was all about threatening me about you. Not that that's come to anything."

"Thank God for that."

Brody handed her the flat white. He hadn't managed to get the fancy leaf design the good baristas manage, but otherwise it looked the part.

"I hear Klara was released without charge?"

Brody had talked to her yesterday. She was in her family's

apartment in Italy, awaiting the imminent arrival of her parents. A property developer had already made a good offer for the family bookstore, despite its burnt-out condition.

Brody had offered to help teach her how to cover her tracks online and, more importantly, in the real world. She hadn't realised that Vorovskoy Mir could easily track her down in Italy and take revenge for running out on them. She had accepted Brody's offer and he had promised to start advising her tomorrow.

"Yes. Her role in fixing the code was significant and went in her favour. Apparently, with the comments removed, none of the existing MedDev Labs staff were comfortable they knew what they were doing."

Brody was running out of work-related talking points. But there was one major one left. "And Manchester?" He tried to make it sound conversational, but the answer would form the crux of their night together as far as he was concerned. He couldn't see her going, not with Da Silva out of the way, but maybe there was more to it than he knew. If there was one thing he understood about Jenny, it was that he didn't understand her at all. But he was willing to keep trying. However, that required her to want to do the same with him.

Jenny sipped at her coffee and nodded appreciatively. "Not bad for a trainee barista."

Brody waited, busying himself with making an espresso on the huge machine. He took his time. He wasn't going to press her.

Eventually she cracked. "I'm staying in Holborn. McLintock wants me as DCI."

He had his back to her, which helped to hide the huge beam that had formed on his face. By the time he turned around, he thought he had it under control. "That's great news. Congratulations."

She smiled and held his gaze. "And Cheltenham?"

He couldn't look away.

Whatever doubts the panel had about Brody following his interview a week before — and there were many, according to Victor Gibb — they were all dispelled thanks to his role in cracking open the medical device hack. GCHQ had taken a lot of stick for not having any idea about the threat. Brody had received a formal government letter this morning offering him the role on the Russian desk that he had demanded. He had the means to go after Contag10n and Vorovskoy Mir.

"I turned them down."

It was true. Victor had been devastated, but recovered quickly and pointed out there was definitely an upside for him. He knew that if Brody joined GCHQ, his reputation as a recruiter would be forever tainted as the guy who brought in 'that crazy maverick'.

But what no one knew was that Brody now had a whole arsenal at his disposal to begin dismantling Vorovskoy Mir's empire and avenge Danny's death. James Butler had been as good as his word. Deep in his digital lair was all the information Brody needed to wage a one-man cyberwar against the Russian cybergang. And he had one more angle as well. Klara had told him about Dmitry Zakharin having real-world access to Contag10n. That was a lead well worth following up. He could wage his war against Contag10n online, where they were probably fairly well-matched, but if Brody could track Contag10n down in 'meatspace', then that was where he would be weakest.

Brody no longer had any need for GCHQ.

"Well, well," she said. "It looks like we're back where we started."

He leaned forward and they kissed, gently but insistently.

Eventually they parted and retreated to sipping their coffees. Brody then added, "Actually, we really are back where we started. Leroy moves in here tomorrow."

Jenny spurted out coffee. "Really? That's fantastic news!"

"I don't know about that. Living with Leroy is hard work. But he got the part in the *As You Like It* show that he auditioned for last week and he needs somewhere to stay."

"You two are good for each other." She thought for a moment. "So what are you going to do with yourself?"

"Well, amongst other things, your predecessor offered me an

advisory role to the Met Police as a cybercrime expert. I was hoping to convince his successor to follow through on that."

Jenny looked at him suspiciously. "Are you being serious?"

"Actually, yes."

"You want me to knowingly invite the most unorthodox, rule-breaking, anti-authoritarian, doesn't-know-right-from-wrong lone wolf to work with me and my team?"

Brody had never thought of himself in those terms, but they all sounded like compliments to him. "Yes, that's exactly what I'm asking."

"Well, you'll have to pass the aptitude test first."

Brody was confused. He wasn't aware of any tests for external advisors. "What test?"

"Is your living room still set up for the *Call of Duty* challenge?"

Understanding dawned and Brody grinned. "You think you can take me?"

"I do, actually."

"But I might have hacked it to bend the rules in my favour. I believe you missed off 'always-cheats-the-system' in your list of my various accolades."

"True, I did. Regardless, I can still take you."

Five minutes later, Brody and Jenny sat opposite each other, the two screens mounted back to back between them.

"If I win, you hire me as an advisor."

"Agreed. But what if I win?" she asked.

He leaned over to look at her. "What would you want?"

She thought for a moment. "I want a fortnight's holiday with you in an exotic place that has no mobile phone signal, Wi-Fi or internet."

Brody shivered at the thought. That was a serious bet.

"You're on."

THE END

AFTERWORD

Thanks for joining Brody and Jenny in Taking Up Serpents. Enjoyed the story? Here's what you can do next.

If you loved the book and have a moment to spare, I would really appreciate a short review where you bought the book and/or on Goodreads. Links to leave reviews can be found here: http://bit.ly/ReviewSerpents.

Your help in spreading the word is gratefully appreciated - it really helps authors get discovered by other readers.

You can also sign up to be notified of my next book, as well as pre-release specials and giveaways at: http://bit.ly/TUSMailingList

In case you missed it, Brody appears in two previous adventures. A short introductory novella called *Social Engineer* and a full-length novel called *Invasion of Privacy*. You can download the eBook of Social Engineer for FREE at: http://bit.ly/GetSocialEng.

Thank you for reading Taking Up Serpents.

Brody and Jenny will return.

Ian Sutherland, London, October 2016.

ACKNOWLEDGEMENTS

Writing my second novel was an entirely different experience to writing my debut novel. The first was written over many years, with lots of false starts, iterations, and always with me in that beautifully blissful state of naive ignorance because, until I published it, no one would ever know if it was any good. Finally, I did publish it and that introduced new concerns. Would people read it? Was it actually any good? Was I fooling myself that I should be an author? But after its launch in August 2014, Invasion of Privacy slowly found its audience, the reviews were incredibly positive and I began to believe I could do this for a living. That was, until the day I sat down full of enthusiasm to write my second full-length novel, staring at a blank page. I experienced different doubts. Could I really do this again? Could I match the quality of the first book? But this time I had much more going for me. I was writing a sequel and so I knew the characters intimately. I had a better understanding of the craft of writing, although I still push myself to improve every day. But, most importantly, during the writing of the second novel's first draft, I had an army of cheerleaders to spur me on. As always, there was my wife, Cheryl, and my daughters Laura and Raquel, who kept my motivation high. But now, there were many other family and friends who'd all read the first book and demanded more. There were also many, many readers (people I've never met) emailing and tweeting me for the publication date of the sequel. In short, there were far too many people to let down and so I took the plunge, wrote my way past that blank first page and carried on until Taking Up Serpents was done. And when the first draft was complete, I had a ready-made team to take it through the publication process and make the book as professional as its predecessors. My editor, Bryony Sutherland (no relation!) whose love and passion for the integrity of the characters and the story, made the book much, much better and completely consistent with its prequels. My cover designer, Stuart Bache of bookscovered.co.uk, offered up a striking eye-catching design, probably the best of the series. I now even have a team of fans who proofread and give feedback right up until the last minute, all helping to make the book as good as it can be. And then there's you, my readers. Without you, there'd be no point.
Thank you!

ABOUT IAN SUTHERLAND

Ian Sutherland was brought up in the Outer Hebrides, remote idyllic islands off the west coast of Scotland. In an effort to escape the monotonous miles of heather, bracken and wild sheep, Ian read avidly, dreaming of one day arriving in a big city like London. And then, at the tender age of twelve, he was unexpectedly uprooted to Peckham, inner-city suburb of South-East London. Ian quickly discovered that the real London was a damn sight more gritty and violent than the version he'd read about in books and watched on TV. Undeterred, Ian did what he did best, and buried his head back in his books, dreaming of other places to escape to.

Roll forward some years, and Ian can still be found with his head in a book. Or, given that he enjoyed a successful career in the IT industry, an eBook Reader. And now, having travelled a fair bit of the globe in person and even more of it via the internet, Ian lives with his wife and two daughters in a small idyllic village, surrounded by green fields, copses and the occasional sheep, yet located just outside of the London he finally came to love.

Here, he writes gritty, violent crime thrillers full of well-rounded characters, set in and around London and its suburbs. His stories also feature the online world that most of us jump into blindly each day, but Ian exposes its dark underbelly and dramatically illustrates just how dangerous the internet can be for the unwary.

Learn more about Ian at
www.ianhsutherland.com

Join his mailing list at:
http://bit.ly/TUSMailingList

Follow him on twitter at:
www.twitter.com/iansuth

Like his Facebook page at:
www.facebook.com/ihsutherland

Printed in Great Britain
by Amazon